T • H • U • N • D

The pristine coral sea of th
Whale National Marine Sanc
explosive eruption at Keahol
coast. The ordinary lives of the inhabitants of the small town of Kailua-Kona are tossed into turmoil. A series of accidents occur, leading to suggestions of murder.

Kiana Kilolani, a very beautiful but demure Hawaiian schoolteacher, is plagued with daunting daytime apparitions and haunting nightmares. She fears she is slowly going mad as the spectres persist. Her alter ego bewitches men with soul-searing kisses. Or is it her alter-ego? Her impeccable reputation in the town is quickly being eroded.

Chung, Min-Ho, a greedy ex-North Korean marine commando who got his start as a ruthless entrepreneur by defecting with a Shark-class submarine, looms menacingly. He and his company, Global Sea Marine, keep turning up like bad pennies.

Manny Manetti, a comical, small-time marina operator, has big-time ambitions - he has wheeled and dealed his way into a SeaTruck submersible dealership.

Kimo Kekuna, Hawaiian Chief and a former Navy SEAL who served in Central America and Desert Storm operations, gets involved to help his former buddy.

Dr. Sarah Leikaina, volcanologist, rock climber and a SeaTruck submersible pilot exploring the deep vents off Vancouver Island, tantalizes men with her voluptuous body and enticing kisses.

Rune Erikson, formerly in the service of a shadowy government communications agency, is lured off his sailing ship, the ketch *Valhalla,* in Victoria's Fisherman's Wharf by the subterfuge of a former colleague. Rune is sucked into the vortex of this intrigue that is scented with the myths and legends of Hawaiian culture, quickly falling into the erotic embrace of the strikingly-beautiful Hawaiian volcanologist.

THUNDERSEA

Ernie Palamarek

Enjoy Rogers' chocolates while READING my novel.
Ernie Palamarek

Trade Winds Productions

THUNDERSEA

A Trade Winds Production
tradewindsproductions@home.com
First softcover edition: 1999
Printed in Canada

Canadian Cataloguing in Publication Data

Palamarek, Ernie
Thundersea

ISBN 1-55212-251-4

I. Title.
PS8581 . A4863T58 1999 C813 ' . 54 C99-910502-7
PR9199 . 3 . P312T58 1999

TRAFFORD

Suite 2, 3050 Nanaimo St., Victoria, B.C. V8T 4Z1, CANADA
Phone 250-383-6864 Toll-free 1-888-232-4444 (Canada & US)
Fax 250-383-6804 E-mail sales@trafford.com
Web site www.trafford.com TRAFFORD PUBLISHING IS A DIVISION OF TRAFFORD HOLDINGS LTD.
Trafford Catalogue #99-0020 www.trafford.com/robots/99-0020.html
10 9 8 7 6 5 4 3

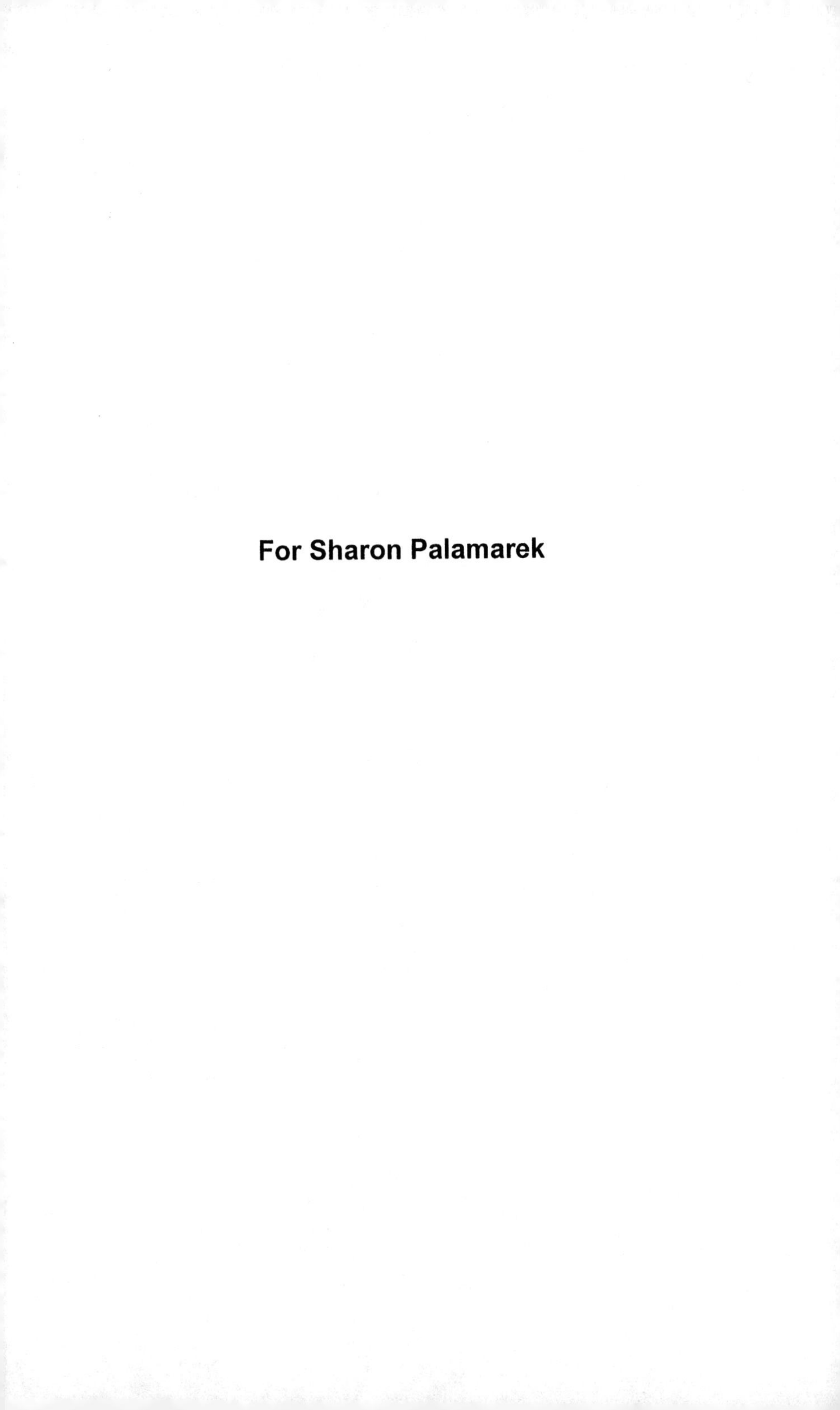

For Sharon Palamarek

CONTENTS

CHAPTER ONE

VALKYRIE

FISHERMAN'S WHARF, VICTORIA, BRITISH COLUMBIA. She came softly down to me enshrouded in a shimmering veil of mist and a luminescent halo. We were brought together by some unearthly force of hers; I felt completely powerless. Embracing me with unbridled passion, her energy flowed between us, now unimpeded by distance. Her delicately-scented, ivory body intertwined with mine. I was overcome with desire as her silky, long red hair cascaded over my wondrous face. Fine flashes of blue sparks crackled in the dim misty light, jolting our bodies as her firm breasts brushed my bare chest. Her long fingernails raked my back. Soft slender fingers caressed my neck. She spoke into my ear with a sensual whisper, in a foreign tongue that I was struggling to understand, yet couldn't. But I could feel her revelations flowing through me as pulsing libidinous thoughts and spiritual sensations and now I could understand. Her moist lips met mine. My body relaxed and surrendered totally as I felt myself melting and flowing as one with her. We rose together, borne upon a misty swell of sultry softness. I would have gone with her this time, I desperately wanted to go with her, and if it was not for the intrusion upon my senses, I would not have come down from those ethereal heights.

It was the slight creak of the rigging as the ship rolled gently at my Fisherman's Wharf berth that woke me this hot autumn afternoon. A boat passing through the channel had set up a series of small waves that bulged through this motley collection of sailing ships, power yachts, fishing vessels, packers, crabbers, house boats and float homes tied to the slips.

I had been having a nap in my hammock which was strung topside near the wheelhouse in an area between the two masts aboard my 65-foot ketch *Valhalla.* I was having the most beautiful dream again. A dream about an exotically-beautiful woman with a curvaceous body and long flaming-red hair.

It was October. I was taking full advantage of the last vestiges of

Indian summer - we had one overnight frost already - before the rains of November would be beating down upon us in this temperate rainforest on Vancouver Island.

Slowly opening my eyes, I waited for them to focus, then looked up through the rigging into the deep blue of the darkening sky. Lying there, I tried to come to terms with my erotic dream, trying to make some sense of it, wishing that I was still there, wherever *there* was.

This latest vivid dream aboard the *Valhalla* unnerved me; it seemed to be very real. It ragged on my mind like a missing piece of an intricate puzzle while it was being filed within the recesses of my memory to be fast-forwarded back into my thoughts at some inopportune moment at a later date.

Yawning after my nap, I carefully rolled out of the hammock, my bare feet hitting the warm wooden deck. I yawned again, stretched and looked toward the west. The hot afternoon sun had just settled below the Sooke hills on the horizon, leaving behind a swatch of glorious clouds with brush-strokes of red, gold and orange. Moving unsteadily, I stretched my tightened muscles. I turned around and watched as a scattering of lights came on in the portholes of other boats tied up nearby. And farther down Fisherman's Wharf, at finger one, the larger windows of the float homes were ablaze with reflection from the fiery sunset. Beyond were the hotels and restaurants ringing the Inner Harbour. There was the Coast Hotel, then the Laurel Point Inn and beyond, just around the point, the Empress Hotel sat regally above the causeway at the far end of the harbour. To my left, the red light of the buoy marking the rock in the channel flickered on and off.

Clumsily, I made my way into the wheelhouse and stumbled down the companionway to the saloon. Something drew me over to my library. Taking down my ancient leather-bound dictionary from the bookcase on the bulkhead, I went over to the galley, held it up under the light and flipped the thin onionskin pages as I searched for the word. I read the notation for *Valhalla*. Then a phrase "borne by the Valkyries" leapt out at me from the text. Then *Odin*. My fingers flipped back to the *O* section, then down past *Odesa* to *Odin* and read: "In ancient Norse mythology, the god (a supreme deity) of art, culture, war, and the dead." Hurriedly, I fingered my way down the column until I came across the word *Valkyrie*. I read: "In ancient Norse mythology, one of certain maidens who ride the air currents and choose the heroes from among those combatants slain in battle, and who are then borne by her to Valhalla (the great hall of the dead); chooser of the slain." This raised the hair on the nape of my neck. Could the exotic woman in my dreams be a Valkyrie? And what did it mean if she was? Did it mean that I was dead or close to death? That I had a near-death experience? If it did, death was going to be wonderful, I thought morbidly. Or was it simply 'la petite morte' - what the French sometimes call the act of love? I shivered in the cool of the evening, trying to come to terms with what all this meant. These Valkyries were maidens who rode through the air and chose only the bravest of the heroes from amongst those slain in battle.

I certainly felt battle-weary after having been in the international service of my country for what seemed to be an eternity but in reality was a relatively lesser number of stressful years that hardly qualified me for an inadequate pension. During those times I had indeed felt like I was dying.

In Valhalla, these heroes were received by the god Odin where they would start an even more glorious life of feasting, carousing and doing battle.

Puzzled, I tried to envision the angelic woman of my dreams again. Her face, her windswept hair, and her voluptuous body seemed to be so familiar, somehow more familiar than just in my dreams.

Then it struck me! I scrambled topside, hurried through the wheelhouse, along the deck and down the gangway onto the dock where I rushed forward to the bow of the *Valhalla*. There she was! Right under the bowsprit! She was the carved wooden figurehead!

Startled, I reeled, stumbling backwards. Goose-bumps rose on my forearms. In the twilight, I stared slack-jawed at her lovely hewn curves and painted figure. It was her! The woman of my dreams. She was the Valkyrie!

Stunned by this revelation, I slowly made my way back up the gangway, on board and down below.

As I passed through the saloon, out of habit, I flipped a Stan Getz CD into the stereo. In the galley I looked through the larder, trying to plan my supper but was distracted by my thoughts. Shivering, I didn't know if it was from this latest revelation or just from the chill of the evening air. I went back into the saloon, crumpled up a section of the Times-Colonist newspaper and put it and some kindling into the small fireplace. Taking a few logs from the wood bin, I arranged them on top of the kindling. I got a wooden match from the holder on the mantle, struck it on the hearth and set the paper aflame. Soon a bright and cheery glow of warmth settled into the saloon as the flames took hold.

That would take care of the chill.

Going back into the galley, I turned my attention to the cold food locker and pulled out some chilled fresh salmon that I had just purchased off one of the fishing boats earlier in the afternoon. I turned the oven on to heat.

A nice hot rum after my meal. That's what I really need to warm me, I thought. Opening the liquor cabinet in the saloon, I selected a bottle of Cockspur light rum from Barbados for later. I retrieved a small bottle of wine from the wine rack for now. Throwing a salad together as I baked the salmon in the oven, I poured a glass of the Okanagan Valley Riesling wine to go with the fish.

Corcovado (Quiet Nights of Quiet Stars) was playing. Astrud Gilberto's sultry voice was accompanied by Stan Getz's mellifluous tenor sax. Dining by myself is not something that I enjoy, so I try to make the best of it.

In any case, I had a reception to attend later tonight. It was one which I had promised my old friend, Coop - a marine biologist - that I would be attending.

Laying out the linen and the silverware, I didn't bother with candlelight. Unless the electricity has gone out or if my lamp is out of fuel when berthed or moored someplace remote, I reserve that special effect when I have female guests. And lately I have had none. Or did I? I mulled this over as I slowly ate my supper. Stan Getz's jazz rendition of *I'm in Love* surrounded me.

Later, I put the kettle on and got out a stout mug. Finishing with the ingredients of the rum toddy, I took a cautious sip. Perfect! I thought as I went into the saloon, sat in my favourite chair and put my feet up. I hunted down the remote, retrieved it from the side of the cushion where it had slid down, then flicked the TV on to channel 50 to catch the latest happenings on CTV News1. ". . . those were the results of the latest poll in Quebec. He dejectedly commented that he really didn't think much of the polls in this case, that it was the polling booths that really mattered and that one day there would be a majority - of one!" Then a news flash was broadcast. "This just in. Moments ago there was an explosive eruption just offshore of the Kona International Airport on the Big Island of Hawaii. First reports indicate that the explosive eruption was of sufficient force to cause some damage to the surrounding area. We have a crew from the local TV station, KSEA channel 4, on the scene. Stay tuned for a live feed later from Hawaii."

Hmm, I thought.

I flicked the remote, landing on CNN. ". . . that was according to the president who later commented that contrary to that old saying, sometimes life is indeed a bed of roses - thorns and all! . . . Now with late-breaking news from the Big Island of Hawaii. Early unconfirmed reports show that there was what has been described as an 'explosive eruption' in the sea next to the Kona International Airport. There has been some peripheral onshore damage reported. We will have a live report from there as soon as possible. In the meantime, stay tuned as we will be having updates as they occur. Meanwhile, in Iraq . . . "

I flipped channels over to the CBC on channel 2. ". . . in answer to some challenges during question period in the house today, he stated that while he did 'approve of salt pork', he asked you to 'take this latest protest incident with a grain of salt but I do not approve of pork barreling, nor peppering reporters, for that matter!' he hastily added to much laughter from the benches behind him." They had nothing new to add.

I flipped back to channel 50 where CTV News1 still did not have their live feed from Hawaii. Oh well! I'll keep tuned in as the evening wears on, I thought. I took another sip from my rum toddy and got up to wash the few dishes that I had.

"We now have that live feed from Carrie Kahakua, KSEA - TV, channel 4 news direct by satellite from the Big Island of Hawaii where an explosive eruption has occurred in the sea just off the Kona International airport." I glanced up from putting the dishes away, grabbed my hot toddy, went into the saloon, and sat on the arm of the sofa, my attention now totally focused upon the news report on CTV News1.

"Good evening from the Big Island of Hawaii. Just minutes ago we experienced an explosive eruption in the waters just off Keahole Point. Keahole Point is where the Kona International Airport and the adjacent Solar/Sea Energy and Aquaculture/Agriculture Lab complex is located. The SSEAAL complex, as it is called, and the Kona International airport, where we are right now, are just seven miles north up the coast of the town of Kailua-Kona. We are on the tarmac just outside the arrivals area. In the background you can see emergency equipment and personnel helping passengers evacuate Pacific Northwest's flight 1204 from Seattle which was just landing when the explosion occurred, sending the plane skidding out of control and nosing it onto the lava beds upon which this airport was built. The different noises you hear in the background are from the hundreds of car alarms that had been set off as a result of the shock force that also blew through the car parking lot. The main terminal's alarms had been activated as well but first reports are that they were accidentally set off. Our cameraman, John Lukeala, was taping the arrival of an advance team from the mainland. They are going to handle details in order to help us host the upcoming World Oceanic Organization's Pollution of the Seas conference, WOOPS for short, which starts later this month in our town of Kailua and at the adjacent SSEAAL complex. We will roll some unedited video shot as the explosive force occurred. Can you roll it now? Okay! Here is that unedited video clip from earlier: 'I am standing out on the tarmac waiting for the advance team to arrive for a conference on pollution of the seas later this month. We have been told that in a significant portion of the Pacific Ocean, plankton, which forms the foundation link of the food chain, are disappearing. Although scientists are unsure of the cause, they tell us that human pollution is one of the major factors, with about three-quarters of a million gallons of toxic chemicals being dumped into the oceans each year! These pollutants run the gamut from industrial chemicals such as PCB's, pesticides and fertilizers to city sewage and the crankcase oil that some backyard oil changers dump down their drains. This is a contributing factor in the ecological upheaval in these oceans which causes them to lose the ability to generate the oxygen upon which life in the oceans depend. Oxygen is released from carbon dioxide during photosynthesis. This oxygen is normally released into the biosphere. Some scientists have even said that the oceans, the cradle of all life here on earth, are dying. While this may sound . . .'" The TV reporter's live voice cut in. ". . . Okay, here you can see the jet landing normally, braking and using its reverse thrusters. There! You can see the camera jiggle. The plane starts to swerve and veer out of control. The shots here are difficult to see as the cameraman was thrown to the tarmac along with his camera. Here he gets back up on one knee to resume filming. You can get just a glimpse of me in the lower left corner of your picture trying to stand up after having been blown off my feet. The video is quite shaky but you can still see the plane skidding then see its nosewheel run onto the lava beds as it came to a rocking halt. It's a tribute to the captain and to the makers of the jumbo jet that there wasn't a more catastrophic situation here. We're now back with a live, long-distance shot. All of us here were thrown to the ground as the shockwave hit, both through the air and along the ground. There appear to be some injuries among the passengers who slid down the slides - bruises and scrapes and so on

- no doubt some of them WOOPS team members, but no reports yet of anything more than that. We are now noticing that smoke is coming from the plane's landing gear and firefighters are frantically trying to control that. We're not sure if there are flames but there is definitely smoke and increasingly so! At the moment, we are still unsure of the magnitude of the damage and exactly what it is that occurred here without warning. At this point it is pure speculation that there may have been a dangerous-goods ship explode offshore or perhaps some type of underwater volcanic action that may have resulted in an earthquake and a shockwave. Some are even speculating that we took a direct hit from a small meteor. There are streaks of mist in the sea and on the land further along the coast toward the town of Kailua-Kona and up Mount Hualalai but they don't appear to have come from the SSEAAL complex itself. We will have further reports on damage as they come in. In the meantime we will try to get closer to the damaged Pacific Northwest plane to bring you more detailed coverage. This is Carrie Kahakua, KSEA, channel 4 reporting live from the Big Island of Hawaii."

"There you have the dramatic footage and the live report of the mysterious explosive eruption from Keahole Point in Hawaii. Stay tuned for further reports as they come in," intoned the news anchor from CTV News1.

I flipped over to CNN but they too had just finished what appeared to have been the same live telecast from Kona International Airport.

My mind wandered back to the invitation to tonight's reception. My friend Jonas Cooper, the marine biologist, had phoned me a couple days ago.

"Where have you been hiding?" Coop had asked. "I haven't seen you in some time."

"Well, I've been extremely busy lately what with one thing and another . . . "

"Rune Erikson!" Coop admonished, "you should get out more often! How would you like to attend the unveiling of a black smoker?"

"A black smoker? I don't think so, I've stopped going to those sorts of things years ago, Coop. They're so juvenile!"

"No! No! It's not what you think, you ignoramus!" he laughed. "My wife is coming with me too! For your information, a black smoker is actually a chimney-like structure of built-up minerals on the sea floor. It is through these newly-discovered natural structures which hot volcanic fluids are vented as distinctive plumes and minerals dispersed into the surrounding area on the seabed. And we got a new one! It's got traces of some new mineral. We're putting it on display in the atrium at ORCA. We brought it up from the depths of the Juan De Fuca Ridge. You know, from the undersea thermal vents 500 kilometers off Vancouver Island, the ones I was telling you about."

"Oh! You mean where you guys, well really, the girls and you, found those tube worms and all."

"Yeah, that's the place! And don't make an issue out of the sexist thing. We're all equal at what we do. We're a team."

"Yeah, well, I'd rather have them on my team than you! They're a whole lot prettier!"

"So, does that mean you'll be coming then?"

"Sounds good, I'll be there hotshot."

I glanced out the porthole. It was pitch dark now save for the wharf lights and the little dots of soft yellow lights here and there that leaked out from the other boats. I went across the saloon, up the companionway, into the wheelhouse and peered out, seeing hazy stars overhead despite the glow from the lights of the city of Victoria. Going out on deck, I made my way to the bow where I looked eastward. A huge, brilliant harvest moon was just starting to emerge, rising quickly from behind lofty Mount Baker in Washington state. A wide yellow moonbeam was reflected onto the calm waters of the Inner Harbour. It would be a nice moonlit drive out to the reception at Patricia Bay out on the Saanich peninsula tonight. I turned around. To the immediate west, the pale yellow lights of Esquimalt. Farther to the west, the lights from the stately Hatley Castle in Colwood and the posh homes of Triangle mountain rising behind it, twinkled from across Royal bay. A necklace of magenta sky adorned the black, rolling crowns of the silhouetted Sooke hills as the evening settled onto Vancouver Island. This too was Heaven!

CHAPTER TWO

VALHALLA

KAMEL POINT, VICTORIA, BRITISH COLUMBIA. These erotic dreams, although extremely pleasant, had only begun after I had received the *Valhalla* as payment from an exceedingly grateful client in Seattle. I had done some work in retrieving his daughter and only child from the clutches of the prostitution and drug culture in Los Angeles.

A good friend of theirs had been down in L.A. on business and had seen their 16-year-old daughter working the street like a fifty-dollar whore. She had been one of the many thousands of newly-independent, lemming-like lasses who run away by taking the bus down to Tinsel Town. There they wander starry-eyed, waiting to be discovered, only to end up in desperate straits sailing aboard some film director's yacht on the weekends. They are mere child playthings for them and their cronies. Cruising through California's Channel Islands, they are fed a steady diet of mind-altering nose candy and sex. From that point on, it is the inevitable comedown from the inevitable letdown. Soon they are out on the streets looking for a job, any job, for they usually are too proud to admit to their parents that they have failed and need help - both emotionally and financially. They also need to support their new drug habit.

Eventually a significant number end up being taken in by the fast talk, ready supply of drugs and false promises of love and a quick fortune by some guy who would turn out to be just another slimy pimp/drug pusher who crawled out from under a damp rock, threw on some trendy clothes and acquired the other trappings so necessary to youthful fads. Now they have to pay back the pimp's largesse by selling their bodies to rich prospects from Rodeo Drive to Marina del Ray.

Or starring in porn films.

Or both.

The drugs take their toll quickly enough so that it is only a matter of time before they are supine in some dirty back alley taking someone on for a ten or a twenty for that is all they are now worth on the market -

if they are lucky to still be alive - if heroin and crack haven't done them in yet.

My client, a friend whom I had met while he was working for the U.S. military, was an aeronautical engineer. I suppose that because of his forbearing nature and analytical mind, he had something to do with driving his precious teenaged daughter away from home and into the clutches of the wolves by whom she was slowly being devoured.

He was in dire need of help. I was in the book. He phoned and asked, "Is this Rune Erikson? The one that used to work in Washington, D.C. occasionally?"

The one and the same. Did I remember him? Sure! Who can forget a brilliant friend from the old days? How did he know what city to find me in? Simply by remembering that I had once told him that I was born on the west coast, on Vancouver Island, in Victoria.

He got on a scheduled Heli-jet in Seattle - one of their Sikorsky 76's - and flew straight to Victoria to see me. It wasn't long before the navy-blue and gray chopper set down with a clatter at Kamel Point Heliport. The chopper was the one with the large Seattle Mariner's logo emblazoned upon its side - my favourite ball team after the Jay's.

As the passengers were filing off and walking to the terminal to attend to Canada Immigration and Customs formalities, I recognized him straight away despite the years that had gone by. Even if I hadn't recognized his features, I could have identified him solely by his wooden walk, his distracted demeanour and his pinched face.

We walked across the wide expanse of parking lot and slipped through the small gate in the security fence to get to the Ogden Point Cafe at the breakwater on Dallas Road. I believe that walking is good for the soul; it was a gloriously sunny day.

He was an athletically-trim man with dark hair graying at the temples though his forehead was lined with creases giving him an expression akin to perpetual puzzlement. I suppose that the creases came from years of trying to solve complex aeronautical problems. The baggy, sunken eyes ringed with darkness and set in a pallid face, told of many sleepless nights and anxious days. There was a certain sadness in his eyes, a beaten look.

We selected a corner table with a breath taking view. If the personal conversation became awkward, there would always be the changing sea, the marine traffic or the majestic Olympic mountains to which we could avert our eyes.

He tearfully recounted his sad tale to me over coffee - he had a latte,

I had a mocha. We had read the menu but then completely forgot about ordering some food. He said that it was even tearing apart his marriage to his wonderful wife of twenty-some years. To lose one woman in his life was unbearable but to lose two would be absolutely unthinkable. "If there is no recourse . . . well," he said as his slumping shoulders heaved with racking cries as I sat across from him. I had no doubt that he could not live with that and that he was verging on being suicidal. Where they had once had an orderly life, there was now chaos. What they had built upon and built up, was now being brutally torn apart. I leaned over and put my hand on his shoulder in sympathy. A table of four business types in suits and a couple of skimpily-clad joggers at another table looked over at us, wondering what I could have possibly said that had sent this grown man into a crying jag.

I stood up and clutching his arm, said, "lets go for a walk."

We trudged out onto the breakwater - that massive structure of cut granite blocks - where the salt water breeze put a new perspective on our conversation. He talked; I listened.

A red and white Marine Pilot boat was tied up at its own jetty nearby, while its sister boat sped out to an approaching deep-sea freighter to put a pilot on board for the rest of the voyage through the Juan de Fuca and the Georgia straits to the Port of Vancouver. Masses of brown, bullwhip-like seaweed floated here and there in the frothy green sea. The British ship *M.V. Seaspread*, which lays and maintains international cable systems in the Pacific Ocean, was tied up at the Ogden Point cruise ship terminal. We stuck to the middle of the rail-less structure. The breakwater angled right, then further along, right again.

Twenty minutes later we were at the end of the breakwater where the blinking red navigation light sat upon its red and white concrete pedestal which was debased with initials and other graffiti. We looked down at the tops of the heads of a trio of fishermen who were casting for rock cod and who, perhaps, if they were lucky, would hook onto a nice-sized salmon or at least a fat rock cod for their supper. Their tackle boxes and bait cans were set behind them on the enormous stepped granite blocks which resembled, in size, those of the pyramids.

We circled the light tower and retraced our steps. He continued talking. I broke in here and there with a question seeking clarification for this point and that. The cadence of our walking kept the conversation flowing without him breaking down. It was a soothing substitute for hand-wringing, jaw-clenching and other nervous gestures of the extremely distressed.

A red Canadian Coast Guard helicopter returning to its nearby base from one of the lighthouses clattered by overhead with a truck-sized payload of equipment slung far below its belly. Out in the Strait of Juan de Fuca, I could now see the stern of the bulk carrier. Streaks of rust ran down upon the lettering but I could still see that it was registered in Monrovia. Below us, two scuba divers in brightly-coloured wetsuits emerged from the depths of the jade-green sea.

By the time he was through telling me all that he had bottled up inside of him, we had reached Dallas road again. He suddenly stopped and wheeled around to face me with despairing eyes. Grabbing my arm in a death grip, he said, "I know that you used to work for your government on special assignments," he continued, releasing my arm to daub his glistening eyes and then blow his nose on his handkerchief. "I also knew how impressed my bosses were with your work. You say that you are sort of retired now," he said as he looked at me with imploring eyes, "but please, I'm begging you! It's my only chance! See if you can get our daughter back to us! If anyone can do it, you can! I'll pay you anything you ask! Anything!"

"I'm not a private detective," I replied looking him squarely in the eye.

"I don't want a private eye. I can't afford to have the job botched. The way I've got it figured, there's only one chance to do it right."

"Have you tried the police?"

He scoffed, "The police? They are understaffed, especially with their caseloads of runaways."

I mulled it over in my mind. What the hell, I thought, what else am I doing that is more important at the moment? I'm just kicking around anyway! It just seemed to be the right thing to do. So I said I would try to help them. I bolstered his courage to wait and see what I could do for him, if anything . . . no promises.

"How much do you want?" he asked, a glint of hope appearing in his sad teary eyes.

"Just expenses," I replied, "and if I'm successful, we'll figure something out afterwards that will be mutually agreeable."

He shook my hand like a drowning man reaching for a life preserver in the middle of the ocean.

Armed with a photo of their beautiful, innocent-looking daughter and little else other than that old, tattered last letter to her mother saying that she was sure a big break was soon to come her way, I flew a commuter jet down to California from Vancouver.

Surprisingly, it didn't take long to find her in L.A. The problem turned out to be not in the finding but in how to persuade her to return to Seattle with me. Even through her drug-induced foggy mind she would never willingly let me take her back home to her parents. That was a given! So I didn't even attempt it.

What I did do was to become somebody else - somebody dripping with cash and driving a fancy set of wheels just like her former Johns did when her market price was still high. I had rented a Ferrari, bought myself some designer sunglasses, loaded myself down with gold jewellery, and stuck a fat Montecristo Double Corona cigar in my mouth. It was an acquired taste that I hadn't acquired. Then I went to seek her out.

To get the street patter down I stopped curbside to talk to a few of the girls, trying not to let myself be entrapped by some eager, young female cop working undercover vice. And I didn't want to flash her photo around either and possibly scare her into hiding, or worse yet, have her pimp come looking for me with a .44 automatic or a sawed-off shotgun. It was not that I couldn't handle pukes like that but I didn't want anything to interfere with my goal of bringing her back to her parents safe and sound as soon as possible. Wanting her to disappear as quickly as she had originally appeared on the scene in L.A., I tried to eliminate the possibility of some slime-ball coming after her and suddenly appearing on their doorstep in Seattle.

I found her in the evening of the second day of looking. She was no twenty-dollar back-alley hooker - she had not sunk that low yet! But she was on her way down, working the streets just the same! There was no mistaking her in spite of the ravages that she had gone through in a short time. A few golden words out of my silver tongue and she slid into the seat next to me.

She was high on something, speedballs perhaps. Her eyes were glazed and her speech was slurred. I flashed a wad of cash and asked her if she was interested in a wild week. She was on me like a bear on honey. I backed her off with one arm while I was wheeling the Ferrari through the streets of Hollywood looking for the route to the on-ramp for the I-5 freeway north to Seattle.

"Wassa matter?" she whined as she tried to grope me again.

"I just want to talk for a while, I like that," I replied.

"Oh, one of those, are you?"

"Until we get there anyway," I countered.

"Where we goin'?"

"I thought we'd head to Canada . . . to Vancouver, it's really happenin' up there, baby!"

"Cool, but I don't know if I got enough candy to last. Gotta have my candy!"

"Don't worry, we'll do a buy in Vancouver, maybe even get something better. I hear that a new shipment just came in from South East Asia. It's much better up there than what's goin down here."

"Cool," she said for the tenth time in five minutes, "I haven't been there in a while."

I didn't know if I would be able to stand to listen to the "cool" word for the rest of the night, let alone the rest of the trip. But I knew one thing - she was still a "baby" in a certain sense, especially to her mom and dad.

So she snorted some white powder up her nose with a coffee straw and chattered away into my ear. She was like a cat on hot pavement. The confines of the car grated on her. Squirming, her short dress kept riding up until she had no modesty left. Fiddling with the stereo and some CD's I had previously bought especially for her, she talked incessantly. When she came down from her high she became cranky, popped a sedative and slept. I dug through her purse to confirm her identity. It was her all right. It wouldn't do to deliver the wrong goods.

Not wanting to risk her fleeing some motel in the middle of the night, other than supervised bathroom breaks at gas stations along the freeway, I drove straight through to Seattle, timing it so that she was asleep when we arrived there.

It was all arranged ahead of time. I had made a quick call on my car phone, giving a prearranged code to notify them when we would be there. I arrived, bleary-eyed, at the front door of an imposing private substance abuse center high on a hill overlooking Lake Union. Bewildered and in need of a snort, she awoke and was met by the sight of her grateful but distraught parents and a host of medical staff. She put up a struggle trying to kick and scream her way out of the trap she felt herself being caught in.

And this too will pass, I thought as I looked back at them entering the clinic through those massive front doors, those are doors to freedom - for a lucky few.

Much later, when all the dust had settled and the three of them slowly got their lives back together, her Dad paid me another visit.

"Just name your fee and it's yours," he stated.

"Ah, it's not the money. I didn't take it on for that. Just the expenses and the difference between the look on your face then and now . . . well, it's all worth it to me."

"My wife is so happy now, it's unbelievable! And our daughter! She owes her life to you! She sent you this note!"

It read "To a really cool guy" and ended with "Thanks for caring enough!" There was that word "cool" again I thought as my eyes misted over, dropping a few tears onto my cheeks.

"And I owe my life to you too!" he stated as he grabbed my hand and pumped it with both of his. "I shudder to think what I may have done if it weren't for you! I was that close to . . . to . . . " he declared as his voice broke up with deep-seated emotion.

I put my other arm around his shoulder and said "I'm just glad that I was able to help you." And life goes on - if you're lucky, I thought.

"I'll tell you what," he stated as he regained his composure. "I've got this old wooden boat that I had totally overhauled a while back - an old ketch. My wife never did like to sail, nor our daughter much for that matter and I want to spend as much time as possible with the two of them as I can now. So it's yours. That is, if you want it."

"Sure," I glibly agreed, thinking that I couldn't turn down a gift even though it was an overhauled old tub.

"Fine!" he said. "You come down next weekend and we'll sail her back. I'll show you the ropes and I'll have one last fling with her."

"You've got a deal," I said to let him complete his end of our original agreement.

So the next weekend I took the Clipper catamaran down to Seattle. I was worrying a little about the seaworthiness of the old sailboat and was wondering if it was big enough to sail through any winds and resultant waves that might come up, especially when we would leave the sheltered waters of Puget Sound and get into the more open Juan de Fuca strait as we neared Victoria. It could be very treacherous near Trial Island and Brotchie Ledge farther on depending on the tide and the winds.

I needn't have worried though. She was a beauty! Some 65 feet long, she had a beam of some 17 feet and displaced 65 tons. A real classic! She was no old tub! She was a ship! And she was recaulked and had new rigging; her masts were sturdy. She was totally refinished and refurbished inside and outside and her diesel engine was brand new too! Built by Leehausen and Sons in Oslo, Norway in 1905, she was used as a fishing vessel in the North Sea. During W.W. II, the Germans had seized her and because of her wooden hull, used her as a mine tender in the Baltic Sea. Gaining her freedom after the war, she saw service as a coastal freighter. In the sixties, she had been brought over from Bergen, Norway to Seattle by way of the Panama canal and lavishly converted for use as an occasional hide-a-away by a Seattle newspaper baron. He was a little eccentric, having built in some unusual features and a number of hidden compartments, some of which I'm still finding as time goes on. The rest of its colourful history will take a little longer to unravel.

I was astonished to say the least! Then reality sank in as I thought about the cost of berthing it back in Victoria.

"I can tell by the look on your face that she's a little more than you bargained for. Well, I've had years of pleasure with her. Now she's yours. And to help you with the maintenance and the port berth fees, here's a cashier's check for you. I'd hate to see her wanting for anything in the future."

I opened the envelope, did a double-take and picked my chin up off the deck. I made a quick mental conversion into Canadian dollars, then calculated the investment interest. Out of that alone, I found that I had annual berthing fees, had the maintenance and that I was now officially retired. That is if I wanted to be! "This is way too much money," I protested.

"No, it's not. I've been very fortunate with my investments. And over the years I've taken out and still hold a number of patents. Hell, with my stock and stock options just from the aircraft manufacturing company alone, I've got more than I could ever spend in my lifetime or my daughter's lifetime for that matter. It's a funny thing, though," he said as he looked intently at me, "I know it's a tired cliche but money just doesn't mean very much to me anymore."

And that was how I came to own the sailing ketch *Valhalla.*

I had, for some years, owned a cap made of cotton with a suede bill that had the name *Valhalla* embroidered upon it. But it was the name of a mountain climbing and hiking outfitter's store that I had frequented in Victoria. Being half Norwegian, I knew that it had great meaning for the Norse, who are the Vikings of Norway, Iceland, and the Faroe Islands - the West Scandinavians. In Norse mythology it was the great hall - a heaven, if you will, into which the souls of Viking heroes who fell bravely in battle were borne by the Valkyries. It also meant an edifice where the remains or memorials of deceased heroes of the nation were placed - a great hall of the slain. So It did seem to be foreordained in that I had owned this particularly-named billed cap. But usually one acquires the boat first, then gets the cap with the name of the boat on it. In my case, I got the cap first and then, by chance, acquired the ship!

CHAPTER THREE

THUNDERSEA

KEAHOLE POINT, KONA, THE BIG ISLAND OF HAWAII. It was the most peculiar thing that the two boys had ever experienced - seeing perfectly-curling waves under their surfboards suddenly turn into quivering tongues of salty water. They looked in vain, out to sea, searching for the cause of the calming.

Farther offshore, a tourist scuba-dive boat was slowly making its way back to Honokohau Harbour after the day's dive. It left a bubbling white wake as its rasping diesel engine propelled it through the water parallel to the beach beyond where the surf line was but moments ago. From its radar tower, it was flying a red dive flag with a white diagonal slash. The stars and stripes flew on its stern.

Billy and Mike saw divers lounging on the afterdeck. Each time the boat rolled they could see rows of air tanks and scuba gear lining the low bulkheads.

To the north, above the horizon on the far side of the airport, they saw two sets of brilliant white landing lights descending out of the azure sky as a couple of wide-body commercial jets prepared to land a few minutes apart.

On this side of the airport, they noticed that the workers at the energy lab complex were no longer tending to their tasks at the various sites on shore. The few trucks and industrial equipment at a construction site were idled and the workers had quit for the day. The black smoke that had billowed out of their machine's exhausts was now gone. Everything looked quietly normal.

Except for the surf.

The two teens were surfing at their favourite spot - up the coast from Pinetrees beach - not far from the seaside Kona International Airport, and just down the beach from the Solar/Sea Energy Agriculture/Aquaculture Lab (SSEAAL), just as they had on countless days before.

They enjoyed this beach despite the intermittent noise. The huge jets would thunder right over their heads on takeoff, their roar muffled only by the cadence of the breaking surf.

The popular beach was only seven miles from Kailua-Kona, where they both lived. It was a sleepy tourist town whose populace was only now waking up to benefits from the increased capacity of the updated international standards in place at the new airport outside town. It meant that larger aircraft could land here and that meant that countries whose airlines used the more cost-efficient larger planes on their longer international routes could now avail themselves of these facilities. The variety of aircraft using the airport, whose runway ran parallel with the beach, intrigued the two boys, sometimes causing them to pause, look up, and gaze in awe at the huge silver birds. The throaty roar of their powerful engines as the planes ascended into the sky for foreign destinations was something that they could readily relate to.

The townsfolk were also slowly sitting up and taking notice of the research lab's varied business tenants on the complex that comprised a wide area of almost a thousand acres. Two separate research labs had originally been funded twenty years earlier. They were merged a number of years ago to form one coordinated research effort that included spinning off research applications to private-sector businesses.

The land upon which it sat was typical of this whole side of the island. It was composed of sloping lava fields of both the rough lava - called a'a - and the smoother, pancake-like lava - called pahoehoe. Both black and brown lava stria mingled here and there in various types of flows that had last flowed about two hundred years ago from a vent far up the slope near the crater of Mount Hualalai. These more recent black flows lay finger-like upon older reddish-brown lava turned that shade by thousands of years of oxidation. The older reddish-brown a'a lava flowed between 5,000 and 10,000 years ago; yet only a few scraggly trees and silky pili grass grew on these open fields.

The maze of pipes and machinery at the research lab on the shore next to the airport lands piqued the two boys' curiosity. Here they often wandered among the businesses, going from site to site along the beach road. They visited the interesting people who worked hand in hand with the friendly guys in the white lab coats over at the main SSEAAL building. They liked poking around the varied types of operations going on, talking to the security guards and seeing all the neat equipment that they used to manufacture or grow their products. And soon they would qualify for and had plans to join one of the high school programs where they could work and study full-time with staff and mentors on various research projects on the SSEAAL site.

Out on the surf, the two boys who had been gliding down that awesome wave on a clear turquoise sea, were now idle; Mount Hualalai, in the background, was bathed in gold. A high-level cloud of volcanic dust that the locals called vog swirled westward around Mount Hualalai from the spewing Pu'u 'O'o vent below the Kilauea crater on the slopes of Mauna Loa in the unseen distance, hidden by the 8,271-foot peak of the adjacent Mount Hualalai.

They were about to call it a day as the sun was slowly sinking toward the sea behind them. Suddenly, when all the waves had flattened into silky folds and then rose into tongues rather than curling and breaking near the shore as they should have, the powerful cresting waves under their boards turned into vapid liquid. A feeling of uneasiness washed over them at this strange occurrence as their boards ominously foundered beneath their feet.

Disappointed, Mike decided to paddle the last remaining distance to shore through the darkening seas rather than make Billy's mom wait for them as they had on one occasion. It was the last time that they had ever made her wait. Even though she was of Hawaiian stock, she didn't let her easy-going nature spoil her son. As she was in the habit of picking them up and giving them a lift home, she had let them know in very specific terms what she expected of them in the future and where their responsibilities lay. Mike could still feel the hot burn of shame on his cheeks and hear the stinging words resounding in his head from the scolding the two of them got from her. Marsha, Billy's mom, was a working single parent who brooked no backtalk and in Mike's opinion was too protective of Billy to suit him. Billy's dad, who had been born in hills of Tennessee, had joined the navy to see the world and had married Billy's mom after falling in love with her during one of his shore leaves. They had an ideal family life after his dad, who was a dive specialist, quit the Navy and found work at a marine contracting company nearby. However, ever since Billy's dad died a while ago in a tragic industrial diving accident not far from here, she became tougher because she had to. And she missed him terribly. The nights were especially torturous to get through. Billy missed the special relationship he had with his dad. They used to be the best of buddies. He sought out Mike more often now that his dad would never be by his side again. Life wasn't as good as it once was for them and never would be, Mike could see that. At the same time, he was glad that he had both his parents and a brother and a couple of sisters, which was nice to have these days.

"I'm goin' back, you comin'?" Mike yelled out to Billy who was some distance over.

"Yeah, you go ahead. I'll catch up to you on the beach."

"Okay!" Mike yelled back as he dug his cupped hands into the water at his sides and pushed back, propelling him toward shore.

Mike thought back to earlier in the afternoon when they had taken a break from surfing. Having brought along their snorkeling gear, Mike and Billy spent an hour or so exploring the crystal clear sea around the pillow lava and the coral reefs. They had seen some colourful Moorish Idols, a comical-looking Lagoon Triggerfish, and loads of Yellow Tangs. A school of small fish, the name of which escaped him just then, had been using a large brain coral as a place of refuge from larger predators. Each time they had neared the brain coral, the little fish would disappear within its protective folds. They had made a game of scaring the little fish back in with just a wave of their arm. They were chuckling so hard at the fishes' antics that they started choking on salt water as their lips burst open with laughter, breaking their lip's seal on their mouthpieces. A serpentine White-Mouth Moray eel had flashed its fangs at them from its niche between two chunks of coarse a'a lava as they glided along. Later they played tag with a couple of green sea turtles who went swimming clumsily by, nudging them out of their way with their hard shells. They watched in fascination the actions of a couple of snorkeling spear fishermen as they hunted their prey. It was then that they decided to resume their surfing lest either one of them accidentally got hit by a stray spear.

"C'mon Billy!" he yelled again.

"I'm coming, don't bug me!" Billy yelled back.

Mike and Billy had been best friends for some time now. After they had finished snorkeling earlier that afternoon, they had sat in the shade of an umbrella-like Beach Heliotrope that Billy's mom had called tahinu. They popped open a couple of cold Pepsi-Colas that they took out of their small cooler. With their backs to the gnarled tree trunk, they talked about surfboards and girls; cars - although they weren't quite old enough to get their licences - and girls; computer games and girls; waves they had caught . . . and girls. Billy had reached over his head into the tree branches and picked off a bunch of tiny green berries and started lazily chucking them at targets here and there.

"You know?" Billy asked slowly. "There's that new girl at school, the one with the dark hair and the freckles . . . I kind of like her . . . Do you?"

"Yeah, she's all right, kinda cute," Mike responded as he watched Billy toss another green berry into the water.

"Yeah, I kind of like her ... a lot. I think her name is Cassandra or something like that," Billy said in a confidential tone of voice.

"Ah, ya nerd! I think you're fallin' in love or something!" Mike taunted as he ducked a shoulder punch in retaliation.

"Am not!" Billy shouted back, readying his fist for another playful punch.

"Are too!" Mike blew in his face as he rose and ran down the beach with Billy right behind him and gaining. Billy got him into a headlock from behind and wrestled him down.

"Give! Okay, okay! I give!" Mike yelled out. "C'mon, let's go surfing again."

Mike's reverie was broken as he finished recalling their tousle earlier and was paddling into the shore.

"C'mon Billy, let's go. Your mom will be here soon and you know what happened the last time we made her wait!" Mike shouted over his shoulder to Billy who was still on his board in the water some distance behind.

"Yeah ... but we're comin' out tomorrow ... okay?" Billy agreed as he shouted in response. A hint of resignation was visible as his shoulders slumped and his lips pursed then curved slightly downwards at their corners.

Mike, whose slightly furrowed brow showed that he was still perplexed at the unusually sudden calming of the waves, thought about this as he paddled along. He threaded his board through channels in the lava-rock jutting up through the surface of the sea. A brilliantly-hued Spectacled Parrotfish flashed in the sunlight just below the surface then turned and glided out of his way. Bumping over a submerged smooth pahoehoe lava rock, Mike darted through the water and came to a grinding halt on a small patch of white coral sand on shore. He lifted himself off the board, stood up and with his right hand still clutching the board's edge, hefted it to his side and under his arm with one practiced motion.

"C'mon, Hillbilly!" He called him that because Billy's dad had been raised in the hills of Tennessee. "Let's go! It looks like your mom's car up there," he teasingly shouted without looking back as he trudged along.

Then he realized that something was wrong. It was too quiet. And

Billy had not come back at him with a crude retort as he usually did when they started teasing each other. Nor was there noise of the surf breaking but there was an odd bubbling sound coming from behind as if from a pot at the boil on his mom's stove. Quickly, he turned around.

Wide-eyed, he stared out at Billy who was just kneeling on his board in the little bay, looking out to sea, his arms hanging down at his sides, his mouth slack-jawed. Mike was mesmerized and stunned by what he saw. The wave-subdued sea was roiling all around Billy, but especially so farther offshore where balloon-sized bubbles were bursting as they surfaced, releasing a gassy fog like sea smoke. Spikes of water leapt straight upwards head-high at Billy from the surface of the sea.

Meanwhile Marsha Tucker, tired from her long day at work, had just arrived. Getting got out of her car, she looked down the beach for the boys, expecting to see them wandering along on their way up, carrying their boards, their towels, and their cooler. She saw Mike, but where was Billy? She looked out onto the sea. Her blood ran cold at the sight.

"Billy, Oh, my God!" she yelled in horror as she spotted him frozen on his board at the far edge of the little bay with the water all around him spouting upwards as if some giant's hand had banged the side of the container that the sea and he were in. And what was that strange mist rising from the bubbling surface?

"Billy!" she yelled again as she broke into a run down the smooth pahoehoe lava slope to the beach. "Billy!" she screamed as she staggered along. She stumbled and fell to one knee, picked herself up and continued running. Blood trickled down from a scrape on her knee.

"Billy!" shouted Mike, finally coming to his sense. He dropped his board at his feet and broke into a run toward the water. Finally Billy tore his eyes away from the boiling sea and looked back at his friend and his mom farther back, running toward him on the beach.

"BILLY!" they both screamed again. "PADDLE IN! QUICK! PADDLE!"

"MOM!" he managed to scream from deep within his throat as he frantically dipped his hands into the water to propel him to shore.

That was when they first heard it!

The reverberating sound came from far down below the sea. It started off as a low, heavy rumble then very quickly grew into a roaring, all-engulfing rolling thunder that exploded from the sea like a banshee out of the deep!

"Billy! Oh, My God! Bill . . . !" was all she got out of her mouth as she tried to scream yet again.

Then it happened!

In an instant the roiling waters turned from an angry gray into an iridescent green, then an electric blue, then as the flash point was reached, the sea turned into a deep, fiery yellowish-crimson.

The rolling thunder from the sea now accompanied a howling moan as wind was sucked offshore, as if in an implosion, just before the full force of the explosion occurred. Marsha and Mike were windswept as they strained to brace themselves as they ran with the sucking wind pulling them along. Bits of loose, low bush mixed in with the flying white sand stung them, then ran with the wind to the sea.

Billy was pulled seaward on his board.

For a split second the gassy grayness morphed into a mass as though it had features like the huffing cheeks of some sinister apparition, then just as abruptly the wind reversed as the offshore explosion blew with a shockwave force onto the land creating a shrieking banshee's wail as it backlashed. The sky turned into a ghastly electric arc brightness creating eerie strobe shadows which were cast onto the shore and upon the streaking shafts of mist.

Marsha and Mike were sent rolling back up the beach slope, alternately tumbling across white coral sand and smooth black pahoehoe lava, and through the silky pili grass and the low scratchy bushes.

The land trembled and shifted and banged, creaking with lifelike contortions and groaning in agony as the shockwave from the explosion rumbled through from the sea, then inland up the rough lava fields of the slopes of Mount Hualalai high above the sleepy town of Kailua.

Billy was torn out of the sea as if by a giant hand. Still clinging to his surfboard, he was flung ashore with such force that it was as though he was actually surfing the glowing waves of exploding misty air.

CHAPTER FOUR

STRATOSFEAR

HIGH ABOVE THE PACIFIC OCEAN NEAR HAWAII. Captain Jack Wardel had over thirty years of commercial flying time logged and was contemplating retirement in the near future. As a senior captain at Canadian Transpacific Air out of Vancouver he had his choice of routes. He chose this one because he liked Hawaii and he liked the shorter hop than most of the other routes the company flew. It had become an enjoyable milk run.

And he liked flying the wide body jets too! This one had a maximum range of twenty-nine hundred nautical miles. His first officer, Nick Lee, had pulled runs with him several times. Nick, who was of Hong Kong Chinese extraction, was a man of smaller physical stature who had just met the minimum height requirements for pilots. Capt. Wardel really liked Nick and sometimes kidded him by asking him if he wanted a pillow to enable him to see out of the cockpit window. Nick would parry, giving a quick thrust back by asking if he wasn't a little long in the tooth to still be a jet jockey.

It had been a long time ago that Jack had first cut his teeth by flying bush planes - those pick-up trucks of the north - by the seat of his pants in the tundra. There were many close calls and a few emergency landings where they would have to sit and wait out a storm on some isolated frozen lake. And there were white-outs so bad that the only reason he was able to set his plane down was that he had lady luck and his common sense riding with him. When situations became tight, Jack realized that panic was his greatest enemy. He relied on calmness to provide him with a clear head which provided him with the opportunity to use logic and reason. Every now and then he had been called upon to go in and rescue another pilot who had set his plane down permanently, or worse yet, where the pilot had set himself down permanently. And the cold! It could be horrific. But he had survived those times and many more in the high arctic flying Beavers and later Hercules into the likes of Inuvik, Iqaluit, and Kaktovik. Now, they were just fond memories and shoe boxes full of photos from his younger days that he and his wife looked forward to sorting through when he retired.

Nick, on the other hand, was a Richmond boy. Raised right near the Vancouver airport; it was natural for him to have caught the love of flying. Unlike Capt. Wardel, he started off flying the feeder flights from Victoria International Airport to Vancouver. They weren't very long - about 15 minutes max - but he got a lot of experience landing and taking off frequently and in all types of coastal weather. Fog, wind, heavy rain, and occasionally ice and snow were his enemies. It was a proud day when he graduated to the bigger birds! He was looking forward to his upcoming marriage to Susan Choy whom he considered to be the most beautiful Chinese girl that he knew. He counted himself lucky to have her as his fiancee.

Still at cruising altitude, their flight from Vancouver to Kailua-Kona was almost at an end, They had been bucking a fierce, high-altitude headwind and areas of clear-sky turbulence for most of the way. The head wind had just recently abated. They checked their instrument panel to scan its readings. Their flight would now take almost six hours. This put their arrival time into Kona International some forty-five minutes behind schedule. The passengers wouldn't be happy at this, to say the least.

The wide-body jet had a maximum cruise speed of 454 knots at 37,000 feet - its two IAE V2500 engines developed a maximum of 26,500 lbs. of thrust - but they had spent a lot of fuel just changing altitude and going around turbulent areas that they had detected. Technology to detect clear-sky turbulence had just been perfected and was recently installed in this commercial aircraft. It worked by a type of radar which sensed the turbulent movement of invisible dust particles in the air. It hadn't come too soon for Jack's liking.

Judging by the fuel gauge, their reserves upon landing would be marginal at best as they were fully loaded to maximum with 180 passengers.

Jack and Nick prepared to get on their glide path to Kona International Airport. In the cockpit they had two primary flight displays, two navigation displays, an electronic centralized aircraft monitor called an ECAM, and two multipurpose control and display units.

The Kona International Airport they would be landing at was the newer one, about seven miles out of Kailua-Kona. The old Kona Airport, which had been outside the town, was now in town and a little too short for safety factors for the bigger jets. But Jack still remembered flying in there. They would be following a Pacific Northwest Air jumbo jet that was just arriving from Seattle. And somewhere behind both of them was a wide-body jet belonging to NorCal Air Charters flight number 1502 out of LAX.

"Okay, let's get this baby down!" Capt. Wardel said to his copilot after they had finished listening to the Kona Air Traffic Control giving final glide path instructions and clearance to land to Pacific Northwest's jumbo flight number 1204. They were somewhere ahead, already on their final approach.

"Kona Air Traffic Control, this is Charley-Fox-Sierra-Zulu-Zulu, Canadian Transpacific flight 807," said Captain Wardel. "Requesting permission to begin our descent."

"Kona tower," they responded. "Canadian Transpacific 807. Turn left, heading two-two-zero. Descend to 10,000."

"Roger, changing heading to two-two-zero. Descending to 10,000 feet."

"Roger, Pacific Northwest 1204 preceding you, NorCal 1502 following."

"Roger that, out."

"This is Captain Wardel," he said over the plane's public address system. "Presently, we are cruising at an altitude of 35,000 feet. It will still be about thirty minutes before we land. We apologize to you for the long flight. We will be running about forty to forty-five minutes late into Kona International due to the headwinds and turbulence that we have encountered along the way. In a moment we'll bank to our left and begin a descent down to 10,000 feet. The airport is currently reporting a balmy temperature of 82 degrees F and winds are calm. If my math is correct that temperature should be about . . . uh . . . 28 or 29 degrees C for those who think in metric. Thank you."

He glanced over to Nick for a descent check.

"Pressurization?" Jack asked.

"Checked," Nick answered.

He reached and flicked the seatbelt warning light on. He eased the yoke to the left and worked the right pedal as they banked sharply to the left, the nose tilting downward from its cruising altitude.

The cabin stewards, under the supervision of the senior attendant, Patsy Mitchell, were making their last minute rounds of the restless passengers, making sure that their carry-on luggage was properly stowed, their seatbelts secured and their trays in the upright position.

Patsy disliked her nickname, her name was Patricia but her uncle hung the moniker on her when she was a toddler and unfortunately the name stuck. She was looking forward to her days off as soon as they returned to Vancouver. She and her husband had planned to go up to Whistler and stay in their condo even though the ski season had not quite started. Lately, they had just wanted some peace and quiet from their hectic lifestyles. The serene beauty of the mountains drew them back in the quieter off-season as well.

Invariably, a few passengers would still be dozing, in spite of the announcement, their seat-backs would still be in the downward position. There was always something!

Amongst the passengers seated on the starboard side of the plane was Florence Clarke - Flo to her friends - and her sister Mavis Brown. This vacation was a seventy-fifth birthday present from Mavis.

They were traveling together as both their husbands had since passed on leaving them comfortable enough but certainly not rich. And a life of frugality, which had been taught them by the Depression of the Dirty Thirties and the deprivations of the Second World War, let them have, at this late stage of their lives, some measure of enjoyment and pleasure. They were both God-fearing, church-going souls who attended regularly to hear the fire and brimstone message from the pulpit. And so they were off to the big island of Hawaii for some fun to tour the churches and to see the volcanoes - sort of a tour of heaven and a glimpse into hell.

At 20,000 feet Captain Wardel ran into some turbulence again. Nick Lee finally caught sight of Pacific Northwest 1204 far in front of them.

Nearing 15,000 feet, the plane resumed gliding smoothly again. They were back far enough so that the turbulence of the jumbo jet ahead wouldn't rock them as they came in behind on the glide path. The setting sun was still some ways up in the sky, enough so that they would be landing in the sunlight but the huge, glowing red orb would be off to starboard, so it wouldn't bother their vision.

"This Captain Wardel again. We are at 10,000 feet now. We will be coming up to the Big Island of Hawaii shortly, passing by the Kohala mountains on your left with the famous Waipio valley farther to the left. On the far side of the mountains are the town of Waimea and the vast lands of the world-famous Parker Ranch."

The mile-high Kohala mountains rose sharply out of the Pacific

Ocean on the port side as they passed over Upolu Point. The deep slash in the land further to the left was the fascinating Waipio valley. They could see a river flowing down the cut, then curling through the small delta to the sea. Frothy white water cascaded like ribbons from the cliffs on the sides of the valley. They passed by the mist-enshrouded green ranch lands on the mountaintop. Then the land fell away again to the small town of Waimea.

The verdant Parker ranch lands, the largest in the world, spread out before them to the left as they culminated in sweeping up the sides of the towering, two-mile-high Mauna Kea volcanic mountain in the distance. Clusters of white-domed observatories sat amidst the snow-capped peak giving Jack a flashback to his bush pilot days in the land of the Eskimo and their igloos.

At 5,000 feet they did an approach check.

"Altimeters." Jack asked.

"Set." Nick replied.

"V Bug."

"Set."

"ECAM status."

"Checked."

"Approach briefing."

"Complete."

Flo, who was the birthday girl and the older sister, had the window seat and was remarking upon the beautiful coastline that contrasted sharply between the greenery of Upolu Point and the black and brown lava on the land, which looked like freshly-ploughed fields, and the creamy patches of contrasting beach sand and white surf separating the aquamarine ocean from it.

The wide-body followed its path in, dropping to 4,000 feet as they cleared the point, past the bay on their left, and swung over the sea again heading for Keahole Point.

"Canadian Transpacific 807, Kona tower. Change heading to one-niner-zero."

"Roger, 807 changing heading to one-niner-zero."

"Let's do our landing check now," Capt. Wardel suggested.

"Okay," replied Nick.

"Approach frequency and courses."

"Set."

"Radio altimeter."
"Set."
"Auto brakes."
"Armed."
"Engine mode selector."
"Ignition."
"Missed approach procedure."
"Checked."

In the hazy distance, they could make out a slash of smooth grey runway amongst the rougher black of the lava fields that abutted the single landing strip. Tiny dots of the terminal buildings were clustered on the left side.

Farther along was the growing industrial layout of the solar energy lab complex on the right side.

Rising to the left in a steady incline were the volcanic slopes of Mount Hualalai. A brownish-gray river of light cloud wound its way from the far side of Mauna Loa in the distance and hooked its way around Mount Hualalai before dispersing into the west horizon. The cloud layer was at the same elevation they were now at. The Islanders called it *vog* - a term for volcanic fog.

Underneath them was a designed inland town and the posh, seaside resorts of Waikoloa. The Queen Kaahumanu highway was a gray ribbon that followed the coastline into the horizon where a small grid work of streets delineated the sloping Sunday kind of town of Kailua-Kona.

"Look, Mavis! I can see the coral under the water as plain as anything!" Flo remarked with the giddiness of the adventure. "And I think I caught a glimpse of the runway up ahead on that point!"

In the cockpit, Captain Wardel had just received his penultimate instructions from the tower. He lowered the landing gear. The gear engaged with a hydraulic whoosh then the wheels snapped into place and locked with a deep, resounding thunk.

"Gear."
"Down."
"Flaps."
"Set"
"Speed brakes."
"Armed."

Three minutes from landing and on the beam, they watched the small white body of the Pacific Northwest jumbo jet meet its shadow as it touched down with a puff of blue smoke streaming from behind its wheels as the tires suddenly screamed into rotation. It fairly rocketed down the white centerline but from this distance back and from this altitude, it looked as if the huge jet was just out for a leisurely drive.

The Pacific Northwest's captain in the plane ahead, was a pilot with an unblemished service record. In all his years of flying in and out of California airports, there was only one time that he had experienced anything even remotely close to this. And that was some five years ago when a 5.8 quake had struck just as he was taxiing to the John Wayne terminal causing his plane to shudder and sway. If there was an earthquake, you wanted to be in the air when it happened. Coming in for the landing was routine at Kona, Captain Chuck Runcey had done it many times. The only tricky part usually was an occasional gust of wind that had to be contended with. In fact, earlier he had mentioned to his copilot, Larry Schindler, that their routine here - landings and take offs - were rather boring and that was something to be monitored also, as a sense of complacency could easily set in under these circumstances.

This time the routine was no different as they were on their final approach.

"500 feet," the first officer had called out.

"Flaps to 30," the captain said.

"Set."

"Gear down."

"Down."

"400 . . . 300," called out the first officer.

Minimum an electronic voice called out. They increased their airspeed.

"200 . . . 100 . . . 50 . . . 40 . . . 30 . . . 20 . . . 10 . . . 5."

Touchdown. There was a slight jolt as the wheels brushed the pavement. Then the nosewheel settled onto the runway as lightly as a feather.

"45, 55, 65, 70 . . . 80 knots, 70 knots."

"On the body gear steering."

"Body gear steering is on."

Capt. Runcey applied the reverse thrusters.

"Manual breaking," the captain said.

"Manual breaking," the first officer repeated as the plane shook off the effects of rapid deceleration.

It had been a picture-perfect touchdown, right on the numbers on a dry runway, no rain, no gusty winds, still daylight. They were about halfway down the runway when Chuck immediately felt something go terribly wrong. It felt as if an unseen hand was steering the plane in a wobbly fashion as they were still decelerating.

Now at three thousand feet on the glide path, Jack in the wide-body following, was intently watching the progress of the tiny white shape on the runway ahead as it neared the halfway mark.

In the cabin, Flo was just as intently watching the surf along the coastline ahead as they descended. She thought it was strange that the three lines of surf that were normally along the shore were missing for a short distance farther up the coast. Suddenly, as if her eyes were playing tricks on her, the aquamarine waters beyond the airport turned a vaporous sullen gray for a while, then quickly flashed to a bright green, then to a blue, and then into a yellowy-red mass. "Oh!" was all she said as she quickly sat upright and pulled at her glasses thinking that she had not been wearing them. She was though! She looked again and saw the devil at work. Her pulse started surging and her heart began a drum-like pounding.

The wide-body jet continued its descent.

"Coming up on two thousand feet," informed Nick.

Jack adjusted the flaps further.

Meanwhile, even though Jack had been watching the instruments intently, a flash of colour caught his eye and directed it forward, out toward the five o'clock position. Nick was already staring blankly out the angled right window of the cockpit, his lower jaw hanging open. Jack had just caught the flash of green in the sea past the airport. The flash covered about a square mile as best that he could judge from this height. A diaphanous veil muted the intensity of the colour as if it were a lingering patch of ground fog in the face of the morning sun. But this wasn't the morning and there was no fog anywhere else. In the milliseconds before it happened, he noticed a minute shape which appeared to be a white boat in the middle of the patch. The green turned to a vivid electric blue, then in a state of fluorescence, changed before his eyes into an outwardly-spreading, yellowish-red hue. The boat was lazily lifted out of the water as if on a giant pedestal where it hovered in the air for a moment before settling back down onto the sea.

The misty vapour streaks first sucked inwards then blew outwards from the center in spoke-like trails of silky voile which ran onto the shore, into the Solar/Sea lab complex, onto the airport runway, past the control tower and up the slope of Mount Hualalai.

Captain Wardel was startled to see the distant white body of the jumbo jet career, shimmy, then overcorrect in the opposite direction, then back and forth again, veering off course as it went into a slow sideways slide. This took the plane to the right side of the runway where it came to a bouncing halt at a crazy angle to the tarmac with its nose over the rough lava.

"What the bloody hell?" exclaimed Jack in astonishment as he watched trails of smoke rise from the plane's landing gear on the runway ahead.

The white vaporous fall-streaks that had radiated over the sea and the land stopped momentarily before dissipating as they slowly drifted out to sea on a soft current of the prevailing wind. Ever so gradually the disturbed sea turned to a rusty-red, then returned to its normal aquamarine blue. Then deep rollers from farther out worked their way across the still-quivering patch of sea to again form three breaking surf lines near the shore.

Larry Schindler, in the Pacific Northwest plane on the Kona International Airport tarmac, had yelled out "What's happening?" as the yawing started. They felt the body of the jumbo jet being buffeted by a tremendous gust of wind. They noticed that the runway was moving like a slowly twisting snake. First this way, then that way, making it difficult to keep the plane under control at this most vulnerable time. Finally, no longer able to maintain a straight line forward, they felt the giant plane yawing in increasingly wider positions until such point as it was impossible to control it at all. The big white bird went into a sideways skid to starboard, away from the airport terminal, blowing some of the tires. Sparks showered out from behind the bare metal rims raking the asphalt. Heavy black smoke billowed out from the ragged blown rubber tires as they were haphazardly dragged and flopped around their rims in a jouncing fashion. As they skidded almost to a stop, the plane's forward rotation of its rims caught and carried the nose and the nose-wheel into a forward arcing turn into the rough a'a lava beside the runway bouncing the fuselage as it came lurching to a smoking rest.

Chuck and Larry sat still, momentarily stunned from the abrupt bouncing on the lava. Then they both quickly sprang into action to start shutting the plane's fuel off and engines down as fast as they could. Wisps of smoke filtered into the cockpit. The fear of fire crept like a stealthy griffin into their very souls, shaking them to the core. Chuck opened the side window to clear the air. The plane had survived remarkably intact for what it had been subjected to, although at that point the two pilots had no way of determining the extent of their good fortune due to the sturdiness of their well-built craft. They quickly ran down the emergency checklist, flipped the fire control switches to stop the oil flow and incapacitate the electrical and hydraulic systems. With the fuel control switches deactivated and the engine master switches shut off, they turned their attention to their cabin crew.

A flushed flight attendant flung the cockpit door open to reveal clamoring passengers trying to escape as quickly as possible. A burst of stinking, burning rubber smoke blew in from behind her, cooling their sweat-drenched brows, but fouling their air further.

Frantic flight attendants were snapping the last of the exit doors open. Billowing chutes sprung out to the sides like the tethered balloon figures at a Macy's Thanksgiving Day parade. Panicking passengers jumped down onto the chutes in a pell-mell fashion, some tumbling out of control in their haste.

Wailing crash trucks screeched to a halt, their red lights flashing in urgency. Silver-suited firefighters jumped off the trucks, running to deal with the wheel fires that resulted. Luckily, only the shredded rubber tires were aflame, and these were soon under control; their billowing black smoke made the fire look worse than it actually was. The melting rubber formed great gobs of black on the tarmac. The red-hot rims melted the asphalt under them, creating deep, sticky depressions under each wheel.

The sinking sun bathed the clusters of silvery, space-suited firefighters with splashes of red. Elongated stick-figure shadows were cast upon the tarmac by the ragtag lines of limping, sooty passengers helping each other get to a safe distance away.

This was not the Hawaiian aloha they had expected.

"Abort landing, go around!" Jack needlessly barked at Nick in the Canadian Transpacific wide-body jet moments from touchdown.

"Aborting, go around."

"Flaps!"

"Set."

Jack hammered on his throttle, increasing his air speed. It took about five or six seconds to spool it up enough to regain part of his altitude.

"Kona tower! What is going on?" Jack fairly shouted into his headset. "This is Canadian Transpacific 807!"

There was no reply.

"Tower! Come in! This is Canadian Transpacific 807! Do you read?"

Silence.

"Jesus H. Christ!" Capt. Wardel swore under his breath in frustration.

A few moments later the stunned and bewildered voice of an air traffic controller acknowledged the urgent transmission. "Canadian Transpacific 807, Kona tower. We have an emergency. We've been hit by an earthquake or a shockwave of some sort. There is also an emergency on the runway. Pacific Northwest has been blown part way off the tarmac onto the lava beds by a blast which rocked us down here. One of our plate glass windows shook loose and fell. You're going to have to divert and proceed to Hilo. I repeat. Emergency! Divert and proceed to Hilo!"

"Roger. Divert to Hilo."

"Did you see what happened?"

"Roger, tower. Something exploded out in the sea, just past the airport offshore of the SSEAAL complex! It covered about a square mile or so!"

"Roger, out!" Then . . . "NorCal 1502, Kona Air Traffic Control."

"NorCal 1502."

"Did you monitor?"

"Yes."

"Divert to Hilo as well."

"Roger Kona tower, NorCal 1502 diverting Hilo."

The lumbering wide-body was now closing in on the airport. They could see silver-suited crash crews hanging onto emergency trucks. Strobe lights persistently flashed as they sped down the tarmac toward the jumbo jet now awkwardly run part way onto the rough a'a lava beds at the far right side of the runway. White and black smoke wafted up from the wheel areas as reddish-orange tongues of flame licked out from them. Pillowy escape chutes shot out from the plane's sides; the leading forward chute lodged at a crazy angle atop the rough a'a lava. The Canadian Transpacific wide-body soared slowly over the runway, through the rising smoke columns from the jumbo jet's wheels and along the edge of the Solar/Sea complex, slowly rising as they gained some air speed.

Flo began perspiring. She glanced out the window at the emergency vehicles rushing along to the shocking scene below. Her already-pounding heart shifted into fibrillation with the shock of what she was seeing. She managed to gasp "I can't breathe . . . it hurts," then clutching at her chest and slumping forward, she hit her forehead on the plastic tray clasp as she lapsed into unconsciousness. A fine mist of blood sprayed out from a cut on her brow, sullying the fabric of the seat-back with ribbons of crimson which ran down the raised plastic tray in tiny red rivulets. As Mavis reached over to stem the flow, blood oozing through her fingers, she let out a pleading scream for some aid for her sister.

"My sister needs help!" Mavis shouted. "Someone, help me! Please!"

What now? Thought Patsy as she quickly got out of her jump seat and ran to see what all the commotion was about, her irritation turning to fear as she surveyed the bloody scene. Oh, my God!

"But what about the fuel?" Nick asked with consternation. "We've burnt up a lot of fuel fighting that headwind, remember? It'll be touch and go if we can make Hilo safely!"

"Eh? Damn, I'd forgotten about that!" Jack replied gravely. "Hmm!"

"What's our alternative?" asked Nick with consternation.

"Well, there's the airport at Waimea but I think it's too short. Then there's the airport at Bradshaw Army Base on the other side of Mauna Kea, but it's a mile high and I don't know how long a runway they've got."

The cabin door burst open. A pale-faced Patsy Mitchell pushed her way in. "Captain, there's an emergency in the cabin. I think a passenger is having a heart attack and she is bleeding profusely from a head cut. She's unconscious! She needs immediate medical attention!"

"God, no!" Jack's body stiffened involuntarily. "Not at this time! There's been a plane go off the runway. We're supposed to be diverting to Hilo! Get on the intercom and ask if there's a doctor on board. Okay? It's a good thing you've been certified as an EMT."

"Got it!" Patsy replied as she struggled to compose her emotions. Then she announced . . . "Your attention please! We have a passenger medical emergency on board. If there is a doctor or other medical personnel on board please make yourself known to either myself or one of the other flight attendants. Also, due to circumstances beyond our control we are diverting to Hilo Airport. Please stay buckled up and in your seats. We need the aisle free! I repeat. Please remain calm and stay buckled in your seats!"

But no one came forward.

Patsy felt a momentary stab of panic as she informed the captain by intercom phone that there were no doctors or other medical people on board, then went back to help with the victim. She quickly returned to the cockpit to report that the elderly female who had been unconscious had now regained consciousness but was still in considerable distress with a suspected heart attack. The elderly lady was complaining of chest pains, her throat and lower jaw had a deep pain, her left arm hurt and she could not breathe properly. Added to that, she was covered in blood before they were able to staunch the flow from her spurting head wound. They now had her clothing loosened and had her reclining in her seat. They had given her some oxygen but it didn't seem to have helped very much. Her distress was overriding their efforts at first aid. They had even given her a tab of nitroglycerine from the medical kit and put it under her tongue but its effect was marginal.

Patsy burst into the cockpit again. "Captain, she needs emergency help now or she's going to die! What are we going to do?" Patsy implored with a sense of helplessness as her eyes dampened with spontaneous tears. "I've got to get back to her now!"

Her words brought Jack out of his concentration with the cockpit readings. He took a deep breath to fight the rising panic. Now calmer, he reasoned his way through this latest problem. Their fuel requirement to get them there was questionable at best. The heart attack victim probably would not survive the delay in getting to Hilo. That would not do!

Then just dead ahead was the old Kona Airport runway. It was now used as a long parking lot to accommodate the state park beach next to it. It looked nearly empty. What cars and trucks were there were parked off on the beach side, well off the faded centerline of the old runway. The beach-goers had mostly gone home and the nighttime party crowd had not yet arrived in any appreciable numbers. This gave him an idea, admittedly a somewhat crazy idea, but an idea nonetheless. His only chance to save the woman would be to land here. There was a hospital only a minute or two away. But was the runway long enough? It just might be. And he definitely had enough fuel to land here but he was unsure if there was enough fuel to get them safely to Hilo. As he came up on it he judged that, though it would be close, there would be enough length and the tarmac was dry which would help with the stopping distance.

Let's see . . . ideally we need a runway 5,630 feet long and a maximum landing length of 4,750 feet, he thought. Damn, I can't recall the length of this one.

But as they overflew and neared the far end, he could see that they had built a low, metal pipe fence across its width. But there also was a wide, open gate in the center which was to be closed when the park was closed late at night. He figured that he could thread the needle if it came to that. They had a wingspan of about 112 feet but the wings themselves would go over the fence. He calculated that the tires just might go through the open gate if they had to go that far along the runway.

"Nick? I'm thinking of setting her down here. What do you think?"

"I don't know. I've never landed here before. That was before my time. Is there enough runway? Are you sure it's okay?"

"Nick, I've landed here hundreds of times, but with smaller planes. This is a little different. If I didn't think I could do it I would never have suggested it. We're low on fuel and it's her only chance to get to a cardiac unit in the hospital quickly. For the record, I'm going to override your objections if you have any. It'll be solely my decision. Understand?"

"Yeah," he said with a resigned shrug of his shoulders. He felt the tension magnify between his shoulder blades and thought to himself: If anyone can do it, you can!

"Kona tower, Canadian Transpacific 807."

"Tower, go ahead 807."

"We are low on fuel with absolutely no appreciable safety margin to make Hilo - we burnt a lot of fuel fighting the headwinds on the way over. We also have a medical emergency on board - a passenger with a cardiac attack - which precludes diverting to Hilo. I am informing you that we will make a pass then go around out to sea and set down on the old Kona Airport runway. It looks fairly clear of vehicles."

Silence.

Then . . . "Are you sure?" the controller asked in an incredulous voice. "What about the length? And then there's that fence thing across near the end!"

"Yeah. I've calculated that into my plans. I think we can do it. Is there anyone you can contact at the old Kona Airport that can keep any more traffic from going on to the tarmac?"

Silence.

Then . . . "Yeah, I think so. There's still a port office staffed there at the far end. I'll phone over to advise them to assist."

"And see if you can have at least one ambulance out there to try and meet us - it's an elderly woman with a heart attack. She's in bad shape. I know you guys got your own problems just now but . . . "

"Don't worry. We'll also get a fire truck out there from town. We'll take care of it. And captain?"

"Yeah?"

"Good luck!"

"Roger, tower. I'll need it. Thanks." Jack quickly swung his head toward his copilot and barked, "Nick, get Patsy in here, okay?" Nick talked to her on the phone. She hung up and came straight in.

"Patsy! How is she doing?"

"Not very good at all. We're doing all that we can for her but she doesn't seem to be responding too well. I'm afraid she won't last long!"

"Okay. Here's what we're going to do. You know the old airport runway in town - the one we just flew over?"

She nodded her head up and down, her face puzzled at his question.

"Well, we're going to try to land there . . . just like the old times! It's our only chance for a safety margin on the fuel - we're running low, maybe too low to make Hilo with a safety margin - and it's her only chance of timely cardiac care by the looks of it."

Patsy's eyes grew wide with surprise. "Okay," she slowly said.

"So get one of the other attendants buckled in next to her as best as they can and get your patient settled in and make her as comfortable as you can. She's going to need the best care that we can give her until we get on the ground. We'll go around first, then land. The landing will be a little rough, given the shorter runway and the lack of runway maintenance over the years. Tell our passengers what we're going to do, when we're going to do it and then get everyone to prepare for an emergency landing!"

Patsy hurried back to her patient. "Everything's going to be fine! I've talked to the captain and he is going to land the plane in a few minutes. There'll be paramedics there as soon as we stop," she promised Flo while unsure whether she believed her own words or not.

Captain Wardel went around by making a slow lazy turn to starboard, west over the Pacific Ocean. His mind was going at warp speed, calculating and recalculating the mechanics of the landing. This one would have to be done without the aid of the latest landing electronics.

He felt butterflies in his stomach, like he had thirty years ago when the going got rough during his bush pilot days. Then, it was usually just him, some freight, maybe a few others, and his gut feeling. But now it was a plane-load of people and a full complement of crew.

He kept turning the plane in a wide circle, bringing the big bird back over the shoreline, lining himself up with the tiny runway in the distance for the one-shot approach.

"Nick, keep a sharp eye out for any vehicles or people on the tarmac, eh?"

"Yeah. I hope that it stays clear!"

"Well, here goes my pension!" He momentarily thought of his wife.

Nick shot him a quick glance in sympathy, gave a quick panicky thought to his own career and his fiancee, then strained his eyes to scan the stretch of asphalt dead ahead. A few cars were parked along the right side. One was leaving the far end and would be gone before they landed. It looked like two cars were parked at this end of the runway but they could overshoot them.

"Captain. Everything looks good. Some cars are still parked on the right and one is just leaving on the far end. Other than that, there are two parked right at this end but I think we'll be able to clear them."

"Okay. That should be good. I'll keep it high enough so we can just slide over the top of the two cars parked on this end. And call out our altitude and airspeed, eh? I'm going to have to concentrate on my visuals!"

"Okay."

"Flaps."

"Set."

Captain Wardel settled the lumbering wide-body jet lower and lower, slowing to near stall speed, lining it up exactly with the faded centerline of the old runway which sprouted a few tufts of pili grass here and there.

Sweat beaded on his brow; there would be no room for error.

They could see a pick-up truck at the far end of the tarmac with its yellow light flashing and a lone figure waving his arms to block traffic from using the entrance to the tarmac from the street. Other figures were standing near the buildings at the far end. Downtown he could see an ambulance's flashing red lights wending its way through the busy streets to get to the abandoned airport. It was followed by a careering fire truck with a bank of sparkling red lights atop its cab.

Suddenly their yokes started vibrating. They incurred a shaker indicating that they were in imminent danger of stalling. Jack increased his airspeed.

"The numbers, Nick, the numbers!" Jack requested in a calm but forceful voice. Nick again called out their altitude and airspeed in response.

At the last second Jack again increased the airspeed slightly and nosed it up to just skim over the two cars right in front of him.

But, unknown to the pilots, the two cars were actually revving their engines loudly - unaware of the fast-approaching plane behind them - in anticipation of a fast start in an impromptu drag race. The two drivers watched each other intently, cigarettes dangling out of their loose lips, looking for that hint that the other would display a moment of weakness.

Their girlfriends and a gaggle of hangers-on stood off to the sides, behind the cars. One sunglass-clad youth stood in front of the two cars, midway between them. In his hand, in place of a checkered flag to start the race, was a bikini top, which he was going to set spinning into a circular motion over his head to start the drag race. The small crowd off to the sides raised their arms and shouted encouragement to their respective friends.

Just as the heavy jet was almost over them, the starter finally saw but still did not hear, the looming jet headed straight toward them. The starter dropped his arms in fright and lurched forward, crouching down to get out of the way of the incoming plane.

Seeing this, the two drivers gunned their engines and popped their clutches. With a squeal of tires and a trail of blue smoke, they were off. Suddenly their world got really dark as they were now traveling at speed directly under the fuselage of the descending plane. As they accelerated, the huge jet overtook them, its fiery exhausts showering the cars in oily, flaming smoke and then buffeted them, sending them into wild gyrations as their front ends rode up off the asphalt with the lift provided from the exhausts of the roaring behemoth directly in front. The cars acted like out-of-control, supercharged funny cars at the drag races except that their drag chutes were actually two huge jet engines in front of them. Then the two dragging cars slammed down onto the tarmac, the force and the turbulence setting them into spins like they were whirling dervishes that only time and distance could stop.

The heavily-loaded wide-body jet hit hard but stayed down. Normally, they would have set it down quite a distance beyond the leading edge of the runway but they hit well before that to shorten their stopping distance. The nose wheel bounced sickeningly. They were in danger of losing control for a moment but managed to overcome the wobble. Jack immediately threw his thrusters into full reverse and jumped on the brakes hard, really hard! The giant aircraft shuddered down the lumpy tarmac still shooting down the faded centerline. The fuselage chattered and squealed in protest as it was squeezed by the rapid deceleration forces working upon it.

They rocketed down the runway.

The brakes began to turn a deep red, then a brighter cherry red as they grew hotter and threw a shower of sparks behind them. The halfway point was coming up fast. A group of surfers packing their boards into the rear of their Toyota SUV turned and gaped slack-jawed at the huge jet as it screamed by them in the long parking lot. The fellow with the last surf board let it slowly slide down toward the tarmac until it dropped completely out of his grasp and fell the remaining distance onto his toes.

The low pipe fence that spanned the width became clearer as they rolled closer to the end. Now Jack clamped the brakes on as hard as they would go. Wisps of white smoke trailed behind each set of wheels. The brakes groaned with an eerie low moan. The fuselage screamed as it twisted, bent and bucked under the tremendous strains exacted upon it, but it held together. Still, the fence loomed in front of them. Realizing that they weren't going to stop short of the fence, Jack lined the nose of the plane up with the center of the open gate. Now that he knew that they would have to thread the needle, he hoped that his calculations had been fairly accurate. Thundering down upon the fence, the nosewheel threaded the gate but the rear wheels smacked the horizontal pipes with an abrupt metallic bang. The pipes tore loose in a shower of fiery, hot sparks and were sent flying off to either side.

But the landing gear held.

Jack now concentrated on the upcoming end of the runway. He needn't have worried; they managed to get her stopped with a sudden jolt just short of the end of the tarmac.

Now licks of flames ran up each smoking wheel. The wailing fire engine pulled up alongside and started dousing the undercarriage with fire retardant foam and made quick work of putting out the initial fire. However, the fires kept restarting as soon as the oxygen got to them again. A tire blew on the left main landing gear with such an explosive force that it sounded like a shotgun going off. Now they sprayed more foam on the brakes to bring their temperature down. The hot metal sizzled, crackled and sputtered. Clouds of steam joined the smoke in billowing white clouds around the fuselage.

The flight attendants opened the emergency exit doors, activating the escape chutes. The paramedics hastily got the firefighters to back their truck up and put a ladder up to an open door so they could provide a first response for a gasping Flo, the heart attack victim.

In the cockpit, Captain Wardel slowly pulled each of his white fingers off the yoke in turn.

"Fuel pumps!" he yelled.

"Off."

"Engine master switches!"

"Off."

Captain Jack Wardel momentarily slumped in his seat as the engines shut down. They had done it! "YEAH!" he shouted out, weakly throwing one fisted arm into the air, then reached over and jubilantly gave an ashen-faced Nick Lee a hearty slap on the back.

CHAPTER FIVE

SHOCKWAVE

KEAHOLE POINT, KONA, THE BIG ISLAND OF HAWAII. The spirulina tanks at the SSEAAL complex near the Kona International Airport were already being agitated by the several huge paddles that resembled those of an old sternwheeler riverboat. The tanks were huge, each of them a block long, wide as a house and head-high. They resembled the oval shape of the Daytona race track except that Spirulina Pacifica algae-laden water, not race cars, coursed through its ways. The paddles kept the green water moving in one direction around the oval.

When the shock wave hit, the force halted the oncoming water. On the opposite side of the oval it pushed with the water forcing it into a high wave that failed to negotiate the gentle roundness of the end of the oval. There it sloshed over the curve, spilling a large quantity on the lava beds upon which the oval was built. The spilled water did not flood down the slope toward the far-off road, but mostly found small holes and fissures in the lava beds where it ran down into the depths of the earth.

On the opposite side of the oval, what water did force its way around the curve without spilling over the edge, now joined force with the water that was pushed and held back by the explosive force. In the lull of the immediate aftermath, this massed green water surged back in its original direction, and upon reaching the other curve, spilled over onto the adjacent road where it floated a parked pickup truck, carrying it off the road and down onto the lower lava beds, leaving the pickup splashed with a coating of green algae residue. It was stranded askew atop a crazy jumble of sharp 'a 'a lava.

Luckily, the two people who were the evening shift this Friday night were only knocked down by the force. They were not totally inundated with water from the oval as they had been monitoring their equipment from the side rather than at the ends where it was the most dangerous. Their injuries consisted of bruised arms and skinned elbows. Picking themselves up, they were awestruck by the enormity of the force and were oblivious to their soaked green clothing. They looked like two figures from the movie, *Creatures from the Black Lagoon*, however in this case, it was a green lagoon.

At another site farther down the road, a blue lobster skittered along on the concrete walk making scraping and clicking sounds, an escapee from its holding tank. The blast had propelled it out of the tank much as a surfer is moved along with a curling wave. There were more lobsters spilled farther on. They were unsure of what to do now that they were free of their confines but also out of their artificially cool, watery element. A silent alarm went off at a security company which in turn triggered an employee's pager to go off as he was just about to sit down to dinner with his family.

Next door, the spat hatchery plant's alarms sounded shrilly when the jolt hit the facility. The baby oysters, which would eventually grow black pearls, were rocked back and forth but other than losing some chilled water from their tanks, they survived quite well.

The giant black pipeline that carried chilled water from the deep and ran up the lava beach onto the land at the SSEAAL lab complex reacted to the force of the explosion as if it were a giant water snake that twisted in agony. It moved sideways, pushing their deepwater stabilizing abutment anchors from side-to-side. Farther on shore, the pipeline writhed as if it were alive, whipping and snapping with minute movements.

The cold-steam electrical generating tower beside the research lab swayed back and forth as the ground undulated beneath this squat three-story form. The shock force that rushed through the air and through the ground rocked it off-center for a few moments as it went by. It resumed its swaying after that, but owing to superior construction on this quake-prone island, the tower held its place and did not leak.

The security guard had been making his rounds of the SSEAAL complex in a golf cart. He thought that he was okay, though a bit shaken as he surveyed the cart which had been blown over with him in it. The cart had lodged itself amongst the stair framework that rose on the south side of the cold-steam tower. Although still dazed, the security guard checked himself for acid burns from the cart's leaking batteries but could not readily see any evidence of acid wetness on his clothes. However, as a precautionary measure, he ran for the emergency shower in the adjacent research lab where there was a mirror to check himself out. There was one lone technician on monitor duty tonight and he would check on him just as soon as he was satisfied that he was all right. He noticed that his arm was starting to swell and turn purple. It felt a little funny too.

He didn't know it but it had been broken when he had reached out to protect himself as the cart went tumbling over and it had rolled over onto his outstretched arm.

CHAPTER SIX

SEA DOG

OFFSHORE OF KEAHOLE POINT, KONA. It had been a perfect day for Jennifer and Doug Andersen. They had signed onto the dive boat *Sea Dog*, a 45-foot cruiser, along with five other couples for a day of scuba diving, sun tanning and relaxing. Now they were making their way back to Honokohau Harbour after having explored the reefs of the Hawaiian Islands Humpback Whale National Marine Sanctuary off the coasts of the Kona and the Kohala districts on the Big Island.

Jennifer had first read about the sanctuary in an article in a National Geographic magazine a while ago. It had piqued her curiosity. Doug thought it was a great idea, one in which they could take a much-needed vacation and indulge in their favourite sport at the same time. She had read that the National Marine Sanctuary System, of which the Hawaiian sanctuary was one of about a dozen scattered along the coastlines of the United States and its protectorates, was managed by the National Oceanic and Atmospheric Administration - NOAA - itself a division of the Department of Commerce. Resource protection is its mandate. The marine areas themselves are not parks in the traditional sense of the word. Generally, you can't drill, dredge, mine, dump effluent into, nor remove artifacts from these areas. However, they still allow a multitude of other uses. You can conduct a commercial fishery, set traps and dive for seafood, sport fish, and spearfish.

Basking in the late afternoon sun, Jennifer thought back to many years ago when she was a little girl. One of her brother's friends had playfully pushed her off the dock at the lake one summer back in Wisconsin, instilling a deep-seated fear of the water. It took a number of years and plenty of her mother's encouragement and patience before she was able to take swimming lessons at the local pool, and even more time for her to graduate to actually swimming in the lake. Being from the Midwest, her family had taken her out to the Oregon coast for a vacation one year. Her old fear of the water came back to haunt her once again. Seeing the roiling waters of the surf, she was suddenly overcome by thalassophobia - an abnormal fear of the sea - which remained with her throughout her teen years.

When Jennifer met Doug, she was somewhat disconcerted to find out after she fell quickly in love with this jovial man, that he was a scuba diver. Her old fears came back to haunt her. However, through his love, devotion and perseverence he gently taught her to love the sea as he himself did. Soon, they were scuba diving together. She lost all fear of the sea.

Or so she had thought.

Jennifer was ensconced in a comfy chair near the stern; the throb of the diesel engine and the warmth of the sun were conducive to sleep. The soft music coming from the stereo - the Eagles' *Hotel California* just began - put her into a mellow mood.

Little did she know of the terrible forces that were soon to be exacted upon all of them.

She lazily opened both eyes to glance around her. Doug was talking diving with a couple of the other divers. They were having cold beers to slake their air tank-induced thirst. What had caused her to wake up from her daydreaming? She wondered. Then she realized that they had motored into an area of calmer waters. The skipper was up on the flying bridge, his mate was stowing the gear down below and tidying up. One girl and her hunky partner were sunbathing on the forward deck. A couple of the other girls were chatting about their kids back home in Toledo. She remembered that her regulator had been a little balky on their last dive so she decided to take a moment and check it out. Maybe someone will know what the problem is, she thought.

Jennifer slowly rose and padded over to her gear bag, extracted her regulator, and sought out an air tank that wasn't empty. She looked over at Doug. He gave her a wink with a twinkling eye. "I'm going to check out my reg. . . . It was sticking a little on our last dive," she informed him. He nodded. She walked over to Timotea, the mate. "Tim," she asked, "which tank has some air in it?"

"That one clipped into the rack, the blue one, is one of the two spares. It should still be full," he replied with a friendly smile.

She hunkered down and screwed her regulator onto the tank, leaving it clipped onto the rack on the bulkhead. There was a reassuring hiss when the air entered the lines as she opened the valve. Popping the rubber mouthpiece in, she closed her teeth gently on the custom-formed bit. She took a few tentative breaths, feeling the air surge into her mouth from the tank. From the corner of her eye, she noticed Doug coming toward her.

That was when it happened!

Jennifer noticed Doug quickly glance away from her to the sea. She saw his smiling face quickly turn to wonderment, then to puzzlement, then a slight expression of concern fleetingly appeared before it turned to one of abject fear. She swivelled her head to follow his gaze, the regulator still stuck in her mouth. The sea was literally boiling. Huge breaking bubbles released a white, gassy mist into the air causing the waters to jump up in towering tongues, splashing water against the gunwales of the boat. She looked on in horror. Jennifer became aware of a heavy rumbling sound that grew in volume until it completely overwhelmed the throb of the engine. The boat shuddered as it cruised along, as if it had entered heavy water. The sound became a shriek, then a mighty roar as it emerged from the deep as the waters roiled in grayness, then turned into a luminescent green, then a bright blue. The roar became thunderous as the sea turned a sickly shade of red as it culminated with an explosive thunderclap that shook them to their very bones.

Jennifer's last sensation before losing consciousness was that of being violently flattened against the afterdeck as the dive boat rose to meet her.

The *Sea Dog* was blown out of the water, straight up on a salty column of sea. There was a rising wall of white in a veil of congealing mist, the vapours were drawn toward them. As the forces exploded, the raging shockwave blew the mist outwards in shreds of shrieking flames and white mist that hit the land some half-mile distant and continued through the SSEAAL complex, across the airport facility and up the slopes toward Mount Hualalai.

The *Sea Dog* settled back down upon the sea, its diesel engine stopped dead. There was a resounding silence save for the reverberation of the explosion and muted music. Slowly the soft breeze dispersed the waves of mist and brought a more gentle appearance to the land and seascape. Gradually the incessant offshore waves worked their way toward shore, once again bringing the heartbeat of the sea back to this forsaken place. The *Sea Dog* drifted and wallowed like a seasick hound. It pitched and rolled and yawed, seemingly lifeless upon the sea.

Adrift!

Jennifer thought that she was a child again with her mother gently rocking her in her arms and softly singing a lullaby to her:

Rock-a-bye baby

In the tree top
When the wind blows
The cradle will rock
When the bough breaks
The cradle will fall
Down will come baby
Cradle and all.

Jennifer, the little girl, became alarmed when the rocking took on a more erratic nature. She tried to cry out but the sounds came out only as a nightmarish low moan. Her brain tried to make sense of it, the synapses and neurons kick-starting each other with sparks that hit and missed then finally started firing the cylinders of her soul, gradually bringing her back to this world. She had a foul taste in her mouth. A rubbery taste and a sensation of a choking dryness in her throat.

Her eyes opened slit-like and stared vacantly, trying to make sense of the weird angles and shapes that were in front of her.

Her ears rung.

With a start she saw a hulking prone form near her in the dimness of her sight. Then she saw other forms farther on, lying on the white deck.

Crazy angles.

Beyond were pencil-points of light glowing in an array of colours - white, red, green, yellow and orange. She tried to make sense of this innocent dream that was turning into a nightmarish scene.

She couldn't though.

Jennifer tried to move but could only manage a slight roll of her body in time with the roll of the dive boat. But it was enough so that she could recognize the familiar features of her husband Doug. He lay comatose, his face covered in thickening blood.

She tried to scream but the rubbery thing in her mouth strangled her voice.

Panicked, she tried to rise, but managed to elevate herself on one elbow only. She lost her balance as the deck tilted, throwing her down again. Again she tried to get up. She managed to sit up. She tried to scream again but that thing in her mouth prevented the sound reaching her other than inside her head.

Groggily, she steadied herself with one hand on the gunwale. With the other she reached up to her mouth and pulled the rubbery mass out. She felt queasy. Saliva dribbled out of her numb mouth. It took a few moments for her brain to recognize the thing in her hand as that of the regulator mouthpiece and that it was attached by a length of hose to an air tank which was clamped onto the bulkhead near the gunwale. It's my regulator, she thought.

Jennifer took a deep breath of air, then gagged as it tasted bitter and foul. She heard a ragged scream, then realized that the scream had come from within her.

Coughing, she had the presence of mind to jam the regulator back into her mouth, sucking greedily at the sanitized air.

Her heart was racing. Her mind was now working at warp speed trying to comprehend her surroundings. She kept hearing something. Or was it that she felt it more than heard it? Like the heavy bass of rock music from a distance. She touched her ear. It felt numb. She drew her hand away. It was sticky with her blood. Jennifer began screaming. Horrified, she touched her ear again, feeling it with her fingers. Some of the blood was removed from her ear canal. She heard her scream from outside of her head now, startling her even more. Now she could also hear the music - the Eagles' *Hotel California.* Where was she? She heard sloshing sounds that seemed to upset her equilibrium. Then she realized - she was on a boat! She heard nothing else.

She reached over to Doug. She shook him. He just rolled from side to side. Blood dripped from his mouth and caked his ears, pooling on the white deck under him. She put her fingers on his neck, feeling nothing but the warm blood covering it. She shook him again as if to rouse him to life.

Nothing!

She felt for his carotid artery again, this time finding it under the sticky blood covering his neck.

Nothing!

Nothing!

Wait! What was that? Was that a pulse? Or was she just imagining this nightmare?

Jennifer tore the regulator mouthpiece out of her jaw. She leaned over Doug's supine form and pressed her lips to his bloodied face and blew. Her breath bubbled red out of his nostrils. She breathed in the air and again choked on the contaminated air. It was slightly better this time but still tasted foul. She jammed the regulator back into her blood-smeared mouth and breathed deeply.

Holding her breath she had the presence of mind to pinch his nostrils shut this time, remembering to tilt his head back slightly. She saw his bare chest rise as she blew. She continued drawing breaths from the regulator for both of them in turn, hoping against hope that she could resuscitate him. She thought she could detect shallow breaths coming from him but she wasn't sure.

She continued.

He seemed to be trying to take shallow breaths on his own. Then Jennifer got the idea to supplant her breathing for him with her regulator. She eased it into his mouth. He seemed to be able to draw a breath much better now, albeit shallow. She was left gasping for air. Withdrawing the regulator once again to take in a supply of air for herself, Jennifer quickly jammed it back into his mouth.

Looking around for a second air tank and regulator, she noted that the air tank she was using was still clamped to the bulkhead and wouldn't roll around. She looked around further.

She still didn't see one.

Seeing her husband's dive bag under a bench at the bulkhead, she crawled to it, unzipped the bag and fossicked inside, finally coming up with his regulator. She dragged it out. One of the gauges got jammed on some gear inside. She tore it loose and crawled over to the row of air tanks strapped to the bulkhead. She cranked the valve open.

Nothing!

She grabbed at the next one in line, opening it.

Hiss!

Good!

Jennifer threaded the line on, opened the valve, and jammed the regulator into her mouth, greedily sucking at the air. She glanced over at Doug's form on the deck. Her regulator was still stuck in his mouth. She thought she could detect a very slight rise and fall of his chest.

Then the unthinkable happened!

Her tank ran out of air.

Which one was the other spare? She thought frantically.

Fumbling with their valves, she tested the other tanks that were strapped down on the bulkhead. Finally she found the right one, quickly switching her regulator over to it.

The air quality outside was marginally better but still not suitable for continuous breathing. Jennifer tore at the strap holding the air tank down, breaking her nail in the process. She didn't even notice. Dragging the tank over to where Doug was, she felt his pulse. It was weak but stronger than before. His breathing was not so shallow anymore, but he still was unconscious.

The pitching boat caused her air tank to roll around the deck. She got on her knees, grasped the tank by its valve, balanced herself with it then picked it up and rose to her feet.

She reached over to a chair and surveyed the scene. Keo, the captain, his mate, and her fellow scuba divers were sprawled all over. The captain was lying with his head hanging down the ladder from the flying bridge, blood from his ears dripped down onto the lower deck. The two who were sunning themselves on the forward deck were nowhere in sight. The others were heaps of greying, bluish flesh tainted with red about their heads. If only she could save them, she thought. Their only chance would be for her to get the boat away from the poisoned atmosphere. She tried without success to resuscitate first one, then another.

Frantic, she dragged her air tank to the main deck bridge. The light rock resonated eerily from the stereo - *Heartache Tonight*. Struggling to find the stereo dial, she snapped it off so she could think clearly. She stood by the captain's chair looking at all the glowing buttons and dials. She wondered why she didn't hear the motor, then realized that it had stalled, probably for lack of oxygen. The key was still turned on, the lever pushed full ahead. She fiddled with the controls but nothing seemed to work.

Glancing up, she was startled to see that the waves had carried them closer to shore. They were in danger of foundering on the coral reefs or the lava beds for there were no wide, sandy beaches here. Ominously, dead fishes floated belly-up around the dive boat.

She redoubled her effort at trying to start the boat. The motor turned over but would not kick into life. Again and again she tried.

No luck!

Then she spied the radio. Luckily it was still monitoring the emergency call channel 16. Not hearing anything, however, she punched buttons with different numbers coming up until all she heard was some static, not realizing that this noise was probably coming from afar rather than up close where she would be heard when she broadcast. Nor did she realize that the battery was being severely compromised with the draining load demanded of it. Fans and other appliances were still drawing current from it. She saw the button on the mike and realized that she had to push it to talk, she knew that much. She pulled the regulator out of her mouth.

"MAYDAY! MAYDAY!" she yelled into the mike. "This is an emergency. Please answer!"

Silence.

Some static gave her fleeting courage to try again with no response to her pleas. She stuck the regulator back in her mouth and drew in the clean air before taking it out again to talk. She punched the channel button again, repeating her frantic message.

Static!

She cried out with frustration. "Damn thing!" She threw the mike down onto the deck. It skittered along until the tethered cord reined it in. She blamed herself for not having taken the time to learn how to use a radio before this.

She glanced out at the water again. The lava rocks in the distance loomed a little closer. It wouldn't matter if she made contact only to be dashed to their death against the sharp lava at the shore. Finally she decided to use logic and starting on the low side of the numbers, kept working at them. Eventually, through trying the channels in turn, she set it back on the emergency channel 16 again.

"MAYDAY! MAYDAY!" she screamed, not knowing that their weakened batteries were having little success in broadcasting very far.

She gulped more clean air from her regulator.

Luckily, a fishing charter boat which was heading for Honokohau Harbour caught the faint signal while monitoring channel 16.

"This is the fishing boat *Happy Hooker*. What is your emergency?"

"Oh, thank God!" Jennifer sobbed into the handheld mike. "This is the *Sea* . . . something or other. We are in danger of crashing onto the rocks. Everyone else on board, including the captain, is unconscious. The air is bad and I can't start the boat."

Jennifer began a violent fit of coughing. She sucked at the regulator in her hand to stabilize her breathing, then continued, "It won't start! There was an explosion in the water or something." Finally, she realized that she should stop talking if she wanted the captain of the other boat to answer her.

Silence.

Seconds ticked by.

Still, silence.

She decided to give it another try. It was only then that she realized that in her haste and nervousness she had forgotten to let go of the talk button. Her thumb was still depressing it and had turned white with the effort.

As soon as she did so, she could hear the other captain responding plainly. ". . . boat! *Sea* boat! What is your location? I repeat, what is your location? Over."

"This is the *Sea . . . Dog*! This is the *Sea Dog*! We are just down a ways, offshore from the airport."

"Roger, *Sea Dog*. I'll contact the Coast Guard rescue unit straight away! I'll make my way over there too but they will be able to get there faster than I can. Hang in there and stay on this channel, you promise?"

"I promise."

A ray of brightness shot into the gloom in her mind. Maybe we can be rescued before we hit the rocks, *s*he thought. She turned her attention back to Doug. He was moaning slightly despite the regulator still in his mouth. Jennifer swung her air tank over to where he was and knelt down beside him. She kept daubing at his bloodstained face with her tee-shirt, talking to him, not knowing if he was hearing her. Finally, she was able to discard her regulator completely as the air became sweet again. She took Doug's regulator off too so that he would have clean air to breathe without the regulator's restriction.

She first heard the whine of the engine, then the *whup, whup, whup* of the rotors of the Coast Guard search and rescue chopper. Then she saw it in the distance. It had flashing strobe lights and had its searchlight stabbing the dusk.

Glancing out again, she could see the frothy white surf dash against the sharp black lava boulders on shore.

Shortly, a white-helmeted figure was lowered out the door of the chopper and dropped down to her in a buffeting downdraft like a guardian angel descending from the heavens.

Jennifer broke down, blubbering, as his feet hit the deck. "Thank God you're here!" she shouted amidst the clatter of the chopper overhead, "my husband is breathing and is coming around . . . the others, I don't know."

The paramedic did a quick assessment of the condition of all on board. "I'll take your husband up first, then come back for you!" he shouted into her ear. "The others if I can!"

Doug was still groggy and not making too much sense as he tried to talk to her. She watched as his weakened body was harnessed to the paramedic and lifted up. Shortly, the paramedic came back down and put her harness on and attached her to him. She felt a sharp yank as she was lifted into the twilight from the pitching deck of the dive boat and into the maw of the whirling bird. Again, the paramedic descended as another worked on Doug while they were still hovering.

By this time, a Coast Guard vessel had arrived. They threw a line to the stricken craft. The paramedic made it fast, then harnessed a limp body and hauled it up to the chopper as well. There was no sign of life from the ashen form. Jennifer shivered with fear as she saw the bluish cadaverous body.

"We're going to fly you folks to the hospital now," the helmeted paramedic shouted at her. "Our guys in the rescue boat below have your boat in tow. They'll work on the others after they get towed away from the rocks. Your rescuer in the other fishing boat is standing by to lend a hand if needed. It's lucky he heard you. The batteries on your boat were wearing down quickly!"

"But what about the others?" she shouted over the roar of the chopper.

"We'll get you guys to emergency. We'll fly back later and check on them but . . . " his voice trailed off as he simply shook his head side to side indicating that it would be to no avail

The others were dead!

CHAPTER SEVEN

BLACK SMOKER

OCEAN RESEARCH CANADIAN AUTHORITY (ORCA), ON PATRICIA BAY, VANCOUVER ISLAND. I had taken a gold-dusted Jaguar XKE out of the motor pool earlier today so that I could attend the champagne reception for the unveiling of the new black smoker. Tonight I had put it through its paces on the way out along the Pat Bay highway to ORCA on the Saanich Peninsula. Somewhat high-spirited it was, but fine just the same as I blew a little carbon out of her along the way.

I don't own this car or any car for that matter. But I've been fortunate enough to have a good friend, Howard Bergman, who owns an exotic car museum in downtown Victoria. Howie is an old friend from way back. During my in-service years, they had the need for me to appear as someone else. Whether it was someone down on their luck, or a middle-income worker, a high-powered businessman, a scum-bag, an investor or just someone of unlimited wealth. For this, I needed both clunkers and classy cars. Exotic cars too! I needed all the trappings of the rich and famous. And they are trappings, believe me!

We used Howard's Exotic Automobile Rentals. He was the only one who could supply all types of autos on short notice and knew how to keep it a low profile. His office is now moved to Victoria, just behind the Empress Hotel. In his younger years his company was called Howie's Zowies Car Rental. Of course they weren't exotic cars back then, they weren't even classy cars for that matter. They were clunkers! But that's how he got his start. Then he got into franchising his car rental business, classy car rentals as well. He was into exotic cars too, but only as a single-business sideline that wasn't franchised.

Becoming wildly successful was the problem.

To get his financing in place, he hooked up with a questionable finance company. One thing lead to another and he was in a sweat - a cold sweat! It seems that their financing had flexible terms - too flexible! Every other month they were tinkering with the terms of their line of credit that they had extended to him. The interest rates kept rising. They kept tightening the screws on him until one day, just when he should have been celebrating his new franchisees' successes, they turned the screws just a little tighter so that he was being forced to turn over his business to them because he could no longer keep up to their terms of payment, their interest rates, and exorbitant demands.

It was extortion, pure and simple.

He called me. I got him an eager-beaver legal counselor who specialized in franchises, and a highly-experienced accountant who would sort out the wheat from the chaff. After an audit was quickly done to see where he stood, I paid a visit to the finance company. It seems that after we had fully understood each other's intentions and points of view, they felt that, indeed, they had misstated their original terms of late. They were only too happy to forgo any action against Howie's company. In fact, they immediately refunded all the monies including interest that were collected in error, plus a sufficient sum of money to pay for his expenses, time and worry.

So his business was saved from the vultures. In this case they were also the predators.

He ran that business until he got an offer that he just couldn't refuse. No, not like the other one. This one was legit. This was a case of a big fish swallowing a smaller fish. They only wanted his new car rental company.

He sold.

So then he spun off his clunker division to someone else. But as a result, this smaller fish became somewhat wealthy and retired to Victoria. To keep his hand in the car business, he saw a niche market here and stayed involved in exotic cars, his true love.

I'm waiting for him to start franchising the exotic car museum operation. He says not, though. He just wants to putter around, to give him something to do. Besides, he said that he has his hands full with the museum and with renting his exotic cars out to the burgeoning movie industry in Victoria and Vancouver.

I declined any monetary recompense for my efforts and as a result he gave me carte blanche on using any of his exotic cars whenever I wanted them. This suited me just fine. No payments, no maintenance, no worry about storing them when I'm not around. Just phone and ask what's available. He gets the benefit of having his cars driven occasionally and I don't charge him for my time to do that.

I guess an avaricious tax man would likely see a taxable benefit in there somewhere so I've left that up to my harried accountant to worry about.

I parked the Jag and went into the glassed-in reception area which connected all the wings to each other. Going over to the center of the three-story atrium, I went to see what the black smoker was all about. It was still veiled with black satin and certainly did have a mysterious aura about it. I looked around, saw my friend Jonas Cooper in a group off to one side and walked toward them. I took a proffered glass of champagne from a server with a silver tray. A string quartet played softly off to one side.

Jonas looked up.

"Rune!" he called out. "Glad you could make it."

"Hi Coop!" I replied as I approached them.

"Everybody, this is Rune, Rune Erikson, a good friend of mine. Of course you know my lovely wife," Coop said.

"Hi, Susan," I said, giving her a peck on her cheek.

"Rune, how very nice to see you here."

"And this is Dr. Albert Auchincloss, head of the department and my boss. And his beautiful wife Zoe," Coop said, continuing with the introductions.

"Oh Jonas, you're such a sweet-talker!" she blushed.

"Doctor," I said. "Pleased to meet you. A tremendous facility you have here."

"Rune. Nice to finally meet you. Jonas here has been telling me a lot about you. It seems that you have quite an interesting background!"

"And Mrs. Auchincloss."

"Call me Zoe," she gushed.

"Zoe," I acquiesced and smiled at her in greeting.

"And I believe you know Dr. Greenlea. Ellen's the one who piloted the submersible on our last dive where we got the new black smoker."

"Of course, Ellen, how are you. So nice to see you again. That was quite a coup! Congratulations!" I leaned over and gave her cheek a peck. She smelled delicious, as usual. It evoked memories of her from so long ago.

"Thank you, but I was just part of a team. I'm afraid I can't take sole credit for this one," she graciously stated.

"And this is someone whom I don't think you have met yet. This is Dr. Sarah Leikaina. Sarah is visiting us from Hawaii. She is a volcanologist doing research with us on thermal vents in the Juan de Fuca Ridge. Part of the research going on there is a joint ORCA/SSEAAL project."

She was drop-dead gorgeous! "I'm so pleased to meet you," I said with my sincerest of smiles. She was even more gorgeous than she had appeared in their group photo which had run in the papers earlier touting their discovery. Her almond eyes were perfectly set on her dusky face. Her silky dress, simple, yet elegant. It showed off her firm breasts and highlighted her smoothly-sculptured dancer's legs.

"The pleasure is mine, Mr. Erikson," she said easily.

"Please, ca . . . uh, call me Rune!" I finally managed, stumbling with my speech like a tongue-tied schoolboy on his first date.

"Rune. I've heard so much about you and now, finally, I get to meet you in the flesh!" she said with a mischievous smile.

It was my turn to blush, which I don't easily do. I was under her spell and I think she knew it. She fixed her gaze on me with her beautiful eyes. I returned her gaze. I was spellbound.

Hell, I was smitten!

"Speaking of Hawaii," Coop asked, "did you hear about the explosive eruption there today?"

I couldn't avert my eyes from Sarah.

Coop repeated, "Rune, I was just asking you if . . . "

"Actually . . . y . . . yes," I managed to stammer as I slowly turned to him, "wasn't that intriguing?"

"Yes!" Dr. Auchincloss added, "we were just talking about that when you arrived. I think it is a very peculiar occurrence. We will be following it closely!"

"Yes, a most peculiar situation, to say the least!" I remarked.

"Oh, and this is Chung Min-Ho," continued Mr. Auchincloss. "Mr. Chung heads a marine group with worldwide interests. He just happened to be here on business so I invited him along. Please excuse me, but I must go to the podium."

"Mr. Chung, pleased to make your acquaintance," I said as he pumped my outstretched hand with an iron-tight grasp that was needlessly strong. "You have a very strong grasp," I added as I slowly increased the pressure of my handshake.

"Yes," he agreed. "Tae kwon do!" he bragged.

I kept my eyes on him, to try to see into his soul, something by which I could measure the man. I found nothing. An empty void. Or was it a wall? He winced in pain as I squeezed his hand even harder than he had mine. "Rock climbing!" I countered as his porcine brown eyes peered at me through tinted, round wire-rimmed glasses. His shaved head gleamed under the floodlights. Oddly, two lone wispy strands of black hair hung down some two inches from his Adam's apple. A single braided gold earring hung from the lobe of his left ear. Two gold rings, one on each hand, provided balance.

The ring on the little finger of his left hand was an exquisitely-cut, brownish-red stone of a type unknown to me. "Interesting looking stone on your ring," I commented.

"Yes, it's Manganotantalite, quite rare really," Chung responded. It was cut in the regent style.

"Try saying that quickly after a couple drinks," I joked. Chung remained stone-faced. The other on his right hand was an unusual but flawless diamond in a Kohinoor cut. It wasn't that it was so unusual in itself. What was unusual was that a man of his obviously considerable wealth would wear anything other than a River, the rarest of white stones. Or at the very least a white Top Wesselton. This one was definitely only Top Cape because of its slightly yellowish colour.

"Your diamond ring, Mr. Chung. I couldn't help noticing it . . . the unusual colour, " I ventured.

"Ah, yes! It is a sentimental stone only. It was chosen by me because it is the very first diamond that one of my companies found," he said as he smiled.

"And what is it exactly that you do, Mr. Chung?" I said to the little man.

"Do? Mr. Erikson. Do? I don't do! My companies do!" the enigmatic man said with a slight bow tilted forward which further highlighted his waxy chrome dome. I could see now why he wore the lightly-tinted shades. He hid behind their partial obscurity. But then, up close, his eyes betrayed his smiling face as a distinct look of hatred flickered from them for just an instant, then was gone. They said *beware, for I am dangerous.*

Rudely turning his back to me, he faced the others in the group and said, "Now don't forget about your invitation to my yacht on Sunday in the Inner Harbour in Victoria. Cocktails at five."

"Only if Rune is invited as well," pouted Sarah.

"But, of course!" he said as he wheeled about in my direction again. There was that flash of anger in his eyes that belied his smiling face. "I will look forward to another encounter," he said cryptically.

I took an instant dislike to him. It was simply gut instinct triggered by a scant few indicators that there was something drastically wrong with the man. He and his ilk had the ability and the power to charm someone if it was in their best interest at the moment. Conversely, they focused their energy with deadly force against you if they perceived you to be a potential threat to them. Likewise if you were of no further use to them or if you had no apparent value to them to begin with. They are the most dangerous type of person. They ooze sincerity in front of others but are cunning back-stabbers when other people's backs are turned.

I was about to respond when we were interrupted.

"Ladies and Gentlemen!" Dr. Auchincloss boomed from the podium. "I would like to present to you tonight the daring trio who made up the undersea team on these fantastic dives to the depths of the Juan de Fuca ridge some five hundred kilometers offshore and some two kilometers deep, retrieving this magnificent specimen for us to study

"Before I introduce them to you, I would like to say that we are on the dramatic threshold of a new era and now have a new dimension to discover and explore, for after all, less than 1 per cent of the Juan de Fuca ridge has even been looked at, let alone explored.

"These are exciting times we are living in. It has only been but a few decades since scientists exploring in the bathyscaphe Trieste dove to the deepest spot in the world - the Mariana Trench - near Guam in the Pacific Ocean. It is so deep there that you could hide Mount Everest in the Challenger Deep section which is 35,800 feet down! That was the moon shot for us oceanographers. That's over eleven kilometers or seven miles down! We can concentrate on the rest of this frontier now that this goal has been achieved. This frontier stretches from the depths of the Mariana Trench to the shallows of the shores and by shallows I mean just a few hundred meters - just beyond normal scuba range.

"And what is in this frontier besides the sea? Well, just the largest geological feature on Earth. It is an immense, single undersea mountain range that circles the world. It runs continuously through the Atlantic, the Indian, the Arctic, and the Pacific oceans. It runs for a mind-boggling 31,000 miles!"

He surveyed the assembled crowd for their reaction to this statement, took a sip of water, swiped a hand over his lips, then continued.

"These undersea mountains were created by the uplifting actions of plate tectonics. Along these plate perimeters or fault lines are rift zones which are marked by cracks, faults, and vents. Around these hydrothermal vents grow exotic life forms never thought to exist only a few years ago. Tube worms, sulphur-eating bacteria, clams. And previously unheard-of marine plants and fishes. All species that are new to us and of immense commercial interest to the biotechnological industry. It is at these newly-discovered hydrothermal vent sites that black smokers are often found. Black smokers are the mineral factories of the seas. Here we have commercially viable minerals including diamonds, gold, silver, cobalt, copper, iron, manganese, nickel, to name a few. Just think of the possibilities! And not just known minerals but new minerals as well!

"Offshore, on the continental shelves and deeper, are oil deposits too! This is the Klondike gold strike; this is exploring the deepest, darkest jungles of Africa for exotic pharmaceuticals; this is the Oklahoma oil strike; this is the land rush of the 1800's; this is the scaling of Mount Everest; this is the moon shot - all rolled into one!

"These truly are exciting times!

"And here we have a new black smoker. As you can tell, despite its shrouding, it is just a little taller than we are. There are black smokers known to be fifteen stories in height, that's stories! But as you can appreciate, the logistics of raising one of that height would be daunting, indeed. And just think of the height of the atrium we would need to display something that tall!"

A smattering of chuckles riffled through the glittering throng of champagne-sipping socialites surrounding the podium.

"Without further ado, I introduce you to the three crew members of this Juan de Fuca dive. The leader and pilot of the sub on this dive, ecologist Dr. Ellen Greenlea from ORCA, her fellow crew member, volcanologist Dr. Sarah Leikaina from SSEAAL, and the third crew member, biologist Dr. Jonas Cooper, also from ORCA."

A loud rumble of applause filled the atrium to its peaked glass roof as the three scientists strode to the front and faced us.

"And now a drum roll please." There was scattered laughter as there was no drum at all to roll. A beaming Dr. Auchincloss yanked the corner of the black satin shroud down to reveal the black smoker. Specks of reflected light glistened here and there like diamonds upon its rough exterior. There were oohs and aahs from the assembled crowd of splendidly-attired people. Then there was a sustained round of applause for all three scientists. Flash cameras flickered bursts of bright light over the black smoker and the three intrepid scientists.

It looked like one of those towering African termite mounds. The exception was that the black smoker was chimney-like in that it had a round hollow core. Although bathed in the glare of the spotlights, it did have a rather exotic air about it.

"If any of you have any questions, we will be happy to answer them for you," Ellen said.

"Sure! I have one," a young woman said. "Why is it called a black smoker if it is brown?" There was a smattering of chatter throughout the crowd showing that it was precisely what many of them were thinking as well.

"A very good question, yet one that has a simple answer. In this case, the black pertains to the black plume of superheated minerals that flow from the top hole of the chimney and not necessarily the colour of the chimney itself. Yes, you have a question over there?"

"Yes," said a diminutive lady who held a reporter's notebook in her hand. "What did scientists know about the deep ocean floor before people went down there?"

"Not much, but it was presumed by most to be a desert of sorts, totally devoid of marine life, which is definitely not the case. You have a question?"

"So how do you see down there?" asked a young lad.

"With our sub's lights. Otherwise, it is pitch black down there. The only light that can be seen is the red glow from the lava vents, if we are in an area of flow."

"Cool," he replied.

A bookish sort of fellow gained the floor and stated, "Dr. Auchincloss mentioned sulphur-eating bacteria. Who discovered them?"

"Well, actually, they were discovered more than a century ago by a Russian scientist. He found that a certain marine bacteria by the name of . . . Beg . . . uh . . . Beggiatoa - if my memory serves me correctly - fed on hydrogen sulphide. The scientific term we use for this is that it is chemosynthetic rather than photosynthetic which means that it gets its energy, its food so to speak, from chemicals - in this case hydrogen sulphide rather than from the sunlight."

"I have a question," a bespectacled science writer from the Victoria Times-Colonist newspaper stated. "What is the black smoker made of?"

"It's made of minerals that came from the Earth's outer core and mantle."

He persisted, "But specifically?"

"Specifically, we're not sure yet. Each black smoker can and usually does have a slightly different mineral composition. This one hasn't been tested yet. We hauled this one up a few weeks ago and have only had it here for a few days. Samples have been taken but they haven't been tested as yet. You'll know as soon as we know."

"You mentioned the black smoker plume," stated a bejewelled matron, "what else besides minerals is emitted?"

"Methane and hydrogen sulphide." The matron's face soured.

"How would you describe the life around these hydrothermal vents?" asked a young female sporting green hair and a bogus-blond punky young man on her arm.

"Incredibly varied and teeming, definitely teeming."

An elderly gent asked, "So how hot are these vents or chimneys or whatever you call them?"

"Hot! It's 350 to 400 degrees C. And the vents actually glow!"

"So how do these things live in that hot a temperature?" asked a schoolteacher type.

"The temperature of the seawater goes from 350 degrees Celsius to just above freezing in only a few meters distance. They all adapt to whatever comfort range that agrees with them."

There was a slight pause.

"We're going to take a break but please ask us any questions that you may have as we relax. I've got to sit, my feet are just killing me from all this standing around!" A ripple of laughter erupted at this revelation. The noise level of conversation increased as people mingled and talked in small groups here and there. Uniformed caterers made the rounds with trays of glasses of white wine, champagne and assorted hors d'oeuvres. The celebrated threesome mingled then came over and sat on various sofas and chairs that were grouped together. The string quartet resumed playing. I felt as if my heartstrings were being plucked.

My eyes were drawn back to that ravishing creature again.

She returned my gaze.

"So, Rune, what do you think of our black smoker?" Coop asked.

Sarah was still holding my gaze in her limpid pools. I felt like I was a kid again. Through the fog I could hear Coop talking, trying to get my attention.

"Rune, I was asking . . . what do you think of our black smoker?"

"What? Oh! I'm sorry. I wasn't paying attention."

"I could see that!" Coop interjected with a knowing smile that contained an obvious touch of envy.

"Uh, interesting, very interesting, indeed. And I'm sure even more so when it's explained to me in further detail," I said as I hoped to get

Sarah away from the group.

"Well why don't I give you a personal tour of it then," offered Sarah.

"Why not?" I agreed, still in seventh heaven.

"Shall we?" she asked as she stood and gently slipped her arm through mine. Her delicate perfume hinted at a sense of the exotic as she and I walked over to the display.

"And this, Rune, is a black smoker," she lectured, pointing to the floodlit strange-looking structure that had been recently raised from the deep.

"What's it made of again?" I asked as I continued my charade.

"Touch it and tell me what you think it is."

It looked like someone had poured a very quick-setting course mix of dark brown sandy concrete mix from a ten-foot height around a central open core. It felt like rock or cinder material and had a rough texture with folds of smoothness.

"Feels like rock, sort of."

"Well, it is rock of sorts. It's made up of minerals deposited over time."

"So where did the minerals come from?"

"They come from the reaction of superheated sea water - 400 degrees centigrade - with hot magma that has just been expelled."

"Magma, that's from the Earth's center. Like from volcanoes."

"Right, except that this is undersea."

"So where does this occur?"

"Pretty much anywhere there is active hydrothermal vent activity."

"Anywhere?"

"Anywhere in the oceans all over the world. That is where there are mid-ocean ridges and back-arc basins."

"So what happens?"

"These are areas where lava or magma is being vented. It's very hot, about 4,000 degrees Fahrenheit. The magma is expelled from the Earth's core into the cold sea water which is instantly heated to about 400 degrees C. The hot water reacts with the magma to dissolve and carry away many elements including sulphur, which you may already be aware of, and economically-strategic metals like gold, copper, zinc. Vents are often sites for these chimney structures that build up over time where hot fluids carrying sulphide minerals form plumes much like factory smokestacks spew smoke."

"That is fascinating, but not as fascinating as your eyes! Has anyone told you that you have beautiful eyes?"

"It's been mentioned once or twice before," she laughed.

"I'm sure it has," I answered feeling the heat rising within me.

"I detect a bit of the rogue in you."

"It's my devilish tongue, that's all. It's the sailor in me coming out."

"Ah, a sailor! So where's your boat sailor? "

"I live aboard a ketch that I have berthed in Victoria . . . at Fisherman's Wharf."

"Sounds intriguing. And what does this sailor do for excitement?"

"Excitement?"

"Yes, what do you do? What fills your sails?"

"What fills my sails?" I asked, stalling for a witty reply to come to mind.

"Yes, what turns your rudder?"

"Well, I'm a great believer in indoor sports!" I said with a mischievous twinkle in my eye. Too crass, I thought.

"I'll bet!" she said with a lascivious smile.

"But seriously, hmm," I back pedaled. "Let's see. I'm semi-retired. Used to work for the government - took a very early retirement of sorts. Now I work when I feel a need to, I guess. I like to sail, of course. I like to ride my Harley. They are both great at clearing one's mind of all the clutter that accumulates over time . . . "

"Ah, a biker too!" she interjected.

". . . and I like to do a little rock climbing now and then. You compete against yourself using your mind and your body. It keeps me in shape and heightens my sense of awareness."

"I like that, '*heightens* my sense of awareness!'" she said, catching onto my choice of words. "I heard you mention rock climbing when you were talking to Mr. Chung. I rock climb too! Trouble is that there is no rock out there in the ocean depths to climb. Well not above water anyway. And I'm out at sea for weeks at a time, months sometimes. As a matter of fact this sailor just got back into port this week. I need to get some practice in."

"Rock climbing, not just bouldering?" I asked as I thought about the double-entendre.

"Rock climbing!"

"Are you a good belayer?"

"I like to think so," she answered with a smile. "Are you good at belaying as well?" she asked in return.

"I use some of my best techniques when belaying."

"Great!"

"Well, would you like to do some climbing then?" I asked as I glossed over but was fully aware of the scintillating conversation.

"Sure!"

"Tomorrow too soon?"

"No, I've got the day off. That would be great!"

"Perfect!"

I hoped that it would be perfect but was there someone else in her life at the moment?

CHAPTER EIGHT

ROCKIN'

THE MALAHAT, VANCOUVER ISLAND. The shriek of the Cooper's hawk riding the thermal currents far below us on Malahat Mountain was the only sound interrupting my thoughts. Thinking my next move through, I visually traced my intended route up the rock face of the mountain, noting cracks, handholds, and angles - its every nuance.

I slowly started my pendulum swing by running back and forth, my sling of hardware clanging like a crazed wind chime in a hurricane though this was the still of the morning. My breathing became ragged as I ran the mountain cliff back and forth slung on my dynamic kernmantel rope. In ever-increasing arcs, I struggled to increase the height of my dead-point each time.

This was the crux of the climb.

I was at the point of giving up for the second time. My shaking legs were starting to do the *Elvis* when I gave it one last mighty swinging run. I snaked my right arm out at the dead-point, just grasping the jug with the tips of my fingers. Hanging there, I panted like a wounded animal. I glanced down searching for a toehold of any size, found a slight crack and dug my right toe in.

But I wasn't home free yet.

"Slack!" I yelled down to Sarah as I was literally at the end of my rope. "Okay!" I yelled as I felt the rope ease off which would allow me to make my next move in order to get into a position where I would be able to set up my next belay. I saw another toehold farther to my right. To do this I would have to change feet in the crack, then match my hands in the jug. My right arm was starting to burn with the effort of hanging on rather than just being used for balance. I changed my mind and decided to set up a hanging belay there, shaky as it was. I chalked up. Switching my hands in the jug, I unhooked a piton from my shoulder sling and jammed its point into a fissure near the jug. Reaching down, I grasped my hammer and drove the piton home with solid ringing chinks. It was awkward going - perched off-center as I was - but finally, it was seated to my satisfaction - snug but not overly tight. I decided to do some aid climbing. Reaching down, I got a carabiner off my sling and locked it onto the piton wedged into the crack. I clipped my rope onto the crab. Having secured my protection, I fastened a foot sling from the piton and let it trail down. I crossed my left foot over and threaded my toe through the bottom of the sling. Still holding onto the jug with my left hand, I tested the sling with my right foot. It held! I stepped up into it and rested by hanging on my protection.

Now I was consciously aware of the rivulets of sweat that trickled under my brain bucket and got caught up in my sodden head band. I always use a protective climbing helmet as it is the smart thing to do. You never know when pebbles or rocks will suddenly rain down on you from above, especially if you are not in the lead position. My temples were pulsing with torrents of rushing blood. My beleaguered body got rid of its muscle burn. I looked down at Sarah as she held my belay.

"Okay! I'm going to catch my breath," I shouted down to her. "There's a ledge above me that has a good chicken-head on it."

"Okay!" she yelled up to me.

Having shaken some new blood into my hands, I was ready again. I had reached a dead end earlier, so I secured some pieces of protection, including a camming device and a chock, to set up a belay there. I had descended enough to allow me to pendulum-swing to where I was now resting on new protection - a single piton. Here, we could find sufficient holds to ascend again to get to the ledge.

My mind wandered back to last night's champagne reception where I had met Sarah. I could still feel her soft touch and smell her delicate scent. Her teasing words replayed in my head. My ragged breathing subsided somewhat, enough so that I could continue.

"Climbing!" I shouted down to her.

"Okay!" she answered.

"Slack!" I called out as I felt the rope hinder my movement.

"Okay!"

I changed feet in the sling. Raising my body sufficiently higher to enable me to finger-stack a vertical crack with my right hand, I was able to gain purchase and look for a crack for my right foot.

Found it.

Lodged it.

Put some weight on it.

It held!

As I was reaching with my left arm higher up in the crack to jam my hand in, my right foot slipped out of the crack. It happened so fast that I didn't have time to react. My right hand, not fully wedged, slipped out of its finger-stack as I was falling. In a flash the rope attached to my harness held as Sarah kept a secure belay. My chin hit the rock face as my fall was suddenly halted though mercifully softened by the rope's stretch. I was left lying in a head-down position, relying solely on a single piton to which my rope and crab were attached. My left foot was still hooked in the seat of the sling. Scads of tiny debris rained down upon Sarah.

There had been an awful cacophony of jangling sounds coming from my remaining pitons, chocks and carabiners on my rack at my waist. I was feeling a little gripped but certainly not vapor-locked.

The piece held - for the moment anyway!

My heart was trying to jump out of my rib cage. I was now running on pure adrenalin! As she kept the tension on, I carefully pulled myself back up by my rope until I could stand up in the sling again.

"You okay?" Sarah yelled up at me.

"Yeah, I'm okay. Thanks. Are you okay?"

"Just a few bits of crud fell."

Chalking up, I did it all over again until I was back up in my original position again where I finger-jammed my right hand and put my right toe into the crack. This time I locked my toe in more securely using an extra twist to seat it. I reached up again with my left arm to put my hand in the same crack. I did a fist-jam where the crack widened. Pulling my right hand out, I reached up to where there were two diverging cracks. Whacking in a slotted piton, I added two more pieces of protection to the setup and roped these in with cordelette to my carabiner.

I rested again then managed to climb the diverging cracks until I could feel the ledge where I found a good in-cut slope. I grasped it, released my right hand from its fist-jam and gained a two-hold purchase on the ledge. Kicking my left toe out of its crack, I raised myself by my arms. Using my toes, I lifted myself to the point where I could swing one foot onto the lip. Doing so, I found a wide ledge where I could sit comfortably. I fastened a rope around the protruding chicken-head rock and hooked a crab onto that to set up my belay. I hooked myself onto this and sat back down to rest.

"Okay! I got bomber protection here!" I shouted down to her.

"What?" she yelled back.

"It's so secure that you could drop a truck off it and it still would hold. It's tied to the chicken-head."

"Oh, okay!" she called up.

I could feel the intense heat of the midmorning sun as it beat down upon me. I could smell the rock heating as the rock face was starting to lose its night time coolness and take on the sun's heat. Wiping the sweat off my face with the sleeve of my cotton shirt, I noticed a little blood come off my chin. I was dead-dog tired.

Images of the ground rushing toward me flickered through my mind, interspersed with my last look at the sky as I tumbled, hurtling downward, the rock face rushing by me with grainy gray streaks at warp speed. Then black nothingness as I envisioned myself splashing at the base of the mountain so far below. I blinked to clear the terrifying image from my brain.

It seemed like only yesterday, but it had happened a number of years ago. You don't forget your friends. They were both experienced climbers who had climbed together numerous times and knew what each other's techniques and limitations were. They had flown out from Ottawa to climb in the Coast mountains surrounding Vancouver. Nearing the top of a 150-meter face, the leader stepped out of his foot sling at a critical section much like the one I had been in when he had both his handholds break away. When he fell, the pitons had held for a second or two, breaking his momentum. Unfortunately, the pieces zippered. As his pitons came out he went straight down in midair without touching rock. His climbing partner, my other friend, stopped him with a dynamic belay some 30 meters down. He slammed into the rock face sustaining massive bleeding from his ears and nose. His head injuries proved to be fatal even though his helmet had stayed on through the fall.

It was a sad loss, this jovial friend of ours. Tears welled up in my eyes at the thought. And here I was, in the company of a beautiful woman, climbing on a perfect morning. And he wasn't. Why did I still feel guilty? I hadn't been there. There had been nothing that I could have done. However, the guilt was still there. But he would still be in my heart and my thoughts. Forever!

I looked toward the horizon which was capped by an incredibly blue sky. Snowy Mount Baker sat majestically in the east, flanked by lower but sharper-spiked snow-capped peaks. These were flanked farther by the rugged Coast Range mountains on the mainland - some sixty miles away - which surround Hope, Vancouver, and Whistler to the north and the snowy Cascade mountains to the south in Washington state. My eyes lowered, following the slopes of Mount Baker, to the series of rolling blue hills and then groups of islands which grew in intensity of misty blueness the nearer they were.

Hulking freighters plied the waters of the strait between the islands, leaving slashes of white wake behind them. An enormous B.C. Super ferry was pulling out of its berth at Swartz Bay enroute to the mainland. The puffy white sails of boats skimming along contrasted with the deep blue sea which lay smack against the shores of the quiet town of Sidney which lay on the far side of the Saanich Peninsula.

In the center of the peninsula, long strips of gray runway marked the Victoria International Airport. On this side of the peninsula, a low-slung series of architecturally-designed offices and research laboratories sat on prime waterfront real estate. This was the home of the Ocean Research Canadian Authority (ORCA). On the foreshore were enormously-high boat sheds, parking areas, a heliport, and stationary docks. A string of variously-sized work boats and research ships were berthed alongside.

Off to the right, in the middle of Saanich Inlet, was a gleaming white ship of unique profile and undetermined use. The vessel was too far away to make out its name or port of registry. It was sharply-raked with the classic lines of a luxury yacht, but there was something unusual about it. There was what looked like a helicopter sitting on a landing pad just aft of midship. It had too much industrial gear on it for being just a yacht. It was bristling with electronic equipment on its mast. Its stern, rather than being truncated as normal, was indented to form a small dry-dock.

I looked straight down at the ghostly-gray assortment of strung-out buildings of the old abandoned Bamberton cement plant. I could just see part of the chrome of my Vivid Black and Champagne Pearl Harley-Davidson Fat Boy. It was parked in the lee of the mountain under a lean-to that was attached to a large derelict shed. This abandoned site was now home to birds, bats, and rodents. The occasional deer, bear, and cougar wandered through here as well. Except for them and the odd hiker, it was deserted.

If you listened really hard, you could hear the faint echo from years gone by of the machinery rumbling and grating and creaking as it made cement. By the same token, but with less effort, you could see the white plume of cement dust rising above this operation because its effect had been to permanently whiten the dark face of Mount Jeffrey. The face rose steeply to form a part of the Malahat Ridge of mountains.

Gentle creases of white surf broke on the shoreline next to the site. A dock ran out into a jade ocean. The crowns of the trees below us were mere patches of open green umbrellas in a compressed vision viewed from this overhead angle.

I looked down at Sarah's helmeted head below me and shouted down, "Wonder what kind of ship that is in the middle of the inlet, the white one with the chopper."

"I was wondering about the same thing myself," she called up to me.

I did a final check on my belays and called down to her, "Are you just about ready to come up? I've checked my belays."

"Give me a moment to get ready."

"Okay."

A minute passed. "Climbing!" Sarah called up.

"Okay!" I carefully kept sufficient slackness to allow her freedom to move but not so much as to let her tumble very far in case she slipped. I could hear her occasionally grunting with the effort of the climb as she swung, lunged and pulled herself up the steep face. Even though I was the leader on this pitch and she was the second, she was physically and psychologically a better climber than me. Her body was somewhat lighter and thus more effective at climbing than is my more muscular form. But our sizes were not so much different as to cause a problem when she was anchoring me with a belay during my climb. And she had infinitely more patience than I had. I tended to act by instinct while she tended to analyze and carefully think things through as scientists like her are wont to do. It was simply our plan that we change lead on each pitch - 200-feet, the length of our ropes - rather than just have one of us continuously lead on every pitch all the way up the face.

I kept a keen eye on Sarah's form and on the technicalities of her climb but still my mind wandered a little. I thought back to how she was dressed when I had first met her last night.

These visions of sugar-plums quickly faded. "Hold!" she shouted. I snapped out of my thoughts and back into reality, bracing myself for her fall. "It's okay . . . Take!" she called out again. I took up all the stretch slack and pulled tight to allow her to get an assist from the rope.

My mind wandered again to the events of last night. Sarah had felt wonderful by my side as she tried to explain the black smoker to me in some detail but this pupil was somewhat preoccupied and couldn't keep his mind on the subject, well, that subject anyway!

"Tension! I need some tension!" she called out from down the rock face as she struggled through a particularly tricky section.

"Is that okay?"

"Yes, just hold it there."

"Holding."

"Okay! Slack now. I need some slack!" Sarah said as I watched her continue up the face of the mountain.

"You okay?"

"Just fine." She struggled through the last few maneuvers near me.

"Made it!" she cried out in triumph at having reached the ledge I was sitting on. "I've been exercising on board ship but obviously not all the muscles that I am using here!"

"You all right?" I asked yet again.

"I'm fine. I feel great!"

Sarah clipped herself onto the carabiner for protection.

"Feel like having some lunch then?"

"Yes, I'm hungry now."

Sarah took a damp cloth out of a zip-lock bag, patted her glistening face and wiped her hands on it.

"Here's a cloth. Wipe the grease and grime off your hands before we eat," she ordered.

"Yes, Mom," I teased.

Sarah made a face at me, playfully gave me a shot to my arm and then flashed me a winsome smile with her full lips.

"Careful, now. It's a long way down! You may still need me."

Sarah stuck out her tongue at me and reaching over, dug into the day-pack we brought up with us. She handed a ham and cheese sandwich and a can of Pepsi to me. She brought out a BLT and a can of Diet Pepsi for herself.

"So tell me a little about yourself," I said as I unwrapped my sandwich.

"Where do I start?" she asked as she pulled at the tab of her can of Diet Pepsi.

"Why don't you start at the beginning?"

Sarah took a long drink from the can, then swiped at a few drops that had run onto her chin. She said that she was born in Kealakekua Bay on the Big Island of Hawaii, went to grade school there, more schooling in the town of Kailua. Then it was off to college for more education, a few degrees and eventually back to Kailua-Kona where she was fortunate to land a good position at SSEAAL.

"So what's a beautiful volcanologist like you doing at SSEAAL anyway?" I asked.

"Doing volcano research and advising on the ongoing effects of volcanos and how they can help achieve our goals and fulfill our mandate. After all, the Hawaiian islands owe their existence to active volcanos which are literally under our feet there."

"Which reminds me," I suddenly said. "I still haven't fully grasped how deep oceanic vents and chimneys occur. I was a tad preoccupied last night. The more I think about the black smoker I saw, the more intriguing it becomes."

"Well," Sarah said, "why don't we start at the beginning like you say. Or in the middle as it were. At the very center of Earth is a metallic core which is at a temperature of more than 6000 degrees C and is some 1500 miles in diameter. The pressure there is greater than three million times that of the air pressure on our bodies at sea level, which is one atmosphere. The outer metallic core which surrounds the central core is kept in a plastic state by intense pressure and an enormous temperature of 5000 degrees C. It is some 1400 miles thick. Then there is the lower mantle of plastic rock, which is also at high pressure and temperature. It is also 1400 miles thick. The upper mantle is next and is 400 miles thick. The earth's crust is some 2 to 45 miles thick. It is through this solid rock that fault lines and pyroclastic venting of molten rock or magma as we call it, occurs both undersea and on land."

"So, are you telling me that Jules Verne's story, *Journey to the Center of the Earth,* couldn't have occurred?"

"Only in our imaginations, I'm afraid. Not with the enormous pressures and intense temperatures that occur there."

"What a letdown. I suppose that next you're going to tell me that there is no Easter Bunny either?"

"Well now, that depends," she laughed as tiny crinkles formed at either side of her exquisite eyes.

"Okay, so how does the molten rock or magma get so hot in the first place?"

"It's made below the mantle by heat generated mainly from radioactive disintegration of uranium, thorium and potassium."

"Uranium, that's dangerous!"

"It can be. Rocks of all types, including volcanic rocks, contain minute quantities of radioactive elements but they are in concentrations so low that, in most cases, there is absolutely no danger at all."

"So how do diamonds fit in here?"

"Ah, a girl's best friend . . . after the right man, that is, diamonds fit very well! Diamonds are formed when carbon is subjected to intense pressure and heat deep within Earth's mantle."

"But how do they get to the surface?"

"They ride the magma flow spewed out by volcanoes and other fault vents."

"They survive?"

"They do extremely well!"

"Hmm, volcanoes just release magma and diamonds?"

"No, they also release gases such as water vapour. They also release methane, sulphur dioxide, carbon dioxide, hydrogen, carbon monoxide, hydrogen sulphide, and, uh, hydrogen fluoride. These are what are so dangerous to inhale at vent sites. They are part of volcanic fumes."

"The rotten egg smell."

"That's right!"

"If the magma is released on the surface of the mantle, what takes its place down below?"

"Volcanic magma, that is, magma that is released to the surface, is composed of anywhere from 80 to 95 per cent core magma."

"So where does the other 5 to 20 per cent of the magma come from?"

"From the mantle, the Earth's crust. As the core magma touches the mantle, partial melting takes place. Certain minerals in the mantle melt first or melt only, as the case may be, because they have different melting temperatures."

"I get it, but still there is a huge imbalance there."

"What also happens is that subduction replaces the lost magma in the molten core."

"Subduction, huh. That's where one plate of the Earth's crust slides under an adjoining one."

"That's right. It slides under and begins melting into the molten core as well. An example of this is the Juan de Fuca Ridge. It's 300 miles off the coast of Vancouver Island."

"And this is going on all over the world."

"All over the world. That's right. It's called plate tectonics. It's where Earth's crust is broken into about ten huge fragments or plates. They move slowly about shifting continents over a long time, forming new land mass, melting old land mass, and also stimulating volcanic eruptions."

"So nothing gained, nothing lost."

"No net gain or net loss," she corrected.

"And old mother Earth stays the same. So the black smoker is composed of minerals."

"Well, everything is. That is other than animal or vegetable."

"Okay."

"There are white smokers too! It depends upon what is being expelled. There are more than three thousand known minerals and dozens more new ones are discovered every year. They are the building blocks of the universe. From ice to salt to rocks and soil. They all contain minerals. And they all have their unique crystal structure. They are our history books, our evidence recording what has happened here on Earth in the last 4.5 billion years since it was created."

"Hmm, I never thought of it like that."

"It blows you away when you think about it."

"Sure does! So all rocks come from volcanoes."

"No, that's not correct either. Sedimentary rocks originate from weathered rocks and are carried on the surface of the Earth or along the ocean bed and then compressed over time to form rock such as sandstone and shale. Igneous rocks were formed as magma cooled and solidified. Basalt and obsidian, for instance, were produced and cooled quickly at the surface. Granite formed when magma cooled slowly at depth, then thrust upwards as a solid. The third class, metamorphic rock, was formed by being subjected to heat and pressure at depth. This is how new minerals form and others crystallize again. Examples are quartzite, marble, and gneiss. Some of the changes can take place in the solid state, not by melting, but fluids are usually present, surrounding each grain as they metamorphose. These metamorphic rocks at depth, in turn, may later be partly melted to become an igneous rock as well."

"Quite complex, really."

"Yes, sometimes I think I should have become just a geologist rather than a volcanologist, it's that interesting."

"I can see why. One thing puzzles me though. What is the attraction of black smokers and vents in general as far as minerals go?"

"Why new minerals, of course. That and the fact that we do not have the technology nor the resources to drill and sample deep within the Earth's mantle and molten core. The black smokers and vents and the volcanoes bring these minerals to us from those depths."

"But why is that so important?"

"They all have their own unique properties. Some minerals are so rare that even a small quantity is worth a fortune. I'm talking not only about gemstones and gold and such. There are other rare minerals that make mining these areas feasible. For example, ancient vents in the now-uplifted Ural mountains in Russia are being mined right now for gold, silver, and copper. The rare minerals from that site are unknown to us at this time. And underwater sites are being jealously kept secret and coveted by those who would plunder them for their minerals."

"It's the last frontier then."

"You could say that. And at times it looks like the wild west."

"The wild west?"

"There are some cowboys - in this case, bad guys in black hats - out there who have complete disregard for the laws of the sea and the laws of mother nature too!"

"Cowboys?"

"Oceanic plunderers, cowboys - pirates, whatever you want to call them. And I'm not talking about over-fishing, that's another problem entirely. In parts of the oceans, huge trawlers set nets with very fine mesh. They trap everything over the size of plankton. What they don't use for food gets ground up into meal and is fed to farmed fish and shrimp. Draggers scour the ocean floor and destroy sensitive ecosystems like bulldozers do in a forest. Still other fishing companies set drift nets which indiscriminately trap fish, seabirds, dolphins, turtles and sea lions to name just a few. I'll tell you about them sometime. It makes me sick!"

"What are the laws regarding minerals in the ocean?"

"Most countries have staked their claim to seabed and sub-seabed resources within two hundred nautical miles of their own shores. In accordance with the provisions of Article 76 of the United Nations Convention on the Law of the Sea, your country, Canada, has been working toward defining the feasibility of extending their sovereign rights over resources of the seabed and sub-seabed beyond the two hundred nautical miles. Much work has to be done - from utilizing knowledge of bathymetry, morphology, to assembling, rationalizing, and analyzing data about the sea floor. In addition, offshoots are mapping, pipeline and cable routing, modeling the circulation of bottom currents, which little was known about until recently, studying the effects of glaciation and sea level changes."

"I guess that's important too."

"It sure is! Look at the effects of El Nino and La Nina."

"And the race is on," I said with resignation.

"And the race is on. But mostly it is not really a race. The U.S. is doing the same thing too. In many cases we are pooling our resources to study our natural resources and exchanging and sharing the information world wide."

"And how do you fit into all this?"

I am part of a joint ORCA/SSEAAL research project. That's what I was doing at the Juan de Fuca Ridge. There were other projects on which Canadian, U.S., and German scientists were working on a British research ship using a Canadian sub and American lab analysis instruments. Now that's cooperation! We were also testing out the new SeaTruck submersible"

"SeaTruck?"

"Yes, it's a new submersible developed and manufactured right here in Victoria. It's a wonderful machine. It handled and performed just beautifully."

"And what did you do personally?"

"I study volcanos, both on land and those under the sea. There, they were under the sea. And there are things living there, like tube worms and blind shrimp, that until now were never known to exist. They are found at some sites in the deep where newly-discovered hydrothermal venting occurs."

"Tube worms? Ellen was telling me all about them," I said.

"She and I work closely together. It's a fascinating subject. It's been a great joint project but I have to return to Hawaii shortly. My stint here is up. For now anyway."

The distant whine of a helicopter's engine came from across the mouth of Saanich Inlet. It increased in volume as it crossed over the sea toward us. Then a whupping sound was added as its blades beat the air nearer to us. We stared at it as it closed the gap. The noise became deafening. It hovered facing us as if it were some giant dragonfly examining its intended prey. Waves of air beat down upon us from its giant blades. Sunlight glinted off its rapidly spinning rotor at the rear as the chopper rotated and showed us its side. As it turned, we noticed the letters "ORCA" emblazoned on it beside which was affixed a stylized collage logo of a black and white Orca whale leaping out of the sea in which there were a sub-sea mountain ridge, a black smoker, an underwater volcano and numerous other marine life.

Two helmeted pilots worked the controls in the cockpit while a crash-helmeted and dark-goggled female crew member in a form-fitting jumpsuit stood in the open doorway tethered by a harness attached to the bulkhead of the craft. In her fist was a hand mike, a long crinkled cord attached to it. She was shouting into it but with their nearness and the cacophony reverberating among the cliffs, we couldn't make out her instructions over the external loudspeaker.

Bits of dust hampered our vision, the rushing air brought tears to our eyes. I gave the universal sign of uplifted arms and turned-up palms indicating that we couldn't understand their instructions. The crew member went back into the bowels of the craft. A few moments later she appeared in the cockpit wedged between the two pilots, holding a hand-lettered sign that said "We need you now!"

I turned to Sarah and shouted, "Looks like they have something urgent for you!"

"I can't imagine what it could be!" she answered incredulously.

Then a second sign appeared, "Lowering cable hoist!"

"Looks like they are serious about this. Okay we'll get you ready," I said to her. I pointed to her, motioning that she was getting ready when a third sign appeared in the cockpit window.

"Both of you!"

"Both?" I mouthed the words at them.

"Yes!" they indicated with a nod of their heads.

"Both?" I turned to Sarah and shouted, puzzled as to this turn of events.

She raised her shoulders and arched her eyebrows suggesting that she had no idea either.

"Lets pull up our rope and grab the rest of our gear. We can come back another time and clean the pitons off the face," I shouted to Sarah.

The crew member reappeared in the open doorway, a winch shot out, telescoping out through the open doorway on a sturdy metal arm. The chopper rose into the sky above us and a cable was lowered as we stood on the ledge temporarily tethered to the side of the mountain.

Grasping the cable, we hooked our harnesses to it facing each other and held onto the cable. The air screamed upon us in a downdraft from the blurred rotors above. A slight tug and we were free of the mountain and were being hoisted up with the electric winch. Then a further jolt occurred as the chopper rose into the blue sky and pulled back from the dangerous position it was in. We clung to each other, Sarah's soft curves pressed tightly to my body. She felt wonderful!

The rock face dropped away, soon we were above the ghost-like assortment of derelict buildings that had been the old Bamberton cement plant. Now we were above the sea heading across Saanich Inlet to where the sprawling ORCA facility is at Patricia Bay or Pat Bay as it is called by the locals.

Reaching the chopper, we were pulled into the maw of the noisy machine, the wind sucking at our bodies as we entered the relative calmness of the cargo bay. The crew member got us tethered onto the bulkhead, handed us crash helmets with headsets, then got the winch stowed into its locked and stored position. Then tugging at her dark goggles, pulling them off her eyes and positioning them on her helmet, we were surprised to see that it was Ellen. Her lithe body looked marvelous in her white jumpsuit. It brought back fond memories from a different time, a different situation. What could have been, should have been, wasn't - much to my chagrin.

Did she feel the same way?

If she did, she didn't suggest it outright. But there had been times when we had seen each other from a distance when I caught her gazing at me in a pensive mood. I must confess that I was caught up in the same emotions as well. Then reality would intrude.

"Hi guys!" Ellen shouted to us through our headsets over the din inside the belly of the metal monster. "Bet you didn't expect to see me today!"

"We were having a really nice, quiet time of it too," Sarah said.

"What's up?" I asked.

"Update on the explosion on the Big Island of Hawaii. Seems that things are more puzzling than they first thought," Ellen shouted over the din. "We are having a briefing at ORCA in fifteen minutes!"

She motioned us into jump-seats opposite from the open door.

CHAPTER NINE

ORCA

OCEAN RESEARCH CANADIAN AUTHORITY, PATRICIA BAY. The giant whirlybird pulled into a tight bank as it reached the ORCA facility, the G-forces pressing our bodies tightly against the vibrating seat-backs. I looked through the open doorway, seeing only asphalt below us, indicating that we were in a very tight turn! We leveled out, hovered, then gently settled, landing with a slight bump as the chopper's wheels touched the tarmac.

We bent to pick up our gear stowed under our seats.

"Just leave it there," Ellen said, "we'll fly you back after the briefing." We jumped out and followed her in a crouching walk away from the whirling blades over our heads. Straightening up once we were away, I unsnapped the chin strap on my helmet and pulled it off my head. My ears still rang from them being unprotected during the short haul up the winch. The women did likewise. Tucking the helmets under our arms, we trudged up the slope to the ORCA complex.

To our right and behind us, was a series of docks jutting out into the sea, a multitude of ORCA research ships and work boats of various sizes tied to them. Wafting up from the shore was the tangy smell of salty brine and seaweed mingled with the sharp smell of tarred dock pilings. To our left was a cavernous boat shed. Within it was an ORCA catamaran work boat which sat propped up on a wood framework stacked in square columns under her twin hulls. Mechanics and shipwrights clad in grease-stained coveralls worked on her from stem to stern. It must have been an urgent job - it was the weekend.

In the bay next to it was a much smaller craft that looked like something out of the movie, *The Deep*, only far more compact and far more complicated. A Plexiglas bubble hatch was propped in the open position. It looked like a submersible; a decal on its side said SeaTruck.

A winch tractor, looking like a preying mantis, maneuvered its way here and there in the yard with boat parts swinging from its mouth. It was picking at the contents of a dryland bone-yard of inventory. Spools of cable and wire, piles of gigantic linked chain, anchors, and shrink-wrapped pallets of machinery and spare parts sat here and there.

Farther back, rusting parts sat out in the open, grass growing through them, suggesting that this was the end of the bone-yard.

I followed the two women into the air-conditioned coolness of an entrance in the research complex, into a short hallway, then over to a bank of elevators. There was an almost imperceptible odour of formaldehyde, alcohol, and other lab chemicals in the air. And that faint peculiar taste of mineral dust.

Ellen stabbed at the UP button with unusual impatience, lighting it as she did. She turned around, smiled and said "I hope we're not inconveniencing you too much but the director called the meeting. Highly unusual for a Saturday, I must say."

The elevator doors opened, we got in, then held the door for a running figure in a white lab coat.

"Thanks," he said as he gave us a quick smile of appreciation. "Going to the meeting?" he asked as he puffed from the exertion of the short burst of speed he had put on.

"Yes," Ellen answered, "and you?"

"Yes, later," he said with a nod of his gray-haired head. An ORCA I.D. card pinned to his lab coat identified him as Dr. Steven Jenkins. The deer-in-headlights photo adorning the card accentuated his translucent face. "Rather an intriguing event," he said cryptically as the door opened again. He exited, turned and went off in the opposite direction.

I expected us to be led down to a lecture hall or a boardroom for the meeting. However, Ellen led us down a short hallway, then into a plush outer office reception area staffed by one harried girl Friday. She hurriedly glanced up and greeted us, patting at her hair as she did. Ellen introduced Cherisse to us. She responded with another smile, then said, "There's an executive washroom just off Dr. Wampole's office if you would like to freshen up. I'll show you into his office now. He'll be along in a few minutes or so. He just called from his carphone to say that he's running later than he thought. I expect that this latest thing has got him in a tizzy."

We were taken into the comfortable office that was decorated in plush burgundy carpeting. Across from us was printed old rose polished-cotton drapery tied back from each tall window. Cheery flames flickered in the fireplace to our right surrounded by dark oak paneling and a trophy-and-photo-adorned ornate mantel carved out of a single piece of oak. Two rose-hued sofas sat on either side of the fireplace facing each other, a low table between them. The darkness of the wood wall was contrasted by the cream of the two adjoining walls. Old English hunting prints showing the various stages of a foxhunt were hung, each print bordered in dark green triple matte and ornate oak frame. A heavy antique brass chandelier hung down from the ceiling at the center of the office. A large oak desk with brass fittings sat off to the left. An antique swivel chair with a broad cushioned seat and gently-curved back sat turned slightly sideways, as if the occupant had just got up from it and intended on sitting back down shortly. Beside the desk, nearer the window, sat a large floor globe of the world held by a sturdy oak frame. The wall behind was covered in oak bookshelves upon which sat literary tomes, sets of geology books, and an assortment of other technical reference texts. Heavy drawers were built-in below that. Various specimens of minerals sat upon the counter. To our immediate left was a low credenza upon which sat a crystal decanter of golden-hued liqueur sitting upon a silver serving tray. Another silver tray contained crystal sherry glasses. Flanking them were a number of different reduced-scale models of research subs. On the wall above, a forest of framed diplomas were hung along with a number of framed photos shot in various locations of two's and groups of smiling people all looking at the camera. His ego wall.

Cherisse, his girl Friday, motioned to us and said, "You'll find the washroom door just beyond the credenza. I'm sure you'll find everything you need there."

"Ladies first," I said as I offered Sarah the use of the executive washroom ahead of me. I walked over to the windows and peered out onto a magnificent view of the facility and the small harbour. My curiosity somewhat piqued by what I could see in the office, I walked over to the bookcase and inspected the volumes to prejudge the man. They suggested a distinct love of literature and geology. The one subject usually soft and occasionally intangible, the other subject usually hard and incredibly tangible. I looked for the unusual title that hid the lever for the concealed doorway but could find neither the book nor the lever. I moved down and pulled open a door revealing a roll-out computer system complete with monitor and keyboard.

"Rune!" Ellen admonished in a stage whisper, "don't snoop! He'll be here at any time."

"Okay," I conspiratorially whispered back as I winked at her and kept right on poking into cabinets here and there.

Sarah rejoined us. She looked refreshed. Her hair was tidy, her face was clean and fresh and she exuded a slight scent of a delicate perfume. How do they do this? Where do they keep all this stuff to do this? It's just one of the abilities that all women have that adds to their mystique.

I went into the washroom.

Nice!

Plush white carpeting, gold-plated fixtures, antique mirror, corner shower - good for those days when you have too many functions to attend and no time to rush home to change. I took care of business. I looked in the mirror seeing the start of a few wrinkles around the eyes surrounded by a face made grimy from rock climbing and sweat. Oh, and the small scar that I got years ago, but that was another story, another time. Right now I felt somewhat like a fish out of water, dressed as I was for climbing. Splashing some water on my face, I rubbed the dried blood off my swollen chin. I reached for the white towel on the adjacent rack. I wiped my face on it, then my hands, leaving streaks of dirt here and there on it. Washing my hands again, I dried them once more and folded the towel, dirt side in and hung it neatly back on the bar. I patted my hair down, turned my head sideways in both directions and nodded approval to myself. I rejoined the others.

"He's not here yet," Ellen informed me.

"Nice bathroom," I said.

Going over to the ego wall, I saw: diploma, diploma, diploma; letter of commendation from some mandarin in Ottawa, letter of gratitude from some cabinet minister; a scroll of recognition signed by the Prime Minister for his 25 years of dedicated service to the department; photo of a skinny guy standing beside a small basic sub, photo of the same guy now a little heavier standing with another guy with a newer looking sub, photo of a now-chunky guy standing with a threesome around a state-of-the-art sub, a typical convention photo of two guys with stogies stuck in their mouths, drinks in their hands, and their arms around each other's shoulders. It was inscribed: "To Harry, a hell of a friend! Jack."

I turned my attention to his desk. A gold metal frame sat off in one corner. It featured a photo of a dark-haired woman with an easy smile sitting in an armchair and two smiling teenagers sitting on either chair arm. I took them to be his wife, his son, and his daughter.

I came upon a small wooden chest which sat upon the desk's highly-polished surface. It was superbly crafted as it was hard to find the seam where the lid was. The wood had an unusual coolness to it in addition to its fine patina. The chest displayed intricate exotic wood marquetry upon its exterior. In the center of the lid, on its top side, was an ornate solid-gold map of the world. Finding the lid seam and trying to flip it open, I found it to be locked. I puckishly pulled open the middle desk drawer and found a small brass key in a concave tray. Taking it, I inserted it into the small keyhole in its front and turned. It unlocked. I lifted the lid to reveal that the chest was actually a humidor. A small hygrometer was attached to the inside of the lid to monitor the humidor's humidity level. Over a dozen fat cigars lay inside, each hand-wrapped to perfection. This was no abstemious man! I picked one up - it was about seven inches long - and read the cigar band. Cohiba Esplendidos, it said. This was the type of Cuban cigar that you buy at the old E. A. Morris Cigar Shop down on Government street. Even if you dropped a fifty-dollar bill on the counter, it wouldn't be enough to buy just one of these babies. I drew in its heady aroma as I ran the cigar under my nose.

"Can I get you a light?" asked the deep voice of a man standing somewhere off to my right.

I wheeled around. I recognized the portly figure standing in the open doorway to the office. The voice belonged to Harry.

"Sure, that would be nice," I said, unsure of whether he was angry and facetious or just facetious.

He was neither.

Harry came over, selected a cigar for himself and motioned toward the women, "Ladies?" he inquired with bushy arched brows. He was asking if they would like a cigar as well as is now the fashion in some circles. He got polite refusals from both. Bringing out his cigar cutter, Harry carefully snipped the end of his cigar then held the cutter out to me to do the same to mine.

"That's an interesting looking device. It looks like a miniature guillotine," I said as I clipped the end of my cigar. "I wondered how you used it."

Harry leaned over and in a hoarse voice, stage-whispered, "It helps if you're a Rabi!", then broke out in a series of ragged guffaws as he poked my arm with his elbow.

Tearing a narrow strip of cedar off the veneer layer that separated the levels of cigars that had come with the original Cohiba box, Harry walked over to the fireplace. He held the cedar strip into the flame, waited for the flare-up to subside, then held it up for me to draw a light. I went over, held the end of the cigar higher in the flame where it burned hottest, drew in the flame to light my Cohiba and blew out the first puffs without tasting them. Harry did the same. Clouds of cigar smoke wafted over our heads, then quickly disappeared. "Don't worry about the smoke ladies. The air conditioning here is state-of-the-art. It won't bother you," Harry said in a matter-of-fact tone.

"Why don't we all have a small sherry? I like a sherry with my cigar." Without waiting for our approvals, Harry magnanimously poured sherry from the cut-glass decanter into four small sherry glasses. Raising our glasses to his raised glass and clinking them, Harry said "Cheers!"

"Cheers!" we saluted back.

"One thing about the Havana cigars though . . . " added Harry. He called them Havana cigars rather than Cuban cigars.

"What's that?" I asked.

"They are more susceptible to change."

"How so?"

"They possess a certain delicacy . . . a certain delicacy of flavour that is unique to Havana cigars."

"Is that so?"

"Yes! You'll never find that certain something in cheaper cigars. Therefore, a Havana cigar needs to be handled with the utmost of care. You wouldn't want to get them tainted."

"I wouldn't?"

"Good heavens, no! You must keep them cool and at the correct temperature and humidity."

"I must?"

"You must!" he vehemently insisted.

"Okay," I meekly acquiesced.

"That's why I keep them stored overnight in that small bar fridge at just the right temperature."

"So that's why the wood was cool to my touch!"

"I just had them taken out before you arrived. My girl Cherisse here, she knows to take them out of the fridge and put them on my desk just before I get to the office. That's a firm rule around here!"

"Ah," I said with a knowing look.

"And one must not dally before an open humidor while choosing one's cigar."

"One mustn't?"

He shot me a look of disgust as if I was a hopeless student and he was the stern, all-knowing professor. "Of course not! Otherwise, they could be tainted!"

"Of course! Silly me!" I said with a suitably enlightened expression upon my face.

"Why, every time you open the humidor, whatever taint is in the air, floods into it and is taken up by the cigars inside."

"Every time?" I asked.

"Every time!"

"Is that so?"

"Yes. I'm afraid so. When the Havana cigar is hand rolled at the factory, it possesses a certain freshness, a certain delicacy of flavour, not just from the leaf itself, but from everything that the leaf came in contact with through the air in that part of the tropics. And once that cigar is otherwise tainted or has lost its freshness, it can never regain what it has lost."

"It can't?"

"Good heavens, no! It can't!"

"So that's why when you see a cigar that has spots on its wrapper you know that it has been tainted," I volunteered brightly.

"Oh no! That's something else again entirely. What that is . . . is a particular fungus that forms on growing tobacco leaves in a certain remote tobacco growing area of the world, an island in Indonesia, south of the Malay Peninsula. Sumatra, I think it's called. Why, in the old days they used to replicate those spots on perfectly good wrappers!"

"How did they do that?" I asked.

"They would dissolve washing soda in hot water, add chlorinated lime, and heat the mixture to a boil for three minutes or so then cool the mixture to later be sprinkled on the wrappers and left in the sunlight and in the air to make them bleach."

"Sort of counterfeiting cigars."

"That's right, counterfeiting of cigars still goes on today. It's been said that half the Cohibas out there are not genuine Cohibas."

"So how do you know that these Cohibas are the real McCoy?"

"Because I know cigars and I know Cohibas! And these Cohibas are genuine!"

"I can't argue with that," I acquiesced.

"Oh!" added Harry, "I suppose that we should be introduced, although I feel as if I already know you - briefings and background checks and so on, you know. I'm Harry, Harry Wampole," he said as he set his glass of sherry down, transferred his cigar to his left hand and held out his right hand.

Briefings? Background checks? I thought.

"That's Dr. Wampole, Director of ORCA," Ellen interjected as she looked at me.

"Just call me Harry. There is too much work to do around here for us to be bothered with formalities and titles and so on. We're all a team. One person is just as important as the next. We all have our jobs at which we do best," he said as he pumped my hand with a firm grip.

"Rune, Rune Erikson, and I feel as if I already know you as well," I mentioned.

"Oh?" he responded, as a trace of puzzlement flickered across his face.

"Your ego wall," I said with measured succinctness.

"Ah! One has to assuage one's vanities, you know," he said forthrightly. "Of course, the three of us know each other. And I understand that the three of you know each other as well," he added with a slight trace of a smile and an elbow poke.

"We do," I said with an enigmatic smile.

"I understand that we found you and Sarah across the inlet at Bamberton. Rock climbing, I think they said."

"Yes, we were having a good time of it until your people showed. In fact, my Harley is still parked at the site."

"We'll get you back there in the chopper as soon as we can. My apologies to both of you!"

"It's okay, Ellen already mentioned that. Sarah and I were somewhat surprised by the sudden request for our presence here."

"Well, I'll get right to the point then," Harry went on as he tapped the ashes off the end of his Cohiba into the ashtray on his desk. "As you probably already know, there was an explosion yesterday just off Keahole Point in Hawaii. That was the reason that I missed the unveiling of the black smoker last night. Too busy with accumulating the reports and conferencing with my colleagues. Then there were the logistics of the joint project to work out. Oh, and I took a call from the Prime Minister as well. Top priority this!"

He took a deep puff on his cigar for emphasis, held it, savoured it, then gently forced the smoke out.

"First reports were sketchy and further reports weren't much more enlightening. Some news reports suggested that a new volcanic undersea vent had opened with pyroclastic force. Others speculated that an inter-island tanker had exploded just offshore. Still others speculated that a small meteor hit offshore. And then there was an early report that a cargo flight had crashed and exploded upon impact with the ocean but that was discounted right away as there was nothing on radar, nothing reported overdue, and no oil slick. However, we do know this. Something of cataclysmic proportions did take place out there. There was an explosion of sorts. There were injuries. There were deaths. And quite frankly, we don't know what in the hell caused it!"

"Yes, but how does ORCA fit into all this?" asked Ellen.

"Good question!" Harry replied. "Let me give you some background on this first. The area in which the explosion occurred is in a highly sensitive area. First of all there is the ocean. It happened right in the middle of a designated marine sanctuary. That is very politically and ecologically sensitive. Dead marine life floating in a marine sanctuary makes for some graphically-dramatic and politically-damaging photos. Secondly, there is the Kona International Airport right there beside the sea. And I don't have to stress the importance of tourism to the Hawaiian Islands. Just look at how important it is to our own Vancouver Island right here. Thirdly, there are our counterparts there as well - SSEAAL. That actually stands for Solar/Sea Energy Aquaculture/Agriculture Labs, Rune. They operate a little differently from us here in Canada in that associate private enterprise is located on their site whereas ours are scattered here and there according to their needs as they are not dependent upon an on-site location. There they are dependent on near-freezing water brought up from the deep. Their research, their basic technology and ability to provide a center with the means, in this case chilled water, have resulted in dozens of spin-off businesses producing new products and products new to that latitude. This in turn provides much-needed jobs to the populace there as a whole. Then there is the historically-sensitive tourist town of Kailua-Kona, itself only some seven miles distant."

"But where do we fit into the picture?" Ellen asked again.

"I'm just coming to that. Quite frankly, nobody has any idea of what occurred. That is, nobody who is in a position to know and nobody whose job it is to know, knows," he said enigmatically.

Turning, Harry said, "It seems, Sarah, that your President and his government authorities want this thing taken care of quickly and in a low-key manner. Their people will conduct the official tests with a minimum of personnel to try to determine the cause. To go in like gang-busters would likely damage the confidence of all affected. That may cause the tourist industry to overreact and the tourists to stay away in droves when there is absolutely no reason for them to do so. They feel that the best approach would be the low-key approach and that's where we fit in. Officially, we, ORCA, have just embarked on a new joint research project with our counterparts in Hawaii - SSEAAL. The official purpose of the project is to evaluate the new SeaTruck submersible. You may or may not know, Rune, that the SeaTruck technology was our new technology that was spun off to private Canadian enterprise a few years ago. The research technology was originally incorporated into our Canadian deep-dive submersibles for which we are justifiably proud of our track record and our work the world over. The prototype SeaTruck was originally tested right here in Saanich Inlet before it went into limited production. It assisted in the drilling for core samples through 10,000 years of sub-seafloor sediment in the unique Saanich Inlet basin. There have been some sales to a select few world-class companies, including two already in commercial use in Hawaii. The firm is poised to go into full production. Therefore, we can kill two birds with one stone, so to speak. My apologies if you are bird lovers. I was only using an old saying to illustrate my point. Haw, haw!"

"Would that be the Victoria firm of Armstrong Robotic Machines in James Bay that makes them?" I asked.

"Why, yes it is," Harry responded. "Do you know them?"

"Yes, a friend of mine works there. I visit him there occasionally to test out his gadgets and have seen parts that could have been for the SeaTruck, but have never seen it assembled."

"Ah, so then you know a little about that which I speak."

"It was all quite hush-hush really!" I added.

"Yes, it had to be, what with industrial espionage and the like, you know. Everybody likes to look over the next person's shoulders to see what they are doing. And countries are no different from humans in that respect - as you well know.

"The folks at Armstrong Robotics will certainly bring you up to speed on the latest technology and operation of the SeaTruck. I know it's short notice and all that but we really don't have the luxury of time on our side. Arrangements have been made and they have generously agreed to have their facilities and one of their scientists at our disposal on Monday morning."

"Okay, but how do we fit in then?" asked Ellen.

"You, Ellen, are going to be the coordinator of this project and will be directing and co-ordinating from right here and wherever else this thing may lead us. Sarah, you will be the official pilot of the SeaTruck that you two will have completely at your disposal from the dealer in Hawaii. Jenkins will fill you in with the technical details of that as soon as we are done and he will be on 24-hour call to help you with anything that might come up. A very capable man, really.

"Officially, you will be getting your instructions from SSEAAL but your actual day-to-day reporting will be to Ellen - every day. And Ellen reports to me - every day. I, as her director, have our direction and authority from both governments, from the highest level in each case, I might add."

"And unofficially?" she asked.

"Unofficially, we are there to check things out just like we are supposed to but at the same time we will be doing quite a bit of snooping around in the guise of evaluating and collecting research data. You both will have a relatively free hand to go where this probe takes you. Anything related to this second part is strictly secret and on a need-to-know-basis only. Is that understood?"

"Yes, but what does this have to do with me?" I asked.

"You, Rune, are our newest marine technical evaluation specialist."

"I'm what?" I asked incredulously.

"Our newest marine technical evaluation specialist," he repeated.

"What's that?"

"A new type of scientist," Harry responded.

"Sounds like a damned bean counter to me!" I exploded. "I detest bean counters! I detest being one even more!"

"Your job is to observe, ask to see everything you can and ask a lot of annoying questions. Oh, and judging by your record, don't get too involved in things if you can help it!"

"But I've definitely not applied for the job nor any job for that matter. In fact, I'm retired!" I said with some exasperation.

"You have been brought out of retirement!"

"Says who?"

"Don't fight it, Rune, because you have already been temporarily reinstated into the service of your country, similar to your old job, as I understand it, with full benefits and your usual expense account. As a matter of fact, when we are finished here, we have a complete package for you to pick up from Cherisse, my indispensable assistant."

"This isn't the military, you know. You can't just toy with someone's life like this, even if you do provide a good cigar, a passable glass of sherry and up until now, pleasant conversation!"

"By the way, the cigars are excellent. Good doesn't apply as a descriptive word in their case," Harry said. "It wasn't my decision, Rune, after all, I didn't even really know you until a few minutes ago!"

"This is bull!" I replied. "Tell them to give their head a shake!"

Harry wheeled around, strode to his desk, flipped the intercom and barked into it, "Cherisse? Make the call!"

A half minute went by. Cherisse buzzed back. "He's on the speaker phone in your office."

"Yes, thank you Cherisse." Harry punched a button then without speaking into the phone, turned back to me and said, "It's for you!"

"For me?" Puzzled, I stepped over to his desk and spoke, "Hello?"

"Why, hallo maan!" a male voice slyly said.

"Who is this?"

"Is this the irascible Mistah Erikson?" the voice asked.

"No, this is the irrevocable Mr. Erikson . . . wait a minute! I think I know who this person is! Speak!"

"You're a very perceptive maan, Rune, getting warmer?"

"You're damn right I am! If I'm not mistaken, it's a fellow by the name of Mr. Wright, Mr. Jackson Wright. Right or wrong?"

"Right!"

"But the girls didn't call you Mr. Right, did they! Nor was it Action Jackson either. If I recall, it was Mr. Wrong!"

"Careful now, Rune, we're on a speaker phone and I think we are straying into personal territory within earshot of the others!" he admonished.

"So how the hell are you anyway?"

"Fine, maan!"

"And what are you up to? Where are you? Last time I saw you, you were just going to get a quick coffee and be right back. I haven't seen you since!"

"I'm in Ottawa, working my butt off on the weekend as usual."

"Are you now one of them mandarins we hear about from time to time but so rarely see?"

"Something like that."

"Well, what's this nonsense about me being reinstated?"

"My recommendation."

"Your recommendation?"

"Easy now, maan!"

"Well, just who in the hell are you?"

"Let's just say that my recommendations are highly sought after now and are rarely turned down, I might add. In fact, I can't recall the last time one actually was turned down - by either party! You were the first!"

"So what makes you so sure I won't turn you down personally?"

"I got a marker, maan!"

"You got a marker?" I turned, rolled my eyes and said in exasperation to the others in the office, "he's got a marker!"

"I got a marker!" he said.

"Look, pal, everybody's got markers. I got markers. You got markers. Everybody's got markers."

"But I'm holding your marker."

"My marker?"

"Yes, your marker!"

"Now wait a minute! I paid that marker off a long time ago! Remember the time that you got into that jam down in Jamaica and had nowhere to turn?"

"Yeah maan, but I paid that one off a couple years later when you ran afoul of that diplomat over in Spain during the turbot war."

"I forgot about that one. So that makes us even-Steven then, doesn't it?"

"Not quite. There was also that dustup in Dhahran. They were downright touchy about things over there in Saudi at the time!"

"That was you? I had forgotten about that one too," I sheepishly acknowledged.

"That was me. So, as I was saying, maan, welcome back! It's always nice to see a stray sheep return to the fold just when it least expected to. And you will notice I omitted the word black!"

"Rather than a sheep, I feel like a lamb being led to the slaughter," I replied.

"Oh, come now! You've got it really good now, too good, in fact!"

"Do I detect a touch of envy in your voice? Or is it the climate in Ottawa that has affected your brain? Or is it the fact that I'm retired and now live back out on the balmy West Coast?"

"Yeah, well, look maan! We really need you on this one! Not a word of a lie! You're the best there is for the job. And you've worked with the people stateside many times before. You got all the contacts. You know the ropes. Speaking of ropes, you still rock climbing?"

"Now and then. Keeps me in shape."

"Good stuff! So we can count on you then?"

"Well, okay, I'll do this thing for you, but no whining and no quibbling after the fact. And keep the damn bean counters off my back!

I'll give it my best shot, as I've always done."

"Nice to be working with you again, maan! It's just like the old times!"

"Likewise, I'm sure!"

CHAPTER TEN

DRAGONFLIES

SAANICH INLET, VANCOUVER ISLAND. The chopper's binoculars were highly powered. I had intended to check out the large white ship that we had seen earlier in Saanich Inlet but it was gone. I could not see it anywhere.

As we crossed the inlet and neared the other side, I was scanning the cliff face to see if we had gotten all our gear off the ledge and from the scree patch at the bottom of the face. This was enough climbing for one day, interrupted as we were. I would go back later to clean the pitons off the face. Swinging the field glasses downwards to the shore then over to the old Bamberton buildings, I tried to see if I could spot my Harley Fat Boy. We had left it parked there under a lean-to that was against one of the buildings. I could see one corner of the building but at this angle could not see the bike at all. What did startle me was to see two figures running around the corner of the building.

"What the heck is going on?" I exclaimed.

The headset in my crash helmet buzzed with the electronic voice of one of the pilots who asked, "What's up?"

"Somebody has been around my bike parked under the lean-to over at the plant!"

Then Ellen's voice came on my headset. "Where?"

"Right over there behind that building, the one with the lean-to on the far side of it. That's where Sarah and I parked the bike before we went climbing! You probably can't see them without the field glasses!" I said as I pointed in the general direction of the old plant.

I followed their progress as they turned down a lane, ran between two ramshackle buildings where I temporarily lost sight of both of them. Picking them up again as they emerged on the other side, I saw them running toward an open area where a small black chopper was parked. They hurriedly opened the doors and slid in. The rotors started turning slowly, then became a blur as they picked up the revs. Meanwhile, we were closing in on the site.

"Where did you want us to land?" the pilot asked.

"Anywhere in the old plant that would be suitable to you would be fine but I'm really concerned as to what those two jokers were up to. I don't like the looks of that at all!"

"We can check them out if you want," the pilot offered.

"Let's just see what they do, now that they know we're coming."

"Looks like they're getting ready to hightail it out of there!" Ellen said.

We steadily closed the gap. Their rotors were now at full revs throwing up a dust storm all around them. Dust clouds drifted into the dark open doors of the derelict sheds and storehouses. It was difficult to read the numbers on the chopper's tail as they were in dark charcoal gray on the black body.

We came screaming in over the plant. The pilot put the chopper into a tight turn to swing around, trying to force the other chopper down as it lifted off. Instead, they went forward as their chopper rose slightly, keeping low enough so that they were afforded the protection of the swirling dust from the street and the old buildings on either side. Our pilot kept just back of them as they shot forward leaving us to contend with the dust. We rose higher. The black chopper reached the last block of the street then made a sharp right turn inland down another street and hovered, then circled the old wooden tower.

We came in closer.

They dropped down, hovering under the sloping conveyor that had trundled millions of tons of limestone and clay to the top of the tower for calcining, later to be made into hydraulic Portland cement. The structure was flapping here and there as loose boards were buffeted by the rotor wash.

"Damned idiots!" the pilot cursed. "All it would take would be for one board to come flying down into their rotors and it would be all over for them!"

As if on cue, the small chopper ducked out from the protection of the sloping conveyor and darted around the far side, making a run for it. They were anxiously looking over their shoulders looking for us as they did. We tucked right in behind them. They veered right hugging the mountainside to try to shake us off. Their strategy worked as our chopper being much bigger, could not safely get in as close.

We followed them as they flew south past Sheppard Point, then right, past McCurdy Point and around to the mouth of Spectacle Creek. It was here that they made another run for it. They crossed the waters of Squally Reach to Elbow Point on the steep shoreline cliffs of Jocelyn Hill. We tried to force them back by maneuvering ahead of them to no avail. Reaching the point, they skipped around Repulse Rock in Finlayson Arm, then kept going south, hugging the shoreline.

We were like two dragonflies, one chasing the other. When the pilot got to the cliffs of Holmes Peak, he cut across the arm again to Christmas Point on the opposite shore of the narrowing inlet. It was a poor choice as the terrain's steepness lessened here. They cut left, going farther up the inlet past Misery Bay. Here we tried to force it down again, but again they recklessly maneuvered their way along, boldly challenging our much larger craft.

As we came upon Sawluctus Island in the middle of Finlayson Arm, they set their chopper onto the only clear and level patch of terrain on the tiny forested island. As they settled down right in front of an old, rustic log cabin, we hovered and pondered our next move. It was a standoff of sorts as we could not land and they could not safely fly.

They waited.

We waited.

No one made a move.

The cat and the mouse.

It soon became apparent that our fuel would probably be exhausted before theirs would be. It was now our move.

"Well, any ideas?" asked the pilot.

"How about hovering around the back part of the island for a while. We can return every so often. Maybe we can flush them out that way. If not, you can always lower me into the woods there during one of our maneuvers and I can come up from behind them on foot."

"Okay!" the pilot said.

We hovered over the cabin then slowly moved back.

They lifted slightly to rotate their chopper around somewhat to view us better but still afford them forward movement for takeoff. They settled back down.

We hovered, partially hidden by the trees.

They waited.

We came forward again and hovered over them.

They sat.

We returned, hovered at the back of the island, then returned to hover over them.

They still sat.

Back we went again. This time I was harnessed for descent on the cable hoist which shouldn't have been visible to them. I quickly went down, disengaged myself from the cable and using the woods as cover, ran toward the rear of the log cabin.

I waited until our chopper resumed its position in front of them where the plan was that they would distract them while I snuck up on them from the rear. The pair must have sensed that something was up. Challenging our chopper again by bullying their way up a little, they moved left toward the protection of the tree line on the small island along its shore. Circling the island, our big chopper in pursuit, the small chopper quickly gained speed. It stayed just above the water as it shot toward the end of the arm, past Hall's Boat House. Then it skimmed over the tidal flats and followed the safety of the gap in the towering trees lining the Goldstream River as it rose into the mountain gorge.

It was a situation where they just said "Oh, well!" The crew and the girls came back, settled down upon the island and picked me up.

"Too bad they got spooked on that last go-around," Ellen said.

"I thought we had them this time!" Sarah said.

"I think I could have got to them, given half a chance," I said.

"You win some, you lose some," the pilot commiserated.

"I think we've seen the last of them anyway," the copilot said.

We retraced our route back to Bamberton, where my bike was stashed, hoping against hope that it was still there and intact. We set down amidst a cloud of swirling, choking cement dust left from years of operations. The two women and I walked over to the lean-to. The bike was still there. It looked intact.

I quickly checked it over and upon closer examination, found that they had been trying to tinker with the bike. The wheel lugs had been dangerously loosened, something that I normally would not have checked before starting back along the highway with its tight corners and sheer cliffs. I worked on the bike with my wrenches and got the lugs secured again. We rode along while Ellen walked back to the waiting chopper for her return flight. We said that we would see her tomorrow, most likely for cocktails aboard Chung's yacht in the Inner Harbour.

"You guys going to be all right?" Ellen shouted through the chopper door. We nodded our heads in the affirmative. She spoke to the pilots who gave us the thumbs-up through the cockpit window, which we returned, then backed-off out of range of the rotors but not the choking dust. We watched as the large craft rose, moved forward, then shot skyward at an angle. It made a wide perimeter check of the area before heading directly across Saanich Inlet back to the ORCA complex helicopter pad.

"Well, that was enough excitement for one day," Sarah said as the silence settled around us, though our ears still reverberated with the clatter of the big chopper.

I gave one final check of the bike and stowed our gear in the saddlebags. We donned our leathers and helmets and sat astride the Harley. I hit the starter and the machine immediately roared into life. The bike throbbed under us. My Fat Boy is 631 pounds of shimmering muscle. Driven by an 80-cube Evolution engine, it spews out 76 foot-pounds of torque at 3500 rpm through dual shotgun exhausts. I waited for the engine to idle down, then kicked it into gear. The bike leapt forward, eager to be on the move again. I could feel its every nuance as we navigated the pot-holed road on the way back up the mountain toward the Trans-Canada Highway. We made a couple of sharp turns around corners where the road shoulder fell away to the sea far below. The bike handled really well as it normally did, even with two of us on it. With loosened wheel lugs we may not have navigated those dirt-road, cliff-hugging hairpin turns quite so well!

Sarah gave me a comforting prolonged hug from behind as we neared the highway that would take us back into Victoria.

As we reached the crest of the hill, we saw a cloud of dust. Then as we topped the hill we saw a sight that chilled the blood in our veins. The black chopper was hovering just over the crest of the hill and was directly in our path on the dirt road. Now it was moving menacingly toward us. I could see the crazed grins on the faces of the two men inside. Jamming on the brakes, I threw the bike into a sliding 180-degree turn and sped back down the mountain to the abandoned plant site. The buzzing black chopper blades were right behind, ready to make mincemeat out of us.

I gunned the bike through the deserted streets then into the abandoned elevator. Spotting a counterweighted hoist, I ran the bike onto its deck. Using minimal effort, I pulled on the rope pulley, hoisting Sarah and me and the Fat Boy up to the top of the elevator building.

The chopper dropped off one thug who ran into the building directly below us. He spotted our tracks in the dirt, then looked up. Pulling a pistol out of his belt, he started firing rounds wildly at us. He couldn't see us but sooner or later he was going to get a lucky shot off and hit us. I got Sarah back on the bike. I started it and slowly made my way along the catwalks near the ceiling until we came to the conveyor leading down to the ground. We had no other choice than to trust the dilapidated structure, hoping that the framework was solid even if some of the outer boards were falling off at crazy angles.

Sarah screamed, "I hope you know what you're doing because I'm in this all the way!"

I ran the bike down the steep incline at an appropriate speed so that any weight would be momentary rather than lingering upon any one given span. Now we had to deal with the chopper as well which was trying to throw us off the conveyor with the rotor wash or make mincemeat out of us.

It worked! I said a silent prayer as we made the bottom.

As we got to the first building, I did a sliding right turn, gunned the engine, fishtailed and sped along, then made a quick left, a quick right, then left into the open doorway of a storehouse and out the other side, across the lane into a second building.

We stopped.

I waited for my eyes to adjust to the darkness, surveyed the interior, shut the bike off.

Silence . . . except for the buzzing of the searching chopper that lurked between the rows of buildings near us. The chopper settled down at a nearby intersection in the deserted ghost plant.

"I've been through a lot, but I'm scared!" Sarah said.

"This isn't exactly the way I had planned to spend the afternoon. Just hang in there and do what I say and we'll probably get out of this one all right!" I replied in as confident a tone as I could muster.

"Okay," she whispered.

We left the bike hidden in the corner of the building and went over to a crack in the wall boards and peered through it at the chopper. We saw one guy walk around the corner in the road while the other, the pilot, sat at the controls as the rotors continued to whip around at high revs.

There was something black in the right hand of the thug on foot. He ducked below the scything blades and crouching, ran in our direction. I looked around for something to use as a weapon and spotted a short piece of two-by-four board lying on the floor. I picked it up and looked through the crack again. We could hear our heavy breathing over the distant roar of the chopper as it sat waiting. The thug came closer to the building that we were in. I could now make out a mean-looking pistol in his hand. He was looking down in the dirt, no doubt checking for the bike's tire tracks. Finding them, he glanced up and looked directly toward us.

"Oh!" sobbed Sarah as the brute stared in our direction.

"Don't worry. He can't see us. At least not yet," I whispered to her and gave her a comforting hug. "Just stay back in the shadows in the corner, okay?"

"I will," Sarah whispered back, looking at me with frightened eyes.

Steeling myself for what I knew was to come, I crept up behind the wide door which was swung inwards. I peered from behind it into the shaft of sunlight that streamed in, seeing only his shadow cautiously making its way toward the door. As he neared, his shadow preceded him and grew longer, making his appearance more ominous to us. The shadow of the gun in his extended hand led the way in.

If his shadow had eyes, he would already have noticed me behind the door, it was that far into the building already.

But it didn't!

The cacophony of the roaring chopper receded far back into my brain and became silent to me as time stood still. He stood unmoving, unsure of himself. He took another step in, now revealing the actual gun to me as he stood trying to let his eyes focus in the darkened structure we were in.

I stood still, mesmerized by the sight of the weapon as he was not quite far enough into the room for me to be effective and do what I knew must be done.

He waited silently except for the occasional sniffle from his nose as he tried clearing the dust from it.

Sweat beaded on my forehead. Time stood still. I stifled my ragged breathing as I studied the pistol which I immediately recognized because of it being so unusual. I had come across one a few years ago. It was its bulbous nose that I noted. Chinese Type 64. Silenced. Made by Chinese State Arsenals. Selective semi-auto or single shot, your choice - semi-auto, this one; blowback type, integral silencer. Strictly an assassin's gun. It looked like some kid's wooden toy pistol that had been held together with black electricians' tape. But it wasn't. It was deadly! If I recalled correctly, the silencer was aided by the unusual subsonic velocity of the bullet. But here, the silencer was unnecessary - the remoteness, the chopper noise. A rivulet of sweat trickled down my brow, around my eye, then down my cheek and onto my chin where it ran into the small open cut there, stinging me into alertness.

As he moved to take another step in, I poised to strike, something akin to a ball player up to bat. But I wasn't playing for the Jays nor the M's; this was no game! Luckily, due to injuries during my younger ball-playing years, I learned to be a switch hitter. This time I had no choice either. I had to hit left-handed! As his foot was just settling back down and his body came into my vision, I wound up with the lumber and hit the gun out of his hand then continued forward, hitting him in his stomach and knocking the wind out of him.

Instinctively, I cold-cocked him. He crumpled into a deflated heap. He had managed to get off a wild shot at the moment of truth but it was a reflex action only. I picked up the pistol from the dirt floor and shoved it into my waistband at my back, not wanting to have to deal with the unfortunate consequences of an accidental weapon discharge if it was stuck in front.

I knelt down and felt for his pulse. He had one, was breathing after thirty seconds, but remained out cold. Grabbing his limp body, I dragged him out into the street where the pilot of the waiting chopper could see him. I went back in, started the Harley, and with Sarah seated behind me, ducked in and out and around buildings making our way back to the dirt road up the mountain, daring the pilot to chase us again. Seeing the gun tucked into my belt at the back, he wisely decided to remain where he was. Once we made the top of the hill, we saw him go to collect his partner and drag him back into the chopper.

I waited for the traffic to clear then roared out onto the Trans-Canada Highway and climbed it to the summit. I opened it up on the top of the Malahat or just *the Hat* as we call it here and leaned into the gentle corners before slowing for the descent into Goldstream Park. Sarah was hugging me tightly as if I was her security blanket. The wind rushed past us picking off the bits of bad memory from our minds. We rode along enjoying the spectacular view of the sight of our earlier chase - tiny Sawluctus Island in the middle of Finlayson Arm far below with its picturesque log cabin. On the horizon, the snow-capped Olympic Mountains rose on the far side of Juan de Fuca strait, some twenty miles away on the Olympic Peninsula in Washington state.

We were happy to be so alive!

The highway took us directly into Victoria. We rode down Douglas Street, through the downtown, hung a right behind the Empress Hotel, along the Inner Harbour, following the contours of the Inner Harbour's coastline for a few blocks until we reached Fisherman's Wharf. We parked the bike in the lot overlooking the federal facility. I looked over at the *Valhalla* tied up to finger nine. She looked magnificent even with her sails furled. Sarah and I carried our gear down to the ketch.

I was glad to be home.

"Welcome aboard!" I said as we walked up the gangway steps and onto the ship's deck. Unlocking the wheelhouse door with the hidden old brass key, I swung it open, allowing her first passage across the threshold. "Mind your feet, the sill is rather high - a necessity on sailing ships I'm afraid. Keeps the water out of the wheelhouse when waves wash over the deck in a high sea."

"Ooh! This is a lovely old ship!" Sarah exclaimed as she surveyed the wheelhouse. She went over to the huge wheel, grabbed the spokes with her hands and began to steer the ship straight into an imaginary storm.

"She sure is!" I heartily agreed.

"Avast, Matey, trim the sails! Ha, hah! Or I'll make you walk the plank, you son of a landlubber!" Sarah shrieked then laughed at her foolishness. She had the giddiness of a child that was perhaps brought on by the tense moments at the Bamberton plant this afternoon.

"Oh, will you now?" I challenged. "Well, I'll just have to mutiny and throw you over my shoulder and take you below!"

"Is that a promise?" she asked with lowered eyes and a breathless voice.

"Only if you want me to," I replied reticently.

"Please do," she simply said.

"I'd love to but I don't think the companionway will accommodate both of us at one time," I said with regret.

"Oh!" she said with some disappointment showing on her moist pouting lips. "What is that brass thing there?"

"That plate there? That's the builder's plate."

"What does it say?"

"Read it."

"Leehausen & Sons, Oslo, Norway, 1905. Good God! She really has aged well!"

"And well built too! With any luck she'll last another hundred years or so at least," I proudly said. "Ready to go below? I'll show you around."

"Aye, Aye, Captain," she replied throwing her hand up to her brow in a mock salute, then giggled. "You'll have to go down first and help me down so I don't slip in the darkness down there."

I went down the companion ladder first. I turned back just in time to catch her as she slid down the steep side-rails and crashed into me. Her soft body melded into mine. Her heaving breasts tracked down my beating chest. She was helpless; I was hopelessly stricken. Then our lips found each other and ground tightly together like two hungry diners at a feast. We came up for air sometime later.

"Oh!" she said over and over in soft kittenish mews as we kissed again. Then urgency overcame us with the suddenness of a squall at sea. The sofa became our safe haven. We shed our clothes quickly, casting them aside in little clumps here and there in the dimness of the saloon. The storm bore down with sudden force. We took refuge and received tumultuous fulfillment at the height of the intensity. As the storm abated, we clung to each other, savouring the aftereffects of its lingering fury.

"You did say that you were going to show me around but I didn't expect it quite like that," she whispered in my ear, then tongued it softly.

"That was just the beginning of the tour. There's more to come!" I said softly to her.

"You promise?" she asked.

"Yes, and I'm one who usually keeps his promises."

"Do you have a shower here?" she asked.

"Why, yes, and a large tub as well."

"Show me the way," she asked.

I replied, "Let me turn some lights on low so we can see where we're going."

"Okay," she whispered in reply.

Clinging to each other as we moved aft, we were like two people who had been cast adrift hanging onto a life preserver in a stormy sea.

We were aft, in the master cabin off which the sumptuously large bathroom was situated. It was complete with a bath for two and a cosy corner shower.

"Oh, I didn't expect this on board," she exclaimed as she took in the finely appointed head.

"I'll run the water, then get a couple glasses of white wine to have with our bath," I presumptuously said.

"That would be a lovely idea," she replied.

I took my time finding and selecting the white wine from the small cellar on board. I returned bearing two glasses and a bucket of ice from the freezer to keep the bottle chilled. She was already ensconced in the tub overflowing with bubbles.

"Your wine, Madam!" I declared, playing the French wine steward.

She replied innocently, "Oh, pour moi?"

"Mais, oui!" I answered.

"We most certainly may!" she said with a mischievous smile. "Why don't you join me?"

I joined her. The old claw-foot tub was specially made in that the gold taps were situated on the far middle side while the ends were both suitably sloping to afford two people the most luxurious bath in total comfort.

We talked. We sipped. We kissed. We played. We whispered sweet words. What we shared was pure bliss.

After a time we got hungry. I threw on a polo shirt and white trousers and lent her a white cotton shirt and an old pair of white dungarees that I had on board. She slipped the several-sizes-too-large trousers on, then put on the shirt, leaving the collar up and tying the shirttails around her beautiful bare midriff.

Walking down the dock, we came to Barb's Place Fish and Chips - it's a floating shack that is tied up to the dock near one of the shore ramps. We both ordered oyster burgers with a green side salad and Pepsi-Colas. We selected a patio table under an umbrella right on the floating dock as here there are no inside facilities other than the kitchen. Both ravenously hungry, we whiled away the time waiting for our orders by amusing ourselves with watching the seagulls making a nuisance of themselves as they fought for scraps flicked to them by other patrons.

"Does anybody else besides you live here year-round?"

"Sure, there's my friend Logan who has been living aboard his sailboat, much like I do, for years now."

"Where is it?"

"It's that one there," I said as I pointed it out.

"What is the name of Logan's boat?"

"It's the *Grumpy II,"* I replied.

"Is he grumpy too?" Sarah asked with a broad smile.

"Sometimes, but mostly he is just a really likeable guy. Everybody has their occasional bad moments. He's no exception. He's a great guy! I would trust my life with him!"

"What does he do?"

"He retired early, just like I did, except that he is somewhat older. I sometimes call him the Old Man of the Sea or just the Old Man to bug him. But he used to be a stock broker. Now he plays the stock market just for himself. The high level of constant stress as a broker was taking a toll on him. He had to retire on account of it. Doctor's orders."

"That's too bad. Does he do well in the market?"

"Most often, but Logan has his trying times. That's when he's usually grumpy, when the market is going down and he didn't sell in time. I can tell what the market is doing just by observing him. He's like a barometer on a ship. If he's grumpy, the market's down but he got out on time. If he's really grumpy, the market's down and he didn't get out on time. Of course, if he's bought short, well, who knows? It's about that time when my expertise and my understanding of the stock market part company. But Logan keeps trying to educate me about the subtle nuances of the market anyway."

"What are those houses there?" Sarah asked as she turned her head to the side and pointed down toward the far end of the dock.

"Those floating ones tied up to the dock on the far side?"

"Yes."

"They are float homes. Their owners live here year-round much like we do. It's their permanent home. We'll take a walk that way later so you can see them. They're quite cute really. Some have small planter gardens and low picket fences. All are unique, that's for sure! One of my friends there even grows her own herb garden."

"Really?"

"Yes. Her name is Rebecca. She has lots of different kinds of herbs! Every now and then she brings something or other over to me to try out. Some she grows herself, others she buys down in Chinatown."

"Like what?"

"Well, the other day Becky brought some Wu wei zi over for me."

"Some Wu wei what?"

"Zi! Wu wei zi. In Engrish, your humble servant calls it schisandra," I clowned using my dreadful Charley Chan accent.

"Schisandra? I've never heard of it!"

"You have now. It's an old Chinese tonic herb."

"What's it do?"

"It, uh, uh, well . . . It's, uh, said to be good for one's, uh . . . drive." I cautiously fumbled before blurting it out.

"One's drive? Like . . . oh, I get it!" she blurted and blushed.

"Indeed, you did!" I replied with measured repartee. Her face turned even redder.

"But you don't need that sort of thing, do you?"

"Works, doesn't it?" I winked.

"Sure did!" she laughed lustily. "Does it work for women too?"

"It's supposed to."

"Wait a minute . . . she brought this over for you?"

"I guess there has been a dearth of women over at my place lately - none, in fact - and I guess Becky thought that I needed something along these lines to pick me up, so to speak."

"And so Becky just happened to have some and came over to take care of your, uh, intimate needs?"

"Rebecca is a very nice young lady but I don't think that was her intention. Nor would her current boyfriend appreciate her and I getting involved in that sort of thing. And even if he is the salt of the earth, I'd be willing to bet that he's not that tolerant. Besides, I have a distinct liking for my personal well-being."

"So, do you think I could try some?"

"Careful now! Amongst other things, it's also said to have been used to alleviate the discomforts of diarrhea and dysentery!" We laughed until our sides ached.

"What else is it good for?" she asked.

"Let me think. It's also said to be good for relieving stress."

"That's what I need."

"And it's also said to be good for improving concentration and coordination . . . "

"Need that too."

"and for sleeping . . . where you have insomnia or are disturbed by dreams."

"Interesting!"

"And it's said to be good for use in the treatment of depression and its attendant cousin, irritability."

"Ah! We can leave some for your friend Logan on the *Grumpy II* in case of a sudden downturn in the market," Sarah joked.

"We will! And it's also supposed to be good for . . . for, uh, I can't remember . . . uh, let's see . . . forgetfulness, that's it!"

"We'll take it right into our old age!" Sarah fairly glowed as she said it without immediately realizing what she had so presumptuously implied. She suddenly became quiet. Our orders arrived just then, breaking the awkward silence and bursting the bubbles of intruding thoughts around us.

"Will you stay the night?" I asked back aboard ship as we sat in the saloon, finishing off that bottle of wine from before.

She replied with a soft whisper, " Yes, I was hoping you'd ask. But I don't have anything to wear to Chung's cocktail party tomorrow."

"Don't worry. Tomorrow I'll get a car and we'll drive out to your place in Sidney and get them."

"Okay."

I picked her up and carried her aft, into the master cabin. I gently laid her upon the faux-fur spread that covers my custom-fitted oval bed at the stern. I reached over and switched the dim light off as we slipped out of our clothes. I opened the short woven-wood blinds that covered the sections of small square windows that were set in the transom, letting square shafts of moonlight fall at a raked angle upon her beautiful naked body. She was seemingly bathed in a golden aureole. Her long black hair was fanned out in a halo-like fashion about her. Her creamy skin rippled to my light touch. She looked at me with her dreamy almond eyes as I reveled in her natural beauty, caressing every soft curve. She moaned softly and drew me to her. I joined her in the golden shaft of moonlight as a chugging tugboat passing up the middle of the channel sent gentle waves rippling through us and set the *Valhalla* into a rhythmic rocking motion.

CHAPTER ELEVEN

COCKTAILS

SHIP POINT WHARF, INNER HARBOUR, VICTORIA. The late afternoon sun bathed the cityscape surrounding the Inner Harbour with the golden hues that makes outdoor photography a snap. The trees lining the streets and those that lay in clusters around the harbour paths and the many small parks were ablaze in the reds, yellows, and oranges of autumn.

Being such a nice afternoon, Sarah and I decided to walk the path around the harbour from the *Valhalla* at Fisherman's Wharf to the cocktail party aboard Chung's ship. The *M.V. Scorpion* was to have been docked at Ship Point Wharf near the foot of the Empress Hotel.

"I'm going to slip these flats on for the walk, they're more sensible," she said. "I'll throw my heels into my handbag for later."

"Good idea," I said as I locked the *Valhalla* and hid the brass key in its secret cubby hole on board. "Oh, try to get Chung to give us a tour of his ship. It might prove to be interesting."

"I'll do my best, my darling," she cooed.

We walked down the dock, up the ramp and past the baseball park where a game was being played. Cheers and shouts of encouragement rose from the small bleachers that flanked home plate. We strolled past the Coast Hotel where some whale-watching boats and pleasure craft were docked in the little bay just around the corner from Fisherman's Wharf.

Rounding Laurel Point, we saw that the *Scorpion* was tied to Ship Point Wharf across the harbour. This is the dock where the small pocket cruise ships tie up with their fifty to one hundred passengers enroute to Alaska or perhaps to the fabulous Princess Louisa Inlet on the mainland. There were none there today. Instead, this equally-large working yacht with its gleaming white raked hull and ultra-streamlined superstructure took their place. She had to be more than a couple hundred feet long, maybe even three hundred. At the moment, she was the biggest ship in the Inner Harbour.

It looked to be the same ship that we had seen in the middle of Saanich Inlet yesterday, but this one had a truncated stern and not the indented stern that the other ship had. This ship appeared to lack a helicopter and a landing pad. Where there had been a helicopter pad on the other ship, this one had a structure that appeared to be a sundeck which was just aft of midships. Glass walls on both sides of this deck protected guests from cooling sea breezes. Coloured party lights were strung around this section, deck tables and chairs were set out around the perimeter. The lower afterdeck was outlined with a necklace of coloured lights as well. Contrasting white lights were strung from the bow of the ship, then swept high up to the two electronic masts and down again to the stern.

"I just love the smell of the salt air here!" Sarah remarked. "It mixes with the fragrances of the flowers and the shrubs. Out on the ocean you usually just have one natural scent. Here you have two so that your nose can compare their differences."

"I never thought of it that way, but you're quite right," I concurred. At the moment I would have agreed with anything this lovely creature had thought to say. It was the result of the blending of the late afternoon's ambience and her entrancing effect on me.

The paths led us around the second little bay in front of the Laurel Point Inn. I chose the path that runs past the totem pole hidden in the foliage. I am in the habit of touching base with its mystical presence and usually give it a familiar pat as I walk past. We stopped while Sarah read the plaque out loud: "'Kwakiutal Totem Pole carved at Alert Bay, B. C. by Mr. James Dick. Donated by the native Indian people of British Columbia to commemorate the centenary of the Union, July 20, 1871 of the province of British Columbia with Canada.' So what is that figure on the very top?" Sarah asked as she shielded her eyes from the sun that cast the totem in gold.

"I think it's a raven."

As we walked the perimeter of the Inner Harbour, the sun turned the colour of the gaily-lit ship from a cool gleaming white, to a deep gold, then to a hot salmon shade. The little green and white harbour ferries flitted here and there carrying passengers from one part of the harbour to another. A red Seaspan tug under shortened tow-rope pulled a gravel-laden barge under the upraised lift sections of the blue bridge on Johnson Street to enter the industrial section of the harbour. A couple of huge seagulls got a free ride as they sat on one of the three peaks of gravel, impassively surveying the harbour scene as they rode along.

"Oh, look at the gargoyles up there!" Sarah said in amazement as she pointed to the roof that was held up by the columns of the classic old building that now houses a wax museum and government offices in the several floors above.

"Yes, aren't they something? Tridents too. I believe that they are of King Neptune, the roman mythological god of the sea. Before, it was the old C.P.R. Ferry terminal building. Their ferries ran to and from Seattle and to and from Vancouver. Those were the days of waiters in proper attire brandishing serving linen on their forearm while setting out tables with real silver cutlery and fine bone china. This was the ticket office as well as the Immigration and Customs Hall. A lot has happened behind those columns over the years. If only the walls could talk! Now its just wax figures, just a bunch of dummies in there. And they can't talk at all!" I joked.

She mercifully laughed at my poor attempt at humour and gave me a hug and a light kiss as we walked with our arms around each other's waist.

We made our way past the nightly impromptu entertainers: comedians, jugglers, singers, musicians, animal balloon makers, assorted other entertainers and buskers and the tourists who were clustered in small groups around the lower Causeway. Portrait artists were intensely drawing their paying subjects under wide canvas sun umbrellas before they lost thc afternoon's light. A handful of people crowded behind each artist watching their progress. The artists who did the cartoon portrait drawings elicited smiles and occasional snickers from the crowd and turned the heads of passers-by like us while the embarrassed subject tried to read the faces of the onlookers for clues as to the artist's comic rendition of their appearance.

Alongside the *Scorpion*, we were met at the gangway by a white-uniformed quartermaster who consulted his guest list upon inquiring as to our names. A deep bass rhythm emanated from a hidden sound system. He did a quick scan, found our names, then ushered us on board with a hint of a deferential bow and a slow sweep of his arm. We were escorted into the main saloon by a second crewman who asked if we would be needing anything before being taken astern to the afterdeck where the host was entertaining the earlier arrivals. Sarah said that she needed to freshen up a little and, being shown the way, said she would only be a minute or two.

"Take your time," I said hoping that I could scout out this part of the ship while she was occupied. I had barely begun to stray when the crewman cleared his throat and suggested that I should stay put as he would be taking us aft shortly. He was not the friendly type at all, nor did his bulging muscles suggest that.

"All set darling?" I asked as Sarah returned.

"Yes, thank you," she replied as she took my arm.

We were escorted aft across the sun deck where clusters of people were gathered at patio tables along its sides and down a wide exterior staircase that lead to the open lower afterdeck.

The setting sun bathed the guests in soft, reddish sunlight as Mr. Chung Min-Ho was holding the attention of a gaggle of guests from the local marine industries who were awestruck by his obvious wealth and mesmerized by its attendant power. He held a cocktail glass in one hand while his other hand gesticulated now and then while holding the longest, fattest cigar that I had seen. It gave him a comical appearance, this gnome with the shaved dome who held sway before this enraptured group. One would have thought that he was the Messiah surrounded by the liberated. Our own escorting crew member went up to him and whispered in his ear. Chung immediately wheeled around to face us.

"Ah, Sarah! How nice of you to accept my invitation this evening. And how beautiful you look tonight, my dear," he said as he gave her a quick peck on her cheek forcing him to tiptoe in his elevator shoes.

Turning to me he said with a snarl, "And you, Mr. Erikson, we meet again." Turning back to those assembled, his grinning moon face beamed pleasantly in a show for the assembled crowd. It belied his hatred for me.

Turning back to Sarah, he said, "Your cocktails will be here shortly. They are being made just now over at the bar. Forgive me for taking the liberty to order for you but I insist that the first cocktail be one of my concoctions. I'm sure you will like them."

"That will be fine," she said.

"It's no problem at all," I added, though I wondered whether it was just his ego that demanded this overbearing gesture or whether he had some sinister motives to his insistence.

"That's an interesting looking cigar that you have there," I commented as I took the proffered cocktail from the silver serving tray held by an immaculately-attired waiter.

"Yes, it's a Casa Blanca Jeroboam," he stated authoritatively as he held it up with a flourish. "It's hand made," he said rather proudly.

"Cuban?"

"It's an international cigar, just like my companies. I like to spread my business around different countries."

"International?" I questioned.

"Yes, the filler is a blend of the Dominican Republic and Brazil, while the binder is Mexican, and the wrapper is from Connecticut."

"You like a big cigar?" I pointedly asked. The damned thing had to be about ten inches long.

"I smoke these because I like the taste of them," Chung stated acidly. I doubted his statement. The stogie smell hinted of herbs. If I recalled correctly, they were economically priced at around four or five dollars the last time I was in E. A. Morris's cigar store. I go there occasionally to soak up the atmosphere and the unique smells of the different tobaccos from around the world even though I'm not a smoker as such. They were such comically-huge stogies that they stuck in my memory. I figured he smoked them because they were big and fat and in his mind made up for his diminutive size. "Could I interest you in a Casa Blanca, Mr. Erikson?" he asked.

"No, thank you. I don't smoke cigars very often but when I do I prefer Cohiba Esplendidos," I said nonchalantly, trying to flaunt my recently-acquired knowledge.

"Cohiba Esplendidos? Why, I give them away by the boxful to people I do business with. If I have any business to do with you, you'll get yours in due course Mr. Erikson," he said with narrowed eyes and a thinly veiled threat. He puffed at the fat tan cigar with the red and gold band then blew the smoke up at me.

Hmm! I thought as I wondered if this was from whom good old Harry Wampole of ORCA got his box of Cohiba Esplendidos. Let's see, at more than 50 bucks a stogie, that's worth several thousand dollars. And his humidor had to cost a grand at least! Just how much business did Chung do with good old Harry? And what kind of business was it?

"You have a lovely ship, Mr. Chung," Sarah said. "I'd like to see the rest of her."

"Why don't I show you around then?" Chung smiled as he took her arm.

"You don't mind if I tag along, do you?" I asked.

"Why, not at all, Mr. Erikson, not at all. We'll start with the bridge."

He took us to midships. There he led us under the deck with all the tables and umbrellas then further down the corridor that led to a larger hall where he punched a button on the wall to call for the elevator. It arrived with a soft hum, the doors glided open to reveal a rather smallish, four-person lift. Here the elevator music was the same as that which was playing out on the afterdeck. I noted that there were six buttons inside for the various decks. We were at number 3 deck, leaving three below us and two above. He reached over and stabbed at the top button marked number 1. After a few moments the doors silently glided open to reveal a bridge crammed with electronics and some standard brass gauges as well. There was not a chart to be seen save for the ones on the glowing monitors. There was some very sophisticated equipment here!

"I like cutting-edge technology, as you can see," Chung stated smugly.

Two crewmen in white duck uniforms stood watch on the bridge, tending to the onboard computers and monitoring the ship's requirements at dockside.

"Oh, look! He's got GDOC." Sarah exclaimed.

"What's GDOC?" I asked.

"It stands for Global Display Operations Computer."

"Ah, just like my charts, only on a computer monitor," I replied.

"As I said, I like the latest technology," Mr. Chung reiterated.

I read the GPS Navigator readout from the satellite: N48 degrees 25.281; W123 degrees 22.288. This is something I've got. I'll have to look into the GDOC though.

"Mr. Chung," Sarah said. "As you know, I pilot submersibles as part of my work at sea. Could you tell us a little about what all these other fantastic-looking pieces of equipment do?"

"I'm afraid not. You see I leave all that up to the captain and he is now off watch. He's in his quarters below, sleeping, actually."

"Well, perhaps the crew can briefly tell us what all these other instruments do."

"As you can see, the crew is rather busy. Besides most of the equipment is on and in use only when we are actually at sea."

The crew did not look all that busy. It was just a lame excuse on the part of Chung to not explain anything at all.

What did he have to hide?

"Why I brought you up here first was to provide you with an unfettered view of the Empress Hotel. It is at it's most spectacular at sunset in the fall. Come out onto the bridge wing for a better view."

"Oh, look, Rune! Look at the ivy on the Empress! It practically covers the whole of the front of the hotel!"

"It is spectacular, isn't it?" I agreed as I put my arm around Sarah.

"Look how red the leaves are. They are simply magnificent!" She gushed in wonder at the sight.

"Yes, simply magnificent," Chung allowed.

"And look how they turn various shades from the top of the hotel downwards," she added. "There is not very much green left at the bottom. Aren't they vibrant?"

"It is times like these that I am truly glad to be alive, to have my freedom," Chung said.

"Your freedom?" questioned Sarah.

"Yes, my freedom. There was a time, when I was growing up, that I did not have my freedom, didn't even know what freedom was!"

"Where were you born?" I asked.

"In Korea, North Korea," he gravely said as his eyes glazed over in remembrance of his youth, "in the capital city of Pyongyang. We lived there. We were very poor, most people were very poor, but at my young age I didn't realize just how poor we were until I got older. When you are just a child, you don't know any better. You think everyone is enduring the same conditions that you are. But that is not so. There were some more fortunate than others. The people in the party were amongst those more fortunate than the others even though under the communist system everyone is supposed to be treated equally. I soon learned that life is hard. I had to steal to keep my brothers and sisters alive, especially as I got older. There was no choice. Nobody had any choice! In my teens I was recruited to serve in the military. It was compulsory! I found myself in the navy, then in the commandos, and later, attached as a commando to the submarine service. In boot camp we were trained to kill, to kill without remorse. It was kill or be killed!"

"Ah, yes. I've seen photos taken from the observation posts. It did look like a bleak and cruel existence from there," I interjected.

"But the observation posts were strictly for show," he countered. "The real action was supposed to be underground. There were miles of tunnels built under the DMZ into the south. Some were as much as a couple hundred feet below the surface. We could get a division an hour through these tunnels. We were just waiting for the word to invade.

"One good thing about the military was that we got more food so I was able to hoard some for my family.

"One of the worst things about commando boot camp though was the graduation. To pass, we were let off by submarine on enemy beaches in the south under cover of darkness to infiltrate their territory. We didn't think of it as South Korea for it was simply explained to us that it was our territory that had been stolen from us."

"But I thought the Korean War was settled way back in the early fifties," Sarah stated with a puzzled look on her face.

I said, "What happened was that an armistice was signed in the summer of 1953 that brought an end to the official fighting in the Korean War. It created a two-and-a-half-mile deep, 150-mile-long Demilitarized Zone to buffer the South from the North. There were many incursions right after that time."

"Correct," Chung said. "But that was well before my time. However, the skirmishes still went on for all these years, like the one I was on in the hills of Kangnung, east of Seoul. I can still recall every minute of those terrifying times. Crawling our way through razor wire and mine fields, never knowing from one second to the next if it was you who was going to be cut or blown to smithereens or the guy crawling beside you.

"There was an awful noise as the monstrously-large American hydrofoils arrived on the beach carrying troops to search for us infiltrators at night. Later, they were used to carry the troops and prisoners out. They were like fire-breathing dragons! And the deadly helicopters would swoop in over the hills with their searchlights and infrared scopes sighting on us. Then your armed troops would arrive wearing night-vision goggles, walking unimpeded by darkness like some zombie scene from one of your horror movies. Not many of us survived! Fewer still made it back to our lines in North Korea. But those that did were tough; nothing fazed us after that torture test!

"I went back home on leave. The people were poorer still, some had starved and died. My parents were very sick and would soon die as they had given most of what they had to the children. When our former allies, the Russians, moved farther toward democracy, our politicians were paralyzed into inertia; our country became unstable. China tried to help but they had problems of their own and neglected us. Soon the city people were starving. They were eating grass or anything else to stave off hunger pangs. Women were desperately selling their hair and some their bodies for a pittance just to buy some rice or Chinese wheat to boil or to grind into flour to make bread if they had the ingredients. The people on the farms in the country were only slightly better off as they had direct access to whatever little food they could scrounge here or there or that they grew in secret.

"Finally, I could see the writing on the wall. If I was to survive, I had to abandon my siblings to whatever fate dealt them. They were on their own. I carefully made a plan to commandeer one of our 325-ton Shark-class submarines on one of our commando sorties. We couldn't get parts for our submarines. Fuel was severely rationed. Then one night conditions were right. We were sent on a working submarine with adequate fuel. The deed was done. We left the captain, the officers, and some crew adrift in the life rafts. I and a skeleton crew smuggled the submarine into a cove in a small island in the South China Sea. After a time I made a deal to sell the sub. An agent brokered it to an anonymous country. That money was a pittance really, much less than a hundred thousand dollars, but it gave me working capital.

"With the end of the Soviet Union as we knew it, I bought Russian subs, some just junk really, at bargain-basement prices and resold them at a profit. That's how I got into the marine salvage business."

"You are doing tremendously well for just a junk dealer," I prodded.

"I no longer just deal in junk, Mr. Erikson! " he stated as he sniffed and drew in a large draught of smoke from his cigar.

"And what do you deal in now?" I prodded again.

"My companies are world wide!" he spluttered. "We deal on a global basis. Our interests are many and varied. Other than to say that we are also in the marine supply and contracting business and had some business in Vancouver, I don't wish to bore both of you with the details of why we are here on the West Coast."

"And what are your interests here in Victoria?" I asked.

"Why, it's a beautiful port city, of course! And it has some of the most sophisticated marine robotics and technology companies in the world located here. I make a habit of keeping abreast of the latest developments. We want to stay in the forefront, ahead of our competitors. One must never become complacent and in doing so, one must be forever vigilant. In business as well, it is kill or be killed!" Chung stated succinctly while a demonical look flashed briefly across his smiling moon-face.

"I feel a chill here," Sarah complained with a shudder. "Let's go on with the tour."

"Yes, let's," I added.

"I'm afraid that there is not much left to see of the ship. Most of the crew has gone off on shore leave, that is, except for the captain who is sleeping below, the bridge watch and the few crew who are catering to our guest's needs at the moment," he said in dissuasion.

"Really?" I asked.

"Yes," he confirmed.

"That's too bad," Sarah commented, "I would have liked to have gone on the grand tour."

"Another time, I'm sure," Chung said with a broad Cheshire catlike grin.

"Come, we'll take the elevator down again. I'm sure your other colleagues have arrived by now," he said as he took Sarah by the arm toward the lift. I brushed past them as the lift doors parted, held them, and purposely hit all the other buttons trying to make it look as if I could not remember exactly what deck we had been on.

"Confused, Mr. Erikson?"

"Actually, yes. I guess I pushed some wrong buttons here."

"Deck 3 is where we're going!"

"My apologies, I guess we're taking the scenic route then."

"Not at all! All the other decks other than deck 3 and the bridge need to be keyed to be accessed."

"Oh! And why is that?" I prodded.

"Why, not enough crew. Shore leave, remember?"

"Ah, yes. Not enough crew. Shore leave. Of course! Silly me!"

"Rune!" a booming familiar voice called out as we neared the guests on the afterdeck. It was Harry's voice, of course.

"Dr. Wampole," I acknowledged.

"Call me Harry," he boomed again.

"Of course, Harry. How are you?"

"I'm very well, thank you. I take it you now know everyone in our little group here."

"All except that beautiful lady on your arm," I answered.

"Of course, I had forgotten! You haven't met my wife Barbara yet!"

"Hello, I'm very pleased to meet you," she said.

"The pleasure is mine, so nice to meet you," I said.

"I think everyone knows each other now. Rune, I see you've made the acquaintance of our indefatigable host, Mr. Chung."

"Actually, we first met at the reception for the unveiling of the new black smoker at ORCA a few nights ago."

"Yes, damn nuisance that I couldn't have been there!" Harry said.

"Everybody!" Chung called out. "Let's watch the sunset! I propose a toast. To life! And all that it can offer to those who go for the gold!"

"To life!" the assembled crowd called out from both stepped decks.

"You know, Rune," Sarah said softly to me as she grasped my arm and molded her body against mine, "I'm really going to hate to leave. If it wasn't for the fact that you will be there later, I just don't think I could."

"It is an exceedingly romantic city, isn't it?"

"It's not just the city, you dummy," she said through misted eyes.

I put my arm around her and hugged her tightly. She raised her teary-cheeked face to mine. We kissed slowly and passionately.

"C'mon," I said huskily, "Let's find a quieter spot."

"Oh, look!" she said, her almond eyes widening, "The moon! It's just coming up!" The huge golden harvest moon appeared in the cleft between the Empress Hotel and the Union Club, silently floating upwards in a dusky sky as it cast the silhouetted obsidian branches of a gnarled arbutus tree upon its beaming face.

"It's gorgeous! There's a quiet spot over there," I added as I took her in tow to the other side of the deck to see the regal Parliament Buildings across the harbour. "Keep your eye on the Parliament Buildings. As it gets darker, its appearance will change dramatically."

"I will," Sarah whispered. "What is that shiny gold thing at the very top?"

"That's the Golden Boy. It's a statue of Captain Vancouver."

"Interesting. And why are those domes green?"

"They are actually made of copper sheathing. They turn green as they oxidize."

"Oh! Look!" Sarah suddenly gasped as thousands of tiny light bulbs flashed on in an instant, illuminating and outlining the Parliament Buildings in the twilight, "It's like something out of a fairy tale!" she gushed.

"And you look like a princess out of a fairy tale!" I said.

"And I feel like a princess too! Pinch me! This can't be real."

I took her in my arms.

"Ooh!" She moaned softly.

"Is it real?" I asked.

"It's real!" She whispered in my ear as the last of the afternoon's radiance settled over us in an evening waft of warm air off the adjacent shore. There was a sweep of magenta on the horizon where the sun had settled. Just above, the evening star twinkled in an indigo sky.

The golden moon rose higher in the evening sky as the hypnotic rhythm of the pop tunes was interspersed with some slow dance music.

Couples gently swayed to the beat under the colourful lights of the patio deck. Still others slow-danced on the lower deck near the stern. Sarah and I had been dancing cheek to cheek, overwhelmed by each other's touch.

CHAPTER TWELVE

SALTED AWAY

SHIP POINT WHARF, INNER HARBOUR, VICTORIA. I noticed a very agitated Chung Min-Ho taking a phone call. He returned to the party for a brief moment, sought out one of his serving crewmen, then fled back into the bowels of the ship.

"Excuse me, my darling," I said, "but something is definitely up with our Mr. Chung. I'm going to see if I can find out what it is that is bothering him. Find Ellen and your other colleagues and stay with them. If I'm not back in twenty minutes seek out Coop, tell him that I had to leave for a short while but will return. He'll look after you until I'm back."

"Oh, Rune, do be careful! I don't like the looks of him. Promise?"

"I'll be as careful as I can be. Now go and join the others."

"Okay," she whispered, looking deeply into my eyes as we parted.

I swiftly followed in the direction that Chung and his crewman took then thought better of it as I realized that I would probably be walking right into them at the elevator. Deciding to second-guess them, I sought out an exterior set of stairs. I strode up two flights of steps to get to the bridge deck. Reaching it, I tested the door to the inside. It turned and opened. Carefully, I made my way inside the ship.

Not seeing anyone, I made my way forward just in time to see the two men emerge from the elevator and stride onto the bridge. The server immediately began upbraiding the two men on watch on the bridge which was unusual to say the least for kitchen staff to have control over bridge crew other than through their cuisine. Chung joined in the upbraiding and became apoplectic. He struck one of the bridge crew with the flat of the hand across his face turning it red and forming welts from each finger's force. The server angrily picked up a shipboard telephone, dialed a couple numbers, waited for a response, barked into it and slammed the phone down.

A minute later another crewman fearfully scurried out from the elevator into the bridge, a fresh bandage covered his right hand. Surprisingly, he appeared to be the same man that tried to kill us out at the Bamberton plant yesterday afternoon, the one that I had whacked the gun out of his hand with the two-by-four board. His injury looked painful. My curiosity was piqued even more at the sight of him. I edged closer, hiding behind the corner of the bulkhead. I began to pick up a word here and there, especially the ones that were shouted. "Idiot!" I heard a voice call out that sounded like it belonged to Chung. "You were supposed to be monitoring the damn thing, not sleeping."

Monitoring what? I wondered.

"I want a situation report and I want it within the hour. Is that understood?" Chung fairly shouted at the assembled men. "I'll be in my office or down at the party," he called back as he strode from the bridge and angrily punched the elevator button.

I waited for him to go down. He got in and closed the door. The light flashed from one to two then stopped. Wanting to find out more, I tried to edge closer to the bridge but was shut out as someone slammed the door to the bridge shut in anger. Pondering for a moment, I decided to try to check out the rest of the ship, skipping deck two as I didn't particularly want to run into Chung by accident.

I exited the bridge deck by retracing my steps to the third deck where I had no choice but to re-enter the ship. Deciding to forgo using the elevator because of the danger, I found the interior stairwell. There were three lower decks to be checked out. However, I found the stairwell door locked. I pulled out a drapery hook from a set of curtains next to me and fashioned a lock pick of sorts. I sprang the door open on my fourth attempt, went into the stairwell and silently closed the door behind me. Looking around for surveillance cameras, I could find none. I crept down the dimpled steel treads, the throb of the engines becoming louder as I descended.

I reached the fourth deck door. I tested it by turning the handle. It turned and the door gave way as I nudged it. Here in the passageway, the lights were kept a dim red to ease night vision. The air conditioning whooshed out of the overhead vents. I softly padded aft down a passageway at the end of which was another door. I was now directly below the sun and patio deck. Cracking it open, I was amazed to see a small helicopter tethered by its bear trap onto a moveable deck. This looked like the same helicopter that we had chased when we discovered its crew tampering with my Harley Fat Boy motorcycle at Bamberton. Entering, I peered at it in the reddish gloom. It appeared to be the same gray colour but it was hard to tell in this subdued red lighting. Looking at its tail number, I tried to recall the one that I had barely seen. It was difficult, I had not gotten all of it then as the numbers were quite obscure. They were dark gray on a black background. I pondered this discovery.

I decided to take a second look at the deck that this chopper sat on. The perimeter was gapped. It appeared that the whole deck could rise like an elevator. But how could it go through the ceiling? I checked the ceiling out and found that, there too, a gap ran along its perimeter where it met the bulkhead. So that was it! A retractable patio deck that slid forward so that the chopper deck could be elevated for use as a helicopter pad.

I retraced my steps back into the stairwell, going down one more flight to deck five where I found an unlocked door and went through it as I made my way aft. The room contained banks of electronic monitors and equipment. The room opened up as I came to an interior balcony that looked down upon another deck farther aft. Below, there was a small blue submersible that looked to be the same size as a medium-sized pickup truck. It was suspended above the water. It had six fat tires that it used to move on surfaces other than water. I could see room for two crew inside it as well as large exterior jump-seats in its rear box. Emblazoned on its side was the name *Global Sea Marine* and in smaller letters the name *SeaTruck.*

I could smell fresh paint. Someone appeared to have been painting camouflage lines on its blue body. Paint-splattered masking tape was still in place on the sub's exterior. It was the same type as the one we were to be evaluating except that it had a few different robotic tools and manipulator arms attached to it. Its front scoop was larger too.

On catwalks on either side of the opening were some chests of sophisticated tools. I unsnapped the hinges of a large aluminum case and set the top aside. Inside was the top portion of a yellow diver's hard suit. Attached to its back was an apparatus that resembled an air pack. Around it, set in foam packing material, were yellow stovepipe-like arms with black bands where the arm sections swivelled around. It looked like a kind of sophisticated space suit. Below the submersible was sea water. Its level rose and fell slightly in tandem with the surge of seawater just outside the ship with the passing of other water craft. There had to be an opening under water nearer the stern. Somehow, through the use of hydraulics and sliding decks and bulkheads, they had managed to conceal the indented stern for the sub bay as well as its elevator chopper pad.

It was the same ship!

There appeared to be a sloping ramp that led down to the stern where the rear docking port of the ship opened to facilitate the departure and the re-entry of the SeaTruck submersible. The transition of the SeaTruck from the ship to the sea and re-entry could be on the surface or could be done while hidden completely underwater.

What operation were they on that they had to resort to using clandestine measures to accomplish their goal? Why did they want to kill Sarah and I? What was the "situation" that Chung had wanted a report on urgently? And why was he so upset with his crew's inattention to monitor something?

An almost imperceptible click behind me interrupted my thoughts. I stiffened as I felt a rough arm snake around my neck then felt the sharp point of a switchblade knife piercing the skin in the middle of my back. "Don't move!" ordered the surly voice behind my head. The overpowering smell of garlic permeated his breath and exuded from his pores.

Chung's voice rang out over the intercom on the wall beside the door. "Well, look at the rat that we have caught in our trap. It seems that the rat set off the silent alarms on the bridge. I wonder what the rat is up to?" sneered Chung.

"I was about to ask you the same question!" I retorted, angry that I had indeed been caught like a rat in a trap.

"From where I sit, your position doesn't look at all favourable to be asking those kinds of questions, Mr. Erikson!" Chung's voice rang out on the intercom as I felt the arm tighten around my neck.

"So it seems! Tell Mr. Garlic Breath here that he can relax. So where's the camera?"

"Cameras," he corrected. "Look up to the bulkhead. See those little pop rivets? They're all over the ship. Not all of them are rivets. You can't move without us knowing about it sooner or later. We were just waiting for the rat to spring the trap."

"I think of myself more as the cat than the rat. But I was just curious as to why you set your boys in your chopper on us yesterday."

"Well, you know what curiosity did to the cat, don't you? It killed the cat!" he said as he howled out in glee. "I hope you haven't used up all your nine lives yet Mr. Erikson, because you're going to need one of them now!"

"What do you have planned for me?"

"Why, to kill you of course! They will find the body of the unfortunate drowning victim in the Inner Harbour tomorrow morning - long after we are gone. You'll just be a party reveler who had become a little tipsy and had fallen off the dock into the dark waters after saying goodnight to his gracious host. Why, I'm already arranging for independent witnesses to attest to your leaving the ship!"

"So if you're going to kill me, tell me why you had your goons after us."

"It's simple, Mr. Erikson, you are employed in an endeavour which may run counter to the higher aims of my group of companies. I also believe in having first-strike capability at all times. Consider yourself soon to be stricken!" he laughed with a hearty howl.

"What endeavour?"

"Come now, Mr. Erikson, you're not a stupid man, and neither am I. Remember I said that I believed in the absolute latest technology and providing favours to people that I do business with. It's industrial intelligence, pure and simple! You've set out to harm me. You give me no choice but to harm you. Reward and punishment. This is the punishment. It's economic war played out to its fullest extent. Don't you find that exhilarating?"

"Not particularly, but what endeavour?" I repeated as I played for more time.

"I wish I had more time for your games, Mr. Erickson I like the challenge of matching wits and toying with people like you. Unfortunately you have a date with the fishes and I have a tide to catch. Get him ready!" he barked, cutting off our conversation.

With lightning speed I elbowed the knife out of Garlic Breath's hand. I relieved the pressure on my neck by gripping his choking arm with both my hands, one at his wrist, the other at the crook of his elbow. I turned my head into his elbow to relieve the pressure at my windpipe, then snapped his arm down. As I turned, I kicked back with all my force, raked my shoe down his shin and stamped on his instep all in one motion. He let out a yell as the excruciating pain overcame him. Holding his arm, I ducked down and moved into place behind him. I pulled my head free and twisted his arm behind him, jerking it high as I slammed him face-first into the bulkhead, ringing his head like the brawny titan did when he rang the large gong at the beginning in the old movies. He crumpled to the deck with a dull thud.

Spotting the second crewman looking up at me from the deck below, I leaned over and grasping the lower tube of the balcony railing with both hands, swung over the edge. I caught him with a direct blow with both feet to his back, knocking the wind out of him.

I quickly glanced around me searching for a way out. The way forward led into an area of heavy machines, conveyors, and lab analysis setups. I moved through the maze but was cut off by a crewman approaching me from the front. I darted around and ducked down here and there trying to elude the man. It was no use as more crew arrived to help.

There was no other way out than to go back the way I had come down. Retracing my route, I stepped over the groaning form of the crewman trying to suck some air into his deflated lungs. I was about to swing back up to the overhanging balcony when I caught sight of a man with a gun above me.

"Freeze!" he shouted.

I dove into the seawater below the submersible and swam under. Slugs slapped into the water beside me, leaving tiny bubble trails behind. I swam down to the exit which was lit with dull underwater lighting. Reality jarred me hard as I discovered a sturdy stainless steel grid blocking my escape route.

I was trapped!

Surfacing on the aft of the interior dock, I used the SeaTruck as a shield.

"Ah, looks like we have a drowned rat in the pool!" I heard a familiar voice gloat. Glancing over to the deck, I spotted Chung surrounded by his gunmen. They had their weapons trained on me.

I would have been a fool to resist further. "Okay, you got me," I said with resignation.

"Let's get on with it," ordered Chung briskly. "Get that old fishing net, and the rock salt out of the storage locker and truss him up loosely. We want it to appear as if he got tangled in some drifting net after he fell overboard. The net may even drift away from his body. When they do the autopsy and find water in his lungs it'll look like he accidently drowned. Make sure that the netting is wrapped around him several times but is still left loose. Fill the net with the rock salt. That'll keep him weighted down for hours until the rock salt melts, then he'll float up. All they'll find is his drowned body and maybe some old torn netting. That'll also attract and give the crabs some time to do their work on his body starting with the cuts to his hands that he's going to get when he struggles with the monofilament net to try to get free. Too bad there are no sharks right down here to chew him apart when his hands start bleeding. Well maybe a few dog sharks will make their way here. Or perhaps a six-gill shark will find him here. I hear there are some around in these waters. And he will struggle but the net won't break, I can guarantee that! Ha, ha, ha!" he laughed with a wheezing squeak that spoke of him having consumed too many cigars.

"You wish!" I spat out.

"Frisk him!" Chung barked out.

I was roughly patted-down as I stood there dripping wet from my swim. They found no weapons. "He's clean," they said.

"Okay, throw a few turns of net around him!" I was shoved prone onto the cold deck beside the lapping water. The crewman whose bell got rung came to me and kicked me in the ribs. The struggling crewmen rolled me loosely in the netting, threw huge chunks of rock salt around me and wrapped me with more netting to cover the open ends. I searched wildly about me with mounting consternation, looking for a last chance for an escape.

I was truly done for now!

"Open the grid door under the water," Chung ordered. His face was showing extreme excitement as he relished the terror that he was subjecting me to. I could hear the whine of the electric motor as the grid slid open. "Funny how things end sometime Mr. Erikson, but that's life!" he chortled.

"No, that's death!" I corrected.

"Roll him in with the fishes," he ordered. The crewman with the bandaged gun-hand that I had hit the other day tried to swing his foot into my groin. Instead, I rolled and flopped into the water by myself, the chunks of rock salt bouncing around me. Just as I hit the cool seawater, I heard Chung sneeringly call out to me in a strange, morbid farewell, "Aloha! Mr. Erikson!"

I took my last deep breath, fighting against the rising panic within me. The heavy chunks of rock salt sank quickly, pulling at the netting which dragged me down with it. My last glimpses were of the submersible slung above me, then the underwater floodlights rushed up past me before I became mired at the bottom of the shallow harbour in semi-darkness.

I figured I had three, maybe four minutes before I ran out of air and would be forced to suck salt water into my lungs bringing about Chung's horrible prophecy.

I fought the rising panic as I struggled to stand up on the mucky harbour bottom. Being somewhat disoriented, I still managed to float into an upright crouched position, the loose netting allowing me to do so. My mind worked at warp speed trying to visualize a solution to my dilemma. There was no way that I could find the end of the net in time to extricate myself from it by unwrapping it and there was no way that I could smash the chunks of rock salt from around me. I searched my clothing for something to rip the monofilament netting. I opened my belt buckle then discard that idea as there was nothing sharp there at all. The zipper perhaps? No, that wouldn't work fast enough.

A few bubbles of air escaped my mouth.

I patted myself down and felt in my pockets. They had been thorough but not thorough enough as I came across a wafer-like plastic object in the watch pocket of my trousers. It was an Olfa Touch-Knife with a tiny half-inch retractable blade that I carry.

This was one of those times that I was glad that I did carry it!

I slowly extracted the small knife from the watch pocket and carefully pushed on the side button to release the blade. I lifted it and slashed at the netting in front of me which I could feel falling away in layers after repeated cutting. Before I was able to make a large enough slash the little knife twisted out of my hand and floated free. I blindly grasped in front of me in the murky depths as the plastic knife slowly rose with its positive buoyancy.

Panic tried to set in again.

My fingertip brushed against something then grasped at the knife just before it was able to work its way through the netting where it would have been out of my reach forever. With trembling hands, I again set the blade against the net and slashed roughly, opening a gash long enough to slip through.

My lungs were starting to burn now. Losing consciousness was a real concern.

I kicked upwards. A button on my coat caught onto the netting and held me fast. Try as I might, I could not free it quickly. I struggled to shuck my coat, then shot upwards, freeing myself of my bonds and rising above my watery casket. Bumping into the hull of the ship as I rose, I followed it along until I broke the surface of the harbour.

I quietly floated while gasping the sweet air around me. The deep thumping rhythm of the bass music wafted down to me from the decks above. Its cadence matched the thumping of my heart in my aching rib cage. Shivering with cold, I thought of swimming around the ship to where I could lose myself under the stationary dock that the ship was tied to. I discarded that idea as I thought that there would be someone on guard there.

Just then I saw the dark outline of the cabin of one of the little green and white harbour ferries. It was showing a green light to my port indicating that it was headed my way after having left the floating dock in front of the Empress Hotel where it would chug along near me as it passed the ship.

Having caught my breath, I took another deep breath and dove under the chilly water. I swam to where I thought that I could intercept the far side of the little ferry boat. Swimming as hard as I could, I reached the spot. I rose to the surface of the Inner Harbour just as the little water taxi was about to brush past me. Reaching up, I caught the gunwale and dragged myself aboard. There were looks of astonishment from the skipper at midships and an older couple who were sitting at the stern.

"Whoa! What've we got here?" the whiskered skipper asked me in surprise. I could just make out his large white eyes below his arched bushy eyebrows. I put a raised finger to my pursed lips asking for quiet. The Midwest couple at the stern put their arms around each other in fright at this creature rising from the black waters of the harbour.

"What happened to you? Some bad guys chasing you or something?" the skipper asked.

"Fell off a boat. I was doing some fishing," I said in a stage whisper.

"Right!" the skipper said.

"It's an emergency! Take me to Fisherman's Wharf and step on it!"

"Okay! You're the boss!" he excitedly exclaimed as he snapped his arm and set his captain's cap down lower on his brow, then pushed the throttle full ahead on the water taxi. Turning around, he said to the older couple in the back. "Folks, we got a little problem. It's an emergency. Got to change my route. The rides on me. I'll take you to the Ocean Pointe Hotel dock as soon as I take this gentleman to Fisherman's Wharf. Says it's an emergency. That okay with you folks?"

"That's okay, ain't it Tom?" she answered with a nasal twang.

"You're damn right! Yee haw! Let's get this tub moving!"

CHAPTER THIRTEEN

SEATRUCK

JAMES BAY, VICTORIA. Sarah and I had arrived at the Armstrong Robotic Machines lab in order to be apprised of the latest developments and operational procedures by one of their research scientists.

We were buzzed into reception where we introduced ourselves to the security guard at the front desk. He had a bank of monitors of state-of-the-art surveillance equipment arrayed in a semicircle in front of him. He was expecting us but demanded identification from both of us just the same. Setting his half-eaten Twinkie to one side, he wiped his fingers on his trouser leg. He lazily scanned our I.D. before sliding them and a couple visitor tags back to us on the front desk. Lifting his bulky torso out of the padded chair, he escorted us through hallways to get to the lab in the rear of the facility.

"He's at the lab bench at the back," the guard stated as he opened the last door and pointed. He turned on his heels to return to his front desk.

He had his back to us but I recognized him straight away. There was no mistaking his nest of unruly hair which gave him a distant profile of a younger Einstein albeit with funky glasses. The research scientist turned out to be my old friend. You could tell Dr. Slavik from a mile away. He was always in his trademark white lab coat. A row of finely-sharpened pencils arrayed in a plastic pen holder in his breast pocket, he would be hunched over a lab bench doodling on paper, peering, poking and muttering to himself about his latest reconfigured contraption.

If you got his attention, he would look up at you through his smeared bifocals, all the while thinking and completing calculations in his mind as he listened to you. You could usually get his attention but it wasn't always undivided.

I had first met Pietro Slavik at the Bryco Accredited Research Facility, a Bryco Federation Lab in Ottawa, some years ago. There, his nickname was Peter the Slave. And he was a slave too! He was a slave to his work. He had an all-consuming passion for invention and improving upon existing machines. There was no dividing line between his work and his hobby. They were one and the same.

As he invented and developed gizmos, some of which I would have the need to use, I became his test subject, his guinea pig, if you will, and his gizmo tester by reason of convenience - usually his, not mine. He said he had his fill of working for Bryco FedLab and had decided to live out on the coast where he felt his many and varied skills and talents would be more appreciated. Some place where his imaginative and keen analytical mind would not become jaded by the woolly nonsense of politics and the pettiness and cruelty of some egotistical managers who were well-entrenched in the habit of promoting compliant, pretty young women and eager, handsome young men based on their capacity for giving favors and generally sucking up. That refreshing place was Armstrong Robotic. Here, they called him Dr. Slavik.

"Peter!" I called out across the busy lab.

No response.

"Peter!" I called out again as we neared him. This time we saw his head rise slowly then turn in our direction. He squinted to adjust his eyesight to the distance then a hint of recognition prodded his face into a beaming smile.

"Rune! So you're the government guy they were talking about sending me to have trained on the new SeaTruck operation. What gives? I thought you were retired!"

"What can I say? I was forced into it."

"And Sarah. How have you been? I haven't seen you since you were on the training course just prior to your tour of the ridge. Things been working out okay?"

"Just fine," Sarah replied, "the dives went even better than we had hoped. Ellen taught me the detailed workings of the SeaTruck. It's a wonderful machine! We've got enough data and exciting new specimens to keep us busy for quite some time."

Peering over his shoulder, I saw a tiny contraption lying on his lab bench. "What are you working on now? Looks like some kind of bug."

"That's right. It is a bug of sorts but it's supposed to be a fly actually. A bug that is a fly," he chuckled as he picked up the small object for us to have a better look. "You've always wished that you could have been a fly on the wall at times."

"I sure have!" I agreed.

"Well, here's your chance. Take a look at it under the magnifying glass. It can fly. It can walk. It can even be made to talk if you wanted it to!" Peter picked up a thick magnifying glass and putting it up to his eye, held the electronic bug up in front of it. He examined the bug in his hand, his peering eye now huge as seen from the opposite side of the round magnifying glass. "Here, you have a look," he said as he handed the bug and the magnifying glass to me. I held it in my fingers and peered through the magnifying glass, enlarging the bug tenfold. It changed from a fat fly to an awesome feat of miniature robotic engineering.

"See the eye? Video! See the other eye? Night vision! Check the head out. Fuzzy logic! The body? GPS navigation and power! The wings? Propulsion! Legs? Robotic manipulators! Feet? Sticky suction samplers!"

"Take a look at this, Sarah," I said as I handed her the magnifying glass and the robotic bug.

"Can you show us how it works?" asked Sarah after she finished examining it.

"Sure! But the bug still has some bugs in it, so to speak. You'll have to be patient as not all the parts are fully functional yet. Some still have to be designed and others reconfigured."

Peter set the bug on the bench and went over to some electronic controls and monitors. "I'm going to program it for a short flight with a specific destination. See that thermostat on the wall over there? That's the target." He punched some buttons on a keyboard then sat back and said "Okay, watch!"

Nothing happened for a few seconds then the fly slowly rose, a small buzz emanating from its vibrating wings. It hovered for a second then flew erratically toward the thermostat, landing squarely upon the face of it.

"Why does it fly in such a pattern?" I asked.

"It can fly in a straight line but it is more natural if it flies like a house fly does. Its fuzzy logic provides an erratic but mean path until its landing is imminent."

"That's amazing!" Sarah said.

"Incredible!" I added. "But can it read a newspaper?"

"Better than that!" Peter said with a beaming smile. "Keep an eye on the monitor as well." He tapped in a few more keystrokes then sat back. The fly took off again moving erratically to the far side of the bench where a manual lay open. The bug hovered over the open page which could be seen quite clearly enough to be easily read on the monitor.

"What if I want to see what's on the next page though?"

"Okay, I'll just activate its program for doing that." The bug immediately grasped the edge of the manual's page with its manipulator leg and flew it open. It landed on the open page so as to use its light weight to keep the page open so it could show on the monitor and be read.

"This is amazing, simply amazing!" gushed Sarah as she shot me a loving glance.

"Let's have fun with it now," Peter said. He punched in some co-ordinates into his computer keyboard, thought a moment, then typed some more, all the while smiling at his thoughts.

The bug flew off the bench, across the lab then ducked under the closed door. From that point on we followed its course on the monitor. The bug flew at treetop level over a forest of twisted green carpet yarn then ascended to near the cratered ceiling tile as it made its way down a long hallway. It turned a corner down another hallway then dropped down and flew at breakneck speed back over the carpet yarn forest, under a second closed door, emerging on the other side. We could hear music from a radio and plainly see a towering security guard with his feet propped up on the rounded front desk which was lined with banks of small surveillance monitors. The bug steadily rose in looping spirals until it was above the guard. He was reading the Monday Times-Colonist newspaper; his coffee cup was at his side.

"Okay, Mr. Fly, time to do your dirty work," laughed Peter in anticipation.

The fly swooped lower and buzzed him at eye level. The guard took a lazy swat at the fly which immediately took evasive action to avoid his ham-hock hands. Once more the fly buzzed his face, causing the guard to look squarely at the video camera as he took another swipe at it. It promptly flew over to the wall behind him and landed, providing a wide-angle view of the reception area. The guard settled back down to his reading, occasionally looking up at the monitors and keeping a wary eye out for the pesky fly.

"Does it breed too?" I asked with a chuckle.

"Not yet," Peter replied with a laugh.

"Well, you'll just have to come up with a sexy companion for it."

"Rune!" Sarah chastised me while she blushed. "You've got a one-track mind sometimes!"

"I prefer to call it a focused mind in these circumstances." I chuckled again.

"Watch the monitor," Peter asked. "We'll buzz the guard's

proboscis this time." The fly took off again for a last sortie through enemy territory. The guard still was not fast enough on the draw but did manage to swat his rather long nose well after the fly had passed. The bug retraced its flight, going under the door, down the hall, down the other hall, under the second door and across the lab before coming to rest on the bench beside Peter. It was like some pet which did a trick and now wanted its reward.

"How did you get it to work like that?" I asked.

"I took the current technology of miniaturization, solar cells, microprocessors, GPS navigation, and touch sensors and melded it with the theory of chaotic systems and fuzzy logic and the principles of nervous net technology."

"Yes, but how does it work?" asked Sarah.

"So far, quite well, I think," Peter replied with a trace of a smile.

"Any problems?" I asked.

"Plenty, but the most disturbing, or exhilarating, if you will, are the result of emergent properties."

"Emergent properties?" Sarah asked Peter.

"Yes, it's where the robots exhibit an adaptive behaviour in response to their environment, something that was not programmed into them."

"Like what?" I asked.

"Well, it's something akin to having a mind of its own and progressing on to react to stimuli in a totally different way than it has been taught or programmed to do."

"Sort of like a rogue robot?" I asked.

"Exactly!" stated Peter.

"Has it been tested out in the field?" I asked.

"Not yet, although I do have a second bug that I am developing at the same time. That one is a mobile unit with all the necessary equipment - monitors, controls and such - built right into a small case with a laptop computer which is what you'd think it only was."

"Is the SeaTruck a rogue robot to?" Sarah asked.

Peter laughed. "No, it isn't. But let me know if it does something like that, will you? Speaking of which, we had better get you oriented with the SeaTruck submersible, shall we?"

He led us into an adjacent room and flicked a light switch on the wall, bathing the room with glaring floodlights. A gleaming white SeaTruck was parked in the center of the large humid room next to a sunken tank of water which was connected to a water-filled tunnel that ran underground.

"I'm impressed!" I said.

"Yes, it is rather new technology that has come along quite well indeed. We are rather pleased with its development and results."

"So it'll perform as well as it looks?" I asked.

"Yes, it will," said Peter, "There was a definite need for a robotic submersible like this. It is the pickup truck of the seas. The submersibles up to this point have been used primarily for research and as such were quite fragile and singular in their purpose. The SeaTruck is going to become the workhorse, if you will, of marine industries. This is no finicky thoroughbred! It's tough, it's versatile and it's safe! It's meant to take a beating and to bounce right back with a minimum of repair, same as a pickup truck. We will be establishing dealers worldwide. Right now there are two dealers we have established. One is here in Victoria, the other one is in Hawaii."

I wondered where Chung got his SeaTruck from, then decided to shelve that question for later. "What is the main difference between this one and all the others?" I asked.

"There are many differences but one of the main ones is that the SeaTruck can be driven under its own power into the sea, either from on shore or down a ramp from the stern of a vessel at sea. As you can see, it has six all-terrain rubber tires."

"Won't that affect the buoyancy of the sub?" I asked.

"Actually," interjected Sarah, "They can help control buoyancy in addition to the side buoyancy tubes. The neat thing is that the onboard computers can fill the tires with air or sea water, whatever is necessary for the type of environment it happens to be traveling in. Something like a buoyancy compensator vest on a scuba diver. Sorry Dr. Slavik, go ahead."

"Quite right!" Peter stated, "On land they are very necessary; at sea they can be used to travel off and onto a ramp launch or undersea on the seabed or with negative buoyancy on some sub-sea structure such as on a pipeline. They are adjustable and retractable. And there are gravity jets on the roof of the cab as well. They can be used to provide positive traction for traveling within or on a large underwater pipeline for instance."

"It even has a light bar of sorts built into it," I remarked.

"It's a light bar, a camera bar and whatever else we need to hook onto it. There are lights on the front grill as well," added Peter. "For instance there are green thallium iodide headlights to illuminate the area. They can penetrate the sub-sea inky blackness much farther than white light can. There are white incandescent lights for underwater colour photography. Movie, television, video and still cameras can be mounted and controlled from the cockpit."

"Can it adapt to carrying some of the more exotic and heavier types of cameras?" asked Sarah.

"Sure, cameras such as the 360-degree surround-screen types can be mounted on the light bar as well. Imax cameras too! Whatever is required to get the job done. Why, we have even mounted small, shock-absorbing roof wheels onto the light bar for adapting the SeaTruck to work within larger water-filled tunnels or pipelines. These top-mounted wheels stabilize the sub in fast-flowing currents and save the sub from instability and possible damage. For this type of work it can come equipped with ultrasound density readers, electromagnetic sensors and a laser measurement system as well as a vast array of cameras."

"I didn't know all that!" said Sarah.

"In addition to forward-looking sonar, It has state-of-the-art side-scanning sonar as well. There are also strobe lights and a navigation transponder, much the same as on aircraft."

"I see two seats in the cockpit," I said.

"Right. The cockpit is housed within a specially-strengthened Plexiglas acrylic pod similar in shape to that of a small helicopter. It affords maximum protection with maximum viewing capacity. There is a frame and a structural housing which is required for the various operations of the sub. There is seating for a pilot, a copilot, and there are dual controls. Outside in the rear deck of the SeaTruck are two jump-seats for divers wearing self-contained deep-dive suits."

"Why would you need to have that?" I asked.

"Well, sometimes the job, whatever it might be, requires human manipulation, control, and evaluation that can't be done by machines alone. It takes the place of an airlock submersible or of winching the divers down from a ship that hovers on the surface using dynamic thrusters to keep its position. Ships in these circumstances are very vulnerable to weather and sea conditions. It also makes the use of a ship redundant when the work is relatively close in to shore. The SeaTruck can just do a shore entry with the divers sitting in the open back. When they get out and down to the work-site the divers get off, do their jobs, and get back on. If there is more work farther on, say like on a pipeline or a cable for instance, they'll get back on and be transported to that site for more work to be done there. This is especially suitable for use with the deep-dive Hardsuits, although with current technology, the depth capacity of the SeaTruck far exceeds that of the Hardsuit."

"I get it!" I exclaimed. "Sort of like a farmer or a rancher using a pickup truck to make the rounds of his perimeter fences with hired hands, tools, and fencing materials in the back of the truck to make the necessary repairs as they go along inspecting the fences."

"Exactly!" said Peter. "Why, they can even conduct harvesting operations just like on a farm too! We are also working on a new model that has an optional airlock system where the divers' rear deck will be enclosed much like a canopy on a pickup truck does. This will allow even more capacity for divers to work deeper and longer."

"And it has an unlimited array of snap-on manipulator arms as well!" interjected Sarah.

"It has the standard range of robotic arms - seven-function arms, five-function arms - and we can pretty well build anything to fill a client's requirements to accomplish any task. All they have to do is provide us with their requirements. We will write their detailed specifications, design, build and test it."

"Within acceptable limits, of course." I said.

"Of course," Peter said.

"How does it collect specimens?"

"The SeaTruck has full laser equipment including a laser micro probe mass spectrometer that heats rock samples to 6,500 degrees C to identify their elements in four minutes flat."

"Why would one of those be necessary?"

"Why, for instant analysis of seabed rock and black smoker chimney minerals."

"Oh! So something akin to a grizzled prospector and his mule using a gold pan to sample creek beds and such."

"Exactly, only a little more sophisticated to be sure."

"So this could be used to prospect for gold then."

"Sure. It could be."

"And diamonds too?" asked Sarah.

"Yes, the SeaTruck's laser micro probe mass spectrometer could be used for diamond prospecting. It could test for a sub-sea diamond field or a gold field for that matter. It also has a tube suction sampler, filter collectors, water samplers, temperature probe, hot-magma sample probe, bore hole drill, rock drill, and an onboard chemical analyzer. It has a vacuum-assisted scoop in its grill which feeds the specimens or mined objects from the manipulator arms gently along an interior chute to where they are collected and held in a mesh container in the bed of the SeaTruck."

"Much like a goody bag that scuba divers use to collect things in," I said.

"Exactly," Peter replied. "Of course, the remote divers can also add whatever they like to the load on the back. The arms themselves can assist the divers with 500 kilogram lifting capability. It also has winching and towing functions of even greater capability."

"So how do the pilots fare in their cockpit? I take it that it is strictly a dry area, that there is no sub-sea transferring into or out of the cab."

"Precisely correct, although I am planning a model that will eventually incorporate those cockpit specifications into a future SeaTruck but for now we have this."

"Power and propulsion?"

"Power is by a new and still-classified type of fuel cell, with backup provided by electric silver/zinc batteries. She's guided by computer and enhanced by a precision navigation system with acoustic long baseline position tracking and acoustic net scans up to 10 kilometers that can position her to within 3.5 meters undersea or on the seabed. Propulsion is by variable-tilt, horizontal and vertical hydraulic thrusters."

"How fast will she go?"

"The SeaTruck cruises at 10 or 12 knots and goes about 20 to 24 knots flat out. Her forte is her power though, she is very powerful. The pilot can call on jet turbines for the heavy jobs that demand lots of extra muscle. She can be very precisely controlled."

"The side fins?"

"Stabilizers."

"How deep is she rated for?"

"The SeaTruck is certified for 4,000 meters, that's well over two miles deep."

I whistled in amazement. "That's deep!"

"Okay, let's get on with the hands-on training."

Peter led me over to a bank of lockers where he selected a white jumpsuit with a wire harness attached and soft boots at the ends of the legs. "Here, we've already received your measurements. These specially-made coveralls should fit you."

"Why do I need these?" I asked.

"With the SeaTruck there isn't a lot of movement for the pilots like there is in some of the larger submersibles, so reduced body heat and some interior dampness can be a concern. Likewise, poor blood circulation and muscle atrophy is also a very vital consideration."

"Is that what these wires are for?"

"Correct. The wire harness plugs into the sub's electrical system. There are tiny heating wires running throughout the jumpsuit including the boots. You can adjust your temperature much like you can a heat blanket except that there are controls to adjust the heat, or use the cooling tubes if necessary, for specific areas of your body."

"Like if I got cold feet for instance?" I joked.

"Very good, ha, ha, yes, even for cold feet."

"So how long are some of these dives?"

"Sarah, how long do you figure the average dive may last?"

"That depends on the type of work you are doing and the depth that you are working at. There are many factors. For instance, a dive like the one we tested the SeaTruck on at the Juan de Fuca Ridge took about six to eight hours. If it was an eight-hour dive, half that time - four hours - would be spent descending and ascending while the other four hours would be spent on actual work on the seabed. If you were doing work on a pipeline or some other structure that called for exterior divers, the time frame would be dictated by the job and the diver comfort level and safety concerns. Generally this type of dive would take considerably less time."

"Okay? Any more questions? No? Right! Sarah, your jumpsuit is over in an open locker back in the change room." Then turning to me Peter said, "She's going to show you the ropes. She has already had courses and as she mentioned, they have tested a SeaTruck out on the ridge during their last expedition. She is fully qualified as a pilot and instructor on this sub."

"So she has said," I commented. "Need any help with your jumpsuit?" I called after Sarah as she walked to the change room.

"I can manage," Sarah shot back with a coy glance back at me.

"Tell me something," he whispered as Sarah rounded the corner out of sight, "do I detect something a little more than professional courtesy between the two of you?"

"Lets just say that we are very compatible and like-minded in our mutual endeavours," I replied with a straight face.

"Oh," he said, "but I thought . . . well, she is a very lovely woman . . . and . . . oh well, never mind."

"Just leave the minding up to me, Peter. What are you becoming? A matchmaker?"

"No, it's just that . . . "

"Uh, uh, uh!" I warned with a friendly smile.

I undressed to my skivvies and donned the coveralls which resembled a flight-suit. "So what are these flat bands in the fabric?" I asked.

"They have their own separate controls. Plug your harness into this electrical source and turn it on."

I plugged into the source and turned a flat dial on my sleeve. "Whoa! That feels different! What is that?"

"It's a muscle massager. It's so that you don't get muscle spasms. It also promotes blood circulation. You can turn it down low so that it will still work but you will hardly notice it."

"Not bad, but I still prefer a woman's touch!" I commented dryly.

"You would, Rune, you would. Ha, ha, ha! Here is your navigation and communication helmet. It has a pull-down, see-through visor with critical LCD navigational display. It allows you limited-range talk with your copilot, external divers or personnel on ship or shore, but keep the long distance calls to a minimum, will you? We don't have an unlimited budget on this one! Ha, ha!"

"Yeah, sure."

Sarah came around the corner looking magnificent in her white jumpsuit. Teasing, I whistled at her in appreciation of her figure in the form-fitting suit. "Are we ready?" she asked.

"I am," I chuckled.

"I'll bet you are!" she laughed.

"Well, I'm ready unless Peter has more questions for me."

"Uh, no, no, of course not!" he replied with an embarrassed stammer.

"Okay," I said, "let's do it!"

Sarah and I climbed into the SeaTruck, adjusted the comfortable form-hugging seats, hooked up to electrical, coolant and communication sources and ran through the preliminary checklist. The craft exuded both familiar and unfamiliar smells of newness.

"Okay, first thing you've got to remember until you get certified. I'm the pilot and that makes me the boss!"

"Yes, sir! Uh, yes, ma'am! You da man! Uh, da boss!" I kidded.

"I'm beginning to like this instructing even more as we go along," Sarah said with a grin.

"Uh, huh," I dryly agreed.

"Until you get familiar with the controls, watch where you put your hands."

"Don't worry! I'm not going to put my hands where they don't belong!"

"Well, unless I tell you to!" she added with a lusty laugh.

"Can he hear us in here?" I asked with feigned exasperation

"No, at the moment I think I've got the communications turned on to us only."

"I can hear you loud and clear!" Peter's electronic voice said through our headsets in our helmets.

"Oh, oh! Damn!" Sarah exclaimed.

"Women! Eh, Peter?"

"'Mutual endeavours, eh?" Peter retorted.

"What did he mean by that?" she asked.

"Oh, nothing," I replied with a slight grin.

"All set?" Sarah asked.

I nodded and said, "All set."

"Okay, here we go!" Sarah worked the controls as a faint electric hum emanated from the body of the SeaTruck which eased forward ever so gently under Sarah's light touch. She ran the sub down a ramp into the large tank of seawater where we ran through a pre dive checklist and a series of tests in the relatively shallow pool. We flicked an array of exterior lights on, checking them in turn.

These completed, she eased us into a channel of seawater, the bottom of which dropped off to allow us to enter the fully-submerged tunnel. This led us a short distance toward a sub-sea entrance to Victoria's outer harbour. Littleneck clams lined the walls of the tunnel, pebble-skinned starfish groped undersea rocks with a slow motion, while a dull red rock crab went skittering out of our path. We descended along the sloping muck of the harbour entrance, navigating around rock outcrops and thickets of marine plants which leaned over with the tide, then swayed in our slipstream as we rocketed past. Visibility was limited at this point due to the turbulence of the tidal water as it flowed into the harbour through the narrow channel. The water cleared as we made our way over to the vicinity of the breakwater. Sarah put the sub through its underwater paces then handed the dual-controlled SeaTruck over to me.

"Yahoo!" I called out as I tested the capability of the craft. "It feels like I'm riding a spirited horse. Or maybe it's like a good ol' pickup truck back on the farm."

I came to the end of the breakwater where we saw two flashers attached to hooked herring bait on fishing lines. "Want to make some salmon fisherman happy for a moment or two?" I asked with a mischievous grin.

"Don't you dare! Leave their lines alone or else Peter will have a fit!" Sarah cautioned.

"Peter will!" Peter said over the radio. "No stunts today, Rune, this is a training mission only!"

"And what better way to train!" I laughed. "I have to test out the manipulator arms."

Just then something flashed darkly in front of our piercing headlights then was gone. There was another flash, this time much nearer to us. It was a curious harbour seal in for a close-up look at this strange craft. Its large dark eyes were caught in the headlights much like those of a deer when caught in headlight glare on a back road. It was very friendly, coming right up to our cockpit for a peek inside. Its companion joined it for a look as well.

"We'd better not feed them or we'll have friends for life here," I cautioned.

"But they're so cute! Look at their eyes," Sarah exclaimed.

"Aren't they though?" I agreed.

"See them rubbing noses?"

"Yeah! They're really cute!"

I pulled over to the breakwater and using negative buoyancy, steered the SeaTruck along a rough path of submerged granite blocks. I momentarily flipped on the overhead gravity jets to provide more stability and traction. I could just imagine the view from the top of the breakwater as two jets of water shot out from the surface of the sea. I said to Sarah, "I was just imagining a couple senior ladies out for a nice stroll up top seeing the two spouts beside them and one exclaiming to the other 'Oh, look! Gertrude. There are two orca whales spouting right below us!'"

Giggling at the thought of this, we crossed into the middle of the channel where we detected the throbbing of powerful engines overhead going out into Juan de Fuca Strait.

"Wonder what ship that is?" asked Sarah.

"Let's see," I said as I looked at the clock, "it should be the Coho ferry making its midmorning run to Port Angeles."

" I wonder what they'll make of us if they see us on their sonar?"

"An orca whale, I suppose," I said with a laugh.

"In the outer harbour? That'll be a whale of a tale!"

"Won't it, though? But it's possible and it'll back the other ladies' story now, won't it?" I agreed with a chuckle as we banked and headed deeper, farther out to sea, to continue my training.

"As long as it isn't Chung's ship; I hope we've seen the last of him." Sarah stated as she shuddered with disgust.

"They cleared port last night right after you got back to the *Valhalla.*"

"Unless they came back in and are going out again." I wondered out loud, "Is this thing armed with torpedoes?"

CHAPTER FOURTEEN

SSEAAL

SOLAR/SEA ENERGY AQUA/AGRI LABS, KEAHOLE POINT, KONA, THE BIG ISLAND OF HAWAII. The fiery red of erupting bougainvillea flowers lined the coastal expressway, separating the stark black lava landscape from the grey ribbon of asphalt. I was passing the remnants of the long line of the oncoming morning rush-hour traffic that was going into town on the Queen Kaahumanu highway. Following a line of traffic ahead of me, I was on my way out of town to see Sarah at the SSEAAL facility.

Tuning in KBIG-FM radio, I caught the forecast. “A few showers expected over Hilo today and tomorrow. Kailua-Kona partly cloudy, chance of showers upslope this afternoon. Highs around 80. U.V. index is 6. The time now is 9:50 a.m.”

The hot sun felt good on my back as I reined in the four-wheel-drive Jeep from its inclination to charge up the road ahead. Soft breezes cleared out the cobwebs of tiredness from the traveling I had done the day before.

I had landed late yesterday afternoon at Kona International Airport after a direct flight out of Victoria International. Sarah, who had just finished work at the adjacent SSEAAL lab, had greeted me at the humid open-air airport terminal with a hug, a long wet kiss and a Plumeria lei around my neck. I thought the scented Hawaiian air was intoxicating until she wrapped her arms around me. All the romantic memories of the preceding week came flooding back to me. However, the bad memory of the dangers we endured together in Victoria still lurked in the near recesses of my mind.

Daydreaming, I recalled yesterday’s events. I had picked up the Jeep from the rental outfit at the airport. Throwing my luggage in the back, I followed Sarah in her car the seven miles into Kailua-Kona where I checked into a condo at the Big Island Inn. The blue pool, built to resemble a lagoon with a waterfall cascading out of a grotto, looked inviting. We donned swim suits for a few laps around the pool then had a cool drink at the bar while we dried off.

Afterward, it was a short walk to the shops where I picked up a nice selection of Hawaiian shirts and cotton golf shirts to go with my assorted walking shorts. Gotta look good, I thought, especially now that I have a particular reason for doing so!

Dinner that night was a romantic, candle-lit table for two on a restaurant lanai overlooking Oneo bay. Sarah looked especially native in her colourful Hawaiian-print dress. I gave her a Plumeria flower off my lei which she tucked behind her left ear. Her long dark hair flowed off her shoulders and cascaded down her back. Her misty brown eyes were set off by long eyelashes. Sarah had looked ravishing in the glow of the candle light last night.

Later, we slipped off our sandals and walked arm in arm, barefoot in the soft sand on the beach as we made our way back to my condo. The ascending moon coincided with our rising passions as we desperately sought to reaffirm our love for each other in the subdued lighting of the condo. I went to Sarah. Her flowing dress dropped in soft folds at her feet as her silken body touched mine. The scented evening air wafted in through the open lanai doorway enveloping us as one. The cadence of the waves crashing on the beach below us slowly set our aroused bodies' rhythm to that of the waves of flowing emotion.

The blaring blast of an oncoming truck's air horn jarred me out of my erotic daydreaming. A new pickup truck with a chrome roll bar had attempted to pull out into the oncoming lane to pass and was now beside me. I had quickly glanced over to notice the black truck with what looked like a globe company logo on the door. It tried to force me over. I had nowhere to go as the rough lava was right near the edge of my lane. He was forced back in behind me by the onrushing rig. I peered up at my rear-view mirror to see an angry-looking man in attitude sunglasses mouthing words of filth at both the passing driver and me. The sullen driver tailgated me, weaving over the double solid yellow centerline looking for an opportunity to take another chance at what I thought to be a foolish and persistent game of Russian roulette. Seeing none and venting his rage, he closed the gap between us and bounced his reinforced cattle-guard bumper off mine. I wondered what brought this road rage on. Having done nothing to provoke this guy, I thought, so why come after me? I had nowhere to go - there was a long line of cars ahead of me, sharp rocks of a‘a lava on my right.

Another bump.

He was grinning like an idiot who had just found a new sport. I was having none of this. I waited for the third bump, got it, and slammed my brakes on hard, forcing his pickup hard against my Jeep's rear bumper and slowly drove off to the right side, bringing his pickup along too. At the last second, I rapidly swerved and accelerated back, leaving him to bounce along running over sharp lava, instantly blowing his right front tire. I continued while checking out the jerk in the rear-view mirror who by now, had jumped out of his truck back there and proceeded to shake his fist at me.

"Idiot!" I yelled futilely out to the rushing wind for he was far behind me now and wouldn't get the full benefit of my word.

What the heck was all that about, I wondered? And was that a truck belonging to Global Sea Marine? The logo looked about right.

The wide-eyed driver following behind us finally had the presence of mind to flash me a big grin and the universal okay sign. I waved back at him.

I continued for a few more miles, enjoying the sweeping vistas, with lava fields all around, culminating at the peak of Mount Hualalai at my right and the Pacific Ocean a mile on my left. I spotted the highway sign for SSEAAL and turned seaward.

There was an embossed-letter wooden sign set in a lava rock wall on the right. The peeling shellac finish showed the ravages of tropical sunlight and time. But there it was, the name Solar/Sea Energy Aquaculture/Agriculture Laboratory. Underneath this was SSEAAL, Kona, Hawaii. A forlorn, boarded-up security shack gave me a sense of uneasiness. I also wondered at the reason for the decrepit condition of the sign.

A straight, barren road ran for a mile before it turned to the right in the distance near the seashore. I thought that this couldn't be the place where Sarah worked. This looked abandoned, although I did see some clusters of low buildings off in the distance. I decided to drive along the road anyway. It ran through a jumbled lava field that supported tufts of silky pili grass and little else.

Wawaloli beach park was at the end of the road. I made a right turn, noting that the sign said that it was run by the SSEAAL research facility. A footnote warned against kite-flying as low flying aircraft flew directly overhead.

Paralleling the beach, I drove on, noticing clusters of nondescript business compounds on both sides of the road. Huge shade-cloth-covered plots of land. Cars, trucks and buses were parked in company parking lots nearest the road; the various operations' buildings and structures were behind that. Industrial tanks, both open and closed, were set here and there. Vast ponds with rubber liners sat behind security fences that contained strands of barbed wire running along their tops. Oversized Quonset huts sat shoulder to shoulder. Oval raceway tanks with green water were kept flowing and circulating by horizontal rotary paddles. Here, there was evidence of busy operations which refuted the state of the sign's disrepair and the boarded-over security shack out by the highway. After another mile or so, I came to a fenced compound and drove in through its open gate. I stopped just inside where there was a lone security guard sitting in an air-conditioned booth.

"And what is the nature of your business here, sir?" he asked politely.

"I'm here to see Dr. Sarah Leikaina. She's expecting me," I said.

"And your name, sir?"

"Erikson, Rune Erikson," I stated.

"Yes, here we are . . . Erikson, Rune . . . Okay, just pull up on the right into visitors' parking and go on into the main building where reception will direct you to her."

"Thank you," I replied as I started forward. A darting golf cart with two workmen in it overtook me, passing on my left as I rubbernecked my way along. Clusters of one and two-story buildings and structures were set under soaring coconut palms and the stouter royal palm trees which did little to provide much shade from the hot morning sun. Spotting the sign that said "visitors parking", I pulled into a parking stall in front of the two-story administration building.

I walked into the reception area where there was a decided chill in the air. There was a sign on the wall directing visitors, deliveries and seawater pickups. Should I just say that I am here to pick some seawater up and see what happens? I wondered what that was all about. Photos and diagrams of the pipeline construction and the complex lined the walls as I went to the rear where a lone receptionist sat, dwarfed by the high reception counter in front of her. She looked up with a cheerful smile and asked if she could help me.

"Yes," I replied, "My name is Erikson, Rune Erikson. I'm here to see Dr. Sarah Leikaina."

"Just a moment. I'll phone her and let her know you're here." There was a lull while she dialed. "There's a guy here to see you." Then in a whisper she said, "He's a real hunk!" She listened and said, "Oh, okay." Turning back to me she smiled and said, "She'll be here in a minute. Would you like to have a seat?"

"No, thank you, but you could tell me why it's so chilly in here," I asked as goose bumps rose on my bare forearms.

The receptionist laughed, "That's why I wear a sweater in here. All the buildings in the compound here are naturally air-conditioned with chilled water from the deep, from just offshore."

"Ah, makes sense now."

"Yes, sometimes we have to keep the front doors open so as to warm up a little bit. In Hawaii? Can you imagine?"

Laughing, I said, "That's like bringing coal to Newcastle!"

"Pardon me?" she asked with a smile.

"Coals . . . to Newcastle." Her questioning face said that this one flew right over her head. "Uh, never mind."

I scanned the frames on the walls again. Radio station licence, another one, most informative display award, certificate of appreciation, another one.

"Rune! You found your way here," Sarah said as she entered the reception area from a hallway that ran off to the left. "Come with me. I'll show you around and introduce you to some of the other staff. You've already met Anne, our receptionist. Thanks Anne, I'll be busy for the next while, could you please hold all my calls till later? Thanks."

I followed Sarah down the hall to her office. We walked in, she closed the door behind her then wrapped her arms around me. We kissed long and hard. I felt my temperature rising quickly. "That makes up for the chilly reception I got back there!" I said with a mischievous twinkle in my eye.

Alarmed, Sarah said, "What do you mean? You mean Anne?"

"No, silly, just that it was chilly in the reception area when I walked in due to the air-conditioning," I said with a laugh.

Relieved, Anne said, "Oh, that! Yes, it can be quite chilly in here, especially earlier in the day. I couldn't think that Anne would be anything other than very pleasant. Did she tell you the buildings are cooled by chilled water brought up from the deep - from 2,000 feet down where the water is only 6 degrees C, that's only 6 degrees above freezing!"

"Sort of. It's that cold just that far down?"

"It doesn't take much depth to go from the 80-degree F range, which is about 27 degrees C, on the surface down to almost freezing. That's what makes this whole operation viable. You need a difference of 20 degrees C at least." We could hear wooden-clogged footsteps clack down the tiled hallway then stop at Sarah's office door. A light rap on the door caused us to quickly resume our professional appearance and disengage ourselves from each other with a slight look of guilt on our faces.

"Yes? Come in," Sarah said rather too quickly.

The door opened and Anne stuck her head in. She glanced at us and seeing our slight discomfort, blurted out, "I forgot to give you these messages that came in earlier. Oh, and Dr. Kerrigan can see you in a minute or so. He's just wrapping up a meeting with the controller."

"Thanks again Anne, we were just getting ready to go see him," Sarah needlessly explained.

I self-consciously rubbed at the lipstick on my lips. Anne shot a smile at us and closed the door again.

"I feel like a schoolgirl again! Imagine!" Sarah admitted with a blush and a smile.

"And I feel like a schoolboy who just got caught sneaking a kiss!" I admitted as we looked at each other and laughed.

I followed Sarah down a hallway. Snatches of conversation could be heard as we passed by the various offices. ". . . funds for start-up. I take it there is no objection how we do this." The next office was " . . . supply of water. Ask Ray how often . . . " then as we neared the corner office " . . . unless we can manage it, then forget about it. So you're following up on . . . that's right, let's see what we got. What are we doing on our cost-structure and cost-sharing?. . . Fine, Bye."

Sarah knocked at the open door and received a "come on in." We entered a rather austere office in this rather utilitarian building to find the SSEAAL director - it said so on his door - sitting on the corner of his scarred 1980's vintage, grey steel desk. Sarah closed the door behind us. The director stood up and greeted me. "Hi, Stuart Kerrigan, pleased to make your acquaintance," he said as he pumped my hand with a firm shake. "You can call me Stu."

"Rune, Rune Erikson," I said. "Nice to meet you." I glanced down at his desk again and was startled to note that he had a cigar humidor sitting off to one side. It had wood marquetry and a solid-gold global emblem - the same type of humidor as Dr. Wampole had in his office at ORCA.

Stu caught note of my glance and said, "Cigars. You smoke cigars?"

"Not often," I replied.

"Nor I. I just keep them for people who do. I'll have an occasional one. Got 'em as a gift from one of our contractors. I'm supposed to keep them cool and around here that's not a problem. Your Harry is quite a cigar aficionado if I can recall. Turned the air blue in his hotel room with cigar smoke. The maids had a hell of a time with the foul air after he'd been in there awhile.

"Speaking of the devil, Sarah tells me that old Harry still appears to be in fine form. Haven't seen him since the summer at that conference in North Carolina. Talked to him on the phone the other night though. Quite the old boy!"

"That he is!"

"Don't mind the lack of esthetics here at SSEAAL. We Yanks tend to put all of our money into the product which doesn't leave a whole lot for the architecture and design of our facilities."

"Not at all. We Canucks sometimes tend to put too much money into architecture and the interior design of our buildings at the expense of the product."

"But you sure got yourself some nice buildings up there, country's really pretty too! Why, I don't think you'll find a nicer piece of real estate than the ORCA site."

"Glad you liked it, but I don't really work there. I'm just on a contract of sorts for the time being. I was Shanghaied!"

"So I've heard! I took a call from the President after this happened. You come highly recommended! He explained to me the need for an absolute low-key operation. The President doesn't want to start a panic here. Until we know what we're dealing with, we have to downplay the seriousness of it all. You're a natural to deal with this as the evaluation of the SeaTruck will make a good cover, hopefully better than if we had one of our guys in on this. It's good to have you on board. I've heard a lot about you from Harry and Sarah's been filling me in as well. We got a real conundrum going on over here. To be up front with you, we don't have a damn idea what really went on. Oh, we know there was an explosion of sorts and seismic activity but taken together, it just doesn't add up. It's peculiar as hell, real peculiar! In all my years in this business, I've never seen anything quite like this one, that's for sure!"

"So I hear!"

"It happened just out there," he said as he turned and stabbed his finger at the sea beyond the window, "half a mile away. Too bad I wasn't here at the time. Just the security guy was here. Sent him rolling ass over teakettle off his golf cart and into the stairs beside the energy conversion tower. He's okay now, though. Got some of the businesses here too. Sloshed tanks, some product was lost, some product escaped temporarily but overall nothing that we couldn't fix. No loss of life here, that's the important thing."

"That's good!"

"There were some kids surfing down the beach a ways. They got banged up pretty good. The mother of one of them too."

"How are they now?" I asked.

"One kid's still in hospital, the other two were released," Stu replied.

"Anything else out in the water?"

"A dive boat was at what we think was ground zero. There was loss of life there but a couple divers survived. We're still waiting for the final autopsy reports from that incident. Amazingly, the boat was practically unscathed."

"I saw how the airport got hit. It was on TV."

"Yes, the airport got hit too but no loss of life there. One air traveler with a heart attack but through the quick thinking of the pilot, she survived by getting timely treatment at the hospital when he was able to set the plane down on the old airport runway. It was really fortunate. Could've been a disaster, though it cracked up the front wheel of another aircraft during landing. Some injuries from the evacuation onto the lava beds. Lots of fishes and marine mammals floated belly-up onto the beaches."

"I had heard that!"

"Yes, we took some water samples but they are still being analyzed. It happened on a Friday, late afternoon, so not a lot of people were around and available that we could scramble to do immediate tests. By the time we did get out there to sample the air and the water, pretty much everything was dispersed by the wind and the currents."

Sarah said, "It doesn't help much either that the vog is spewing out from the Kilauea rift zone and drifting this way. That pretty much contaminates any air samples."

"I noticed that as I flew in yesterday. I could see a layer of brown air swirling around Mount Hualalai from the direction of Mauna Loa," I said. "Funny thing though, I thought I could see some smoke coming from higher up on the slope of Mount Hualalai. Maybe it was just some ground fog."

"You saw right," Sarah said, "there has been some steam venting for a few years from some fissures on the slope above here. It hasn't been enough to get too worried about though."

"I thought I saw some steam!" I replied.

"Yes, unfortunately, the conditions are not conducive to clean air right now," she added.

"Anyway, as I understand it," Stu said, "we're here to give you and Sarah all the assistance that you may need to accomplish our joint task. We'll continue to do our testing as is expected of us and let you both know the results as soon as they are in. Anything we can do to help out, just ask me. Our facilities are at your disposal.

"In the meantime, I understand that, officially, you two will be conducting an extensive evaluation of the new SeaTruck submersible. Let me tell you right now that we had the use of one occasionally - it belongs to one of our marine contractors - and from all the reports and from what we've seen, it's a magnificent machine. I don't think you'll be disappointed in that regard. We've even got one on order.

"One thing though! There have been a few construction accidents out there, it's a dangerous environment when things go wrong, and we don't want to add to them. Our safety record has been excellent but some of the outside work contractors' safety records have become blotted. There were a few industrial accidents including a few deaths - some suspicious circumstances and so on. Frankly, it put quite a damper on things at the time. So be careful out there.

"Anyway, let's give you an overview of our operations, then we'll show you around the facility."

"Yes," I said, "I'm curious about the operation here. It looks intriguing."

"First of all," Stu said, "What we are doing here at SSEAAL is to tap into our natural resources. We use chilled seawater from the deep, warm seawater from the surface and an abundance of solar light to cope with somewhat high humidity and low rainfall. We develop an alternate energy source to provide electricity, low cost air-conditioning, potable water and through the use of chilled water, provide our associate aqua-culture and agriculture businesses with the ability to produce cold water marine life and grow temperate-climate vegetables and other produce.

"We also do research on thermal vents. That's Sarah's department.

"We've got almost a thousand acres of land here to be developed for commercial users of our resources. We also do pure research and research to assist tenant businesses. And we encourage on-site education. We have one of our associated businesses which provides high-school students with a program that allows full credits for full-time work and study on-site. Mentors help the students with their projects. All of the work and the projects completed at the complex are done in an environmentally and culturally-sensitive manner. Let's have a quick tour of the site. Oh, grab a cigar for later, will you?"

Curious as to the brand, I took Stu up on his offer. I flipped the unlocked lid up to reveal a full box of Cohiba Esplendidos. "Cohibas. They're supposed to be an excellent brand of cigar, especially being as they are Cuban," I commented to see what reaction, if any, I would get from him.

Stu coughed and sputtered out, "Cuban? Cuban? Let me see that!" He picked one up, rolled it around in his fingers as he read the cigar band. "God damn it to hell! I had no idea! Is this somebody's idea of a joke? I could get in serious trouble with U. S. Customs on this one. Doesn't that Chung know about the embargo? Imagine, smuggled cigars sitting right in the Director's office! And Cuban at that! Anne!" he barked out as he went for the door.

Sarah and I exchanged searching glances at the mention of Chung's name.

We followed the fuming director down the hallway to Anne at reception. She took the full brunt of his ire with a smile as if she was used to his occasional outbursts. Then it was left down another hallway which ran past a small office strewn with blueprints. We went through a doorway into a combination warehouse and shop. "This is Rudy, the shop foreman. If you need anything fixed, Rudy's your man." Stu said after he pulled Rudy aside and asked him to give us his complete cooperation with the SeaTruck project.

I grasped the rough hand of the shop foreman who said, "Anything

I can't make hasn't been thought of yet. Anything I can't fix hasn't been made yet."

"I'll keep that in mind," I said with a smile at this boastful man, then got to thinking that it probably was no boast - he was probably right!

Stuart said, "We don't have a big crew, a couple dozen is all, and that includes the office staff. We contract a lot of the work to outside contractors; keeps our costs accurate. It's not any better or cheaper but some of the things we do are a one-shot deal, so we can't afford to be buying all that equipment for just one project. C'mon, let's have a look at the pipeline and the pumping station."

We walked out of the shop, got in a couple of golf carts and followed the SSEAAL director as he sped off toward the sea. We pulled up beside him at the security fence which was topped with strands of barbed wire. He unlocked a gate and led us through. Low scrub bushes grew here and there amongst the putty-coloured sand and jumble of black lava. A red beacon sat atop a whitewashed pillar on the point which jutted into the sea. Rows of black pipelines rose from the deep and climbed ashore like sea snakes only to slide back under loose fill and reemerge farther inland.

"What you see here," said Stu, "is a trio of 40-inch black polyethylene pipes which bring up 6 degree C chilled water from the deep - from 600 meters or 2,000 feet down. This chilled water has very low concentrations of organic matter."

"How is that?"

"The seawater from that depth is below the photic zone and the mixing layer. Therefore, it is very pure. Due to a lack of sunlight at that depth there are fewer living organisms which results in for all intents and purposes pathogen-free seawater," Stu said.

"Photic zone?" I asked.

"The depth to where sunlight can penetrate."

"Ah!" I acknowledged. "And pathogen?"

"Any disease-producing bacterium or microorganisms."

"Ah, yes. Those deadly little buggers!"

"But chilled seawater from the deep has higher levels of inorganic nitrates, phosphates and silicates compared to the relatively nutrient-deficient surface water."

"Is that good?"

"Yes, these nutrients are necessary to grow algae."

"Oh. How far out does the pipeline go?" I asked.

"Roughly a little over a mile or a little over 1.5 kilometers," Sarah responded.

"So it goes out and down at an angle following the underwater slope."

"That's right. You could walk down it with the right diving gear or follow it down with the SeaTruck," Sarah added.

"What holds the pipes in place?"

"The pipes go through rings on cables anchored to the bottom and supported by buoys above," she said.

"And that holds the pipelines in place?"

"That's right," answered Stu, "and those three smaller white pipelines over there are surface warm-water intake pipes."

"And they are needed for?"

"The warm water is used to blend with the chilled water when a specific temperature of seawater is needed for a particular operation whether it is for air-conditioning or for some production function. We also require it for the production of electricity."

"Really?"

"Yes, we'll go and see that operation in a minute."

"And those pipes over there?" I asked.

"They carry the discharged water back to the sea."

"What is your biggest cost here then?"

"Well, the water or source of energy is free. So is the sunlight. Probably the biggest cost is the cost to pump the seawater up and pump the cooled discharge down somewhat to its ambient level. And if we generate electricity from the operation, our power costs are quite low."

We retraced our path, following the route that the intake pipes took to the center of the complex. We stopped at an ungainly-looking three-story industrial tower that sat across the road from the shop.

"Here is where we generate electricity from the sea," Stu said.

"How does it work?" I asked.

"It works on the principle that, in a vacuum, water turns to steam at lower temperatures," explained Sarah.

"Right," said Stu, "and here is where the warm seawater enters the vacuum chamber and is turned to steam. Steam turns the turbine to generate electricity."

"How much electricity does it generate?"

"It generates 210 kw gross, 50 to 100 kw net. Cold water enters here, goes into the center of the chamber, condensing the steam into potable water. The desalinated water is pumped out, ready for drinking or for irrigation purposes. And Bob's your uncle!"

"This is ingenious!" I said.

"Think of this whole operation as a life-support system. A life-support system that can be used around the world at this latitude where you also have these conditions - a relatively steep shelf drop-off which accesses deep chilled seawater, high solar insolation which insures warm surface seawater, low precipitation and high humidity.

"Think of all the countries that could use this technology to better the lives of their citizens! The Pacific islands, pieces of Asia, parts of Australia, some coastline of India, sections of South America, stretches of Central America, bits of the Caribbean, portions of Mexico! This energy plant can provide electricity and fresh water. Where the shelf drops off more gradually, this unit could be built on a moveable barge and set farther offshore with cables running the electricity in to land and pipelines or tankers bringing the desalinated potable water to where it's needed.

"Think of what this operation can do for the comfort, indeed, the very survival of the people! It can cool their buildings at one-tenth the normal cost. It could open up new varieties of cold water aqua-culture production never before possible in the tropics! Oysters, abalone, lobsters, salmon, shrimp, flounder, not to mention edible sea vegetables and spirulina microalgae."

We walked over to tanks of various marine life. I stuck my fingers into their water testing the coolness. It was ice-cold. Blue lobsters skittered on the bottoms of the tanks. Fish swam in others. Each tank's temperature was regulated according to its inhabitants requirements by mixing chilled seawater with just the right amount of warm seawater to produce the desired result.

"How does this work?" I asked.

"Very well," Stu said, "in some species of marine life, we now have the ability to manipulate the seasons and adjust their growth and reproductive cycles. It allows them to achieve more rapid and faster growth including enhanced production of eggs outside of their normal cycles."

"But how would the production of algae be improved?" I asked.

"Seawater from the deep has a higher nutrient level which produces more rapid growth and higher protein content in micro algae and macro algae."

"Amazing! I said. But what about agriculture?"

"Look at these strawberries!" Stu exclaimed as he walked over to another area. I reached down to a leafy row of plants in a raised bed, plucked a bright red strawberry off a vine and rinsed it. I popped it into my mouth, tasting the large sweet berry. Red juice dribbled down my chin. Wiping my chin with my fingers, I then rinsed them with a fresh-water hose.

"They're really sweet!" I commented.

"Yes, aren't they?" said Sarah. "They're grown in sunny, ideal conditions in very nutrient-rich soil which produces a high sugar content."

I moved the leaves aside in the bed to reveal a black vinyl hose running on top of the soil. I dug my fingers into the black loam. It felt cool and damp.

"The chilled seawater is run through these pipes. The salt water never touches anything, it only chills the soil to the ideal temperature for the type of plant or vegetable we grow. In turn the coolness of the black pipe causes moisture from the air to condense on the outside of the pipe and trickle into the soil, thus irrigating it," Sarah said.

"Ingenious!" I commented.

Stu said, "Yes, in essence it provides a continuous drip irrigation. Market gardens normally associated with cooler climates can now produce more than six dozen, that's dozen, varieties of vegetables and plants in the hot tropics. Isn't that something?"

I had to agree that this was a remarkable operation with potentially astounding benefits to a large cross-section of people, especially those in the poorer regions. "But you have to get all this full-scale and into production."

"We already have full-scale production going on all around us. There are associate tenants producing spirulina, baby clams, giant clams, blue lobster, and mushrooms to just name a few. The pearl industry starts their spat here. Flounder is grown here too! Sea urchins!"

"Amazing!"

"Yet, what you see here is only the tip of the iceberg. The best is yet to come."

We got back in our carts and left the compound to tour a few of the associate tenants' facilities, which were all grouped in one section of SSEAAL property. To protect their unique technology and valuable commodities, most resorted to high security to protect their investments. Tours by appointment only, high barbed wire security fences, electronic surveillance, and operation alarm systems were the norm. Wary glances were thrown our way by busy workers as we walked the sites. I could tell that uppermost in their minds was the question "Who is this guy?" as they already knew Stu and Sarah. When the few bold enough to inquire as to my purpose were told that I was a technical evaluator working on the new SeaTruck, my appearance may have belied my stated profession to some. I supposed that the old battle scars that were here and there on me suggested otherwise.

"I would like to see what lies beyond the SSEAAL compound on the other side. Can we do that?" I asked.

"You mean along the shore?" Stu asked.

"Sure," said Sarah.

"Of course," Stu answered, "but perhaps Sarah can take you. I have a rather pressing matter to take care of at the moment."

"It'll be my pleasure," she said with a smile.

"That'll be fine," I agreed.

Sarah and I turned the golf cart to the left off the paved road, onto a path beaten through the scrub vegetation, sand and the lava beds. We followed the tracks over the pipelines, around the point, roughly following the outside perimeter of the SSEAAL security fencing.

Here, by law, there was public beach access. There were only a few fishermen and picnickers. A lone white van sat backed up to the rough black lava beach, its side doors open, its stereo booming but subdued by the noise from the tumultuous surf. On my right was an industrial bone-yard of rusting equipment and parts. I'm sometimes curious as to what people have in their back yards and public corporations' facilities intrigue me no less. Squat sheds stored yet more odds and ends, these not in as rusty a condition as the exposed ones. We passed the end of the fenced compound. I looked to my right into the distance. Tenants' facilities were in evidence by more fenced compounds which contained squat buildings, tanks and lined pits. There was one large warehouse which sat on SSEAAL property but which had its main access off the Queen Kaahumanu highway.

"What is produced at that building, the one sitting by itself way out near the highway?"

"That's the marine contractor's warehouse, Island Pipeline, I think is what they're called. Nothing is produced there. It's just a storage facility for their equipment and stock."

"What do they store there?"

"I've never actually been inside their facility. Come to think of it, I don't know anyone who has been in there. I guess that is where they keep their submersibles like the SeaTruck and their diving gear and things like lengths of pipe and fittings and pumps and valves."

"They have a SeaTruck there?"

"Yes, they have one. They used it to work on the latest pipeline that they had laid for us."

"Why are they situated way out there? You'd think they would want to be right on the shore. There is no direct road to here."

"I suppose so. I never thought much about it. From what I can recall at the time, they insisted on that site. It might have had something to do with better access to the highway and the airport. Because the shoreline sites are at a premium, the director readily agreed to have them lease that area. Come to think of it, they were insistent on not just the highway site but a particular spot along the highway. Strange really, now that I think about it."

"What other kind of work do they do?"

"Anything to do with marine pipeline. They contract work from us and from anyone else who needs their services. They are part of a much larger company who are supposed to be quite big really."

The hazy flanks of Mount Hualalai rose on high but its volcanic peak had a thin blanket of cloud covering it. I wondered, was some of it volcanic vent fumes? The low airport buildings sat a short distance away as well, perhaps a half mile or so. Planes thundered in takeoff; others softly glided in with more tourists. Tourists come, tourists go. It was a never-ending treadmill for the airport staff.

We came to the end of the trail. On the right was a depression in the lava which was fenced-off. "What is that?" I asked Sarah.

"A lava cave," she answered.

"But it looks like just a rough hole in the lava bed."

"The whole area is dotted with holes which lead to lava tubes and caverns, from here right up the slope of the mountain."

"What are lava tubes?"

"They are left over from old lava flows. The dark lava that you see here last flowed about 200 years ago. The reddish lava flowed thousands of years ago."

"Why the difference in colour between the newer and the older lava flows?"

"The iron in the lava has oxidized over thousands of years, turning it red. This black lava, in time, will turn red too."

"And the lava tubes?"

"The lava tubes are in both the newer and the older flows."

"How are they made?"

"They are made when molten lava flows as a surface stream down the slope of the mountain. The top of the lava flow is cooled by the relatively cooler air. The molten lava solidifies on the top as a crust, leaving the stream insulated, hot and still flowing underneath it."

"Sort of like an underground river?"

"Right, except that instead of water, it is molten rock."

"So how does the tube form? Wouldn't the stream harden at some point?"

"It can, but quite often the molten lava keeps flowing down the slope even though there is no more lava to replace it. Therefore, once the flow is finished, an empty tube or tunnel is left behind. They can run for miles and can be quite large. Some are more than 40 or 50 feet in diameter and they can even widen out into large building-sized caverns."

"How are the caverns formed?"

"Probably when lava runs through an existing lava valley of sorts, filling with molten lava then having the top layer solidify while the rest of it keeps running and melting through whatever old lava blocked it temporarily. That whole mass has to stay molten then run through leaving a void - the cavern. Sometimes they will also branch out into other tunnels or tubes. Gravity dictates that lava tubes run downhill toward the sea."

"Do they end up being open tubes right to the sea?"

"They could be. A lot of them would be plugged right where the tube meets the sea or farther up-slope but a number of them could be open underwater. Others can also have openings like the one you see here."

"Where there was an incomplete crust formed."

"That's right or where the crust has fallen through."

"And the fencing is to stop someone from falling down the opening?"

"Right. Or from driving into it. That's happened before. This is a picnic area," she explained.

On our left was a white sign with red lettering. It said "KAPU! NO ENTRY!" It was posted just outside a sandy area along the shoreline which hosted a grove of coconut palms. The area was surrounded by a low lava-rock wall. Inside this area were some larger smooth lava rocks set upright and an assortment of smaller rocks laid out in various formations.

"What is this?" I asked.

"It's a heiau," Sarah said.

"What's a heiau?" I asked, curious, and not being able to recall what they actually are.

"A heiau is a temple where the ancient Hawaiians, my ancestors, worshiped their gods," Sarah replied.

"Do Hawaiians still use them as temples?"

"Yes. There are many heiaus, usually built on points of land that jut out into the sea. They are still very sacred sites."

"Is that why there is a rock wall around the site?"

"Yes. The heiaus were of various sizes and could be anywhere up to five acres in size and enclosed with walls that could be ten feet thick and as high as twenty feet. The walls usually tapered narrower as they rose and were constructed of tightly-fitted lava rock and were topped off with smoother slabs of lava or sometimes with coral."

"What did they have inside this compound?"

"There was a stone or wooden temple which was used for sacrifices. Those sacrificed were sometimes buried here to appease the gods. If I recall correctly, it was called a lukina. No, that's not right. It was called a lu-a-ki-na. Yes. A luakina," Sarah repeated with certainty.

"Luakina," I repeated after her.

"And in front of this sacrificial temple was an altar, or lee, which was made of stone. This sacrificial inner temple was sacred to the priests. Inside was a wicker enclosure from which seers, or kaulas as they were called, issued oracles. These kaulas at the heiaus were sought out by the king or chief when an augury was required. Outside the entrance were images of the main gods. There were also buildings, huts, for the high-priest, or the kahuna, as well as a house for the local chief or the king. Outside the entrance to the outer enclosure was a tabu staff. Nearby was a walled hut where sacrificial victims were slain for the altar. During a battle, the first prisoners taken were reserved to be slain at the altar in this fashion. They would be clubbed to death here, then taken and laid upon the altar. There, the chief or king would get a warrior to tear out the left eyeball of the corpse and have it handed to him."

"Is that all they used them for?" I asked.

"No, they also held services of chants and prayers for the ordinary people at which these people would bring offerings of fruit and perhaps meat and fish. Women were not allowed to participate in these ceremonies but by the same token they were never used as sacrifices either."

"Lucky them!"

"I'll say!"

"Why did they have sacrifices?"

"They were offerings to appease the gods."

"What kind of gods did they worship?"

"Well there are many gods. For instance, there is Kuula, the main god of the fishermen. Ukanipo is the shark-god of Hawaii. There is also Ku-kaili-moku or just Kaili for short. It is the war-god of the kings. It is a wooden image, quite small really, that is decorated with a yellow feather headdress. The image was taken along with King Kamehameha when he was doing battle."

"Sort of a good luck charm."

"It was more than that. Legend has it that it cried out loudly and spurred the warriors on in the midst of the battle. Only the king or royalty was allowed to use pure yellow feathers. King Kamehameha wore a cape made out of pure yellow feathers. Lesser functionaries like priests and chiefs wore a mixture of yellow and red feathers in their capes."

"Where did the yellow feathers come from?"

"From a little black seabird called the Mamo. There was but a single yellow feather found under each black wing of the Mamo."

"So thousands of birds must have been killed to gather that many feathers."

"Sad, but true. So many that the Mamo became extinct. "

"And the war-god must have been the most important god then."

"No, by far, the most important god is Pele."

"Pele! I've heard of Madam Pele before, of course, the volcano goddess."

"Right. She is the one god who is dreaded the most, especially on the Big Island here. Pele lives right in the middle of the volcano. She has five brothers and eight sisters who all represent different natural forces."

"Where does Pele live now?"

"She lives in the Kilauea crater but she moves from one crater to another at her pleasure and can spew forth lava anywhere on the island where she thinks the residents haven't contributed sufficient offerings of food into the crater where she lives. Or perhaps in areas where people have angered her in some other way."

"You say 'she'. Do you mean that she is in the form of a woman?"

"Not necessarily, it has been said that she can take many forms, one of which has been known to be human. In one instance, she took the form of a beautiful woman and as such, lived within the population. She even was involved in passionate sexual relations with men."

"I have heard that!"

"This is what they say."

"Talk about a hot love goddess!" I laughed.

"Exactly, she is supposed to be one fiery babe!"

CHAPTER FIFTEEN

MANNY

THE BIG ISLAND INN, KAILUA-KONA, HAWAII. I was in a deep slumber. Something other than first light caused me to shake off the outer veil of sleep. Not knowing what it was, I waited. There it was again. Fingers lightly patted my hair. Ah, Sarah. I had forgotten that she was in bed beside me. I smiled and gave a soft comforting sigh as I drowsily opened my eyes to see my reflection in the floor-to-ceiling mirrored wall. Focusing on my head, I expected to see Sarah lazily playing with my hair. Instead, I saw a creature, something like a small crab with an upturned tail, perched in my hair. I stiffened in horror as I recognized it to be a scorpion, its deadly curling stinger poised high in readiness. My pulse quickened, my skin perspired. I steeled myself to remain motionless. My carotid artery in my neck jumped with every heartbeat. Seeing my pulsing neck, the scorpion slowly crawled onto my ear and paused, mesmerized by the action on my neck. Silently it sat as if it was sneaking up on its prey. It lunged! A blackness shrouded my eyesight as I struggled to remain calm but I fully expected to feel the sting of the poison to immediately work its way into my bloodstream. I strained to see through the veil that shock had brought over me. I didn't feel any sting. I thought, was I paralyzed? Was I numb with its poison? Is this how it felt to die by lethal injection? Stunned, I could only watch in horror as that thing sat there. It stirred then climbed onto the bedcovers tucked around my shoulder. I flung the covers aside, jumped out of bed and whacked the insect into oblivion with my sandal. I rushed to the mirror. No punctures. Relieved, I looked around. No Sarah. So how did a scorpion get into my room? I wondered.

My image was reflected to infinity in the misty side mirrors as I ran an electric razor over the stubble on my face. I had slept in. My body was still getting over the jet-lag and acclimatizing itself to the heat and the humidity of the tropics. A full-force shower was not necessary for me to wake up. I had been jolted into awareness. Snapping my razor open to clean it, I tapped it clean against my open palm to the beat of

Shave and a haircut, two bits. I drank some coffee, draining the cup. I was settling down.

Looking in the mirror again, I ran a comb through my hair. There was still some puffiness below my eyes as I held my face up for inspection. My nose was somewhat sunburned from yesterday's rays so I daubed some sun-block on it. I slapped on some aftershave on my cheeks and felt its cooling effects. The aroma of the percolated Kona coffee filled the air with its pure essence. Pouring myself a second cup of brew, I turned on the radio to catch the news and the weather forecast. Later, I clicked the radio off, preferring to listen to the morning songbirds outside my open lanai door. Padding over to the bedroom, I shed my towel and stood looking at the closet. I thought, should I wear a golf shirt and a pair of walking shorts or . . . tough choice! I dressed then selected a comfortable pair of sandals. Cup in hand, I walked out onto the lanai of my condo at the Big Island Inn. The sharp salt air set up my olfactory senses. I took a deep breath of the sea air. The sunlight was being filtered through palm fronds which were cast as waving fingers of shadow across me.

I sat in the overstuffed patio chair and scanned the horizon. Little fishing boats bobbed like corks far out at sea, hauling in the day's catch for the restaurants' dinner menu. A few dive boats were already under way with their quota of tourists heading down the coast to the popular dive spots. I picked up my phone from the lanai table and called Sarah.

She answered with a cheery "Good morning!"

"And a good morning to you too!" I replied.

"Oh, it's finally you. The sleeping beauty, " she said as I mumbled my apologies for having slept in. "It's not a problem. I thought you'd need to catch up on your sleep, so I purposely didn't phone you when I realized that you were going to be late."

"That was nice of you."

"That's me, Miss Nice. Did you sleep well?"

"Yes, except for being awakened by a scorpion."

"Oh! Really? There are no scorpions in Hawaii as far as I know," she said, puzzled.

"And there still aren't . . . I killed it. Are we still going out to Honokohau today?"

"Yes, if that's okay with you."

"Sure, had your breakfast yet?"

"Not yet."

"Know a good place for breakfast before we head out?"

"I do. How long will you be?"
"I'm just about to head out the door."
"Good, see you in a few minutes then."

Kids were already splashing in the pool as I walked past on my way to the parking lot. Their mothers were ensconced in lounge chairs, novels in hand and cool drinks beside them. A group of elderly men sat on a quiet side of the garden under a patio umbrella, talking over coffee. Two young girls were bouncing a red ball and singing:

"There was an old man
That swallowed a fly
Oh me! Oh my!
He may even die

There was an old lady
That swallowed a spider
It wriggled, it jiggled
It tickled inside 'er . . . "

Their ball got loose and bounced across my path. I scooped it up and tossed it back to them. "Thanks mister," they said. Wondering if they had a verse about a scorpion, I waved and smiled back. I was alive! I felt marvelous!

The jeep was parked in the shade of a tree. It was relatively cool as I got in, then backed out. Driving to the end of the driveway, I checked the traffic then eased the Jeep onto Ali'i Drive.

"You look great this morning," I said to Sarah who was sitting in front of a hibiscus bush that surrounded the restaurant's lanai.

"And don't these hibiscus flowers look nice too!"

"What kind are they?" I asked as I slathered guava jelly on my toast.

"I think we call these Kokia Aloalo. I'm not exactly sure. There are over a thousand species. They're the floral emblem of Hawaii," she said as she plucked a red flower and tucked it behind her left ear, "and they'll keep for a whole day." She leaned over and grasped my hands as I leaned toward her. We kissed. Hawaiian music played softly in the background. Or was that in my heart? It was hard to tell. The helpful but intrusive waitress came by asking if we would like more coffee.

The spell was broken.

"Tell me a little about this SeaTruck dealer we're going to see today," I asked as I leaned back into my chair. We watched a Pacific

Golden Plover on spaghetti-like legs work an exposed part of the beach. It occasionally gave a clear, two-note whistle.

"I really don't know much about it. Dr. Slavik at Armstrong Robotic wasn't too clear about the arrangements made with these guys other than they are their Hawaiian dealers for the SeaTruck. From what I was told by Ellen, it is a marine sales and leasing place that was given the right to handle the SeaTruck business here in the islands."

"What arrangements did she say were made with them for us?"

"That we were to have a SeaTruck at our complete disposal. If anything went technically wrong that the dealer couldn't handle, we were to call on SSEAAL technicians here or contact Dr. Slavik at Armstrong or Dr. Jenkins or her at ORCA."

"Do you know anything about the owner?" I asked Sarah as she finished her fruit plate.

"Only his name . . . Manny something or other. I have his card somewhere in my purse. Ellen gave it to me as part of the info package. Here it is," she said as she rummaged through her handbag.

"Manetti Marine," I read out. "All major brands of industrial and pleasure boats and personal water craft. New and used. Leasing, sales and service. Giancarlo 'Manny' Manetti, proprietor, Honokohau Harbor, Hawaii."

"Stu said he was okay but perhaps a little . . . eccentric? No, that's not the right word that he used. Odd? No. It'll come to me in a while."

The road to Honokohau Harbor is lined on both sides with palm trees planted in honour of war veterans. It felt like we were driving by a mile-long spiritual honour guard as we swept down this road some four miles out of town and three miles short of Keahole Point.

A forest of sailboat masts and bimini-topped fishing charter boats with whip aerials and tuna towers hove into view as we closed the distance to the marina. We passed what looked like the industrial part of the marina where Manetti Marine had a huge plywood sign with an arrow pointing to the right. I drove past the Port Director's office to the end of the road.

There was another inlet of this huge marina. Sport fishing boat docks with signs like Why-Knot, Hustler and Infinity were vacant as their boats had long ago slipped their lines and cruised out of the harbour for another day's work. Row upon row of white-hulled pleasure craft of all types were snugged up to floating docks in the placid waters of the marina. The odd cigarette boat was counterbalanced by a few fine ketches and stately schooners.

Along the sides of the channel at the mouth of the marina, singlet-clad natives and haoles alike sat on the rocks or perched on the entrance channel marker, working their jury-rigged fishing lines in hopes of a good strike. A sloop entered the channel under engine power, its sails furled. To the left, over a slight rise of pahoehoe lava, I was delighted to discover a small secluded beach that had a nice expanse of soft white sand and a few shade trees which overlooked a promising snorkeling site.

"This is a really nice little beach for a picnic and a swim," Sarah said as we looked down upon the little bay tucked around the corner from the marina.

"It sure looks inviting," I agreed as I edged the Jeep forward. "Too bad we have to work, so to speak."

"Maybe later," she said.

"Let's go and find this outfit." I retraced our route then turned left where a dryland marina sat behind a security fence on the right.

It was sad to see so many boats sitting high and dry out of the water. Boats belong in the water. It was like looking at puppies at the pound. Puppies belong with kids.

We bounced down a pot-holed dusty road to where a public haul-out ramp was built. A boat on a trailer was being washed down by its owner and his fishing buddy to get the brine off before they hauled it home after an early morning's fishing trip. We continued down the road. It ended abruptly at a security fence with an open gate. We drove past another large, garish plywood sign that said Mannetti Marine. They had their own haul-out ramp and towering boat lifter that sat upon four tall, sturdy rubber-tired legs like some monstrous skeletal beast from *Star Wars*. It had a fiberglass yacht slung under its belly and was slowly being walked up the shore like some fearsome creature from the sea that had its hooks deep into its prey. Gleaming new boats sat in rows waiting to be sold or leased. The used boats were parked on the lot at the rear.

We pulled up in front of the showroom and parked. The middle of the large lot was taken up by the showroom where smaller boats and personal water craft like the Sea-Doo were displayed in air-conditioned coolness. The somewhat faded storefront sign proclaimed Manetti Marine in large letters. A parts department was behind the showroom. A grease-stained marine repair shop was run out of the rear of the white building.

The new addition on the right side had just been completed. A gleaming new sign over the new showroom declared *SeaTrucks of Hawaii.* There sat a lone white SeaTruck that glistened under banks of floodlights. A sterile-looking repair shop was behind this showroom. Sarah and I walked into the old showroom as the other one looked deserted. We were hit with smells of newness from the fiberglass and other materials used on the PWC's and other small boats.

"Manny around?" I asked of a couple guys idly talking. They looked like a potential customer and an eager boat salesman. The salesman gave me a grunt during a lull in his spiel and finger-pointed in the general direction of the back. We walked up to the parts counter. Customers leaned against the chipped, greasy counter while parts guys scurried around filling their orders and answered incessantly-ringing phones. I caught the eye of a tall guy who was showing a customer a boat part as he talked into a cradled phone on his shoulder. I asked in a stage whisper, "Manny around?"

I got another grunt and a curved-arm point farther toward the rear. We took the side hallway that led to the repair shop. Here the level of conversation took a decided downward turn as mechanics and labourers joked and cussed their way to resurrecting broken parts and worn-out old engines. There was a drop-off in the conversation as each became aware that there was a female in the shop. The tinny music being played on the radio suddenly sounded louder and was quickly turned down. All eyes were now ogling Sarah's beautiful figure. A couple low wolf-whistles sounded from the far recesses of the shop floor.

We stared at them, they stared at Sarah. "Is Manny ar . . . " I started to ask when we heard this grinding voice from just beyond the open shop doors at the rear.

"Look ya son-of-a-no-good baloney-skinner. Just where do ya come off asking for that, huh?" a short rotund man shouted into his cell phone as he kicked at the lava grit underfoot. "I told ya and told ya. That's the lowest I can go - thirty-two five."

The swarthy little man puffed on the tattered stub of a fat stogie stuck in his wide mouth and twanged his bright red cartoon-character suspenders for effect then winced as they slapped his chest smartly. "I know, I know, but I've already taken that into account." He raised the short sleeve of his red floral Hawaiian shirt - which on him came past his elbows - as if to wipe his nose on it, then thought better of it and pulled a white hanky out of the rear pocket of his white trousers and blew his nose noisily while jockeying his cigar out of the way. He jammed the hanky back into his rear pocket.

By now the men on the floor were distracted by his loud conversation to the point where they didn't know whether to keep staring at Sarah or to stare at the animated fat little man out back.

"Leave Maria out of this, okay? What are ya tryin' to do? Pick my pockets? I got a business ta run and I can't do that arguing with ya all day." He held out his free hand to the sky and gesticulated wildly with his cigar. "That's my lowest price, ya piece of scum, money doesn't grow like coconuts on trees, ya know. It's still thirty-two five!" he said as his face grew redder matching the red floral colour of his Hawaiian-patterned shirt. "Well then borrow it from your rich old man, you gutless wonder!"

With that the diminutive loudmouth angrily slapped the lower hinged mouthpiece shut, poked the aerial down and slammed the phone into his rear pocket. It jammed on his wadded hanky.

"For chrissake's," he exclaimed as he hauled the phone out again and slammed it into his other rear pants pocket. He tilted his straw hat back on his head and looked out to sea, took a deep breath, smiled, then broke out into a big grin. The grin turned into laughter which turned into a chortling belly-laugh.

We all stood stock-still witnessing the amazing performance of this comically-dressed little butterball. He wiggled and jiggled so hard that his trousers would have fallen down if they hadn't been held up by his funny suspenders. He unconsciously tugged at their waistband causing them to ride up. It gave this bandy-legged, midget-sized dynamo a pair of floods.

"Told that son-of-a-garlic eater!" he said to himself as he turned toward the shop, noticing his silently gaping audience for the first time. The laugh dropped off his face like an egg off a tilted Teflon frying pan. "What're ya all lookin' at? Get back ta work. I don't pay ya guys good money just ta goof off, ya know!"

The show over, the men turned back to their work benches and their boats, resuming their hunched over positions and foul but now-subdued language. Someone cranked the radio up a little, taking the edge off the silence.

Sarah and I continued staring at him. This had to be Manny. Da boss.

"Manny?" I asked.

"What's it to ya, pal?"

"We've come to see you Manny."

"Who's the pretty lady?"

"She's with me."

"I can see that, pal."

"Uh, this is Sarah, Dr. Sarah Leikaina."

"A doctor? I don't often get ta meet a doctor and a lady doctor at that. Especially such a pretty lady doctor. Ya make house calls I see!" Turning and sidling up to her while wincing, Manny said, "Doc, I got this problem with my . . . "

"She's not that kind of doctor. Manny."

Turning to me he said with an astonished look on his face, "She's not?"

I shook my head to say that she was not.

Manny turned back to her and asked, "Well, what kind of doctor are ya, doll?"

Sarah flushed and stated, "Well, thank you for the compliment . . . I think. I'm actually a doctor in volcanology."

"What's that? Oh, I get it . . . like in volcano. Yeah, ya do look like a real hot number! Hey babe, wanna see some real fireworks, huh?" Manny said as he did a tripping little two-step.

"Careful now Manny, she's a real lady, something that perhaps you're not used to."

Manny immediately dropped down to one knee, doffed his straw hat and smoothed the ruffled edges of hair around on his bald head. Then he held his hat over his heart and grabbed the stogie out of his mouth with his other hand. He declared with an angelic expression on his face as he looked up at her towering over him, "excuse my uncouth manners, ma'am, but sometimes my mouth races ahead of my brain and gets me inta trouble." He reached up, took her hand and kissed the back of it.

"Well, you're forgiven this time," Sarah said with a trace of a smile as she unsuccessfully tried to hold the mock stern look on her face.

"Why thank ya, I'll have ta mind my p's and q's from now on," he stated as he stood up and slapped his straw hat at the dusty knee of his trouser leg.

"Do you always talk to your customers that way?"

"Ya mean apologize?"

"No, no, I mean what you were saying before."

"Ma'am, uh, doctor, I already said I was sorry and I apologized ta ya for that!"

"No, no, I meant when you were talking on your cell phone. I assumed you were talking to a customer. Do you always talk to your customers that way?"

Manny let go with a little grunt then a snort and finally a raucous chortle as he recalled his conversation of a few moments ago. "That was no customer! That was my dumb brother-in-law!"

He turned serious. "He's a no-good bum. He's married ta my dear sister who deserves better, God knows! That guy is nothing but a money-sucking leech. The things I've done for him. If it wasn't for my poor sister . . . "

"But I take it he's trying to buy a boat from you." Sarah interjected.

"He's tryin' ta *steal* a boat from me! Well, actually it's a pretty good deal . . . for me. Hey, I gotta make a buck too, ya know! That creep's family has more money than they know what ta do with. They been stackin' it away in some mattress for over a hundred years now. Money's been handed down from generation to generation. Someday my poor sister's gonna be a rich woman but until then . . . "

"So you're really making out like a bandit on this deal then?" I asked.

"It's all part of the game," he laughed. "He'll come back and buy that boat here for what I'm askin' for it. Then he'll want something else thrown in for free. And I'll throw it in for free just as he wants. Then we'll all get together at a luau at my place on the weekend, have some vino and some good Italian and Hawaiian home cookin' and all will be well. We're family, ya know?"

He took out his hanky and blew his nose with a forceful honk, then daubed at his misted eyes.

It was quite a performance!

"So what can I interest ya folks in? We got some real nice used cruisers that just came in or do ya folks belong to the sailing crowd? We got some classy overnighters - fiberglass jobs, ya know?"

"That's not why we're here," Sarah stated, "we've come to use your SeaTruck. You were sent out a working arrangement for this project by ORCA and Armstrong Robotics. This is my partner Rune Erikson. He's a marine technical evaluation specialist."

"Say what?" a skeptical-looking Manny asked as he cocked his ear toward Sarah.

"A marine . . . "

"Save your breath, sister, I caught it the first time." Manny said as he turned to me and stated, "Cut the crap, pardon me Ma'am. Mistah

Rrrune Errrikson, just what in the hell is a Rrrune and what is it that ya do?"

I took a deep breath as I attempted to con a con man, albeit a little one. "The name is Rune, it has Viking origins. I'm here to do a hands-on technical evaluation of the on-site performance of the SeaTruck submersible and relate that to the cost structure and the retail selling price or the leasing price, as the case may be. I factor in cost of production, cost of like submersibles, the competition, which in this case there is none yet, profit margins at all levels, and do a recommendation of improvements or changes to the submersible to better reflect economic viability and the client's requirements."

"Yeah, yeah, yeah. Sounds like a bunch of horse, uh, hogwash ta me. I'll tell ya. Me and my accountants, we don't talk the same language. They're bean counters. They use reams and reams of computer paper and can't see the forest for the trees. Maybe with them using all that paper there is no forest left for them ta see. Ha! Me? I do all my figurin' on the back of an envelope. I get the big picture. And I get it faster ta boot!"

Sarah and I exchanged amused glances. "I hate bean counters too, Manny, with a passion. I go at it a little different than they do. What we're going to do is to take a hands-on approach to this thing. We're going to go out and actually see what this thing can do - under a real workload."

"Where ya gonna do that?"

"Just offshore here and up a bit. We're going to check up on the SSEAAL pipeline and maybe do a little more scouting around, see what's down there."

"I'd be careful if I was ya! Haven't ya heard? There was an underwater explosion just up the coast from here. One of the charter dive boats got blown out of the water. Bunch of 'em recreational divers got killed. Skipper and his deck-hand too! Only a couple from the Midwest survived!"

"Yes, we heard. It's too bad. How'd it happen?"

"Nobody seems ta know. The authorities are sittin' around with their fingers . . . uh, their feet up on their desks waitin' for some clues to drop outa the sky or somethin'. If they know somethin', they're not sayin'. I knew the skipper pretty good. Used to bring his boat here for repairs now and then and get it hauled out and bottom-scraped once a year. Seemed like a real good head. His widow's just devastated. Got a couple little kids and a big mortgage and all. We're takin' up a collection to give ta the widow and all if you'd like to contribute a few bucks."

"We sure will!" Sarah said.

"Yeah, it's too bad. One day ya got the world by the tail and the next . . . well . . . you never know. The way I figure it, if ya gotta go, ya gotta go. It's your turn. That's all there is to it. No sense worryin' about it. But the poor widow and them kids. That's what hurts the most!"

"They have any insurance?" I asked.

"Don't know. Nobody's heard yet."

"Wonder what caused the explosion?" I asked.

"The way I figure it, it has ta be somethin' freaky-like, cause this has never happened before in all the years I been on this island. And I been here more years than I care ta remember, I was born right here! Mind you, there has been some scuttlebutt goin' around lately but you hear things all the time."

"What kind of scuttlebutt?"

"Well, before this happened there were a few accidents out there, work-related, ya know, some not, though. There was one scuba diver working on that new pipeline who got some bad air. A real experienced guy, navy-trained and all. He left a widow and at least one kid if I can remember right. There were others."

"Then the explosion!"

"As I said, the way I got it figured it was something freaky-like. Or maybe it was one of our Hawaiian gods, ha, ha!"

"Hawaiian gods, huh? What do you know about Hawaiian gods?"

"Listen pal, I know I don't always seem like I am but I do have one-quarter Hawaiian blood in me, so I do happen ta know a little of which I speak. How's them for coconuts, pal? Bet ya didn't know that!"

"Really?"

"Yup," said Manny as he stuck his chest out proudly and hooked his thumbs under his suspenders. "My grandfather, when he came over from the old country, from Italy you know, he married himself a real Hawaiian girl. A real looker if the old photos do any justice. Take another look at me. I got the best of both worlds. Okay, so I got a little short-changed in the height department but that's life."

"There can be a benefit in being short," Sarah interjected.

"How so?" asked Manny.

"Well, for one, just getting around on boats is easier for a shorter person. We taller people tend to get our noggins rapped frequently when sailing. Also, I find that getting into and moving around in submersibles would be a lot easier if I was shorter."

"Speaking of which, shall we have a look at the SeaTruck?" I asked.

"Yeah, let's go have a look at her. She's a real beauty alright!" Manny exclaimed.

Sarah and I followed Manny's rolling gait through the shop, through the parts department, into the old showroom then into the new showroom where the SeaTruck sat gleaming under the ceiling track-lights.

"This is a wonderful machine. We got it not long ago. It's only been a demo. I've had my head mechanic, who is certified ta pilot this thing, take a prospective buyer or two out and put it through its paces."

"No problems?" I asked.

"None whatsoever," declared Manny as he edged up to the open showroom door and sent a stream of spittle out onto the pavement. "In fact, I'm even thinking of renting this baby out, with pilot, on a daily basis. I could make a bundle on it that way too. So how long do you guys want it for?"

"We're not sure. Until we finish our evaluation of it. Could be a few weeks or so," I stated.

Manny rubbed his hands together and said, "I think I could just manage without my head mechanic for that long."

"Oh," said Sarah, "we're both certified pilots as well. We won't be needing a pilot's services."

"Oh, well in that case, I'll have to see your certificates before I can let either of you operate this on your own."

"Are you serious?" asked Sarah.

"Yeah, it's part of the contract."

"Well, I suppose we could get something faxed here from Victoria. Will that do?"

"Yeah, I suppose. Let's go see Glenda, she'll review the contract with ya."

Sarah and I exchanged puzzled looks then shrugged our shoulders and followed Manny once again.

"Glenda, this is Dr. Sarah . . . " Manny groped for her last name.

"Leikaina," Sarah said.

"Leikaina. She's a Vulcan . . . " Manny interjected.

"A volcanologist!" Sarah declared with some exasperation.

"I stand corrected. A volcanologist. Hey, how come a Vulcan . . . a volcano expert needs a sub? The volcanos are on top of the mountains! Heh, heh!"

"Not all, some are active underwater as well."

"Yeah? Well, I'll be darned. The things you don't learn. And this is, uh . . . What'd ya say your name was again?"

"Rune, Rune Erikson, pleased to meet you." I said to Glenda.

"What the hell kind of name is Rune again anyway?"

"Same kind of name as Manny is . . . only not shortened."

"Okay, okay. I get the hint, pal."

"Viking."

Then turning back to Glenda, Manny said, "He's some kind of fancy accountant or something. Write up our new SeaTruck. Use our standard contract."

"Right away, Mann . . . uh, Mr. Manetti," said Glenda, a dyed-in-the-bottle, honey-blonde as she turned to her desk and pulled out a lease agreement, She started filling it in. Looking up, she asked us with a deadpan face, "Will that be Visa or MasterCard?"

Sarah and I exchanged surprised looks, then she said to Glenda, "That was all supposed to have been taken care of in the instructions and the agreement sent to your company over the weekend."

Glenda looked questioningly over at Manny who was now the picture of angelic innocence again. Manny's cherubic face displayed raised eyebrows and pursed lips as he shrugged his shoulders. "I don't know nuthin' about no arrangement. You folks will just have ta pay by credit card and settle up with your boss later. Ya got enough room on your card for this, don't ya? It's gonna be a few bills, I can god . . . uh, guarantee ya that!"

"Now just wait a minute!" Sarah exclaimed. "This whole thing was supposed to have been taken care of. We're not going to use our cards for this! Can I use your phone? I'll straighten this out right away."

Glenda handed her the phone.

"Thanks," Sarah said. She punched a long string of numbers, waited, then asked, "Ellen? Sarah. How are you? . . . We're fine, just fine. We've got a little problem or misunderstanding for you to straighten out if you could. We're here at Manetti Marine, just as we are supposed to be to arrange for the use of the SeaTruck. It seems that Mr. Manetti has never heard of our arrangement at all. He wants us to use our credit card to pay for the whole lease amount . . . Well, that is just what we said too! . . . Yes . . .Yes . . . Okay, I'll put him on." She looked over at Manny who was slowly shrinking into the woodwork and requested, "Ellen would like to *speak* to you."

Manny took the proffered phone and handled it as if it was a hot potato. He paused as if to collect his thoughts. His clouded face suddenly took on the features of a smiling salesman. “Hello, Ellen?” he beamed. “What seems ta be the problem?” He paused as he listened, then in an innocent tone of voice said, “Oh, really? Ya know? Come ta think of it, I did see something cross my desk on Monday morning that had arrived over the weekend . . . I see. Well, I hardly had any time ta review it. In fact I hardly glanced at it . . . Is that so? . . . Oh, okay. Sure. Oh, for sure! Don’t worry about a thing. I’ll take care of it right away! . . . She wants to talk ta ya again,” he said as he handed the phone back to Sarah.

“Listen, Sarah,” Ellen laughed, “don’t let that little carnival hawker fast-talk you guys into anything! I think he was just testing the waters to see how far he could get with this. The SeaTruck is there on consignment only. It doesn’t belong to him or his company, so we call the shots from this end. Keep me up to date and call me right away if you have any more problems, okay?”

“Thanks, Ellen, we’ll do that, bye.”

“Sorry about that little misunderstanding,” Manny apologized, his halo now somewhat tarnished, “it seems that I didn’t fully understand the instructions. Now, how would you like ta handle paying for the insurancc? Wc havc two levels of insurance which can be paid by Visa or MasterCard . . . ”

“Manny!” I admonished with a threatening voice.

Manny hung his head down, grinned slyly and said, “You know how it is. I just couldn’t resist!”

CHAPTER SIXTEEN

DAYDREAMS & NIGHTMARES

KAILUA-KONA, THE BIG ISLAND OF HAWAII. After having arranged to take the SeaTruck out on sea trials there wasn't much of the afternoon left in which to do some scouting around. While Sarah took care of some things of her own, I played the tourist and wandered the avenues and the back streets of Kailua on foot. Seeing the markets, the artwork and the library, I let my mind subconsciously roam. There were still a lot of unanswered questions about what had exploded or erupted out there in the sea. For the most part, the questions were pretty much all unanswered. It was with some added concern on her part that Sarah asked me if I would have dinner with her and an old childhood friend of hers who had been troubled of late. She thought that perhaps I could help her friend.

The day had been a little tiresome, what with Manny's machinations that we had to deal with just to get access to our submersible. Oh, he was a loveable little rascal but a rascal just the same.

When I agreed to have dinner with the two of them, Sarah's eyes lit up as she thanked me.

"I wouldn't have asked you to take on more problems if I didn't think this was so serious," she said. "I bumped into Kiana the other day. I've known her since kindergarten, even before that. We were childhood friends who never lost touch with each other. Oh, there were times we were away at different universities or later when I was off on deep-sea explorations that we didn't get to talk as much as we would have liked to, but I know her like a sister. Rune, I know there is something very wrong with her."

"Like what?" I had asked.

"Well, she has dark shadows under her eyes. It looks like she hasn't been getting much sleep. Her hands tremble. She can't concentrate for too long on any one thing. She seems very stressed. Frankly, Rune, she's like a frightened little bird. To add to her considerable distress, she and her elderly father were in a car accident recently. She is shook up about that too. Her father was injured but is now on the mend with his arm in a cast. He is still in the hospital. Kiana was hurt too but not as severely, mostly bumps and bruises. I'm concerned about her mental health as she maintains that there was another vehicle involved in the accident whereas the police investigation shows that their car was the only vehicle at the scene. The police may even charge her with giving false statements. And she keeps going on about these bones and something about some stone balls or something like that. I just find it very unlike her and I wish you would hear what she has to say."

"What does she do?" I asked.

"She's a schoolteacher."

"Ah! Maybe the kids are getting the better of her. It's been known to happen. Teacher burnout."

"No, she is a very good teacher and I don't think teacher burnout is the reason. The kids all love her dearly and don't cause her any problem at all. She teaches elementary grades; history is her specialty. She loves her work!"

The Captain's Lookout complex contained a few shops, a handful of bars and a few good restaurants. It was the kind of character building that tourists love and locals frequent. We agreed to have dinner on the lanai at the Blue Lagoon Restaurant. It was handy as it was just down the beach from my condo at the Big Island Inn.

Kiana, who was staying with her mother in Kealakekua just a short drive down the coast from Kailua-Kona, had picked Sarah up at her place on her way to dinner. While her father was in hospital, Kiana decided that she would forego the use of her own condo in town and comfort her mom.

Getting to the two-story restaurant first, I found my way up to the second floor where I selected a quiet table off to one side of the lanai nearest the beach below.

I thought this would be a perfect spot in case Kiana wanted to unload her troubles onto us. The adjacent surf would muffle any sensitive conversation that we may have.

I sat and ordered a cold beer from the friendly waitress. Casting my eyes around, I noted that the tables were starting to fill as the huge fiery-red sun started to take its downward plunge to be extinguished by the sea. Farther toward Ali'i Drive the complex rambled along, another restaurant here, a bar there, some skylights covering ground-floor kiosks where trinkets and jewellery were being sold. A four-story bell-tower rose alone beyond that and was connected to the complex by a web of walkways and narrow tin roofs. Sets of rough-hewn plank staircases ran maze-like here and there including up to the top of the tower. Scattered palm trees soared beside the lanai providing some fluttering shade.

I first noted the presence of the two women by the quieting of the other diner's conversations as they walked onto the lanai. All eyes were turned their way as the alluring Hawaiian women made their way over to me. They were wearing floral-print sheath dresses that hugged every soft curve of their trim bodies. Each of them had a white flower behind their left ear, forming a nice accent for their flowing, silky dark hair. I stood as they arrived.

"Sorry to be late, Rune, but we've finally arrived," Sarah said as we kissed in greeting. "This is my good friend Kiana Kilolani. This is Rune Erikson." I leaned over, clasped her hands in mine and kissed her cheek, noting a faint trace of plumeria-blossom fragrance. In spite of her radiant beauty, it was quite evident that she was very tired as Sarah had said. She was the type of woman who usually wore no make-up and she wore none this time to cover the dark shadows under her eyes. Her lovely hands felt ice-cold; I detected a slight tremble as we had touched. The ladies ordered Chi-Chi drinks while perusing the menu. I ordered a small steak and a garden salad, Sarah had the mahi-mahi and Kiana ordered the shrimp salad.

"So I finally get to meet you!" exclaimed Kiana. "Sarah has been telling me about you. Have you been to Hawaii before?"

"Yes," I replied, "but not to this island. I'm looking forward to seeing more of it. We've been too busy with work to do anything else yet."

"Well, you'll have to change that. First chance you get, see what the Big Island is all about. I was born here but I'm still fascinated with its uniqueness and its history - it has a very rich history. I'd be happy to show you some of the historical sights."

"I hear that you are a teacher, a history teacher."

"Yes, I find history, especially Hawaiian history, so interesting. And the kids! The kids I teach are at a relatively young age where they are not yet caught up in all the trappings of peer pressures."

Sarah said, "She has the neatest kids in her class. She brought them over to SSEAAL for a tour of the facility just before I left for my stint on the joint expedition in Canada."

Kiana said, "You know, it was right after that tour when I started having trouble sleeping! In fact I haven't been feeling at all well since that time that I had those . . . " Our food arrived just as she was starting to get into some of what was troubling her. I put my inquiring mind aside while we ate a leisurely meal and talked. Sarah and Kiana did a lot of reminiscing. I did a lot of listening and laughing with them about their hilarious hijinks together in school. I found that Sarah had a rather mischievous side to her, the extent to which I hadn't really realized until now. It did Kiana good to laugh again - that was easy to tell. She became more relaxed. That, and the drink she had, eased whatever pain this lovely lady was feeling. The evening rolled along. Then some casual word triggered her old anxiety again. She tensed and grimaced.

"Kiana, before our dinner arrived, you were just going to tell us something about that tour that you took your kids on . . . "

"The tour was fine, Rune, and Sarah, you were just wonderful to us. We had a great time! But remember when the tour was over, when I said that I had promised the kids a picnic on the beach afterwards?"

"Yes, you were going to take them to the public beach just outside the compound fence and I, unfortunately, had to get back to work. You remember, Rune, it was where we drove around the perimeter in the golf carts because you wanted to see what was there."

"Right! The beach with the fenced in lava tube skylight and the hi, uh, the hay . . . "

"The heiau," answered Sarah.

"Right, the heiau," I repeated. "The temple, the place of worship, the place where sacrifices were sometimes made."

"Well, we went there for our picnic, the kids and I, another teacher and a couple of the parents, and the school bus driver. That was the first time that I had an anxiety attack."

"Because of the kids?" I interjected.

"No, they were just fine and had a whale of a time. It was me! Only me! After a while there, this feeling started to come over me, something that I had never experienced since I was just a little girl. I began to feel quite anxious, more like a panic attack really! Try as I might, I couldn't sweep this thing from my mind and enjoy myself with my kids. Thinking that lying down would make me feel better, I made an excuse that I had a slight headache and asked if the other teacher and the parents would look after the children."

"Where did you lie down?" I asked.

"On a blanket in the shade of the bus."

"Where was the bus parked?"

"Near the heiau, where we got off to see the sacred site. The beach is right there too."

"You should have come over to the facility, we have a sick room that you could have used," Sarah interjected.

"I thought I would be okay if I could just lie down and rest but the anxiety intensified. I had this feeling of something not being quite right. Then I realized after some time that the intense anxiety was not coming from within me but from without."

"From without?" we both asked in unison.

"Yes. It's difficult to explain. It was like feeling a movie rather than seeing and hearing it. I was being drawn into it mentally. Now, I know you'll both think I'm going crazy, but that's the truth!"

Sarah and I exchanged worried glances, then sought to empathize with Kiana. "Kiana," said Sarah, "maybe you just had too much sun or something. That can make you feel ill, sometimes even cause a person to hallucinate."

"No, I know what that is like. This wasn't it. Remember when you were little and your Mom told you about the Hawaiian legends that were passed down through the generations and you would get so emotionally caught up in them?"

"Yes," Sarah acknowledged.

"Well, this was something like that, only I'm not that little kid any longer. The feeling was the same though."

"Can you elaborate on this feeling a little?" I asked.

"It's difficult to explain and even more difficult to have someone else understand but, please, don't think I'm going crazy, at least, I hope I'm not!"

"No, no! Please try to explain," Sarah quickly said as she reached out and comforted Kiana with a soothing hand on her shoulder. "We don't think you're crazy."

"This is going to sound so weird . . ." Kiana said as she held her head high and glanced away in embarrassment.

"Please try," I said. "It's important!"

"I felt this thing," she swallowed hard and continued, "this presence there . . . at the heiau. It spooked me, at first. Then I realized that this presence was in an extreme state of anxiety. Something like a tortured soul, a poor, lonely, tortured soul, but yet, somehow powerful . . . very anxious, very upset about something. I tried to relax but the more relaxed I became, the more the intense detailed feeling overcame me. This . . . this thing, this presence was trying to convey something to me. I saw something that looked like sticks, white sticks and stones. Well I didn't really see it. I saw it in my mind, sort of like a fuzzy picture, a picture out of focus. These sticks started moving fast, sort of tumbling and coming to a rest all jumbled and scattered, scattered widely apart. The most dreadful sensation came over me when that happened."

"What happened then?" asked Sarah breathlessly.

"I saw this man as if I was seeing him distorted through translucent glass. He was wearing yellow, a cloak of yellow. He had what looked like a spear. But I couldn't make out his features."

"What happened next?" I asked.

"That's just it! Nothing happened! The intense feeling faded just as fast as it had come over me and then the figure disappeared."

"That was it?" Sarah asked.

"That was all!"

"Well, I'm glad that that's over."

"That's what I thought too."

"Thought?" I prodded.

"Yes! I thought that I was fully cognizant. So I got up and made my way over to where everyone was picnicking. I tried to talk, to tell them that I was feeling better now but all that came out of my mouth were a lot of words about sticks and stones. I tried to tell them that there was something evil going on at the heiau. I felt an acute sense of paranoia. I was wringing my hands and glancing wildly about in a daze. The parents were looking at me in amazement and the kids were laughing at me because I wasn't making any sense to them at all. I was so embarrassed that I didn't even mention the figure in yellow. And the bus driver, who knows what he thought? After 15 minutes or so, I finally came around to where I was starting to make some sense to them. It was like having a feeling in a dream, or a dream within a dream. It was weird!"

"And that was all?" Sarah asked.

"Yes, for the time being, that was all. The next few days were very hard for me to take emotionally. There was a lot of gossip. People talk, you know. Oh, they don't mean any harm by it. But there was some talk. I'm afraid I became a little paranoid that this feeling would come over me again. I had doubts that I was sane. I had fleeting thoughts that I would slip into insanity or something! That I would lose self-control. Especially when the other teacher or one of the parents who were there would come up to me and ask if I was feeling better now. All the old feelings would come flooding back to me. Like now!" Kiana said as tears misted her soft almond eyes. Her lower lip trembled. We both put our arms around her and hugged her together. "I'm okay now," she said as she daubed at her eyes with her dinner napkin.

"And that was the end of that?" I asked.

"I thought so. Then later, the following week, one of my young boys in my class, a real cutie pie, came to me at the end of the day and asked 'Are you feeling better now, Miss Kilolani?' I said 'Why, yes, I am! Thank you for asking!' Then he asked, 'Did that man make you feel bad?' Startled, I didn't know what to say except, 'What man?' He said, 'That tall man in the yellow feather jacket and the yellow feather hat.' 'Where?' I asked him. 'When we were at the beach with you,' he said, 'when you were sick. He was standing near you. Didn't you see him?' Frightened and confused, I mumbled something to him about being too sick to see him and said that the man didn't make me sick. 'Good,' he said as he hugged me, 'because if he had I would have gone up to him and kicked him right in the leg and taken his spear away!' I was astounded. He's just a little boy. How would he know to make something like that up if he hadn't really seen him?"

"Do you think that the little boy may have had an overactive imagination?" I asked.

"No, I don't think so. He has never done or said anything even remotely like that either before or after! I'm sure he knows what he saw."

"This is so incredible!" remarked Sarah as she put her fingertips to her lips.

"Is this still bothering you?" I asked.

"That and more!"

"More?" I asked incredulously as I leaned forward.

"A few nights later it happened. I started to get these dreams or nightmares, if you will."

"What sort of nightmares?" asked Sarah with some consternation.

"Sleeping fitfully, I tossed and turned. It didn't cool off much that evening. And it was quite humid too. Then these images flashed through my mind."

"What sort of images?" asked Sarah wide-eyed.

"I dreamt about those white sticks and stones being violently scattered. They turned into a skull and bones. Then these gray things came rolling down this slope toward me. I tried to get out of their path as each thing was knee-high and there were many of them tumbling around. I can still hear the rumbling, clunking sound they gave off as they caromed off each other as they rushed toward me. Then I can remember getting very warm, hot, in fact, as bright rivers of red-hot lava with eddies and swirls resembling faces came flowing down to me. Then this tall figure in a yellow cape would roar at me, his roar turning into cynical laughter."

"What happened next?" I asked.

"Then I woke up in sheer terror, drenched in perspiration."

"Did you talk to anybody about it, about the dream?" asked Sarah.

"At first, I did mention it to a few people, you know, like you do to friends or your co-workers during a break or something like that. I did mention that I thought there was something evil going on around the heiau. But then word started to get around town and the gossip started all over again. People I hardly knew started to ask me personal questions. It just got out of hand, so I stopped talking about it with anyone. You guys are the first ones I've talked to about this in some time."

"Have you had any more dreams?" I asked.

"Almost every night! I'm getting so that I dread having to go to sleep as I know the nightmares will return!"

"You poor thing," Sarah said as she comforted Kiana, "You poor, poor thing!"

"Did you seek professional help?" I asked.

"What a shrink? No! They would only think that I really was crazy then!"

"You mean the people?" I asked. "Hmm! Yes, I guess that is a possibility."

"Sometimes, I have serious doubts about myself too!" Kiana lamented. "I approached a psychologist friend of mine. She said that this sometimes happens to adults but is more commonly seen in children. My friend called it *pavor diurnus* - daytime hallucinations - which result in agitation, screaming or running around. She said it was a fear reaction which arises during afternoon naps and consists of hallucinations of strange people or animals. And *pavor nocturnus* is the nighttime version. The problem with this was that my pupil also witnessed at least part of it - the figure in the yellow feathered cape. She didn't have an answer for that except to suggest that perhaps I was a seer. Oh, I just wish that I could understand what happened to me! I hope I'm not going crazy!"

"Look at me, Kiana," demanded Sarah as she stared at her and held her hand, "you're not crazy! Don't even think like that! Perhaps this is something which you will just have to accommodate in your life. But if you ever do need any help like that, whether professional or otherwise, we are right beside you all the way!"

"You can count on us, Kiana," I added.

"That's so comforting to hear. You're so sweet, both of you!"

"That's what good friends are for, Kiana," Sarah declared as we hugged each other again.

"In the meantime, we're here to help you in any way possible, with any difficulties you may face," I said. "Speaking of which, Sarah tells me that you and your father were in a car accident a little while ago."

A dark cloud of worry shaded her face as she recalled the trauma of that event and her ongoing concern. "It was terrible. My poor father. His health hasn't been the best lately and now this. He could have been killed. We could have been killed."

"He's all right now, isn't he?" I asked.

"His right arm is in a cast. It's broken. And he's got a bump on his head. He seems to be weathering that. Our backs were sore for a few days but mine has cleared up. I hate to have caused him so much pain. He is still recovering in the hospital."

"How did you manage in the accident?" I asked.

"Just some bumps and bruises. The passenger side of the car took the brunt of the force. We slammed into a tree. It saved us from going over the edge. It's a long way down."

"Where did the accident happen?" I asked.

"On the top part of the road leading down to Kealakekua Bay. I was driving my dad home after a visit to his friend's place in Kailua. Having grown up in Kealakekua Bay, I know that road as well as any other, better than any other! That's what is so puzzling!"

"How did it happen?" I prodded.

"I wanted to get Dad home before dark otherwise Mom worries so much about him. But we were running a little late, not that I was speeding to make up the time or anything like that. Things just run late sometimes. This time it was a flat tire. Thankfully, a fellow who happened to be nearby offered to change it for me. It was nice of him to offer to help but he was so slow."

"Maybe he was just trying to get a date with you," Sarah said.

"No, it wasn't like that at all. He wasn't very pleasant but he did offer to change the tire. He insisted that we would be all right to drive home on that little temporary tire. But it bothered me to do that so I drove over to a garage and got the flat fixed right away. That made more sense to me in case I got another flat along the way. But the strange thing though was that the mechanic said that the tire was fine. The only thing he could think of was that there was a leak along the rim of the tire where the sealant might have let go."

"Which tire was flat?" I asked.

"It was the front tire - on the passenger side. Anyway, the sun had already gone down and it was dark by the time the flat was put back on. I was being really careful. The road is quite narrow, steep and winding - you know how it is Sarah. We had gone around a few curves in the road already and I was being cautious because it's a long way down, thousands of feet down the slope at that point. We were coming to another curve, this one to the left. As I said, it was dark, so I had already turned my lights on. Just as we neared the curve, without warning, a pair of headlights suddenly appeared directly in front of us. These lights were wavering and closing quickly as the other car coming at us was going about the same speed that we were. We didn't have a chance! Dad shouted 'Look out!' I slammed on my brakes and cut the steering wheel to the left into the oncoming lane. At the same time, the other car must have seen us and swerved back toward their lane, toward us as well. I could see their headlights sliding along like in a dream. Going into a sideways skid down the road, I remember screaming and closing my eyes at the moment of impact."

"There was an impact?" asked an incredulous Sarah.

"That's just it. I kept waiting for the impact to happen. But it didn't happen. It was like in slow motion, you know. When it didn't happen, I opened my eyes. We were still sliding down the road. I screamed again, this was like a living nightmare. The next thing I knew we slammed broadside into a large tree by the side of the road. The car door on my dad's side was bashed in. That's how his arm got broken, from the force of the door being slammed inward. I remember hitting my head on Dad's shoulder then being bounced back against my door as he and I were thrown back by the force of his door buckling inward. That and the seat belts saved us though. That tree was the only thing that kept us from hurtling over the edge and tumbling down that steep slope for thousands of feet. And it was lucky that I had swerved to the left. We hit a tree farther down to the right rather than turning to the right where there was none. Otherwise, we would have been killed for sure."

"Did the other car stop?" I asked knowing that this was a very contentious issue.

"We were dazed, so I don't exactly recall everything clearly. I didn't see the car stop, if it did. I guess it continued up the hill to the highway."

"Did your dad see anything more than you did?" I asked.

"No, unfortunately Dad's eyesight isn't as good as it once was and he had his eyes closed as well in anticipation of the crash. He was unconscious for a few moments right after the crash."

"So you didn't see or hear anything else?" I asked.

"Hmm, strange, now that I think of it."

"What's that?"

"Well another car came up the hill shortly. It stopped and they gave us first aid and used their car phone to call for an ambulance. They really comforted us. But now that I think of it, I remember hearing voices before I heard the car stop. Funny, I never thought about that until now."

"Before?"

"That's strange! Maybe I was just imagining hearing voices or maybe I was just confused and in a state of shock after the crash."

"What have the police said?"

"They questioned me a little at the scene before we were whisked away to the hospital in Kailua. They interviewed both of us later that night at the hospital and again the next day. I went to Mom and Dad's place after I was released from hospital. They kept me as well as Dad overnight for observation because of our head injuries, but I was okay. Dad, he's going to take a little longer to mend. Mom was frantic with worry about us. If it wasn't for my brother and his family to comfort her and bring her to the hospital to see us, I just don't know how she would have managed. She must have spent a terrible night!"

"Was that all that the police did?" I asked.

"No, apparently they investigated the accident for a couple days then they came back to see me."

"What did they say?" I asked.

" They said that they had investigated the accident and could find no evidence at all that there ever was another car involved."

I questioned Kiana, "But didn't they have your dad's statement?"

"Yes, but they said that he is just an old man who admitted that his eyesight was bad and that he had been bumped on his head. They said that he may just have thought he saw a car or that he heard me saying there was a car so he said there was one too! Can you believe that ridiculous statement?"

"Could the tire somehow have caused the crash?"

"No. I stopped and checked the tire before we got out onto the highway and I stopped and checked it again just before we went down Napo 'opo 'o Road. I was scared of driving down that steep road with a low tire but, no, it was fine. I mentioned that to the police."

"I know that you have school to teach but I'd like to have a look at the accident scene. Can you give me some further directions as to the exact location?" I asked.

"Just drive out to Kealakekua Bay. When you start to go down the long, winding road with the magnificent view of the bay, Napo 'opo 'o Road, it's about the sixth or seventh curve. You can't miss it. There are two large trees close to each other then there is a large tree on the roadside on the outside of the curve just a bit farther. It has been freshly scraped and you'll see the red paint from my car on it."

"Did the police say anything else?"

"It wasn't really so much what they said. It was what they intimated."

"What did they intimate?" I asked.

Kiana started twisting the dinner napkin around in her fingers belying her nervousness. "They said that perhaps I had just made up that story to absolve myself of the blame," she blurted as her lips trembled, "for insurance purposes, you know!" Her eyes started to mist again then turned into tears and she started to silently sob. Here was a woman who was at the end of her rope. She had gone through so much to that point and now this! "That's not the worst of it," she managed through sobs. "They said that they had heard what had happened to me out at the heiau that day and they hinted that perhaps I was losing my mind and had just imagined the other car." Her shoulders heaved with racking sobs as we tried to comfort her.

Other diners had come and gone. Those that were still here now turned in our direction, then politely turned back to their dinners when I stared them down. All except one. The exception was a surly-looking fellow with a contemptuous air about him. He was sitting just inside the open-air restaurant on a stool at the bar behind me. Come to think of it, he had been there about the same length of time that we were there. He was nursing a whiskey and had been chain-smoking cigarettes while talking in low tones with another fellow who had his back turned to us.

We comforted Kiana until she came around and was smiling weakly saying, "I'll be okay. It's just been so much in the last while . . . "

"Maybe we should go," I said. "There's a nosy individual seated at the bar. He seems to think that we're his entertainment or something."

"Which fellow?" asked Sarah who had her back to the bar.

"Don't look now but it's the guy directly behind you. The muscular one with the shaved head and the tatoos on the arms and neck."

Kiana whispered needlessly as the surf modified the sound, "He's been eyeing us all evening. I was just ignoring him. Look at him! He's staring harder than ever now!"

"I'm going to go and have a chat with him, see what his problem is," I stated as I rose from my seat.

Sarah said, "Do you think you ought to?"

"Don't worry, I can take care of myself. Lounge lizards like that don't deserve to ride roughshod over everyone else."

"He looks more like a lounge rat to me," laughed Kiana as she attempted to elevate her mood with a little levity.

"Please be careful," pleaded Sarah.

"I will," I promised over my shoulder as I walked over to the man at the bar.

"You've been staring at us ever since we got here. You got a problem?" I asked evenly.

"You got the problem, Jerk!" he barked in reply.

"Looks like we've got some talking to do, Butthead!"

"Who you callin' a Butthead?"

"If the moniker fits . . . "

"Who you callin' a monkey?" he said menacingly as he rose and started toward me.

"Let's just calm down and talk about it, shall we?" I said. His companion turned around to look at me. He was a prize piece of work as well.

"Suits me just fine, pal. Why don't we step outside over there?" He said as he pointed to another area of the lanai which ran around the corner, out of sight of the one we were on. I thought he might have a change of heart and perhaps would only want to talk to save face. If not, I felt that I could take care of him with no problem.

I turned and went back to the women and said, "I'll be right back. We're going to have a talk about this."

Sarah said, "Be careful!"

"It's him!"

"Who's him?"

"The fellow who fixed my flat. The one that had his back to us. He's the guy that fixed my flat for me. I recognized him when he turned around."

"You sure?"

"I'm sure. A face like that you don't forget," Kiana emphatically stated.

"I'll talk to Beavis later."

Kiana turned to Sarah and questioned, "Beavis?" Sarah shrugged.

I turned and followed Butthead across the lanai while his companion stayed seated at the bar. However, as soon as we stepped out of the line of sight of the restaurant he quickly turned and sucker-punched me once on the jaw. He lined up his second fist for another quick shot at my head. I caught this one before it even got close. I grabbed his clenched fist in mine and squeezed till he winced in pain and let out a little yelp. He struggled loose from my grip, backed off and came at me again with his fists raised. I assumed a boxing stance as he rushed me. Just as he neared, I jumped to my left to avoid his leading fist, landing on my left foot. I leaned far to my left. With my right foot, I kicked him in his gut as his momentum carried him forward, his fist flailing the air, missing me completely. He grunted. I lowered my right leg as I recoiled from my kick. He turned his body back to me in surprise. I pivoted on my right foot, hitting him on his right knee with my left foot as he moved backwards. I grabbed his extended right arm with my right hand and leaned on it, hyper-extending it and forcing him into submission. He cried out in pain.

A moment later, it felt like the whole world came crashing down on me as I was ambushed by his buddy, Beavis, who tackled me from the rear, pushing both of us to the deck. I heard a slight popping noise come from Butthead's elbow as I fell on top of him when we went down. With my arms pinned down by my attacker from the rear, I was cushioned on the front by Butthead as we went down. We landed heavily. I rolled over to try to shake loose my new adversary but he held on tightly, pinning my arms at my sides.

Meanwhile, Butthead decided to have another go at me as he got free while holding his right arm. He backed away then came at me like a football punter with my crotch as the tee. I can remember thinking, oh, this is going to hurt! But at the last second as I still lay pinned from behind on my back, I deflected his extended right boot to the outside with my left foot. With my right foot, I caught him squarely in his crotch and kicked upward hard, letting his momentum carry him forward, up and over the balcony railing. I heard Butthead's anguished scream as his tortured body arced over the railing, sailed through the air high above the central courtyard and went crashing through the glass skylight onto the jewellery displays below. Sounds of glass skylight shattering were followed by the sounds of glass display cases exploding, jewellery being jangled, display cases being flattened and customers shrieking in fright at this sudden intrusion from above.

By this time I felt as if my lungs were going to explode from lack of oxygen as Beavis continued the bear-hugging pressure on me. I kicked at his shin with my heel and slashed at his thigh with my hand causing him to relax his grip slightly. I gasped and sucked in a deep breath of air and clasped my hands together, forcing my elbows outwards. Breaking his grip, I exhaled and slid downwards, rolled and scrambled to my feet.

By now other diners and waiters had come around the corner and were agape at the sight. Beavis, meanwhile, had got to his feet and hightailed it. I ran after him, my footsteps thundering behind his on the plank deck. As he heard me gaining on him, he jumped up on the railing near one end of the open courtyard and leapt across the chasm, landing with a bang onto a narrow metal roof covering a suspended walkway that joined the complex to the lookout tower. He got to his feet and in a half crouch, skittered sideways like a crab along the metal roof. I followed him across the chasm, landing lightly on my feet as I hit the metal roof with barely a clang. I ran along the ribbed metal roof like a halfback football player through the practice tires.

Meanwhile, Beavis got to the bell-tower where he started to climb the square wooden support post to gain some higher ground. He had his arm draped over the railing as I came up behind him and grabbed his foot. He gave a mighty kick backwards, breaking my grasp. Doing a Texas roll over the rail, he fell heavily onto the fourth-floor bell-tower lookout deck. I fairly flew up behind him and vaulted over the railing. He threw a punch at me through the dimness which glanced off my cheek as I completed my vault. He grabbed my neck with his hands and squeezed his thumbs into my throat. I clasped my hands together and brought them up between his arms and pushed outwards to break his hold on my neck. I grabbed him by the neck, pushing his head into a ship's brass bell hanging from a beam and began to ring his noggin with the roped bell clapper giving off muffled gongs each time it hit his head. He twisted around, breaking my hold on him. The brass bell swung wildly, continuing to clang each time the clapper hit the side. Coming at me again, he went for my throat and pushed me backwards across the railing.

I caught a glimpse of the ground some four stories below where people had gathered in a crowd, edging closer for a better look, peering up at us high above them as if this was fight night and they were ringside. I would not be a pretty sight after a fall from that distance. Hearing the railing creak as it bent and strained to hold our combined weights, I prayed that it wouldn't let go. If we both fell, Beavis would likely land on top of me causing my demise.

My world was starting to go black again as I gasped for air. With the last of my strength, I brought my knee up into his crotch. He gave a loud, animal grunt and backed off to the other side of the small lookout. He doubled over with pain as I struggled to get my breath and my balance. With a bellow, he came at me in a full rage like a wrestler on steroids intending to take both of us through the railing to the ground far below us. The split second before he reached me, I ducked down, hit him low on his legs with my shoulder, causing him to go sailing horizontally over the railing. Seconds later, his body came to a thudding halt four stories down. Panting from exertion, I pulled myself up to the railing and peered over into the gloom below. He was spread-eagled, his bald head gleaming in the anthurium flower bed at the foot of the tower. This was a unique variation on pushing up daisies. This was Hawaii after all!

As I leaned over the railing looking at the scene below, the green cast-iron, courtyard clock sounded ten gongs signaling 10 p.m. He didn't rise before the ten-count so I figured I won by a knock out but by the time I got down the stairs, both men had fled.

Who were these guys? I wondered. And what were they after?

CHAPTER SEVENTEEN

THE CHIEF

KAILUA-KONA, THE BIG ISLAND OF HAWAII. I could hear the gurgling jets of the hot tub down by the pool as I sat on my lanai enjoying the stillness of the morning. I was nursing a cup of coffee and myself as I checked my body over again after last night's fracas. Other than bruising and a lot of soreness, I had come away rather unscathed. No broken bones. My chin was bruised and my rib cage creaked. My neck felt raw from being choked. My muscles took the brunt of the punishment and screamed out in protest as I tried to stretch them; I had hobbled around when I got out of bed. I felt like hell!

Doing some stretching exercises, I planned my day, the plans being contingent upon me being relatively mobile. I thought I would go out to the Kealakekua Bay road where Kiana and her Dad had their accident and have a look around. Giving up on the exercises for the time being, I decided that a spell in the hot tub would help to relax me to the point where I could effectively limber up.

I padded over to my bedroom, threw on a pair of swim trunks, grabbed my beach towel and my coffee then went down to the pool grounds. Thankfully, the pool was still empty save for a few lap-swimmers. I found the hot tub over in the corner of the gardens, took a stimulating cold shower then eased myself into the soothing bubbles. I played a water jet over my aching muscles one after the other. Parking myself on the bench between the jets, I slid down, leaving my head above the water. I lay there collecting my thoughts, luxuriating in my rejuvenating condition.

I heard the pool gate creak open and glanced through the tropical shrubbery toward it. A tall, lithesome blonde in a black bikini swivelled her way over to a recliner, set her book and her coffee down on a table and dove into the pool with practiced ease. She was a soothing sight for my sore eyes. The gate creaked open again. This time a tall, dark-skinned handsome Hawaiian man of some bulk came through it and made his way over toward me.

"Good morning!" I said, wishing that he was the blonde femme fatale in the bikini instead.

"Mornin'!" he gruffly replied as he set his cup of coffee down on the ledge of the hot tub. "Looks like another beautiful day."

"Sure does," I agreed. I noted that his bulk was made up of muscle rather than body fat. He wore his coal-black hair in a brush cut but sported a defiant thick lock of shoulder-length hair tied into a ponytail at the back of his head. It gave him a mean presence. But it wasn't this that triggered my memory. It was his voice! Somewhere in the back recesses of my brain his voice triggered something that said that I knew this fellow once, knew him almost like a long-lost brother. "I don't mean to intrude but by any chance were you in Central America a number of years ago?"

"Uh, yeah, actually I was in Central America some time ago," he replied. "I was in the military. Served some time there." He cocked his head toward me and studied my face. "You know, you look like someone I used to know there!"

"You the Chief?" I asked.

"Yeah! You Rune?"

"Yeah!"

"Well I'll be a monkey's uncle!" he declared as he laughed. "I've often thought back to those days over there. I never thought I'd see you again! My name's Kimo, Kimo Kekuna!"

"Small world, Rune Erikson," I said as we shook hands then gave that up as we gave each other a bear hug.

"Ooh, not so hard," I complained, "my ribs are too damn sore this morning."

"What happened?"

"Got into a little scuffle last night with a couple of tough guys."

"Oh!" Kimo said with concern. "You look okay though, 'cept for that bruise on your chin! Oh, and your neck too!"

"Yeah, I was fortunate that there were only two of them."

"Where did it happen?"

"At a restaurant-bar in the complex just down the beach a bit - the Blue Lagoon, I think it's called. One of them was staring at my girlfriend, Sarah, and her friend as we had dinner last night. Come to think of it, there was a little more than what met the eye about that pair of toughs."

"How'd they fare?"

"One guy went down through a skylight to do a little jewellery shopping."

"Yeah? And the other guy?"

"He got his bell rung then went straight down four floors for the ten-count!"

"Ooh!" Kimo said as he winced.

"So, hey, Chief! The last time we worked together was in Panama. That was a hell of an operation!" I said.

"Yeah, and before that, Nicaragua."

"One thing about that for me was that I was in and out of there fairly fast each time but you, you had to stay the course there. I didn't envy you one bit. If the local bad-asses weren't gunning for you and enough of a worry, the lowland diseases would provide plenty of problems."

"Tell me about it. I picked up malaria in Panama. Too much time spent in the swampy boondocks. Damn bug! Comes and goes when it pleases. I guess there's worse things to get these days, though, huh!"

"Whatever happened to that kid that was in your unit?"

"Which one?"

"The one that was always getting into one jam after another and you guys had to bail him out. What was his name? You know the one I mean. The little redheaded kid with freckles."

"You mean Corky?"

"Yeah, Corky. That's it! The Irish kid!"

"He came over to the Middle East with me in the Desert Storm operation but since I retired I haven't heard from him for a couple years. We used to correspond now and then. Yeah, he was a real mischievous kid. Always gettin' into trouble of one sort or another!"

"How'd he come by his nickname? Was it from the place in Ireland?"

"Corky? Naw, forgot to take his gun-barrel cover off one time. Damn near blew him and the cover to smithereens! We kidded him about him trying to use it as a popgun, you know the kind kids have with the cork on a string?"

"Yeah. I can just see it now!" I said with a chuckle.

"Yeah, Corky. Quite the lad! Remember the time we were in that dive in Panama? All the boys were there. We were puttin' back a few cold ones and Corky, he gets the hots for this one babe at the end of the bar?"

"Oh, yeah! What happened? I remember something about him hotfooting it through the door or something."

"Yeah, he got the hots for this latin babe. She was all dolled up and all, showin' a lot of leg and a hint of cleavage and battin' her long eyelashes at the little guy and all. Anyway, the way I remember it,

Corky goes up to her and makes the pitch. Turns out she's really a hooker and wants to get paid to do what Corky is hopin' to get for free. Now Corky isn't thinking straight, cause he's all hot and bothered and now he's got a one-track mind. Corky comes back to the table cause he's come up a little short, in the finances, I mean. So we all throw a couple bills into the pot for Corky as we can see he's chompin' at the bit, all ready to have a go. He goes back to her and she seductively leads him into the back room.

"Meanwhile, we're all makin' bets on how long he's goin' to be in there with her. Well, the pot got to be quite large in a hurry as everybody wanted in. We were all second-guessing Corky's staying power.

"The next thing we heard was a loud shout 'Hey! Come back here!' It was a man's voice.

"Out comes a frantic, wide-eyed Corky from the back room at a dead run right past our table. He's got his tee-shirt in one hand while trying to hold up his pants and in the other hand, in his fist, was the wad of bills which he threw down on the table as he whipped past us and out the door. As he cleared the threshold he turns his bugeyed head to look back over his shoulder and shouts 'she's a he!'"

Kimo gave a long lusty laugh over this recollection.

"Yeah, I'd forgotten about that," I laughed. "What a shock!"

"Yeah, we never let him forget about that either!" Kimo said while he ran his fingers through the stubble of his brush-cut to the back where his ponytail started as he thought back to those good old times gone by.

"What's with the pony tail?" I asked as I took a sip of coffee. "That's something new."

"Just part of the package now. It keeps the young bucks from taking a run at me to get a rep. It seems to intimidate them. I was a challenge to them before. I got tired of teaching them lessons one after the other. Now they just leave me alone. They don't know what in hell to make of it!"

I chuckled then thought of this guy's sixth-degree black belt in Tae Kwon Do karate. He came by his nickname honestly as he indeed was a chief at one time. There was a time he was the chief of a U.S. Navy SEALS special operations craft in Central America. Even though he moved up the ranks the name stuck. There was also some talk at the time that he actually was a Hawaiian chief, none of it confirmed though.

"Did you stay in Central America long?"

"Not too long. I was Commander, U.S. Navy SEALS, special operations, Central America for two years there after you left. Then I got transferred to the Middle East to head a special SEAL unit in the Desert Storm operation. Did some instructing after that, got bored and then took early retirement. How about you?" Kimo asked. "You still operating?"

"Oh, no! Well, mostly no anyway."

"What do you mean?"

"Like you, I took an early retirement. Couldn't see much sense in staying on. The politics were getting to me. So I moved out to the coast, to Victoria on Vancouver Island, where a guy's got some breathing space and a sea to sail in. I live aboard the *Valhalla*. She's a 65-foot ketch. A really classic wooden sailing ship. Got her tied up at Fisherman's wharf in the Inner Harbour there. You ever been to Victoria?"

"Yeah, had shore leave there once. Had a real good time. Real pretty place."

"You living here?"

"Yeah. I bought a condo here. This place has got everything that I'll ever need or want. I can just pack up and go on a moment's notice if I feel the urge. The pool is real nice and the hot tub comes in handy. You staying here?"

"Yeah, I'm here for a while. I got a couple things I'm looking into."

"Do any of those things involve the administration?"

"Well, yeah, one of them does."

"I thought you said you were retired!" Kimo admonished.

"I was. I am. Well, they forced this one on me. Reactivated me. They had to use a little coercion but they're really good at that."

"I know what you mean. You think you're all done with that horseshit but sometimes they have a way of playing underhanded, playing dirty pool. If only John Q. Public knew exactly the way things operated!"

"Oh, well! Such is life! So what have you got planned for today?"

"Not too much. Got some laundry to do, a few things to pick up at the supermarket. Why?"

"Really laid-back stuff now, eh Chief?"

"Well, some things you just got to get done cause they're not going to do themselves!"

"Isn't that the truth? Anyway, I was going to go over to Kealakekua

Bay and check out an accident site. The place where Sarah's friend - Kiana is her name - and her Dad hit a tree. It's a really strange one, so they say. Why don't you come along? You can show me the way."

"Sure, I can also show you some sights and talk about old times."

Kimo and I swung southwards onto Ali'i Drive. It was a glorious morning as we followed the beach road and dodged surfboard-laden youths on the roadside. Dazzling White Sands Beach was just starting to come alive as teens with boom cars started jockeying for road parking to set up their center of activity.

"What's the attraction here?" I asked.

"White Sands? Well, the girls, naturally. The guys all come here because of the girls."

"And the girls?"

"The guys, naturally!" Kimo said as he laughed heartily. "It's also called Magic Sands or Disappearing Sands Beach."

"Why do they call it that?"

"Because come November all the way through April, the beach loses its sand to high surf but the sand comes back in the spring. Actually it's a good body-boarding spot for the more experienced boarders. It's also a good spot for shore-diving a few hundred feet south. There are some caverns and lava tubes to explore underwater."

We came to Keahou then turned the Jeep up Kamehameha II Road to get onto the Hawaii Belt Road.

"This slope is riddled with old lava tubes that run downslope for some distance, like worm holes in old woodwork, only much larger. You could drive a bus through some of them!"

"Really!" I said as we turned right onto Highway 11. It wasn't long before we came to the turn-off at Captain Cook. The road down to Kealakekua Bay was called Napo 'opo 'o Road. Try saying either of those two names really fast from memory! I thought.

The land fell away on the right giving us the eerie feeling that we were in a small aircraft coming in for a landing on a strip thousands of feet below us were it not for the tight turns that the road took every so often. "Count the turns," I asked as I kept my attention on the steep, curving road. "It should be just up ahead. Two large trees on the right on the curve to the left and a third large tree just beyond that with some red paint scrapes and gashes on it."

"This looks like it up ahead," said Kimo. "Yeah, there it is!" he added as he pointed down the country road.

It was a bad corner. Three trees and no barricades. I pulled over to the right and parked just short of the curve so as to be seen by traffic from either direction but yet not cover too much of the accident site itself. There wasn't any shoulder but the view was spectacular.

Kimo and I got out of the Jeep and walked down the road to the third tree. In the glaring light of the day it was difficult to see how such an accident could have occurred. But there it was, scarred tree, red paint and all.

"What do you figure?" I asked Kimo after I outlined the accident as it had been related to me - the flat tire beforehand that delayed them until nightfall, the headlights that suddenly appeared on the corner, the impact that never happened, the long slide into the tree, the voices heard before help arrived and the run-in with Butthead and his buddy Beavis, the flat-tire changer.

"Don't know. It's a puzzler at first glance."

I saw something glint in the weeds in the ditch, bent down and picked it up. "Piece of a car's outside mirror," I explained.

"Got something to put it in?" asked Kimo. "Might see if it'll match up to her car later."

"Yeah, there's a discarded cigarette pack over there. I'll put it in that. That's two pieces to consider."

"Yeah, let's see if there's anything else lying around."

"Okay. I'll start beating the grass from this side."

Despite checking thoroughly, there wasn't much to find, save for a few pieces of chrome strip and some tear-strips off first-aid supplies that we assumed the paramedic attendants had used at the scene. There was a hubcap in the ditch farther down the road that likely came off Kiana's car. We would check those out later too.

"Not much to go on," I said, "why don't we walk back up the road and see if we can visualize what happened at the time to cause this?"

"Sure, that may give us some ideas." The breeze wafted the sweet scents up the steep slope from the produce farms far below us. The sun started to beat down upon us with the warm rays of midmorning. A half-block up we turned around and stared back down the paved road, eyeing the layout of the road, its slope and the position of the trees.

"Okay, let's assume that she's driving down the road in the right lane," I stated. We started walking slowly back down. "Okay, here's where she first sees lights ahead if she's traveling at a moderate speed as she says she was. Then here is where her reaction time is used up before she hits the brakes."

"Here is where the brakes took hold. See the marks? Fairly straight," added the Chief.

"Then she takes evasive action as the car comes directly toward her. She has a choice. Left or right. Right goes directly over the cliff and down the slope. She turned left. Good choice!" I said.

"I'll bet if she had turned to the right the car would have rolled for thousands of feet down this steep slope," exclaimed the Chief as he gazed at the village of Kealakekua Bay in miniature far below us.

"That's for sure. It would have been nothing but a blazing fireball. No one would have survived that!" I declared. "If she would have been driving on that temporary tire, it may have thrown the car off the cliff to the right when she first hit the brakes in a panic. She may not have even had a chance to crank it to the left under those circumstances."

"Good thing she had that flat looked at and put back on," said Kimo. "Okay, here is where she cranked the wheel over to the left but instead of trying to drive around the oncoming car she continued to turn left. Why would she do that?"

I said, "She told me that the other car swerved back into its proper lane just as she was steering into it as well."

"So why wasn't there an impact in the lane here if they were to meet each other in the same lane?" asked the Chief.

"That's what she wondered too. She said they had their eyes closed in expectation of the impact but it never occurred here. Instead she opened her eyes a moment later just before they hit that tree broadside."

"Okay. Here are the skid marks from the four-wheel drift. They pretty much cover most of both lanes of the road. There is no way that they could have missed hitting another car if there was one where they said it was!" Kimo incredulously exclaimed. "I hate to say it but it looks like the cops might be right."

"I hope they're wrong, for her sake. She's pretty shook up about this. I don't see her as a liar. It's not in her character from what I know of her. Let's go over this again from the top, okay?"

"You bet, only this time let's concentrate on the other car's position."

"Okay," I agreed as we hiked back up the narrow road. Then turning around I said, "Well, we pretty much agree from her description, which the skid marks seem to verify, that they were driving in the right lane to this point here. Now, for an oncoming vehicle's headlights to show up as coming directly at them from in front, that car would also have to be in this lane as well. So here is where the skid marks start which means that she first saw the oncoming headlights while they were back about there. That takes care of her reaction time."

"Was the other car just parked here in the wrong lane?"

"No, she was adamant that it was moving at about the same rate of speed as they were and the gap between the two vehicles was closing fast."

"The other car was moving toward them?"

"Yes. It doesn't make sense."

"Especially if the other car then swerved back into its rightful lane just as they tried to move around it."

"Yes, that car would have had to have been actually flying at them through the air from out over the edge to have done that!" I exclaimed.

"Exactly! It's impossible. I don't like the look of this thing for her sake."

"There's got to be a logical explanation and I hope it's not her going off the deep end as the cops are suggesting! She's too nice a lady!"

"I'd like to meet this nice lady sometime, Rune."

"Sure, I'll be glad to introduce her to you."

"Promise?"

"Promise," I repeated as I scratched my head trying to figure out this latest puzzling revelation. "So why don't we go off the deep end?"

"What?"

"Why don't we go off the deep end? I mean, let's suppose that there really was a car coming in from out there."

"You crazy, man?"

"No, let's just run with it and see where it leads. Okay, we've already discounted that there could have been another car parked on the curve for two reasons. One is that there would have been a collision because there was no room for there not to be one on this narrow road. Two is that both Kiana and her dad said that the other car was moving toward them about as fast as they were moving."

"So what are we left with?" Kimo asked.

"We're left with a UFO."

"Get serious, man!"

"I'm not suggesting that there was one but it would fit the description and the circumstances," I said.

Kimo pursed his lips and let out a long Twilight Zone whistle then stated, "Man, I can see now why you're retired but the question is: why did they ever rehire you?" he chuckled.

"Just play along with me on this one, will you?"

"O . . . kaay." Kimo said apprehensively.

"Let's say that there really was something out there."

"There's . . . some . . . thing . . . out . . . there!" he laughed as he mocked me.

"Okay, birdbrain, visualize this! Let's just say that there is an oncoming car. What path would it have to take to do what they said it did?"

"The path from outer space? Sorry, I just couldn't resist." I gave him a pained look.

"Yeah, the path."

"Why, the path would roughly have to be directly from out there in the air just above the slope then run toward us between those first two trees on the curve."

"And onto this lane on the road, right?" I asked.

"Right."

"So . . . "

"So, it's a UFO, right?" Kimo asked with a grin.

"So . . . let's take a look along that path," I said as I ignored him this time.

"For scorch marks, right?" he said.

I shot him an exasperated look.

He said, "Just kidding."

We walked off the pavement and examined the area between the first two trees. It was clean. Not even a scorch mark. "Hmm!" I said. "Let's see what's on the other side of these trees, on the slope." We went around and jumped some three feet down the steep incline. Here the short grass showed some marks as though it had been trampled upon at some point recently.

"Hey, here are some cigarette butts near the base of these two trees." Kimo bent down and examined the butts. "All the same brand."

"One person? Hmm. What would cause a person to spend this amount of time in one spot where they would need to smoke . . . how many butts are there?"

"Three."

"Even if he was chain smoking, that's a half hour anyway, maybe an hour if he wasn't. Do some butts look older than the others?" I asked,

"Naw, they all look about the same."

"Anything else here?"

"Not that I can see. Let's have another look though. Wait a minute. Here's a half-smoked stogie." Kimo bent down and picked it up to examine it. "Cigar band says it's a Sancho Panza, Habana, Cuba. Now what the hell is a Cuban cigar doin' in the good ole U.S. of A.? The embargo is still on!"

I peered at the brown wrapper with the white printing. Sure enough! "Hmm! Cuban cigars turning up all over the place!" I mused out loud.

"What?" Kimo asked.

"Cuban cigars are turning up all over the place. ORCA, SSEAAL, now here."

"Connection?"

"Not sure yet, but it's damn suspicious that anyone would throw away a half of an expensive cigar like this. Cuban or not Cuban!"

"Look, here is an older set of slide marks from somebody jumping down over the edge like we did," Kimo stated as he walked over to the side.

"As in two somebodies?"

"Looks like it," agreed Kimo as he kept beating back the low grass. "This is odd!" he said as he squatted down and peered intently between the two trees. "A perfectly round hole filled with rain water. Something rested here. Left an impression an inch deep. Wonder what could have caused that?" he asked as he examined the hole further. "There seems to be something at the bottom of the hole."

Kimo got down on his knees and worked at an object with his index finger. "Why, it's a rubber cap, like from the tip of a cane. It got pulled off whatever it was attached to."

"A cane? That's really odd. Now what do you suppose two smokers with a cane were doing here?" I asked.

Kimo examined it, twirling it around in his fingers. "If it was a cane," he stated, "it was a new cane."

"Why do you say that?"

"No signs of wear on the bottom."

"Let's see that. Hmm. Not very thick either. Most cane tips are quite thick. This looks familiar though. I've seen this part before. I know I have! It belongs to something that I've got on my boat."

"A boat part? Naw, it's too flimsy. It looks like it's an end cap protector for something, perhaps a piece of tubing or something like that. Well . . . maybe a boat part . . . an end cap for a pike pole perhaps."

"Not a boat part. It's something that I've got on board, something that I use but only very occasionally."

"Maybe for a support pole, like for a sun awning or a rain-catcher apparatus, so you could project it like a telescope and hold something outwards."

"Projector! That's it!"

"It's a projector?" Kimo asked incredulously.

"No! It's for a projector screen. It looks like the end cap for the support pole for my old projector screen. I don't use it much anymore but I've carted that thing around enough times to remember that end cap because it sometimes worked loose. That's why it seemed so familiar."

"You think so? Now why would anybody have a projector screen way out here?"

"Good question, Chief."

"To run a film showing a car hurtling toward them? Naw, I don't think so. Not realistic enough."

"It was dark, remember? All you need would be a pair of headlights to show."

"Naw, even so . . . "

"Maybe they used a set of roll-bar headlights from a four-wheel drive."

"You gotta have power."

"Portable battery."

"Yeah, maybe."

"Kiana said that the headlights were moving toward them as fast as they were and as she spun the wheel to the left, the other pair of headlights swung toward them as if they were mirroring their movements."

"That's it!" shouted Kimo. "That's it!"

"That's what?" I asked.

"You just said it . . . mirror!"

"Mirror?"

"Yes, mirror! There were two guys here holding a mirror. Kiana saw her own car's headlights being reflected in a mirror."

"But the headlights veered off just as she turned off."

"Right. A mirror image. The projector screen pole held up a mirror!"

"Could be, or . . . how about the projector screen pole held up a screen?"

"A screen?"

"Yes, a screen. A role of film, Mylar reflective film!"

"Of course! But the reflection would be somewhat distorted, wouldn't it?"

"Kiana did say that the lights were wavy and sort of slid over, like in a dream."

"Then that's it! That's what happened! Or something similar to that. That would explain a lot of things!"

"Yeah, it's a bit of a stretch but that would explain it. If that's what really happened then somebody was out to murder them. It wasn't an accident at all. Who would want to murder them? She's a schoolteacher, he's just an old man!"

"I don't like the looks of where this thing is going!" declared Kimo as he spat in disgust.

"Nor I!"

"But assuming that this is what happened, how would these two guys down there know when a particular car was coming down the road?" he asked.

"Probably a lookout at the top at the turnoff knew they'd be along or someone was tailing them. Could have used hand-held radios to communicate to each other. As soon as they got the word, they would watch then raise the Mylar roll up at the last second to catch her headlights, making it appear that a car was suddenly coming right at them."

"That would explain the discarding of the expensive stogie."

"Yeah, cast aside quickly to get ready to run the roll of Mylar film up the pole."

"And then hide behind the trees in the unlikely case she drove straight into the lights and between the trees. There's enough room between the trees for her car to have gone hurtling over the edge."

"Or if the car had skidded to the right because it had on a temporary tire on the right front!" I added.

"Then they would grab the reflective film, roll it up, pack up the pole and just walk away."

"She did say that she thought she heard voices well before the first car came down the road and stopped to give them first aid," I said.

"But how would they know they'd be coming up the highway in the first place?"

"Remember the coincidental flat tire that caused them to return after it got dark?" I asked. "Maybe it was not so coincidental after all! Maybe they've been under surveillance! One of the Bozos that I got into a fight with was the guy who changed the flat for Kiana."

"They may have been under surveillance. That may just be! You know? I think I read something years ago, I think it was just a story though, about someone causing an accident like this but I've never seen nor heard anyone actually doing this, if that's how it was done!"

"Who knows?" I said.

"Man, this was a beautiful morning! Now it just got ugly!" Kimo stated as he spat as if trying to get a bad taste out of his mouth.

CHAPTER EIGHTEEN

SHERIFF JIM

KONA, THE BIG ISLAND OF HAWAII. The ride back was somber. Both of us were lost in our own thoughts, trying to come to terms with what we suspected but couldn't prove.

Kimo spoke up first. "Why don't we stop by the police station and see the sheriff? He's a friend of mine."

"You think that'll help at this point, Chief?" I asked dejectedly.

"Yeah, I think it might. He's got an open mind. At least it may stave off the hounds for a while as far as Kiana is concerned."

"Okay. Sounds like a plan."

"We'll turn off onto the Kuakini highway this time. It's faster than going back the way we came out."

"Sheriff Paoluana, this is Rune - a good friend of mine from way back," Kimo said as he introduced me. "We both worked together in Central America a number of years ago. Rune, Sheriff Paoluana."

"Rune Erikson, pleased to meet you, Sheriff Paoluana," I said.

"Call me Jim," said the sheriff who obligingly ushered us into his rather utilitarian office in Kailua. "Where you from?" he asked.

"Canada, from Victoria on Vancouver Island."

"Oh, yeah! British Columbia. Real nice country out there. I was at a police convention in Vancouver a couple years ago. Didn't get a chance to get out to the island though. Next time for sure! I hear the fishing is real good. So what can I do for you guys today?" the Sheriff asked as he motioned us into chairs.

"Jim, I been helping out Rune here who is just looking out for a friend of his girlfriend's," stated Kimo. "And what we come up with has been a real puzzler, in fact, it's raised more questions than we started out with, though we think we've solved a few."

"Sounds intriguing. What's this all about?" asked the Sheriff.

"Well, you tell him, Rune."

"First of all Jim, I don't want you to think that we're here to influence or sway you or your investigation in any way. All we're doing is trying to help someone out who desperately needs our help,"

I cautiously said.

"Which investigation?"

"The accident up above Kealakekua Bay. The one involving the young lady, the red car and the tree."

"Oh yeah! Kiana Kilolani and her dad. At the moment the investigation is still open. But quite frankly, we're going nowhere fast on that one. It's a different one, all right. Not the accident. The explanation. Accidents like that happen all the time. Speed, darkness, lack of experience on the part of the driver, there's lots of reasons. People make stories up all the time too. They say, 'Car came out of nowhere and disappeared.' We get those excuses regularly. It's real easy to see through their stories in short order. Things don't add up, story changes, the people involved can't keep their stories straight, the physical evidence says otherwise or their faces give their lies away."

"Well that's just it. Kiana is pretty shook up about the allegations," I interjected.

"Don't worry about it. Standard police investigation techniques. For a while there we had to act on information that she may have just imagined it and really believed what she thought she saw. There was an incident earlier on a field trip where she was supposed to have seen or heard something near the heiau on Keahole Point which may or may not have happened. We suggest things to people to see how they react and stand up. A litmus test, if you will. So far we haven't been able to shake any of her story or her dad's for that matter. But there's no physical evidence to back up her story. That's the problem!"

"That's why we're here. We were just up there to have a look around."

"Yeah," Kimo interjected, "we found a few pieces of evidence and have a theory that just might fit in with her story."

We apprised the sheriff of the details as they evolved - the flat tire, the tire changer, the surveillance at the restaurant, the shard of broken mirror, the cigarette butts, the significance of the discarded, half-smoked expensive stogie, the crumpled grass on the slope and the rubber tip found in a small round depression in the ground between the trees.

He sat back in his chair, put his hands behind his head and listened. Every now and then he would unclasp his hands and lunge forward as he asked a question or clarified a point we made.

"Hmm!" the sheriff said as he rubbed his chin when we were finished. "It all seems to fit. But who would go to this much trouble to knock off a schoolteacher and an old man?"

"Good question but I don't have an answer for that," I replied.

"I'll get my deputy working on this new angle. In the meantime, if you guys come up with any other suggestions, let us know. I'll likely see Kiana later this afternoon and allay some of her fears."

We grabbed a bite to eat at a Chinese food joint just across Ali'i Drive from the beach. The decor was early fifties but the food was good and the prices were reasonable. The packed house attested to that. I stared out at the sea and the hustle and bustle around the Kailua pier. Tour boats came and went, snorkelers explored the sea life amidst the coral. Tiny, the big Hawaiian reveled in the surf with his little dog Brutus. Down the street the kite guy plied his colourful wares. Meanwhile, Cap, the old artist under the spreading shade tree, put paint to canvas in yet another splendid rendition of a local marine life seascape of dolphins exploding out of breaking surf.

I was trying to plot our next course. There wasn't much we could do at this point. It was in the hands of the Sheriff and his deputies. Then I thought about Kiana's dad still in the hospital.

"Hey, Chief. How would you like to meet Kiana?"

"Sure! When?"

"This afternoon. I'll phone her and see if she's going take some time off work and visit her dad at the hospital. We can let Kiana know what we came up with and see if her Dad has any more recollections from that night."

"I'd like that!" Kimo said.

"I'll call her now."

The hospital waiting room was like all hospital waiting rooms everywhere. There were a few groups of people anxiously clustered together, some solitary ones with pinched faces, the odd one bored with the now-routine process of waiting for interminable lengths of time suggesting a daily visitor to a long-stay patient. We were early for visiting hours. I edged over from my seat beside Kimo and picked at a haphazard pile of dog-eared magazines from a coffee table in front of the lady sitting near me.

"Excuse me," I said, "I've got to read something to pass the time."

"I know what you mean. I've been taking time off work to come here every day for some time. It gets so that your mind becomes numb just sitting here waiting. But the waiting will be over any day now.

He's coming home soon, my son is. He's much better. It was such a terrible thing that happened!"

"Do you mind me asking what that was?"

"Why the explosion, of course, everybody knows about it! It was in the paper and on TV and all."

"The explosion just offshore at Keahole Point?"

"Yes! Billy's friend . . . Billy's my son . . . Billy's friend Mike and I were there too. We weren't hurt like Billy was. We just got some scratches and bruises. But Billy's got broken bones. He took such an awful hit when he landed. His surfboard shattered from the impact but it shielded him. It's a miracle he survived at all! I believe that the gods were looking after him."

"Landed?"

"On the beach. He was on his surfboard in the water and he got blasted into the air and onto the beach. It was such a horrendous force! We were more fortunate. We just rolled up the beach with the force of it all.

"Billy lost his father a while back in a diving accident at work. He was a fine man, my husband was. We sure miss him a lot. The pain is unbearable most times," she said sadly as she blinked a tear back.

"I'm sure sorry to hear that," I said.

"Thanks, they say the pain will eventually go away but . . ."

She didn't continue. I gently asked, "Do you think we could talk to your son?"

"Sure, I don't see why not. It's really close to visiting hours. I'm sure they won't mind at all." She got up and beckoned to us to follow.

I said to Kimo, "I'll only take a few minutes." We followed Billy's mom down the antiseptic-smelling corridor. She walked into a four-bed ward where a young lad was idly flipping through a surfing magazine.

"Hi Billy, how are you feeling?" she asked, her voice softening.

"I'm bored Mom. When can I go home? Can't you tell them that I'll be okay?"

"I'll ask the doctor later, Billy. These gentlemen wanted to see you, to see how you are. I was telling them in the waiting room all about the explosion."

"Hi," he said disinterestedly.

"Hi Billy, my name is Rune and this is the Chief, uh, Kimo."

Billy replied dubiously, "Are you really a chief?"

"Uh, yeah, actually I am," Kimo answered hesitantly.

"Wow! Cool!" Billy gushed then looked at his mom. "He's really a chief, Mom!"

"That's nice. I'm Marsha, by the way." We nodded our heads in unison.

"Sorry about your accident," I said, "I'll bet that it was a terrifying experience."

"Naw, it wasn't terrifying. It all happened so fast there wasn't much time to be scared."

"I'm amazed that you look so well, especially after all you've been through."

"That's what I keep telling the nurses. I'm ready to go home."

"Anxious to start surfing again?"

"Yeah, can't wait, 'cept Mom says my board's broken," Billy said dejectedly.

"Tell you what Billy, here's a down payment on a new board for you," I said as I pulled out a few bills out of my pocket.

"Gee, thanks," he replied as his eyes brightened considerably. "I'll add this to my money I got saved up from my paper route."

I said to both of them, "I gather the explosion was quite a sight. What did it look like?" They took turns explaining exactly what they saw and felt in those critical few seconds before and after the force erupted. It didn't give me a whole lot of new information, just a new perspective from that location to go with what I had already read in intelligence reports and newspaper accounts of some of the other victims. The dive-boat survivor's anecdotes were similar to theirs. They had already returned home to Wisconsin. The pilots who had observed it from the air had described the scene much as the others had, albeit from a lot farther away. There was one thing for sure, something of cataclysmic proportions occurred out there.

Thanking Billy and his Mom, we left them and said that we would see them again sometime.

We returned to the waiting room just in time to see Kiana come through the main door. I greeted her and steered her into the waiting room, then introduced her to the Chief. His mood brightened considerably because of her presence.

"Kiana, Kiana," Kimo said thoughtfully, "I used to know a girl named Kiana in grade school when we lived on a small farm higher up on Puuhonua Road."

"That was probably me, only I don't remember you."

"There was a small schoolhouse down in Kealakekua Bay that we attended."

"Yes, that's right. There was one."

"I think you were just starting school at the time. I was a bit older and was only there for the one year. We moved around a lot. We moved to Honolulu after that."

"Quite likely that was me then."

"I'm sorry to have to meet you again under these circumstances after all these years but it is a real pleasure to do so. Have you been living here all this time?"

"Pretty much, except for university to get my teaching degree. I love it here in Kona. This is home!"

"I know what you mean. That's the way I feel too."

"How about you. Have you lived in the islands all this time?"

"We stayed in Honolulu after that. I joined the navy to see the world. Then I joined the Navy SEALS and served some time in Central America and the Middle east in Desert Storm. Now I'm back."

"Here on the Big island?"

"Yeah, I got a condo in Kailua."

"Me too but I spend a lot of time in Kealakekua Bay with my parents. Speaking of which it's just about time for us to go and see Dad. My brother is going to bring my mom to see him later."

"Just before we do, I have some new information for you," I said. "We were up to the accident site and found a few things. We talked to the sheriff too. Has he talked to you today yet?"

"No, not yet. Why?" she asked with consternation.

Kimo and I explained what had transpired that morning up at the accident site and what the sheriff had said when we talked to him. You could see some of the tension leave her body when we told her that the sheriff was backing off on his allegations and intimations. Her full lips were not set so thinly, the agonizing grimaces in her face were less frequent.

However, this was short-lived as there was a new worry for her, one which we wanted to minimize but couldn't. If there were someone or some people out to murder her, it was a far more serious matter.

The three of us went to see Kiana's dad. He was sitting up in bed, fluffed pillows supporting his head. He was feeling much better, thank you very much, and wanted to go home. The doctor had come by and had given him encouraging words that he could indeed go home that afternoon once the last of the lab test results confirmed his diagnosis. Unfortunately, he couldn't give us any more details about the accident than we already knew. Kiana filled him in with the details of how we had offered to help them out with having a look at the accident site and with having a chat with the sheriff.

"Thanks for everything," her Dad said to us. "When I get settled in back home, we'll have to have you guys over for a real Hawaiian luau. Why we'll get the old pit all stoked up and ready to go. Roast a pig and a bunch of other things. I can just taste it now!"

"That's really nice of you to do that. I can't wait," I said.

"It's been some time since I was at a luau myself," added Kimo.

"We'll get everyone going on it and I'll get Kiana to give you a call when we're ready. That sound okay?" her dad asked.

"Sounds super to me!" I answered.

"Great!" added the Chief.

"You guys go on," Kiana said. "My brother and I can handle getting Dad home this afternoon. You've both been a great help."

The Chief and I left them there with a promise that we would get together for a luau really soon and to call us in the meantime if we could be of any more help.

CHAPTER NINETEEN

WHEELING AND DEAD DEALING

SSEAAL, KEAHOLE POINT, KONA COAST. The sign on the door said *Dr. Sarah Leikaina, Volcanologist.* I eased the door open without knocking, feeling a twinge of uneasiness at doing so even though earlier she had said to just walk in and feel at home. Anne, the receptionist, said that Sarah had gone to consult with the director and would likely be only a minute or so.

On the drive out I tried to put yesterday's revelation into an analytical thought process. That there was a strong likelihood that somebody was out to murder Kiana, was not in doubt. It was the *why* that had me puzzled. Kimo had offered to be her guardian angel and keep a protective screen around her without causing her to feel like she was under constant surveillance by him. After all, he had over half a dozen years experience in planning and conducting special operations. We thought it was only fair that we ask her permission for him to do so for surreptitiously shadowing her was not morally right and could do irreparable harm to her psyche if she had found out about it. Kiana, however, was receptive to this suggestion, having been mentally strung-out for what was an interminable length of time. She said that she would like to get on with her life and her work. She knew this was impossible at the moment, so she was glad for the support Kimo and I afforded her.

This morning Sarah and I were to start evaluating the SeaTruck, using this as a cover for our real purpose - to find out what caused the cataclysmic explosion just offshore from Keahole Point. I was feeling a few butterflies in my stomach as I came to the realization that I would be diving deeper today than I have ever dove before - in excess of 2,000 feet. I felt a measure of comfort knowing that Sarah would be the sub's pilot. After all, though actually few in number, she had as many deep dives in the SeaTruck to her credit as any other SeaTruck pilot.

"Okay! We're all set!" Sarah said as she came in the door, a sheaf of paper in her hand. "We're going to check out the cold intake pipeline to see how it withstood the explosion."

"It's operating okay isn't it?"

"Yes, but the anchors may have become dislodged or some of the cables from the anchors may have snapped. Only a visual scrutiny will really tell."

"So we're going down 2,000 feet then?"

"That's where the pipeline ends but we may go down farther just to see if anything else is amiss."

We drove over to Manetti Marine at Honokohau Harbour, bringing along our specialized, custom-fitted jump-suits that were made for us in Victoria. I mentally ran over the technical aspects of the submersible so that I wouldn't look like a complete idiot to Sarah once we were actually underway.

It was with some trepidation that we made our way into the showroom where we were waved along toward an office door at the rear corner of the showroom. Manny sat in a high-backed executive chair looking much like a big kid in a high chair were it not for the stub of a lit stogie jammed into the side of his mouth. Blue smoke to match his blue language flowed up over his head. His tiny sandal-shod feet were propped up on his burn-scarred desk. This morning he was wearing a blue floral Hawaiian shirt, white ducks with suspenders and a white Panama hat.

"Look! I'm tellin' ya," the little fat man was saying in couched tones into the phone as we entered. "We gotta get more than that out of this rube. He's loaded! What do you mean, 'How do I know?' It's my business ta know. Had his plates run and his credit checked the minute he drove in. The bastard's loaded, I tell ya! We got a live one! Uh, huh. Uh, huh. Yeah, well upgrade him, show him the best unit we got. Get him hooked on the electronic gadgets. Find out what his weaknesses are . . . well, everybody's got 'em for chrissakes! Then play him on that!"

He looked up at us and motioned Sarah and I into two chairs off to one side of his large office. "Goddamn rookie salesmen," he whispered as he continued holding the phone to his ear and listened, "got ta teach them everything," he said with a wink. Then he refocused his attention on the salesperson on the phone and ordered, "just do it! " He slammed the phone down, took his feet off his desk, stood up to his full height of just over five feet, smiled expansively and with open arms said, "Hi guys!"

"Who were you talking to?" asked Sarah.

"Uh, pardon my language, Ma'am, but I get carried away sometimes in the heat of a sale."

"But who were you talking to?" she asked again.

"My salesman, of course!"

"Where is he?"

"Why, he's in the next office, of course, with a ru . . . uh, a customer tryin' ta close a god . . . a."

"Right next door? And please don't start with your swearing again, okay?" Sarah said as she competed with Manny for the floor.

". . . pardon me, Ma'am . . . a good boat deal when he don't even know how ta ask for a sale and close it. Kids these days. Gotta hold their hands! Why, when I was a young buck there was no way I was walkin' away from a deal. Deals are in my blood. I was born that way!" He moved off to the side of his desk and did a little soft-shoe shuffle, all the while singing;

"I think we gotta live one!

I think we gotta big fish!"

Mannie reared back then leaned forward as if he was on the business end of a fishing rod reeling in a big one in time with the tune he was singing;

"When the deal gets done!

Just think of the commish!"

"Sorry, I get a little carried away. It takes me back ta my younger days when I just started out selling boats." Then turning back to us, he scowled and said, "If that rookie can land him, that is!"

"Now, about the . . . " I started to mention as I saw a little light bulb flick on in Manny's devious brain.

"Glenda!" Manny barked into the intercom, "get in here! Now!" Manny's eyes lit up as he relished putting his idea into play. A crafty little grin spread over his face. He started rubbing the palms of his hands together as if he was molding an idea between them.

"Yes, Manny, uh . . . Mr. Manetti," she said when she saw that he had company. She was smoothing her hair back as she gushed, her speech now softened to a sultry whisper, "what can I do for you?"

"Glenda! Glenda! Glenda! Dear girl! I think the poor boy needs to have his confidence bolstered and his importance in this fine organization measurably raised in front of his fine and rich old client that he is trying to sell a yacht ta."

"That's to whom he is trying to sell a yacht," corrected Sarah.

"To whooom?" Manny asked as he emphasized the vowel by puckering his lips. "Why ta that rich old geezer, that's whom he is trying to sell a yacht ta!" bellowed Manny in response. Sarah rolled her eyes with exasperation.

"But how can I help?" asked Glenda in her cutesy, dimple-cheeked way.

"Just be yourself Glenda, just be yourself!" Manny replied as he fussed with some papers.

"Be myself?" she asked in her gushing voice.

"I want you to knock on the office door that the new kid is in. Say 'excuse me, but Mr. Manetti needs some things done right away.' Then go in and file this paper in the bottom drawer of the filing cabinet that's along the opposite wall. Take your time and make sure that it gets filed correctly. Oh, and do that like you normally do, your filing, that is. Then turn around and ask the kid if he can sign these two pages that I'm goin' to give you. Stand behind the kid and make sure that you lean way over and show the client your . . . uh, I mean the kid where to sign. Oh, and Glenda, you look a little tense, I mean, uh, loosen up a little, will ya?"

"I'm not ten . . . Oh, Mr. Manetti! Shame on you!" Glenda said as a rosy hue spread across her blonde-hair-enshrouded face.

"Here's the papers ta file and here's the papers ta get signed. Now get out there and show them your best stuff . . . uh, impress them!" Manny ordered as he gave her bottom a pat to send her on her way.

"Mr. Manetti!" Sarah admonished once Glenda had left. "Is this how you treat your female staff? That sort of behaviour went out with the dark ages. I can't believe what I just saw and heard!"

"Whaaat?" whined Manny. "She's just part of the sales team. If the kid makes the sale, we all celebrate. I make the profit, the kid gets his commish and our dear young Glenda gets a nice bonus. That's women's equality at its finest! We're what I call an equal opportunity team!" beamed Manny in a grin that went from ear to ear across his wide face.

"Can you believe this?" spluttered a wide-eyed Sarah as she turned to me for moral support. "Can you just believe this?"

Wisely, I just shook my head and shrugged my shoulders. You can bet that I was staying out of this one! It was a no-win situation for me.

"I'm in the moolah!
I'm in the moolah!"

Manny sang as he did a little tap dance in time to his song. It was hard for Sarah to remain indignant and watch this comical little man do his routine.

"Manny, some day I'm going to teach you some, uh, manners," Sarah vowed.

He dropped to his knees, whipped his Panama hat off his head and crossed his hatted hand over his heart and asked with begging brown doggy eyes, "Is that a promise, pretty lady?"

"Well, I suppose if she's not offended. But one of these days I'm going to have a long talk with your Miss Glenda!" Sarah said.

"Ooh, ooh, ooh. Touchy! Touchy!" Manny laughed.

"Okay, Manny, the show is over. We've got to get to work. Is the SeaTruck all ready to go?" I asked.

"Yeah, she's all gassed up and ready ta go! Checked the oil and washed the windshield too!" he replied with an angelic face.

"Washed the windshield?" asked Sarah as she looked quizzically at me. Then, as she saw the grin on my face, she said, "Aw, you guys!"

* * * * *

Just across the marina basin from Manetti Marine there are tidal pools in the folds of black pahoehoe lava at the small secluded beach near the entrance to Honokohau Harbour. As the sun rises in the morning sky, it heats these pools, turning them into warm havens for marine life that live there or may have been trapped there at the last tide change.

This morning the denizens of one particular pool had their routine upset. There was a larger creature that had become lodged there, having floated in belly up on the last tide. The shyer fishes stayed away from the creature, unsure of what to make of it. The bolder, more curious fishes would dart up to it before losing their courage and flash away. However, the crabs were not shy at all. They had breakfast in mind, a veritable feast and plenty for all for days to come. They began to rip and tear little chunks of flesh out of the unmoving creature. Flies smelling rotting flesh, buzzed around looking for a suitable spot to lay their eggs. The creature just lay there floating on its back and heating up as the sun rose. The putrid odour increased with the temperature of the bloating creature until it enveloped the immediate area like a fog.

A fly landed on one of its unseeing eyes and jerkily moved around before depositing its eggs in the fold of the creature's eyelid.

This secluded beach was a favourite with the kids who lived aboard the boats and ships that berthed here at Honokohau Harbour on a semi-permanently basis. It had a few shade trees and excellent snorkeling. The surfing was only passable but it sufficed if there wasn't a ride to a better beach. There were turtles here and plenty of fishes so boredom was seldom a problem.

This beautifully-sunny morning held promise for the two young boys as they got up. They had a hurried breakfast and then went to meet each other by the small marina store before heading over to the beach. They walked up the short dusty road as it rose before cresting the rise where they could see the beach laid out before them. Hillocks of lava rock concealed tidal pools.

Few tourists had any idea that this beach was here, hidden as it was. Most mornings as usual, the two boys would check the tidal pools to see what the tide change had brought. This morning was no different as they peered down into a tiny pool and waved their arms over it to scare the fish into action. Not much here. They moved on to another tidal pool. They dipped their hands into the warm water to move some of the loose pieces of lava rock to see if anything was hiding under. One crab under the rocks, three silvery baby fish were under the small niche to one side. They were hunkered down staring into the pool and looking at their reflections in it when one of them sniffed, looked to his friend and said, "Did you let one go?"

"What?" asked the other boy.

"Did you fart?"

"No!" the other boy replied with a grunting grin.

"Sure smells like you did."

"Did not! Must have been you," he replied.

"Had to be you! Wasn't me! Phew!" laughed the first boy.

"Get out of here! It wasn't me!" he replied as he gave the other boy a playful shove that sent him reeling backward, falling toward a larger tidal pool behind them.

"Look out! You almost pushed me in!" he complained with a backward glance. At that moment his eye caught sight of something large floating in the pool that he almost fell into. He stared with disbelieving eyes as he tried to comprehend what he was seeing.

He could only gasp "Aaaah! Aaaah!" in horror at the sight of the dead scuba diver floating on his back with the point of a spear rising out of the dark stain on the lightweight wetsuit over his body's heart. The back part of the spear was pointing straight down, acting like a mooring line and anchor for his body, keeping it tethered and causing it to drift in circles around the spear. Startled, the boy backpedaled to get away, slipping on the smooth pahoehoe lava bed as he did.

The second boy looked over to see what was the matter and catching sight of the grotesque partially-eaten body in the pool began a choking shriek "Eiii! Eiii!" as he stumbled backward to get away from the thing beside them.

Both boys started running back up the rise to the road shrieking in terror as they dug their toes into the sand and then into the folds of the lava to gain speed, skinning their toes in the process. They went down the road at a fast clip, incoherently screaming and yelling for help as if the devil himself was after them.

CHAPTER TWENTY

THE DEEP

HONOKOHAU HARBOUR, KONA. A small crowd of onlookers surrounded the showroom as Sarah and I climbed into our respective seats in the dual-controlled SeaTruck in the Manetti Marine showroom. We plugged the electrical harnesses from our jump-suits into the craft's electrical outlet. This would keep our bodies at an ambient temperature for the varied conditions we would be traveling through on our deep dive.

Sarah and I began with the detailed pre trip checklist. I called out the instructions in order and Sarah turned on switches and confirmed readings on the computers. The two onboard computers could do all of this but in the case of a computer malfunction we would have to control some operations of the craft manually.

We gave the thumbs-up sign to Manny who was watching the procedure like a mother hen tending to one of her chicks. He ordered the showroom door opened and carefully scrutinized our move through it. Outside, our next step was to check out the dryland propulsion and steering. The six-wheel drive worked beautifully as we could spin on a dime. We drove the pickup-like submersible vehicle onto the ramp leading into the placid waters of Honokohau Marina. Then we went down into the water so that only our cab was visible to the fishing crowd who lined the narrows of the rocky marina shoreline.

Our intended destination was the SSEAAL pipeline at Keahole Point a few miles up the Kona coast. Nearing the channel that led to the open sea, we went through another checklist, this one a pre dive list.

We could see the flashing lights of an ambulance as it rocketed up the short road past the marina and stopped with a jolt at the crest of the rise. The doors were flung open and a stretcher was pulled out of the back while the other paramedic ran down the path to the beach with an emergency kit only to come to an abrupt halt at a tidal pool. He slowly set his kit down and waved off the hurrying stretcher bearer with a shake of his head. Two young boys hung back at the crest of the rise, fearfully peering down at the scene as a squad car ground to a halt in a rising cloud of road dust.

"What's going on?" Sarah asked while busying herself with the cockpit controls.

"Accident, I guess. Looks like they have it well in hand."

"Okay," she replied, "I've been looking forward to this. Here we go!"

Slowly we angled downwards into the turquoise waters where our forward propulsion would be easier and our stabilization would be smoother out of the surface waves and the tropical breeze.

Elongated Trumpetfish horned in on us as we submerged. A couple Threadfin Butterflyfish wove their way along as did a solitary but beautiful Moorish Idol. A pair of Spectacled Parrotfish caught the morning sunlight and threw off a rainbow-hued flash of colour. We had entered a world of silence save for the faint electric hum from our lateral thrusters. In the first bay along, we glided over to a bare patch of smooth pahoehoe lava and tested our six-wheel-drive, all-terrain tires and our vertical gravity thrusters as we navigated this uneven formation. We had no problems establishing a suitably-light but positive gravity.

Going around the next point of land, we encountered a pair of Green Sea turtles who were paddling bumpily along, quite unperturbed by our presence. We even altered our course slightly as it didn't look like they had any intention of doing so themselves. They passed very close to us and didn't so much as turn their beaked heads toward us.

We were about a hundred feet below the surface as we crossed the next small bay. A couple of wetsuit-clad scuba divers excitedly pointed toward us to alert their buddies as we silently glided by. We waved at them, they returned our greeting along with the universal okay sign saying that they thought our craft was cool.

A large shadow gracefully glided off our port bow. The huge Manta Ray banked our way to check us out but only viewed us in a nonthreatening manner. Its whip-like tail followed its triangular shape as it turned back onto its original course.

"It is really quite beautiful down here!" I remarked, mesmerized.

"Aren't these marvelous sights?" agreed Sarah. "I hope we get to see a Spotted Eagle Ray too!" she added.

"What are they like?"

"They are practically the same shape, which is typical of rays in general, but its snout isn't forked like the Manta's is and the top of its body is speckled with white dots on a dark, mauve and black background. They're beautiful!"

Our Global Positioning Satellite navigation unit told us that we were nearing the SSEAAL pipeline site. We surfaced briefly to look around then sank back down to the relative calmness underwater, hovering beside the rows of pipeline as they dropped into the sea from the land.

We conducted our deep-dive checklist before descending any farther. Everything checked out just fine with the exception of a balky valve in one tire as the air was displaced with sea water through the tire's axle and rim. We got the valve working after the third attempt. If it had remained stuck, we could have compensated for it by adjusting our buoyancy in other ways.

"Okay, we're all set for the dive," Sarah said. I got a few butterflies in my stomach as I realized that this was it. The big moment.

I mentioned the butterflies to Sarah as we glided downward on a gradual incline. "I get them as well . . . on every dive. They soon pass though."

We followed a path between the warm and cold pipelines which were set some distance apart as they followed the downward slope.

"What is the temperature of the surface water here?" I asked.

"Usually it ranges between 24 and 28 degrees C on an annual basis."

The warm pipeline on the right soon ended and a third pipeline, which returned the used water to the sea, ended well below that.

"That was the warm pipeline," said Sarah, "It looks like it survived the explosion or underwater surge just fine. There was some small shifting back and forth though, but nothing with which we should be too concerned. It's easily repairable."

"I noticed that some of the sediment has been disturbed."

"Yes, it's okay though."

"Does the pipeline suck up fish as well?"

"Yes, when it does there is screening that will protect the fish from harm and block it or allow for their eventual release back into their habitat."

"Is there a lot of muck in the waters here, like microorganisms and such?"

"Actually, the surface seawater here has extremely low levels of inorganic nutrients and organic particles."

We followed the cold water pipelines on their downward run, the sea around us growing darker as we descended.

"I noticed that the warm water pipelines were secured to the bottom of the slope."

"Yes," said Sarah as she adjusted the plane of the SeaTruck, "one was trenched as well."

"Why was that done?"

"We are still experimenting with different anchoring and positioning techniques to see which methods work the best."

"And I notice that there are many cold water pipelines running down here."

"Again, the reason for that is that we are experimenting with different sizes and techniques of pipe laying. For instance, there are some half-dozen or so old pipelines which an old tenant had installed just for their operation. They are the bottom-laid ones over there."

"So some of these pipelines are not used anymore?" I asked.

"That's right. Some could be used while others could be used only with major renovations."

The pipelines ran down the slope into the darkening blue gloom of the deep.

"Then there were other methods of anchoring used. Pendant weighted and buoyant catenary, for instance."

"Buoyant catenary?" I asked.

"Yes, floating or suspended pipelines which are anchored on the slope of the sea floor and follow an arcing line downwards. You can see them over here, those ones attached to floats by cables anchored to those massive sea floor anchors."

"So how do you tell all these different pipelines apart?"

"Sometimes it's not so easy. There are getting to be quite a few now."

It was now twilight several hundred feet down. We switched on our exterior green thallium iodide lights to illuminate the pipelines. Exotic-looking fish flashed their colourful forms in our light beams. We threw on our white incandescent photography lights to take a few shots of these beauties. Some had long luminescent filaments which trailed like streamers. A baby octopus slowly floated by, its transparent colouring alternated by manipulating its pigment sacs called chromatophores. Neon-like lights reflected off its internal organs.

"Why are they so transparent?" I asked.

"It helps them hide from their predators."

The sea became darker by degrees as we descended into the deep.

"Kind of spooky when you get this far down, isn't it?" asked Sarah.

"Yeah, it's a good thing that I'm not claustrophobic to any appreciable degree."

"You? Claustrophobic?"

"Only very mildly, when I was a kid - I couldn't stand to be confined. I grew out of it though. I hope!" Sarah shot a glance at me wondering if I would have a relapse at this depth.

"You okay?" she asked.

"Yeah, I'm okay. I don't think you have to worry."

There was a flash of silver and white as a Great White shark shot by in front of us. It had come to check us out. Its ominous staring eyes flashed green in our lights. Its gaping tooth-encrusted mouth caused me to give a little shudder.

"Whoa! Did you see that?" I asked.

"Yes, they still give me the creeps when they suddenly flash by like that, even though we are protected in here," exclaimed Sarah as she scrunched her body farther into her seat.

We continued our downward descent, occasionally diving down to the sea floor slope from the suspended pipeline as we came upon an anchoring cable. We came to another one and dove to check out its massive anchoring foundation.

"Look at the foundation down there, it looks as if it has been disturbed."

"You're right, it has shifted somewhat but obviously still holding."

"How far down are we?" I asked.

"We are just below the warm layer of the sea, a little over 200 meters deep or well over 600 feet down. We are just going into the colder layer now where it eventually goes down to as low as 4 degrees C."

Soon all that we saw were bits of tiny phosphorescence seemingly rising past our cockpit window. We followed the pipelines and their anchors ever downward on the slope. There was no sense of motion save for the view of the pipeline and the phosphorescence. The anchoring foundations in the cold sea level seem to have held quite well whereas the anchoring foundations near the warm sea level and in the warm sea level appeared to have shifted slightly by the recent cataclysmic event.

As we neared 600 meters deep, the various pipelines ended one after another until we came to the last one. The last part of the descent had become relatively boring. It was the sameness of the black pipeline in view in our headlights, relieved only by the bolted joints of the lengths of pipe. Occasionally, anchoring collars and cables appeared out of the speckled blackness. We followed with a visual inspection of its anchor foundation.

"What now?" I asked.

"Let's descend a little farther down and check out the seascape for anything unusual, that is, more unusual than it is."

"Okay, I'm game!" I said. I adjusted the temperature settings on my jumpsuit.

We followed the rise and fall of the lava slope as it continued downward. Great caverns and cracks were in evidence here and there much like back up on the land. There was more pillow lava here due to the remnants of lava flows having been cooled by the sea whereas on land the lava would be cooled by the air over a much greater time span and distance.

At around 1000 meters deep the underwater terrain leveled out somewhat as we saw the tops of what appeared to be hills or peaks and valleys on our side-scan radar. Some of the valleys fell off sharply into an abyss while others fell away at a very low angle.

"This is very interesting terrain," I remarked to Sarah.

"Yes, what we are seeing here, believe it or not, are remnants of the slope above which have tumbled down for one reason or another."

"Tumbled down?"

"Yes, large and small pieces of the lava slope sometimes break off under its own weight and roll down the slope coming to a rest at some point, usually where the ocean floor levels off."

"But some of these sections are enormous! They are the sizes of buses, some are even the size of domed stadiums!"

"I'm told that there are even some pieces a dozen miles long and several miles wide that have broken off under their own weight and slid down the slope here off the Hawaiian Islands. Sometimes this action is triggered by an earthquake or just a tremor."

"You're kidding!" I said as I looked at Sarah in amazement.

"No! That's the truth!"

"Really?"

"Really!" she answered.

"Wow!" I exclaimed in wonderment at the massiveness of that occurrence.

"Yes, but all that must have happened eons ago."

"Some did and some happened more recently."

"How recent?"

"1975."

"1975?" I asked incredulously.

"Yes!" Sarah emphatically stated. "That year an earthquake caused a part of the south flank of Kilauea to slide about 20 feet down the slope into the sea."

"As recent as that?"

"Yes! A group of Boy Scouts were camping along the shore. A 10-foot-high wave rolled in at night right after the quake struck and swept some of them underwater and out to sea. One of the Boy Scout leaders drowned. One Scout awoke to find himself offshore under water. He struggled through the debris-laden water to get to the surface. Once there, he had to walk on top of trees and branches to get back to the new shoreline. At first light, the survivors were astounded to see that the land had slid into the sea and that only the tops of palm trees of the former shoreline were sticking out of the surf and still visible. I've been told that this particular former scout now lives in Seattle."

"That's incredible!"

"There are many slides, some huge, some very small, some ancient, some new."

"And they cause waves as well."

"One of the largest waves or tsunamis occurred some 100,000 years ago when one of the largest pieces of lava shoreline broke off. The tsunami was a thousand feet high."

"A thousand feet?" I whistled in amazement. "How big was the chunk?"

"It was the miles-long one that I mentioned before."

"Where did that happen?"

"Off the island of Lanai."

"Well maybe they were thrown there in an explosive eruption something like the one at Mount St. Helen in Oregon where one wall of the volcano blew suddenly."

"No! Good idea though. Just not the right one. Our volcanoes don't explode as such."

"They don't?"

"Sorry to disappoint you. Unlike other volcanoes which explode because their magma, their molten rock, is quite dense and their gases are under great pressure and so explode when released, our volcanos in Hawaii have magma which is much less dense and therefore holds less gas under less pressure, so they only ooze and erupt in fountain-like displays of fiery lava."

"But nothing explosive."

"Nothing explosive per se." Sarah corrected.

"So then the underwater explosion here could not have been from a volcanic explosion."

"Probably not."

"Well, how about the gases from an eruption at this depth rising to the surface and causing havoc?"

"Probably not, either."

"Why?"

"The immense pressure at this depth - 1000 meters - would not allow gases to rise to the surface. They are more likely to be absorbed into the water right here."

"So what are we doing down here then?"

"Just looking around."

"Okay."

"You never know what you may find down here, besides it's so interesting just poking around."

"So what are those smoother rocks down there? Are they just pieces of rough debris that have became worn down and made smooth over time?"

"Which ones?"

"Those ones just to the left there. They look like rubble. Here I'll shine the light on one of them."

"Probably not. They could be nodules though."

"Oh?"

"Nodules are minerals that accumulate around a central foreign object which can be anything, much like a pearl is formed around a grain of sand in an oyster except that we aren't exactly sure how the process works yet. They're mainly made up of manganese. Similarly, geodes occur when gases are trapped within a chunk of lava rock as it cools. They are those pretty crystals - violet, blue - that you see encased in nubbly rocks. "

"Strange!"

"Yes, and even more strange is that the nodules, which are usually composed of significant amounts of manganese, can contain lesser quantities of other minerals - some extremely rare and therefore very valuable, far more valuable than gold!"

"I'll bet you that black smokers spit the nodules out along with the mineral smoke after they have been rolled in a chimney gathering more minerals. Something like out of the comic strip *B.C.*"

"You might be on to something there," Sarah laughingly acknowledged.

"Can they be mined?"

"Sure, but there are some drawbacks."

"Like what?"

"I see that there are quite a few here at this level but they are also found in great concentrations at a depth of around 4,000 meters, so that is a more difficult depth to mine."

"Any other reasons?"

"This is a marine sanctuary and the U.S. undersea territory extends 200 miles out. Beyond are international waters. Who would regulate undersea mining there?"

"It's the wild west out there then," I said.

"You could say that."

"Can we analyze one of these?"

"What now?"

"Sure!"

"Well, I suppose that we can. Let's give it a try, shall we?"

Sarah positioned the SeaTruck while I worked the robotic manipulator arm to clench the potato-like rock. I inserted it in the laser hotbox which is actually a laser micro probe that heats a sample of the rock to about 6,000 degrees C. Five minutes later the computer screen readout stated that the Plasma Mass Spectrometer analyzed the nodule's valuable mineable minerals as being 26.1 % manganese, 1.8 % copper, 1.4 % nickel, 0.83 % cobalt and 0.035 % gold.

"An amazing machine!" I declared, "and quick too!"

"Yes, it's the first time that I've operated it on my own. But it didn't test for some of the more exotic minerals. We used it on some dives back in Canada. I'm impressed!"

"Ready to go back up?" I asked.

"Sure, let's do that. Time for some sunshine!"

We rose straight up in the inky blackness, only our computer navigation system telling us where we were. There was no pipeline here to use as a security blanket nor as a guide. Here, there was only a black void.

Or so we thought!

Our first indication that something else was with us was a slight plopping sound that hit the SeaTruck from behind, jarring us slightly. Then a sucking sound worked its way forward. Sarah and I looked at each other with widened eyes, not knowing what was making that awful sound. Sarah and I jerked our heads up and saw a single large fleshy disk, bigger than a major league catcher's mitt, attach itself to the outside of our cockpit-domed window. We watched in fascination, our eyes riveted to the spot. A long second later we heard the same sucking and popping noises as we watched the disk undulate and work its fleshy pad off the window. We quickly glanced at each other again, seeking reassurance that all was well.

But it wasn't!

Sarah let out a bloodcurdling scream as another fleshy pad moved across the bubble window right beside her. Then two fleshy pads appeared behind, attached to the first by a gigantic reddish-orange arm. Rows of huge fleshy pads followed. The SeaTruck shuddered in mid-ascent as the giant arm's suckers stuck onto the window.

I yelled out, "What the hell . . . ?"

"It's a . . ."

"An octopus?"

". . . squid, it's a giant squid!"

"A giant squid? But I thought that those things . . . "

"Were a matter of fiction?" Sarah looked at me with frightened eyes.

"Yeah! Like the Loch Ness monster, like Ogopogo, like the Kraken in Norse mythology!" I said incredulously.

"They're not supposed to be aggressive," Sarah yelled over to me.

"Maybe it thinks we're food what with our manipulator arm and roll bar."

"Maybe it thinks we are a whale. Whales are their enemies as they are on top of the food chain."

The SeaTruck shuddered again. We were thrown violently around, glad that we were securely strapped into our seats. Sarah powered up the thrusters.

We didn't budge.

She tried them again.

Nothing!

We were being controlled.

Sarah shut off the thrusters as they were useless against this savage beast of the deep. I grabbed the robotic arm joystick and worked it back and forth trying to gain an upper hand on the creature but I only succeeded in attracting the attention of another of its tentacles. Then I managed to grasp the tip of one of the arms in the manipulator's hand and squeezed tightly while extending the arm outward.

Becoming aggravated, the ugly giant squid worked its way around farther. We could now see its gleaming eye, the size of a truck's hubcap, staring out from its mottled orange and beet-red head into the cockpit as it writhed and tightened its hold on our sub. We heard the glass lights on the cockpit's roll-bar give way and crack. Shards of broken glass floated down around our super-strengthened Plexiglas bubble window. The sub groaned under the strain of the unequal pressure being exerted upon its framework.

I freed the laser micro probe from its exterior hot box and struggled to point it at the arm containing rows of suckers. The arm was as thick as a tree trunk. I fired off a shot but only managed to burn a small hole through the tentacle. A small cloud of vaporized flesh floated off to one side.

It did no good!

Desperately, Sarah tried to make the contacts work on the robotic arms to deliver an electrical charge from our batteries to the grasping beast.

"That's it. Give it a jolt just like a stun gun! Do you have enough power?" I asked.

"For an instant I do. It should give it quite a shock. Can you manipulate the arm closer to its body?"

"I'll give it a try," I said as I worked the joystick to move the robotic pincer-arm closer. "Let me know when you're ready." I frantically maneuvered the arm closer to its body while retracting the robotic hand and extending the arm's dual pincers forward.

"I'm ready," Sarah shouted, "I've got it figured out!"

"Just a second . . . " I yelled out as the giant squid put the SeaTruck into a downward spiral alternately turning us upside down and disorienting us. "Okay! I've got the robotic pincers close to its head. Fire away!"

"Firing!" Sarah yelled out as blue sparks arced from the dual pincers to the beast's head.

We watched in morbid fascination as the red monster's head was only vibrated by the stinging blow that would normally take down an elephant. On the giant squid it had little effect. The beast shook off the effect of the deadly jolt with ease and redoubled its efforts against us. Its sixty-foot-long tentacles continued working their way around the acrylic bubble window until we looked on in horror into the pulsating maw of the giant squid's mouth. We caught flashes of its thick, dark red body behind its head which now showed us its other eye albeit a much smaller one than the other. The pulsating suckers pulled the SeaTruck still farther toward its deadly maw which was now distending itself to try to encompass the entirety of our submersible. Sarah shrieked in disgust at the sight of the undulating mucused maw, its formidable mouth resembling the shape of a giant parrot's beak. The rasping radula tongue worked back and forth in anticipation of a meal. Slimy suckers slid across the cockpit window as we stared in horror at this fearsome creature that was trying to eat us by attempting to bite us into pieces and swallow us in our craft. We still had some exterior lights and the interior lights that were not yet damaged. This dance of death was being played out under their illumination.

Suddenly, our world went black for a second as our sub was severely jolted. Then the SeaTruck was bounced repeatedly against the side of some fast-moving soft object. We were jounced along as if we were a fishing plug that was set for deep trolling for sea bass and the fish had struck at the bait. The giant squid loosened its grip on us enough so that we could see along its body.

There was one big problem.

We were already taken by the fish, in this case by the squid. Now the tables were turned and the predator was the bait. Water bubbles rushed by our acrylic-domed cockpit as we were sped along by some unknown force, still in the loose clutches of the beast. Our exterior lights caught the side of something enormous, something that was grayish-black with deep furrow lines in its side.

As we twirled helplessly at speed, we caught sight of a jaw full of enormous white teeth within which the body of the writhing giant squid was enmeshed. The squid's enormous appendages, except for the two that held us, were wrapped around this giant's head which sported an enormous eye on this wall of charcoal hide.

"My God! It's a sperm whale!" Sarah shouted as we were flung about, caught as we were in this battle between the two behemoths.

"Give the squid another jolt, maybe it'll let go this time," I yelled to her.

"Is the robotic arm in place?"

"I can't see. You'll just have to hope that it is. Fire it!"

"Firing! I'm firing! Dammit! Let go! Why won't it let go of us?" sobbed Sarah in frustration.

"Give it another blast!"

"Firing!" she yelled out as the beast finally relaxed its grip on us when the whale bore down on it again with its mouth. The enormous suckers slowly let loose one by one and slid across the cockpit's domed window.

I fired up the thrusters as the SeaTruck drifted downward from the death struggle. We looked up at the writhing monsters caught above us in the glare of the sub's lights. The two-ton squid's eight grasping tentacles and its two slightly-longer club-ended feeding tentacles were holding onto the submarine-sized whale's head by its massive suckers. The whale struggled to hang onto the squid's body in its huge jaw. We gave them a wide berth as we rose past them. Then looking down, we saw the twenty-ton Sperm whale's mouth close tightly on the giant squid whose body now hung loosely from the toothed jaw. Strangely, the unmoving suckers still stuck to the body and the head of the whale as if in a final death-grip.

We shuddered as we rose higher and lost the leviathans in the closing gloom of distance. The thrusters worked somewhat roughly now.

"Whew!" I said as we rose, "that was close! That really was a giant squid! I thought that they were mythical!"

"We were very lucky. I can't believe our good fortune!" Sarah declared weakly.

"Have you run into any before this?"

"No, never. They are very rarely sighted as they usually habituate the depths to around 3,000 feet. Their scientific name is Architeuthis. I know a person who is a teuthologist, that's someone who studies giant squids. He told me that fishing boats have reported hauling them up in their nets. There is no intact preserved specimen in the world. There is one that is preserved but it's missing its eyes and pieces of its body and tentacles."

"Holy! Did you see that big glassy eye staring right at us?"

"Yes, it was so freaky! It also had that second smaller eye which some scientists think is used for vision in shallower seas as it has been known to come to the surface at times."

"What was that beak thing in its maw?"

"That's what it uses to bite food into pieces. It's made of chitin because the squid has no bone structure."

"It was disgustingly ugly!"

"You're not kidding!" Sarah agreed.

It was some time later that the SeaTruck broke the surface of the sea. Sarah and I were finally able to relax, though giddiness overcame us from having survived the ordeal. We slumped back in our cockpit seats, exhausted from the struggle and its attendant stress on our bodies. Looking wide-eyed at each other, I said, "We were lucky to have survived!"

"You're not kidding we were lucky, although squid, including giant squid, is the Sperm whale's natural prey," Sarah said.

"I'm glad the whale got the giant squid rather than mistaking the SeaTruck for it."

"Yes, some Sperm whale's stomachs have revealed thousands of undissolved chitinous giant squid beaks."

"That's amazing!" I replied.

That evening we went out to dinner with Kimo and Kiana and recounted our tale from the deep.

"Are we ready to order yet?" Sarah asked as the waiter approached.

"Ready to order?" The waiter asked. "How about an appetizer to start with. The calamari is especially good tonight!"

CHAPTER TWENTY ONE

ANCIENT WAYS

KEALAKEKUA BAY, KONA, THE BIG ISLAND OF HAWAII. The gentle sea breeze carried delectable smells to me from the imu cooking pit. I was relaxing in a large hammock strung between two palm trees on the beach at the Kilolani family compound in Kealakekua Bay. Kiana and her dad had invited Kimo and I to a luau in our honour later that night.

Meanwhile, Sarah had to attend a previously-scheduled weekend conference on volcanology in San Francisco. She could not back out of it as she was the conference's keynote speaker.

I had driven her to the airport early this morning for her flight out of Kona International to Frisco. It was hard to part with this desirable woman even for one weekend but as she was going on this whirlwind round trip, there would not be much time for ourselves if I tagged along.

Sarah said as she was leaving, "Kiana's going to show you around and the luau will be in your honour so I'm sure you will have a wonderful time. Luaus are so much fun. I wish I didn't have to go to this conference but I have no choice. See you when I get back." We embraced and kissed softly for a long time before breaking away from each other as her flight's final boarding was announced.

I savoured her lingering scent as the hammock was swung gently by the sea breeze. Kimo had some errands to run in town. I had spent part of the morning with Kiana's dad. He was almost recovered from his accident and had supervised Kiana, her brother Akoni, their cousin Neki and I as we had gotten the imu ready to cook the food for the luau.

We had dug the waist-high pit near the beach. Meanwhile, we had heated rocks in a fire until they were red hot. Taking these stones, we carefully shoveled them into the pit where we kept far back from their fierce glow and manipulated them so they formed a red-hot liner. On top of this we placed damp grass to provide some shield from the scorching-hot rocks as well as to provide the necessary steam that is a characteristic of imu ovens.

A whole kalua pig had been gutted, scraped, cleaned and washed in preparation for the evening's feast. Hot rocks were also placed in its belly to cook it from the inside out. The pig was wrapped in taro leaves and placed upside down in the center of the imu. Other meats such as beef and chicken were also wrapped in ti and taro leaves and placed alongside the kalua pig. Vegetables were similarly wrapped in many bundles of ti and taro leaves and placed on top of the bundles of beef and chicken. The pile of bundled food was steaming even as we added a layer of banana and ginger leaves. On top of this, we laid woven-grass mats and then layers of soil to contain the heat and steam of the imu.

Kiana showed me how to make poi. She had taken cooked taro corms and using a stone pestle, pounded them on a dished-out board until the pulp was a paste to which she added sufficient amounts of water to attain the right consistency.

I took over the job of pounding poi. Soon, I got the hang of it and became quite adept at maintaining the rhythm needed to make the pale mauve-gray paste.

Meanwhile, Kiana began to make lomi lomi with her Mom. They took fresh salmon and kneaded it under water so that they were able to shred the meat with their fingers. To this, they added fresh tomatoes, onions, sea salt and alai, which they said was a red salt from the island of Kauai.

Finishing our tasks, Kiana, Akoni, Neki and I went for a swim in the bay where we frolicked with the fishes and the turtles that swam amongst the beautiful coral reefs.

"Rune," Akoni had said, "follow Kiana, Neki and me below to the coral. We'll show you some things you probably have never seen before. For the next hour they enlightened me about the denizens of the deep. The underwater life within the first twenty feet was fantastic. Between surfacing for air and talking about what we had seen, I saw things that I had never noticed before. We had no scuba gear - a mask and snorkel were all we needed. Neki, who was in his late teens, impishly teased me by coming from behind to grab my feet like the fearsome shark in the movie *Jaws*. I never did get him back for that. He was too wily and moved too quickly underwater for me. It was a fun time.

As I lay in the hammock, Mr. Kilolani, Akoni and Neki came over and asked if I would tell them about the encounter that Sarah and I had when the SeaTruck was caught in the grip of the giant squid. I told them the story of how we had inadvertently been rescued by a huge Sperm whale which had come along at the right time to do battle with and eat the suckered giant squid. They shuddered at the thought of how close we had come to being killed. The SeaTruck had been built to withstand many forces upon it but obviously no one had the forethought to envision it in a tentacle-to-robotic-arm battle against a long-thought-of mythical monster of the deep. This was no myth. This was real!

It had been late when we had finally returned the SeaTruck to Manetti Marine so we had scant little time to do a thorough inspection of the craft at that time.

The next day, in the light of the morning, Sarah and I had returned to Honokohau Bay to inspect the damage.

"What on earth did ya guys do ta my machine?" Manny had exclaimed as we all stood around peering and poking at the SeaTruck. "Look at the roll-bar! There are no lights left there!"

"Yes, well it's a long story Manny," I had said.

"And it's not your machine Manny, so don't worry about it," Sarah had said. "Think of all the money you'll make repairing it."

"Yeah," said Manny as he rubbed his palms together at the thought of that. "And there's a tire that hasta be replaced as well. It got a little bent out of shape."

I said, "One of the gravity jets is bent as well. That'll also have to be repaired. A thruster too!"

"Check out the robotic arm and the laser while you're at it Manny. We had to use both of those as well. If you need some technical assistance or just plain wrench-pulling, give Rudy at SSEAAL a call. They say he's the best."

"Yeah? I might just do that. So what did happen down there?" He asked.

"It's a long story Manny," Sarah said.

"Look! There's round scuff marks on the exterior paint. They're bigger than dinner plates! The paint has actually been rubbed off in circles. What caused that?" asked Manny, his eyes growing wider.

"Giant squid," I said.

"Giant squid?"

Sarah added, "Yes, a giant squid!"

"Where?" Manny asked incredulously.

"In the deep off Keahole Point," she added.

"In the deep?"

"About 3,000 feet deep," Sarah added.

"No kidding! What did it do?"

"It decided to check us out, I guess, and wrapped its huge tentacles around the SeaTruck. We tried to fend it off with the robotic arm but that just aggravated it. Everything was going fine until it got a little too tense and the exterior roll-bar lights started popping and the frame started creaking."

"Whew! So what did ya guys do?"

"We tried using the laser on it too."

"Zapped the big sucker, eh?"

"That didn't do any good either. We then had to jury-rig a stun gun but it was no match for the beast either."

"Holy smokes! So what did ya do next? How did ya guys get away?"

"We didn't do anything!"

"You didn't? But you're here, ain't ya!"

"Only because a Sperm whale spotted the giant squid and scooped it up in its mouth to eat. Sperm whales eat almost a ton of squid every day, it's their main source of food. The SeaTruck went along for the ride until the giant squid let loose its grip on us as the whale's jaw bore down on it. It was a wild ride until that happened."

"Wow!" Was all Manny could manage to say. For once he was stuck for words but his slack jaw and blank stare said it all.

"Okay," said Kiana breaking into the end of my story, "the food is cooking and there is nothing much to be done until later this evening. Dad, you and Akoni and Neki can look after things. I have to help the Friends of the Kailua-Kona Library give their junior members a tour of the Hulihee Palace this afternoon. Rune, you and I can pick Kimo up at his place and he and I can show you some of our cultural heritage while we are at the palace."

"Sounds great!" I said. "I haven't had much time for that since I got here."

The young group was fidgeting and milling about in the sunlight on the front lawn of the Hulihee Palace. The chaperones, Kiana included, were having a hard time containing the exuberance of their youthful charges. Kimo and I stood back under what little shade was afforded us by a low coconut palm on the front lawn. From the open front door of the palace, a muumuu-clad lady of some regal forbearance strode onto the elevated entrance and raised her arms in greeting.

"Welcome to Hulihee Palace!" she announced. "I am glad that you could come today. It is so heart-warming that many of our young people have taken the time to explore their cultural heritage, of which this palace is but one example."

I glanced around the boisterous group and found that the kids had stopped their horsing around. They fixed their gazes upon this pleasant woman who wore a lei around her neck and who had dark hair cascading down her back.

"Since our Polynesian ancestors came on dangerous voyages from the Marquesas Islands around 1300 years ago in 700 A.D. and from Tahiti in 1000 A.D. to seek a new and better life for themselves and their future generations, of which you are one, they have strived to make these islands self-sufficient by importing plants and animals from their former homelands over a period of some 500 to 700 years.

"They had to make do with what they found here or what could be sustained here. They had no metal tools so their tools were made of bone, wood, stone and seashell. Their clothing and their shelters were made out of the varied leaves and bark that grew on these islands. Their ships were canoes dug out of tree trunks, indeed, that is how they arrived here in the first place from their former homelands thousands of miles across the Pacific Ocean.

"Various head men ruled parts of these islands under a kapu or taboo system of social and religious culture that governed the way people lived. Finally, in the eighteenth century, kingdoms evolved by which Kings and Queens ruled each island and chiefs, both men and women, ruled portions or districts of each island. Warfare between the different kingdoms and chiefdoms were commonplace but throughout the generations Polynesian and especially Hawaiian history was passed on by the spoken word and by chants for there was no written language then as we know it today.

"Around the beginning of the nineteenth century - around 1800 - King Kamehameha united all the Hawaiian islands into one kingdom. Soon after, the kapu system of laws and the heiau, which were the religious temples, were discarded.

"What has survived the last one to two centuries has been the Hulihee Palace here in Kailua Bay in Kona here on the big island of Hawaii, the Queen Emma Summer Palace in Nuuanu Valley, Honolulu and the Iolani Palace in downtown Honolulu."

The kids were starting to fidget again under the glare of the afternoon sun despite Kiana and her fellow chaperones' best efforts to get them to pay attention.

"I know that you are getting restless, so in a moment we will go inside for the start of the tour. In the meantime, to your left near the sea, is the fishpond built for the exclusive use of the king. You can get a closer look at it after the inside tour," she said as she turned and went inside.

We trooped up the entrance stairs and found ourselves in an entry hall which ran from the front to the rear of the palace. It fronted the sea save for another expanse of lawn, scatterings of palm trees and a stone seawall.

The gracious tour guide had us follow her up a sweeping staircase past a display of an assortment of ancient spears.

We toured the upstairs bedrooms first as another tour was still being conducted downstairs at the time. The lady spoke with passion and had a thorough knowledge of the articles she was describing to us. An ornate four-poster canopy bed carved out of kauila wood was the main feature of the south bedroom. Tiny taboo sticks decorated the top canopy board. The four-poster bed was flanked by ancient feather staffs called kahili which were symbols of royalty. The bed itself was set quite high so that it made falling out of bed an adventure.

The north bedroom featured furniture made out of native woods including a large ornate crib once used by the royal baby Prince Albert. A couple rockers sat atop a floor covered with a woven lauhala mat.

The upstairs sitting room contained lanais off the front and back. A large and sturdily-built royal settee was positioned there. It was a gift from Peru.

Downstairs, a sturdy koa wood table dominated the Kuhio dining room. Its large round top was cut with the grain and polished to a high gloss. A setting of Lokelani china was on display.

It was the Kuakini room that caught my eye as memorabilia from a bygone era were featured in display cases: a royal helmet, medals, a guitar inlaid with mother-of-pearl, kapa cloth, stone tools, spears, stone mortar and pestle.

On the floor in the center of the room, was a narrow wooden sled some six feet long, whose sturdy wooden runners were fastened to a framework upon which a woven mat was attached on a slightly raised platform used for sitting upon.

"What is that?" I asked.

"It's a holua sled, sometimes called a papa," answered the guide.

"What is it for?"

"The ancient and not-so-ancient Hawaiians used them for sliding down the lava slopes. They would hold races to see who was the first to reach the bottom of a run. Sometimes they spread grass or rushes out on the slope to make the sleds run faster. It was great fun! Of course, if the sled tipped, the wounds a contestant received from the rough lava could be quite severe. It was much like a bobsled run except there is no ice nor snow to run on and the course was usually straight down. Some of the holua sleds were longer, about twelve feet long, and could hold more than one person."

"Something like the four man bobsled in the Olympics?" I asked.

"Yes, something like that."

"Sounds like they had a lot of fun."

"Yes, sometimes wagers were made as to who would reach the bottom of the sliding track first."

"Did they sit on the platform?"

"I suppose they did but they also lay down on it and headed down the hill face first, which of course, was very dangerous," she said.

"That platform looks no wider than eight inches or so."

"Yes, it's not very wide which would make it even more difficult to control at speed."

"I see the runners extended out in front and are curved upwards at the very front."

"That would have aided in stabilizing the sledge somewhat."

I turned and said to Kimo, "You game for a little holua contest?"

"As a matter of fact," Kimo said, "I did do a little holua sledding when I was a kid but our sled wasn't this well constructed. Of course, we kids were always crashing the things and breaking them."

"So are you saying that you're game?"

"Sure, anytime. We'll just have to find a couple holua sleds," he laughed.

I worked my way down the line of display cases lining the walls, peering and wishing that I could handle some of these fine items. Hearing someone on my right gasp out loud, I looked up and saw Kiana staring, slack-mouthed at a stone ball that was sitting on the floor in one corner of the room.

"What's the matter?" I asked as I could see that she was in a state of shock. She said nothing but weakly raised her arm and pointed to the stone ball which was slightly bigger than a medicine ball. "What's the matter?" I asked again as I saw that she was flustered. I went to her and touched her arm gently.

"The stone ball!" she gasped, "it's the one I have seen in my dreams! Oh!" she cried as she fled the room. Kimo quickly followed her as she fled the palace, going outside where she sought refuge on a shaded bench at the side of the walk.

I knelt in front of the grey stone ball which was a foot and a half wide, perfectly round and weighed some 180 pounds. Peering closely at its grainy texture, I thought that it could be lava rock which had been ejected from Mount Hualalai centuries ago. There was some minute cratering on its surface of the type that could have resulted from it having been rolled downhill or more likely from lava rock having been smoothed down. This would allow the lava's inherent bubble cavities to remain and appear as small indentations on its surface. I gently rolled the ball but could not lift it with casual effort. But then I considered its grey colour and wondered where it had actually come from as I had not seen anything like it on these islands.

I asked the guide, "What was this stone ball used for?"

"We're not entirely sure," she replied, "but King Kamehameha was said to use this stone ball to exercise with. Perhaps it was also used in battle as a weapon."

I went outside where I found Kimo consoling Kiana. He had his arm around her shoulder as small racking sobs came out of her. "I don't know what is real!" she cried out in frustration. "I just can't deal with these images anymore!" she said in anguish.

"You saw the stone ball in your dreams?" I asked.

"Yes! Those were the gray shapes that came tumbling down at me in my dreams. I just realized that now when I saw the stone ball. That's what they were! They were followed by fire or something, Oh, I don't know!" she sobbed as she blew her nose in a hanky.

CHAPTER TWENTY TWO

KEALAKEKUA LUAU

KEALAKEKUA BAY, KONA. The kukui torch-lit grounds danced with the shadows of the party guests. Youngsters ran around while their parents chatted in small groups here and there. They were snacking on puu puus of lomi lomi salmon, butterfly shrimps, rum and plantation-sugared pineapple chunks and freshly roasted macadamia nuts. Beneath the starry sky, they watched the preparation for laying out the luau. Great clouds of steam rose as Kiana's dad directed the uncovering of the imu pit. Bundles of aromatic foods were being set out by Kiana and her mom on giant leaves on the garden lawn.

Earlier, Kiana had put a lei around my neck and had kissed me gently upon my cheek. "Aloha," she had said. I was overwhelmed with the intoxicating fragrance of plumeria.

A faint drum beat rose to a rhythmic crescendo as we prepared to sit down to the feast.

"Aloha! Komo mai e noho iho! Welcome. Everyone, please be seated!" Kiana's dad said. "Enjoy this wonderful feast that we have prepared for our guests of honour this evening - Rune Erikson and Kimo Kekuna."

I looked around at the beautiful women with flowers in their hair and wished that Sarah could have been here too. Kiana was especially appealing as the sparkling kukui torch lights reflected off her glistening ebony eyes. Some men were in grass skirts, others wore loin cloths. We all sported bands of woven leaves on our heads. Orchids, anthurium and attractive displays of fruit graced the spread in front of us.

We helped ourselves to the mouth-watering mounds of food set out on large leaves. Kiana handed me a bowl of mauve-gray poi which I had pounded earlier this morning.

"Now remember, Rune," said Kimo, "you eat poi with your fingers. One finger if it's thick, two if it's thin."

I dipped my hand into the bowl and drew up a finger of poi. It was sufficiently thick. I popped my finger into my mouth and tasted the paste. "Tastes something like the glue that we used to make in kindergarten," I remarked as I swallowed the pasty substance, followed by a swig from my drink.

"Ha, Ha!" laughed Kimo.

"Don't you like the taste?" asked Kiana. "You will, though! Once you acquire the taste for it you'll never look back," she laughed. "Just like Hawaiian girls," she laughed again.

"I'll keep working on it," I said.

"And so you should for tonight you are a guest of honour here. Whatever you wish for, it is our obligation to fulfill," she said with a twinkle in her eye.

"Is that why luaus are given?" I asked.

"Sometimes luaus are given to celebrate an event, like this one. Business people also use it to close a deal. Other times, we have luaus to appease the gods. Of course, the romantic atmosphere has been known to improve one's love life," Kiana chuckled, "and sometimes we have luaus just to eat really well and keep us happy!"

The kalua pig sat in the center with garlands of cherries, pineapple, kumquats and lichees. Kiana's dad began carving the pig for his guests. He handed a leaf to me upon which he had placed a strip of the kalua pig's skin and fat. "Here, this is for you!"

Kimo said, "We consider this a great delicacy," as he was handed his own to sample.

Biting into the skin, I found it surprisingly tasty and chewy but still tender. I didn't care for the fat though.

I was given a large portion of kalua pig meat. It was tender to the point of melting in my mouth.

"Have some laulaus," offered Kiana.

"What are they?" I asked.

"They are some of the things that were cooked in the imu with the pig - beef, fish, taro tops, for instance," she replied.

I helped myself to these aromatic delicacies. "Are these the taro tops?" I asked as I ate something that looked and tasted like spinach.

"Yes," Kiana said, "they have had the stems and veins taken out. Aren't they good?"

"Delicious," I agreed, "I think I like it with salt and pepper," I added as I tried some tender moa chicken. "I'll have moa of this," I joked.

"And this is lawala paluula," she said. "They are baked yams with pineapple which has been sweetened with coconut syrup."

"Delicious!" I said as I tasted it.

"Try some limmu, it's dried seaweed," she offered.

"Why not?" I replied.

"And if you finish all your meal, there are noupio and baked bananas for dessert," she laughed.

"Okay, what are noupios?"

"What is noupio? Coconut cream pudding."

Kiana's dad poured some liquid into small bowls and passed two of them to Kimo.

"Here, have some of this," Kimo declared, "it'll knock your socks off!"

"I've got no socks to knock off, Kimo," I answered.

"Then this will take care of what ails you then."

"What is it?"

"Okolehao!"

"Okolehao?"

"Yeah, it's a rather potent brandy distilled from the ti plant."

"Lea lea kakou," stated Kiana's elderly father as he raised his glass in a toast.

"That means to happiness," whispered Kiana.

"Mahalo," responded Kimo. "And likepuoe," he added.

"Mahalo," I said.

I raised the small bowl of liquid and drank from it. The fiery liquid stung my throat as I swallowed, immediately raising my stomach temperature several degrees. "Wow!" I gasped. "Kimo, you weren't kidding!"

"Wait until it hits your head!"

"I think it already has!"

"Careful now!" admonished Kiana. "That stuff is pretty potent. We wouldn't want you out of commission tonight!"

"Yeah, drink enough of this stuff and you might get to see Pele," Kimo stated.

"Pele?"

"Yeah, the volcano goddess. She can get around," Kiana said.

"Oh?" I said as I felt a little flushed. "She can, can she?"

Kiana smiled.

A group of four musicians led off with a selection of Hawaiian songs followed by a man in his traditional costume, the mea oli, who chanted stories from the past. It was a truly fascinating insight into the Hawaiian culture, though I couldn't understand a word of it. The flickering shadows played on his glistening face as he held the attention of our enraptured group. The mesmerizing chant continued for some time until ending abruptly, breaking the spell.

"Now Dad is going to tell some stories," Kiana whispered to me.

"The chant, or mele as it is called," intoned Mr. Kilolani, "has been with us since time began. Meles that are not danced to are called oli. It is in this way that our people, especially royalty, traced their lineage back to a single god, to Kumuhonua, and to the couple who were denied entry to Paradise by the great white bird of Kane, who is one of the four leading Hawaiian gods. The kahunas, who were the priests, the seers, the medicine men, the astrologers and the great canoe navigators, also had used olis to tether their lineage to the ancient gods. The chants were important. They are our history books, our knowledge. These mele were chanted lacking the rhyme or metre of poems but they have cadence, accents which are denoted by the trilling of the voice changing by half-tones. There were ipos, love songs; religious prayers and prophecies; inoas, naming songs recalling deeds of the newborn's ancestors; and kanikaus, funeral dirges.

"And so, through the years, the royal settlers were blood-related to retain this kinship. To keep order and distinction between the classes, they set rules called kapu. These taboos forbade the ordinary people from doing certain things or consuming certain foods or going into certain places. At the same time, it gave a privilege to the higher classes who were exempt from most taboos.

"Mo'i, kings, emerged. They were the most powerful of the chiefs and having taking power into their own hands, ruled over other chiefs and their lands. The king's family lived in palaces in royal compounds.

"A heiau, or temple, was built in the royal compound alongside the palace. An outer gate of the royal compound led to a raised stone sacrificial lele, or altar, and the entrance to an inner court of the luakina, or temple, of the high priest. Outside this entrance were the carved images of some of our gods - Lono, Kane, ku and others. Other heiaus, which were for the public, were built on nearby land.They were enclosed by massive stone walls up to ten feet thick and twenty feet high. The heiau was run by the kahuna, or high priest.

"Interestingly, the kahuna also took care of the burial of deceased kings and chiefs by steaming their bodies in fire pits until the flesh fell away from the bones. During cover of night, the kahuna would paddle out to the center of the bay and dispose of the royal flesh and organs in the sea as food for the fishes. Two volunteers would be required to hide the royal's bones in the maze of ancient lava tubes which run beneath the old lava beds. The disposing of the royal flesh and organs and then the royal bones in this manner was done so that no other king or chief or person could take them and assume their powers nor denigrate their memories. To keep secret the location of the royal's bones final resting place, the volunteers were sacrificed and became martyrs while their family's well-being was looked after by the royal family.

"King Kamehameha's bones were secreted in a lava tube or lava cavern and to this day have never been found," Mr. Kilolani said.

"The hearts of dead kings were often dropped into the active Kilauea crater as an offering to appease Pele, the volcano goddess.

"Seers, or kilos as they were called, were believed to be able see and talk with the spirits of the dead. The spirits were called unihipili.

"High priests were believed to be able to talk with the spirits of the living, which were called kahoaka. These spirits freed themselves from their bodies while the person slept or was in a state of a trance.

"To distinguish themselves visually, kings, on important occasions, wore the mamo which is a mantle or long cape that drapes down to here." He touched his lower leg. "It was made from the yellow feather of little sea birds who were also called mamo. The mamo seabird had but a single yellow feather under each wing so it took a great deal of time and number of birds to make the royal cloak. Yellow was the colour of the royals. Chiefs wore a shorter cape of yellow and red feathers while the kahunas wore short capes of red feathers." He touched his shoulders as if adjusting a cape.

"Kimo, you are also a chief," said Mr. Kilolani. "Please tell our friends here, especially the children, something of the ancient way of life. Perhaps the wars. It needs to be told." Mr. Kilolani settled back.

"It is my pleasure to do so. There were wars," Kimo said emphatically as he looked at each of us in turn. "Wars were a fact of life then, as unfortunately, they are now. Wars were fought for the same reasons they are fought today. All war is hell." He glared fiercely. "That I can tell you from my personal experiences in the US Navy SEALS.

"The wars that went on during ancient times were no less traumatic, no less gory. There were battles between our own people and later, much later, there were skirmishes against the haoles when they arrived. The only differences are the choice of weapons and the electronic wizardry that is in use today.

"The weapons then? The war club! And the pahoa or what is known as a dagger, in this case, a wooden dagger. The shark's teeth knife could wreak havoc and make a mess of a warrior. Stone battle axes were part of the heavier armament used. The ihe or javelin was effective as well as the spear. And don't forget fists and rocks. Rocks thrown, rocks whipped along by slings, rocks rolled downslope. All methods could be deadly to the enemy.

" Warriors' protection? Not much!" Kimo pursed his lips and shook his head sideways. "A mahiole, a feather helmet which was more ceremonial rather than protective and usually reserved for royalty.

"And his mind. His mind for self-preservation. Although choice in this respect was not always an option, the same as it is today!

"Guile? Cunning? Deception? Subterfuge? Deceit? They were all used then as well as now.

"Psychology played a role in war. King Kamehameha had a war-god. It was called Kaili and was a small wooden figure which wore a yellow feather mahiole. The king took it into battle with him to bolster his warrior's confidence and to terrify their opponents. It has been said that the war god broadcast a battle cry that could be heard for miles over the noise of the combatants." Kimo cast his arm in a sweeping motion.

"One of the great battles was told to me by my father when I was a little boy. On the island of Molokai there was a powerful, but fair chief by the name of Kamauau. However, in time, more warlike chiefs started to move onto Molokai and take control over much of the land and its people. Seeing this situation develop, his oldest son, who was named Kaupepe'e, convinced a battalion of his men to make a naturally-protected, cliff-side compound in Haupu. This wave-lashed gulch cut into the mountain like a notch cut into a tree.

"He had many buildings made to house his warriors on the field-sized mesa which was ideally formed to be defended on three sides by towering cliffs above the narrow gorge and by a single narrow path on a high mountain ridge from inland. Traditional high stone walls were built on the inland side to protect the compound from invasions from the path. An underground lava tube was used as a passageway to bypass the wall. The entrance to the lava tube was sealed off within the compound by a large section of pahoehoe lava which was maneuvered on and off the skylight by the warriors.

"It wasn't all work and no play for there were games - like konane, a type of checkers, for the adults and punipeki for the children."

Mesmerized by Kimo's description, I envisioned a bastion high above the roiling waters of the small inlet where sturdy bronze warriors vigilantly kept a lookout over the seas below. Alongside them, I could imagine rude wooden idols staring seaward. I could see prophets and diviners and astrologers struggling to seek the answers of the future while the sorcerer worked his magic of the moment and the mysterious high priest strutted around sanctimoniously, no doubt plotting, along with the chief, the introduction of their next taboo. Mea oli practiced their historical chants. Musicians played their instruments. Dancers practiced their scintillating moves. Images of warriors flickered across my mind. They were testing their physical prowess by competing in wrestling matches and foot races, spear catching and javelin throwing; glistening bodies straining with their efforts. I saw women tending to the boisterous children and to the mundane cooking tasks of preparing the evening meal. Still others whiled away their time and improved their mental skills with a challenging game of konane.

The Chief continued, "It was said that from this compound Kaupepe'e led raiding parties to neighbouring islands. They got to their canoes by using narrow steps that were chiseled into the cliff-side wall. The paths led down to a small bushy beach where their canoes were stowed away from the pounding surf. His warriors plundered by night in canoe flotillas and seized women and booty by the light of their torches. This continued for several years before a chief on Oahu said that enough was enough and found the island, Molokai, to which the warriors had returned. He decided to plan a counterattack against them. The Oahu chief mounted a force of a hundred canoes, and landing on Molokai, sought out their compound by using Kolea, a plover, and Ulilli, a snipe, to seek their enemy out. The invading force glided into the narrow gorge to battle the enemy warriors after this reconnaissance told them that the fortress compound had only a few dozen defenders at the time. They couldn't believe their luck! In their eagerness, the retaliating force landed their canoes in the narrow gulch in preparation for the assault on the cliffs above. Once the canoes were beached, the defenders, of which there were a full battalion, let loose a torrent of rocks. They rolled these down the cliffs from the lofty compound above and smashed the invaders' canoes, breaking them into mere splinters of wood. The noise of the caroming stone balls was deafening. Rolling boulders rained down upon the invading warriors. Many were killed! There was pandemonium. Confused shouts rose with the din of the tumbling stones. The ground shuddered under the stress of the barrage. A choking dust rose from the bottom of the gorge where the stones had laid waste. Wounded warriors cried out in pain. The startled invading chief believed that the gods were responsible for this torrent of rocks upon them from high above. He ordered what warriors were still able into the few canoes that were still seaworthy. Panicked, they fled the island." The children looked on, wide-eyed with imagination.

"It has been said that in the following years Kaupepe'e raided again, seizing a beautiful woman by the name of Hina. Even though she was his captive, she was willing to live with the chief and did so for almost two decades. She had left behind her husband and her sons. To try to get her back, there was another battle in the gorge involving hundreds of canoes paddled by warriors. A battle-blast by a chief on a shell did nothing to spur on his warriors. They also met the same fate as the others had before them. A prolonged Trojan-horse-like game of wits and waiting began at the inland wall. After a lengthy standoff, there was a storming of the walls, resulting in a devastating battle during which Kaupepe'e was killed by a spear thrust right through his chest."

The people stared at Kimo.

"Hina, who had grown to love this warrior, wept over his death before returning to her family."

The women became misty-eyed, daubing at their tears.

"This is the kind of anguish that results from war." Kimo cast his eyes downward in sadness.

Kiana's father said, "But it was not all devastating in times of war. There were places of refuge called puhonui. They were a part of the heiau. Their gates, which were marked with a white flag, were always open, especially in times of war. Anyone could go there. Those who were able to make it to the gates were given refuge by the priests standing guard there. They were safe from harm no matter who was pursuing them."

"Kiana, my dear daughter. Do you have a story to tell? Perhaps about Pele."

"Yes, father. Pele has always intrigued me, so I will tell a story about her."

"Ah, Pele!" sighed Mr. Kilolani.

"The goddess Pele . . ." Kiana exclaimed as she looked left and right at the seated figures around the luau feast. Reflections from the kukui torch lights flickered across their attentive faces. ". . . is the goddess of volcanoes. She is the most feared and yet the most respected of our gods, for it is here on the Big Island of Hawaii, our island, that she lives. Pele makes her home in the bubbling, molten crater of Kilauea on the flank of Mauna Loa. It is there that she lives in her fiery caverns and molten lava tubes. And it is also there that she consumes the offerings left by those who worship her and schemes to destroy by fire those who would disparage or disrespect her.

"Pele is attended by her five brothers and eight sisters. At her direction, they attend to their many duties including making explosions, steam, thunder, clouds, upwellings of lava and bursts of flaming rocks.

"Her brothers are Kamo-hoalii who is the king of steam; Kapohoikahiola, the god of explosions; Keuakepo, god of the night rain of fire; Kane-kahili, the god of thunder; Keoahi-kamakaua, the fire thruster. Her sisters are Hiiaka-wawahi-lani, Hiiaka-noho-lani, Hiiaka-kaalawa-maka, Hiiaka-hoi-ke-poli-a-pele, Hiiaka-kaleiia, and Hiiaka-opio, all cloud holders of one type or another. There are also her sister, Makoie-nawahi-waa, the fiery canoe breaker and Hiiaka-ka-pu-enaena, the fiery mountain." The children sat with rapt attention, their visions written on their faces.

"Pele and her family would receive their offerings at other places on the island. To do this they roamed other districts and attended at the sites of old craters and lava tubes where molten lava used to run. Thunder, shaking earth and new lava eruptions announced their arrivals and departures throwing great fear into the local people. Here, more offerings of food were made to appease these gods."

Kiana's father interjected, "Ah, that reminds me! In 1882, a wide swath of lava flowed down the slopes of Mauna Loa. It was thought by the locals that it would bury the town of Hilo, which lay directly in its path. The people quickly made deflecting walls but to no avail. The lava still advanced downslope toward Hilo Bay. Chief Ruth Kamehameha went to Hilo where she set up an altar on the slope just above the town. Here she made many offerings to Pele and solemnly prayed to her to stop the lava flow. Shortly afterwards the fiery lava stream halted and cooled to form a massive wall of black lava above Hilo which still stands there to this very day!"

Kiana said, "That is true but I had a different story in mind. Pele morphed into many different forms. One of these was as a beautiful woman. Pele is lonely sometimes and craves human companionship, indeed, she is said to have had many love affairs.

"It has been said that one day Pele was home in the crater of Kilauea when she heard distant drumming. Following the faint sound until it became louder, she searched the islands to the north. Finally she found the source of the drumming on the island of Kauai. Morphing into the form of a beautiful woman, Pele made her new form known to the drummer, who was a prince on the island of Kauai. He was playing the hula drum. Lohiau, as this prince was named, fell in love with this beautiful woman. Captivated with each other, they became man and wife. The nights of passionate bliss went by as if they were living a fairy tale. Lohiau did not ask his new wife where she came from nor whether she had relatives. Her presence turned him into a quivering state. In time Pele had to return to Hawaii and promising to return quickly, got his promise of faithful love until then.

"As the number of days of her absence grew, the love-struck Lohiau became more lonely. He stopped eating after a month's wait. Grief-stricken and starving, he died. No one knew the real cause of his death. However, the probable reason was put forth by a kaula who knew of Pele's ways. He had a vision that the beautiful woman, the wife of Lohiau, was actually Pele, an immortal who became so enamoured and possessive of her prince that she enticed him to death and caused his spirit to fly to her in the Kilauea Caldera."

Kiana's father said, "Yes, Pele is a romantic but she also has her petulant side."

"Indeed she has!" Kiana continued. "It has also been said that there was a young chief named Kahawali. During a celebration of Lono, a holua contest was under way between the chief and one of his young friends. A merry crowd of onlookers were lined up along the holua run. The holua slide was quickened by the addition of pili grasses to its course. Together, two contestants would race each other down the lava slope run on sleds called papas. The papa was anywhere up to a dozen feet long and ran on two polished upturned runners held far less than a foot apart by lashed crossbars which were also used by the participants as handholds and footholds. The racer whizzed down the slope while lying face downward upon the papa. The racers walked up the run inspecting its every bump and pitfall.

Along the way to the top of the slope, the group was met by a beautiful young woman who brashly challenged the chief to race her down the course. The chief, who was quite taken aback by her audacity, tried to belittle her, a mere woman, asking her what she knew about holua racing. She replied that she could easily beat him to the bottom of the holua run. Becoming annoyed at her impertinence, Chief Kahawali asked his friend to lend her his papa. They threw themselves down upon their sleds and hurtled down the grass-strewn course dodging rocks and debris as they went. They were evenly matched. However, nearing the finish line, the less-experienced woman lost her balance and crashed her papa, allowing the chief to finish first. Angered at her stroke of bad luck, she asked for another race. However, at the top of the course the woman demanded that they change sleds as she thought his was the better of the two. The chief refused and threw himself down the holua course leaving her standing at the top. She was fuming mad.

"Enraged at this, the mysterious woman's eyes became a fiery red. A thunderclap sounded, startling all, causing them to look up at her as she revealed herself as Pele. She pointed down the course at the chief and released a river of molten lava. As this beautiful woman morphed, she became engulfed with fire, changing into Pele, the goddess of volcanoes. Lightning bolts snapped and crackled around her."

The children were wide-eyed with wonder.

Kiana continued. "Meanwhile, Chief Kahawali was driven into the sea by the snapping, snarling streams of red-hot lava. By chance, he was able to make an escape by using a canoe which happened to have been left onshore. Still steaming mad, Pele followed him into the sea where she hissed and frothed and threw large flaming lava stones after him. She was not able to cause a direct hit - her aim was bad. Chief Kahawali made good his escape from the wrath of this woman-goddess scorned."

There was absolute silence as Kiana ended her story.

A thumping drummer leapt out of the shadows behind the kukui torches followed by a woman with a rattling calabash. The stillness was shattered. A guitar player, another playing the ukelele, and a singer emerged from the shadows opposite and surrounded us. It was the call for some Hawaiian dancing. Kiana rose and put on a display of hula dancing for all to admire. "I'll teach you the hula 'auana!" Kiana said as she came over and took my hand. I rose and soon felt myself swaying along with Kiana to the rhythm of the Polynesian music. Those still seated laughed with me as I attempted to learn the intricacies of the dance so as to be a suitable partner for Kiana. Akoni got up to dance along with some females of his age. Neki, his younger cousin, did a comical exaggeration of Akoni's dancing to the amusement of all.

The music stopped as suddenly as it had started. A brightly-costumed mea oli started his chanting, the cadence of which rose and fell with the story. Although I could not understand the words, I fell under the spell of his chanting. After some minutes, the mea oli finished his chanting to the applause of all.

The feasting continued. More ancient stories were told.

I recounted my story about the battle with the giant squid and the Sperm whale in the deep.

Wild hula dancing resumed. Kimo danced with Kiana.

More fiery okolehao in a calabash was passed around. Kimo proposed a toast to Laka, goddess of the hula.

Drums pounded.

Gourds rattled.

I drank.

I danced.

The evening glided along until I felt that the land, rather than me, was swaying. The luau festivities were slowly winding down anyway as Kimo and I took Kiana up on her offer of sleeping mats and blankets for the night.

"Come with me," she said, leading us to separate small grass huts that were more like pup tents that I had used as a kid. "These shacks are sometimes used as storage places. You should be quite comfortable here for the night. There is a washroom in the shack next to you. I'll see you both in the morning for breakfast."

Kimo and I bid each other a good night. I tumbled off to sleep as soon as my head hit the pillow.

Feeling a presence, I awoke during the small hours of the night. I looked around the small grass shack and saw no one. Then realizing that why I awoke was probably that I felt the need to use the toilet, I made my way to the adjacent washroom. Upon my return, I noticed a soft glowing light coming from a larger grass shack a short distance away. A woman was standing in front of the strange light, her body in silhouette.

"Come here," she said softly as she beckoned to me with her feminine hand.

I stopped and stared slack-mouthed, not knowing what to make of her request.

"Come here!" she said softly again although with more urgency this time.

"Me?" I answered as I looked around me to see if she was perhaps calling to someone else.

"Yes, come here!" she urged as her diaphanous creamy gown floated around her curvaceous body. She beckoned to me again.

I went toward her until I could make out the finer details of her enticing body. I was uncertain as to what to do, so I stopped.

"Help me!" she pleaded. "Please help me!"

"What is the matter?" I asked with some concern and confusion as I had not as yet shed the effects of the potent okolehao from the luau.

"I need your help!" she pleaded again. "Come here, come here quickly!"

Concerned, I went forward until I felt myself being drawn into the large grass shack although she did not touch me to do so. It was only then that I realized that there was something strange about the light that had backlit her form. The light, like an aura, was all around her body. I could not only see the light but I could feel her warmth and feel her lustful suggestive thoughts through her aura.

I glanced around the peaked grass shack and found myself in a room whose walls were covered in finely-woven tapestries and whose floors were covered in fine woven matting. On the far side of the room was a large raised bed covered with several layers of matting and two layers of finely-woven kapa cloth. Calabashes and ornaments decorated the far reaches of the room. Conches and smaller shells were displayed; anthurium and other cut flowers were beautifully arranged in bamboo vases; erotic wood and stone carvings were set here and there.

I turned back to the woman, trying to see her finely-featured face. It was greatly softened in the misty recesses of her aura which now surrounded her head but had diminished around the rest of her. However, the fleeting glimpses of her dusky body afforded me through her silky negligee was starting to have its effect and aroused me.

"What is the matter?" I asked hoarsely.

"I am so lonely that I could not sleep," she sighed as she wrapped her soft arms around me and drew me to her bosom.

All my protestations were lost in her ample cleavage. Her dark nipples pressed into me. Wrapping herself around me, together, we flowed toward the raised bed and settled upon it. Her hot breath bathed my neck then found my ear as she tongued my lobe. I felt a momentary flash of pain as I felt her nip my lobe with her teeth. I was consumed by rising passion as she covered my lips with hers; her delicate scent washed over me. The moistness of her lips wet mine, suffusing it into a soul-searing kiss. I traced her comely body with my trembling fingers. Massaging her shoulders and her back, I felt her tension fall away. She became supple under my hands. I massaged her nipples and felt them stiffen and enlarge. She openly received me as I gently became one with her.

Glancing at her through the shadows of my eyelashes, I was startled to see Kiana's alluring face emerge on the other side. Jarred by the recognition of her, I slowed.

"Its okay! Its okay!" she whispered in her soft voice which now was ragged with modulation as we journeyed toward the heavens. "Don't feel bad when it feels so good," she encouraged as a way of spurring me onward. "Don't stop us, it's wonderful!"

I was now totally lost and had no recourse but to continue to our ultimate destination. The land below us began trembling. Lightning crackled nearby. Thunder boomed around us. Kiana moaned and cried out repeatedly until she sighed with pleasure as if some all-consuming fire within her was finally being extinguished.

"I'm so sorry!" I said later as it hit me again through my still-foggy brain who she was and what we had done together.

"It's okay. I won't tell Sarah," Kiana whispered.

"I didn't mean for this to happen!"

She pleaded, "Stay with me the night."

Embarrassed and uncomfortable with the situation, I fled back to my own grass shack.

"Please come back," she pleaded. Glancing back, I saw a flicker of anger flash over her eyes which flared brightly then dimmed to two smoldering embers, leaving smudges of red that pierced the softness of her aura. The two red smudges leaked down to form two fiery molten teardrops that traced her ivory cheeks.

I looked upon the moonlit waters of Kealakekua Bay and shook my head to try to make some sense of what had just happened. It didn't make sense.

I looked back again.

She was gone.

I entered my grass shack and lay down to try to think. I promptly fell asleep again.

A dog snuffling after food scents from last night's luau woke me. Drums pounded and gourds rattled but this time they were all in my head.

The rising sun was sending shafts of gold through the palm trees. I rubbed the sleep out of my eyes and yawned. Peering around the corner at Kimo's shack, I heard only his loud snores.

Then it hit me. Kiana! Last night! I groaned as much because I was hung over as because I dreaded the thought of what had gone on in the middle of the night.

How could I face her this morning?

How could I face myself for that matter?

Looking out at the surf in Kealakekua Bay, I decided to go for a swim to clear my head and organize my thoughts.

I picked my way across the pahoehoe lava edging the beach, padded through the white sand and entered the warm salty sea. Fishes of every colourful hue darted around me. I dove under then headed seaward with a brisk stroke. A turtle gave me a hip-check as it clumsily wallowed by me. I swam until my head cleared but my thoughts of last night stayed with me.

Toweling off after having a freshwater shower, I heard a familiar female voice behind me. "Well, hi there! Ready for some breakfast?"

Startled, I whipped around to face her.

"Look, about last night." I apologized as I looked at Kiana, "I'm really so sorry. I was awful . . . "

"I thought you danced the hula just fine and . . . "

"No, no. I mean . . . " I stammered in embarrassment. "I mean after . . . after what happened last night. I feel so bad . . . "

"Did you have too much okolehao to drink last night?" Kiana laughed.

"No, no, you don't underst . . . "

"I think he had too much okolehao last night," said Kimo with a laugh as he came up behind us. "Come to think of it, so did I. I slept like a log!" he added.

"And how did you sleep last night?" asked Kiana as she smiled at me.

I searched her face for some clue that would lead me to understand where she was going with this but I could find nothing, nothing at all. It was as if last night had never happened between us.

"Uh, fine. Just fine!" I replied, mystified.

"And you?"

"I had a wonderful sleep!" she said as she yawned and stretched catlike.

Now I was really confused. I excused myself and went toward the washroom.

"Breakfast is under the palm trees in five minutes!" Kiana called after me.

I looked at my face in the washroom mirror. Doubts hung on my face like bags under one's eyes. Apprehension glazed my eyes. I noticed a raised bump on my ear lobe. It was more like a blister rather than a lovebite. That's odd, I thought, I hope it doesn't get infected. Leaving, I wandered over to the large grass shack that I had been in last night. Entering, I found it to be bare. I looked away, not believing my eyes. I looked back into the shack. It was still bare although there was a raised section where the bed could have been. No tapestries, no erotic statues. Had I been that intoxicated? I wondered. Nothing was making sense to me. Even the floors were covered in sand and not in matting. There was a covering on the raised area but it was stained with blackened matting as if someone had charred a section of it. I could smell the charring as I got closer. Hmm! I thought. This is odd.

After breakfast, I pulled Kimo aside and asked him to go for a walk with me while Kiana and her mother tidied up. We hiked the little cluster of village roads as we talked.

"Kimo," I said, "something is bothering me."

"What's it about?"

"I'm not sure but it is mystifying me."

"Go on."

"Last night I . . . "

"Ah, last night!" he said, fondly remembering the festivities of the luau.

"No, I mean after . . . during the middle of the night after we had gone to sleep."

"Yeah?"

"Well, you see? It happened this way. Something woke me during the middle of the night. I wasn't sure what it was but I did have to have a whiz. Maybe that was what woke me. Anyway, I finished using the washroom and was on my way back when I heard this voice calling me from another shack, the larger grass shack not far from mine. This woman - I couldn't see who it was at the time - was calling to me. I went over to see what was the matter. Here she is in this sheer nightgown, and I mean sheer! I could see her, well, I could see her body. She was gorgeous! But I couldn't see her face well enough. There was this mist or this light, kind of a backlit glow."

"A backlit glow?"

"Right. A backlit glow. I couldn't see her face well enough. I asked her what was the matter. She reached out to me, wrapped her arms around me and said that she couldn't sleep because she was lonely."

"Lonely?"

"That's what she said. Lonely."

"Uh, huh."

"She somehow drew me into the room which was lavishly appointed and one thing quickly led to another and we were making out."

"You son-of-a-gun! You got lucky!"

"No!"

"No?"

"Well, yeah, sort of . . . "

"Sort of? Either you did or you didn't!"

"Well, we did!"

"Well, what's the problem then?"

"Well, the problem is that I opened my eyes during our . . . our lovemaking and finally saw her face."

"So?"

"So, it was Kiana!"

"Oh!" Kimo said as his face darkened at the thought.

"Yeah . . . Oh!"

"I see the problem. You sure?" Kimo asked as his face became more troubled looking.

"Yeah, I'm sure . . . well . . . no! I'm not sure!"

"You're not sure?" he asked incredulously.

"Well, after our lovemaking, she begged me to stay the night but I was so embarrassed and tipsy from the booze that I left her standing in the doorway to the shack."

"What happened then?"

"So she called me again but I didn't go to her. And her eyes. Her eyes sort of brightened and glowed bright red for a moment or so. Then two red tears formed and ran down her cheeks. I couldn't believe what I was seeing. It was so odd. It was more than odd. It was eerie!"

"Hmm!"

"And then this morning I started to apologize several times to Kiana for last night and she acted like nothing happened."

"Maybe nothing did happen."

"What do you mean?" I asked.

"Maybe it was all a dream," Kimo replied.

"Yeah, maybe it was because I went over to look at that grass shack this morning, the one that we, that we . . . that we were in and it was empty. Last night it was lavishly decorated with things that I have never seen here before. Tapestries, fine mats, erotic wood and stone carvings. It was all gone. Oh, there was a raised bed area in there but it was all scorched and everything. I don't see how . . . "

"It was scorched?"

"Yeah, scorched. It smelled like it was recently scorched."

"Hmm!"

"But it all seemed so real!" I said with exasperation.

"Maybe it was," Kimo said slowly as if he were pondering a mathematical equation.

"I thought you said it was a dream!" I countered.

"Maybe, just maybe it was Pele!" Kimo said as his eyes widened in some sort of inner revelation.

"Pele? What do you mean?"

"Pele! The goddess of volcanoes. She has been known to take human forms, especially the forms of beautiful women."

"Get out of here! That's insane!"

"To you, maybe! To me, no!"

"No?"

"Madame Pele is one amorous chick and she can get testy if she doesn't get her way!"

"What? That's just some old tale. Don't tell me that you really believe in that?"

"I do!"

"I told you not to tell me that!"

"Well, I am!" Kimo said. "That would explain her eyes flashing red with anger. The red tears."

"And that would also explain the blister on my ear lobe!" I declared.

"Your ear lobe?" Kimo asked.

"Yes, I thought that she had just nipped it with her teeth but this morning I found a blister rather than a love bite!"

"Whewwww!" Kimo whistled at this revelation.

We found ourselves back at Kiana's family compound on Kealakekua Bay. We passed by the large grass shack. I pointed out the scorch mark. We continued walking down the path. Kiana came up to us to ask if we had a nice walk.

"We did," replied Kimo. "Tell me something. That shack over there. What is it used for?"

"That one? We use it to build canoes in. Why?" Kiana asked.

"Oh, that may explain the scorch mark on the bench there. You probably burnt it while burning out one of your canoes."

"No, we don't burn out our canoes. A scorch mark?"

We walked to the large hut.

"Let's see. No, that wasn't there yesterday. And so big too! It must be a foot by three or four feet. I would have noticed something that large! Hmm! I wonder how that got scorched?" she exclaimed. "There are also some fine strands of golden glass on this matting here. It looks almost as if they were spun, they're so fine. That's odd! I'll have to ask Dad or Akoni if they were working here."

Kimo and I exchanged glances and said nothing.

Sometimes things remain well enough if they are left alone.

CHAPTER TWENTY THREE

RECONNAISSANCE

KAILUA-KONA, THE BIG ISLAND OF HAWAII. The time was right to continue exploring the deep along the coastline off Keahole Point. The SeaTruck submersible had been repaired after being mauled by the giant squid and Sarah was back from her convention in Frisco.

I decided that I wouldn't mention the eerie happening the night of the luau. Oh, she had many questions about the luau all right. How was it? Did you have fun? Anything exciting happen while I was gone? Well, yes and no. I answered her questions as delicately as I could without mentioning the unmentionable. "Oh well, we can have some fun together at the Kona Coffee Festival that's going on this week," she had said. "There'll even be a parade!"

Having picked Sarah up at her condo to go out to Honokohau Harbour for another search with the SeaTruck, I was wheeling the Jeep down curving Ali'i Drive following the downtown shoreline. Tour hawkers were snagging the early-rising tourists walking by their kiosks. "Chopper ride to see the volcano? No? Then how about a tour to the beautiful Waipio Valley then?" Well, at least they weren't running you down on the streets and clutching at your sleeves like they do in some tourist towns in other parts of the world. Here you could just walk on by or stop if you felt like it.

We neared the end of Ali'i Drive. The Kailua Pier was bustling as usual but it had a new addition. A long, gleaming white yacht was tied up to it taking up the entire side of the pier.

"Look at that!" exclaimed Sarah as we drove along the curving drive.

"She's a beauty all right!" I agreed. "Must be two, three hundred feet long."

"Does it look familiar to you?"

"Wait a minute! It sure does! Does the name Chung Min-Ho ring any bells?" I said as I tried to recall the name of this working yacht with the chopper pad and the submersible dry-dock.

"It's the same one we were on for cocktails in Victoria, in the Inner Harbour."

"Yes, there's the truncated stern," I pointed out.

"*M.V. Scorpion*! Yes, that's most definitely the same one!" Sarah said as she read the name. "I wonder what they're doing here?"

"Looks like they are provisioning for something big," I said.

"Lots of activity," Sarah said.

"Up to no good, I'll bet!" I added as I recalled with a shudder the night that Chung had literally tried to put me down. If I hadn't had a mini knife in my pocket, I surely would have been food for the fishes and the crabs.

"That was a narrow escape back in Victoria," Sarah said as if reading my thoughts.

Shipboard cranes were hoisting gear and cargo nets of supplies on board. The supercargo, directing the loading, was shouting orders to longshoremen. Cargo-laden trucks trundled up to the ship and waited their turn to be unloaded. On the bridge, above them all, stood a familiar figure - Chung Min-Ho - his bald head gleaming in the morning sunshine.

"I don't like the looks of this. Wherever he is, there's trouble!" I said to Sarah. "He turns up like a bad penny!"

"I'm afraid so," she agreed. "I wonder what he's up to?"

"I'm sure we'll find out sooner or later," I said while feeling a sense of foreboding coming over me.

"Good morning, Manny!" I boomed as we got out of the Jeep at Manetti Marine.

"Yeah? What's so good about it?" Manny asked.

"It's a beautiful morning. A great day for a cruise," Sarah countered.

"Yeah? Where you going?"

"More sea trials," I said.

"Yeah? Well, I got some advice for ya pal! No more giant squid, okay?"

"What's the matter? Didn't you like repairing the SeaTruck?" I asked with a smile.

"Yeah, we like the work. We got it repaired. What a job! We had to call in Rudy from the SSEAAL workshop like you suggested. He's an excellent technician. These things are tricky to work on. They're not like repairing a boat," Manny complained loudly.

"Well I'm sure your repair bill will reflect that," I pointed out.

"Yeah, it sure will!" Manny agreed as his cherubic face brightened at the thought of all the money he was going to make from this one job.

"By the way. Did you ever sell that boat to your brother-in-law?"

"My sister's husband?"

"I think that was who it was."

"Yeah, he bought the boat all right. He's still a no-good scum though. Maria deserves a lot better than that!" Manny's face was momentarily clouded in concern but brightened as if remembering all the money he made off that deal too. "Made a couple bucks off that garlic grinder, ha, ha!" he added.

"I'll bet you did!"

"Be careful out there! That scuba diver got killed with a spear from a spear gun. He was diving with a buddy about two miles up the coast from here and was trailing behind. Next thing ya know the buddy turns around and no partner. He's gone and disappeared. Two days later there is his partner lying there in a tidal pool just on the beach right here, deader than a doornail from a spear through his heart. Some kids found him. Really freaked them out. His diving buddy swore up and down that he didn't do it. I think the experts proved that it likely wasn't his spear. Word is the cops had a lie-detector done on him. Apparently he came out clean on that one too!"

We did a surface cruise until we cleared Honokohau Harbour, doing our pre dive checks as we went along. Everything seemed to be working just fine, thanks to Rudy. If Manny's mechanic had been the only one working on the repair, I would have had some serious second thoughts about this.

A catamaran dive-boat rode the waves like a cowboy on a galloping horse as it motored by enroute to a coral reef just up the coast. It had the name *Body Glove* emblazoned on its side in large black letters.

Sarah piloted the SeaTruck down so that we would not be affected by the surface waves but still could see with plenty of light as we followed the coral and lava seascape offshore. Blue sky became blue water as we settled, getting a double view as we dropped below the surface. Incredible, though smaller, vistas opened up. A comical Lagoon Triggerfish swam by.

"We call that fish a Humuhumu-nukunuku-a-pua'a," Sarah said.

"Say what?" I asked.

She repeated the name again, "Humuhumu-nukunuku-a-pua'a."

"Humonoko-noko . . ." I attempted to say. "Numohumonoko . . . ah, forget it."

"Needs some work I see," she laughed, "we'll just have to coach you on it."

"Or not."

"No, really. It's a requirement that you learn this when in the islands," Sarah laughed.

"Well, maybe. Where should we look today?" I asked.

"Let's try the area just on the far side of SSEAAL, shall we? Just off the heiau at Keahole Point. That is the next logical place to check out."

"Sounds good to me."

"That is nearer to where the explosion occurred."

"But there are no facilities there, are there?" I asked as I peered into the blue wall of ocean.

"None in use that I am aware of, certainly none on the land anyway. That's the strange thing about it. I would have guessed that facilities of one sort or another would have been the cause or at least a factor in it."

We passed over the multitude of large pipes dropping down the slope into the deep off the SSEAAL complex. I shuddered as I recalled the incredible fight we had with the giant squid here some 1,000 meters deep. I could still vividly see those huge fleshy sucker pads working their way across the SeaTruck's spherical cockpit window.

We were working our way along just thirty feet below the surface as we passed by where the heiau was on shore. Everything looked normal - fishes, turtles, coral, enormous structures of jutting pillow lava and lots of blue water and sand.

We worked the SeaTruck in and out of little coves for half a mile as we passed by Keahole International Airport without seeing anything of interest to us that would indicate a source point for the explosion.

"Well?" asked Sarah after the SeaTruck cleared the surface. "Do we turn around and go home?"

"May as well. There doesn't seem to be anything along here," I agreed.

"Oh well, we tried," Sarah said with some finality.

Sarah swung the SeaTruck around. I said, "Why don't we dive a little deeper and see what the lower sea-slope looks like until we get back to the SSEAAL pipelines?"

"Good idea!" Sarah agreed.

We settled the SeaTruck at almost three hundred feet down. In the growing dimness of the depths, we switched our high-intensity lights on to see better.

We needn't have bothered!

The horizontal gash in the slope was so abrupt that it felt like we were teetering on the edge of a precipice. Our lights stabbed the watery gloom that lay beyond the gash and picked up the other side of the gash more than a hundred feet away.

"Do you believe this?" Sarah shouted out in surprise.

"Is this what I think it is?" I asked

"Something definitely occurred here and recently too!"

"Is this a fault or rift zone?"

"No, I don't think so. It appears that a good chunk of the slope has broken off and fallen away."

"How can you tell?" I asked.

"The angle of the slope on the other side of the gash is greater than the upper slope here. It looks like a chunk of the lava slope has broken off, tilted, and slid down slope for a hundred feet or so. The walls of the chasm are clean when they should have some growth or sediment on them if they were old. Let's see how far it follows the coastline." Sarah kept the SeaTruck moving in that direction. The chunk of slippage finally petered out and the slope became normal again.

"Okay, we'll try the other way again," said Sarah eagerly.

We followed the chasm for a quarter mile. It was if someone had roughly sliced at the slope with some gigantic knife. We continued following it.

"Look at that down there!" Sarah said excitedly. "Recent pillow lava flow down near the bottom of the break." Sarah maneuvered the SeaTruck lower into the chasm. There was a wide strip of fresh pillow lava that bulged out of the upslope sheer wall like a weak spot in an inflated tube.

"Wow!" I exclaimed.

"It looks like the flow has stopped."

"What caused this?"

"Sometimes - it doesn't happen too often on old volcanoes - there will be some residual flow of lava part way down the slope. It can run through an old lava tube underground then surface somewhere far downslope from that."

"Is this an old volcano?" I asked.

"Mount Hualalai? Yes, its last major flow on this side was about 200 years ago. It was a surface flow from on higher. But it could become active and start flowing again at any time."

"What are those bubbles coming from around the pillow lava?"

"It appears that's just some residual gas being released from the lava."

"What kind of gas?"

"I'm not sure. There can be many types, methane gas for one. Also different types of acid can form, sulphuric, hydrochloric, for instance. I'm going to take a water sample as well as some lava samples for analysis back at the SSEAAL lab."

"Can't we just analyze that here with the SeaTruck's own analyzer?" I asked.

"Unfortunately some of the tests require additional procedures in the lab and are beyond the scope of the SeaTruck."

"Okay. Lets check out how far this goes on," I said after Sarah completed the sampling. The SeaTruck's propulsion fans whirred as we rose out of the chasm and followed the edge of the break farther. Shortly the break ended and the natural slope resumed. We retraced our path, dipping into the chasm as we went along. We explored it to the end of the break then silently rose out of the slash to the two hundred foot level and began following the coastline back.

"Will you look at that!" I exclaimed in amazement. "There are four pipelines coming out of that lava tube just above. Look! One of them ends right here. The second and third go a little deeper. The fourth one appears to be headed downslope to the deep. We must have gone under it when we were following the chasm a hundred feet lower. I wonder if it was dislodged in any way when the slippage occurred?"

"Don't know! I never knew we had old pipelines way over here. And all coming out of a lava tube at that!"

"Do you guys do that? Use the lava tubes, I mean?" I asked Sarah.

"Not that I'm aware of. I'll have to check with Stu."

"And look, the rest of the lava tube opening has been closed off around the pipes with a grid, a steel gate."

"Somebody sure doesn't want visitors," Sarah remarked.

"Those don't look like the SSEAAL pipelines, do they?" I asked Sarah as we came up to them.

"I don't know," she replied. "If they are ours, they may have been left over from the initial set-up we had for making electricity years ago. But we surely wouldn't have run them up a lava tube. That part looks newer."

"Where exactly are we?" I asked.

"Just off the SSEAAL site," Sarah replied. "No, that's not right. It's more this way. It looks to be more like just off where the heiau is situated. Yes, that's it!"

"Off the heiau. Hmm," I said.

"I'll have to ask Stu and see if he knows what's going on."

A rushing outflow from one of the mid-length pipelines jostled the SeaTruck slightly as we passed.

"That's strange!" Sarah said, "I really don't get this at all. It's puzzling. There's a second inflow pipeline to supply mixed-temperature water at this level in addition to an outflow pipeline into the layer between the warm and colder layers of seawater. I'm going to take a sample of the outflow water from this pipe."

"Hear that sonar sound?" I asked.

Sarah replied after some thought, "That sounds like an anchor running out."

We immediately looked up at an angle to see a long white hull on the surface cast a dark shadow downwards through the sparkling waters. From its bow, an anchor ran down on a chain until it met the sloping bottom at our level. The bow thrusters maneuvered the ship until the anchor flukes had lodged.

"They seem to be settling in there. Do you think we can go under them?"

"Shouldn't be a problem. We'll just have to watch out for the anchor chain."

We looked around in all directions to the outer edges of the solid blue distant wall of the sea. There were no other craft in sight. Sarah put the SeaTruck into forward, angling upwards. The gap between us and the ship closed until we were nearly under them. Rows of high-intensity underwater lights on the ship's hull snapped on, startling a school of Bandit Angelfish swimming nearby.

It startled us too.

"I think they know we're here," Sarah said.

"Then just keep on going as if we're not concerned."

"Okay."

I looked up at the ship's underwater cargo doors and realized that they were the same ones that I had been hogtied, salted and dropped through in Victoria.

"The *Scorpion*!" I exclaimed. "Chung is up to his eyeballs in crap of some sort or other." Suddenly, a camouflaged SeaTruck, painted in lines of curving green and blue, sank through the open hull doors. There were two pilots. In the back of the submersible were two divers clad in the yellow diver's hard suits that I had spied in their cases aboard the *Scorpion* back in Victoria.

"Let's keep going!" Sarah said.

"Watch it! A diver with a Jet Sled just dropped through the underwater hatch behind their SeaTruck!"

"Is that a spear gun he's got?"

"It's a spear gun, all right, but that's no spear on the end of it. That looks like a small rocket."

"A rocket?"

"Yeah, a rocket or a mini torpedo and he's aiming it at us. Put on some speed!" I shouted.

Sarah frantically jammed the throttle full open and the SeaTruck surged forward as if shot from a cannon. She whipped the steering jets around putting the sub into an evasive zigzag course.

"Step on it!" I shouted as I looked back at the mini torpedo headed our way. In the distance, I saw the diver-laden SeaTruck angle down toward the deep.

"I am!" Sarah shouted back as she put the SeaTruck into fishtail turns.

"Okay, now! Hard left, uh, hard to port, keep it there!" I yelled forgetting for a second that I was in a sub rather than in a pickup truck.

"Keeping it hard to port!" Sarah answered as she tried to see the mini torpedo that was rocketing toward us. The torpedo zoomed by the SeaTruck leaving a turbulent trail behind it.

"Whew! That was too close for comfort!" I said to Sarah. The SeaTruck spun around like a pickup on gravel. I looked back toward the ship, their SeaTruck and the diver but they were swallowed up in the distant wall of blue sea.

CHAPTER TWENTY FOUR

BARSTOOL PIGEON

KAILUA-KONA, THE BIG ISLAND OF HAWAII. The note was written on a torn-out page and shoved under the door at my condo. I found it lying on the marble tile in the entry when I got back late that afternoon. At first, I thought it had been something that I had dropped on the way out earlier this morning. It was crumpled and smudged and stained; the script form was chaotic, as if someone was just learning how to write. As near as I could make out the scrawl, it read: *Meet me at Sonny's Hideaway Bar. I got some info you might be interested in. Ask for Jake. I'm usually sittin on the back corner stool at the bar. Later tomorrow noon would be right.*

Hmm! I wondered. Who is this guy called Jake and what does he know? And how does he know me? I phoned Sarah to find out what street the bar was on.

"Hello?" Sarah answered in her sweet melodious voice.

"It's Rune, Sarah."

"Have I got news for you!" she exclaimed excitedly.

"What's up?" I asked putting aside for the moment any thought of mentioning the note I found this afternoon.

"I talked to Stu. He was sure surprised to hear that there was a chunk of the slope break off, especially one that was almost a half-mile long. They're going to analyze the lava sample to see how old it is and what it's made of."

"What about the water samples that you took?"

"They're going to analyze them too. Oh, and he says that Chung's company, Global Sea Marine, owns Island Pipeline, the marine contracting outfit, the one that laid SSEAAL's pipelines and the one that leases land for their warehouse out off the Queen Kaahumanu Highway. They're here to do some minor repair work to SSEAAL's pipeline anchors, the ones that were slightly dislodged."

"No kidding?" I said in surprise.

"And get this! SSEAAL does not have, I repeat, does not have any pipeline in use offshore of the heiau! There was some pipeline left there as I'd thought but it had been salvaged down to diving depth and the rest was left there because it was too costly to remove at the time."

I gave a long, low whistle in surprise.

"Well, I guess that my own news is minuscule compared to yours."

"What's that?"

"Where is Sonny's Hideaway located?"

"You're not taking me to that place! It's a dive!"

"Well, you're the one with all the dive experience!" I kidded.

"Fuh-ny!" she replied.

"Actually, I was going to go alone."

"Alone? Why?"

"I've got to see a guy. Somebody slipped a note under my door here at the condo. He wants to see me at Sonny's Hideaway tomorrow noon. Says he's got some info for me."

"Oh! We were going to take in the parade tomorrow. It starts at noon," Sarah pouted.

"It shouldn't take too long. I can meet you along the parade route somewhere. Name the place."

"How about down from the farmer's market on Ali'i. I'll try to pick out a shade tree. There's usually a bit of a sea breeze there too. It should keep us cool."

"Sounds good."

"Did the note say what it's about?"

"No, just that he's got some information."

"I'd be careful. It doesn't sound too good. Could be a setup. Remember that pair that you tangled with at the restaurant where I introduced you to Kiana. They were nasty guys. Maybe they're looking for revenge."

"Don't worry. I've already thought of that. I'm going to phone Kimo and see if he can be my backup on this one."

"Good idea!"

"So do you know where this bar is?"

"Yes. It's on one of the side streets up the hill from Ali'i Drive. Check the Kailua map in the phone book. You can't miss it."

"Okay. I got the map page. Yeah. Oh, there it is!"

"And Rune?"

"Yes?"

"Please be careful, both of you!"

"Don't worry, we will. Bye, Sarah."

I hung the phone up, picked it up and dialed again.

Busy.

Redialed.

Rang.

"Hello," Kimo answered.

"Hi, Chief?"

"...This is Kimo."

"Kimo, how are you buddy?"

"...I'm not able to answer- "

"What?"

"...the phone at this-"

"Hey Chief! Pick up the damn phone! It's important!"

". . . time because I'm applying Sex Wax to my latest-"

"Hey there, Rune! Hang loose, huh?"

"Well, well, well. A real live voice."

"How are you?"

"What's this thing about Sex Wax?"

"Polishing my surfboard."

"I'll bet!"

"What's up?"

"What's up is I need some backup tomorrow. You interested?"

"Yeah, I'm interested. Anything to help out an old buddy, you know that. What you got? Another fracas like the last one?"

"No, nothing like that, I hope. Sarah and I were out in the SeaTruck today scouting around off Keahole Point and when I got back to my condo there was a note shoved under my door offering some info of one sort or another."

"About what?"

"The note didn't say. But I'm curious enough to want to check it out. It may lead us somewhere because at the moment we're slogging through the muck and mire when we should be up and running on this case. What do you say?"

"Where and when?"

"Sonny's Hideaway, noon tomorrow."

"Sonny's? That's a real tough bar."

"I'll knock on your door at the crack of noon, not too early for you, is it?"

"Ha, ha! I'll make the effort to get up early. I just hope you know what you're getting into here."

"That's just the problem. I don't. Thanks Chief."

"Yeah, anytime Rune."

I slid into the driver's seat of the Jeep in the parking lot, tucking the laptop computer under the seat. A minute later Kimo came up the sidewalk and jumped in as well. We roared down Ali'i Drive into the middle of town then turned right up a steep lane, parking a block away but still within sight of Sonny's Hideaway Bar. They were right. It was a tough looking bar. A sailor's bar. One that most people try to avoid.

Reaching under the seat, I pulled the laptop out.

"What's that? A computer?" asked Kimo.

"That and more," I answered.

"What's the more?"

"Bug."

"Bug?"

"Bug."

"No, really." Kimo asked.

"Really."

"Really?"

"Really."

"Okay. What kind of bug?" Kimo asked.

"Fly."

"Fly?"

"Fly."

"Okay. What does it do, really?" Kimo said.

"Bug fly," I said as I burst out laughing. I pulled out Armstrong Robotic's miniature robotic SpyFly from its case in the laptop and held it open for Kimo to look at.

"Well, I'll be damned!" he said as he held it, peering closely. "How does it work?"

"It's got video, night vision, GPS navigation, fuzzy logic and a bunch of other things which I forget. It's a robot! Just watch it perform!" I said as I set it on the dash, turned the laptop computer on and banged a rudimentary program out on the keyboard. I slipped my hand into a molded glove that contained a guidance system.

"What's that do?" Kimo asked.

"It gives GPS guidance to it. It gets the fly to its target area, in this case the bar door. Once it's in it uses its own brain - fuzzy logic and nervous net technology built into it - to navigate and send us back video and sound," I said as I set the fly in motion."

"Wow, how does it get back?"

"I can send suggestions to it with this glove. More reconnaissance, target something that I see for a close-up or for it to return. That sort of thing."

"Ever had it not take your suggestions?" Kimo asked.

"I don't know. Dr. Slavik said something about rogue robots doing just that. Anyway, it even comes with its own fake I.D.! Liftoff!"

The fly rose with a faint whir of wings. I directed it to the bar door then let it do its thing while Kimo and I watched the monitor.

"Will you look at that thing?" marveled Kimo. The bug flew over the bar, giving us a fly's-eye view of the interior. Kimo called out as he watched the monitor, "tipsy older woman at the bar, guy at the bar - rummy, another guy - too old and frail, bartender. I don't see any threat to us yet. Hold it, that looks like our guy on the other side at the end of the bar." He looked like an old salt who was still in his prime though somewhat worse for the wear at the moment. We could hear low conversation from the patrons and the clink of glasses as the bartender worked.

I gave the glove a flick with my finger directing the fly to reconnoiter the area at the end of the bar. We watched as the video homed in on the bar counter near the far wall just past our man. It hovered then decided to spiral downward for a landing. The polished surface of the bar gleamed as it rose into view. Suddenly, just as it came in to land on its sticky suction feet, a magnified dome of frothy beer filled the screen. As the fly landed, it skidded right into the amber liquid spilled on the bar counter. The suction pad feet hadn't worked on the slippery surface of the bar. The screen went snowy. Reception lost. Bug lost!

"Shit!" Kimo swore, "I think we got one of them rogue robots!"

"I think we've got a real barfly on our hands," I said. "He's a really thirsty robot. Dr. Slavik will be damned unhappy with this little guy!"

I parked the Jeep in the public lot higher up the slope back of the cop shop. I didn't want to park too close to Sonny's Hideaway in case we were tailed at some point after we left the bar. Heck, we could even have a tail on us right now, I thought. If someone knew where I was staying there was no way of telling how many others knew also.

I turned to Kimo and said, "Okay, here's the plan. There is supposed to be that guy by the name of Jake sitting at the bar on a stool at the far end. Could be the guy we saw, maybe not. I didn't get a chance to see the rest of the layout."

"I know it. You walk in, a horseshoe-shaped bar right in front, turn to your right to follow the bar around which then curves to the left to go to the stool at the far end. A few booths line the outer walls. Small bar."

"I figured that you would go in first and sit someplace where you can keep an eye on us and on the door."

"There's two doors."

"And the back door."

"But they're both near the front," Kimo said as he shifted in the front seat of the Jeep.

"Not so good. No back door?"

"No, that could be a problem."

"How the heck do they allow a bar without a back door?" I asked incredulously.

"Beats me. This one ain't got one, though."

"Well, what if someone's old lady comes sauntering in, you know, lookin' for the old man who sure as shootin' has had one too many and was in trouble even before he entered the bar. How does he duck out the back?"

"Ain't no back."

"Ain't no back? That's crazy. All bars have a back and a back door."

"Not this one. Ain't no back!"

"Ain't no back?"

"Ain't no back!"

"Ain't no back door?"

"Ain't no back, therefore, ain't no back door," Kimo repeated.

"Smarty!"

"This one's built like those little sodas, you know, those little bars in Central America and the Caribbean."

"How so?"

"Two front doors side by side, well, in this case, either side of the curved front wall, no back door!"

"Yeah, you're right too, come to think of it! Well, I'll be a monkey's uncle."

"Careful, I just might agree with you. Ha, ha, Ha!"

I gave Kimo a quick shot to his left biceps and hurt my knuckle in the process. "Okay, here is the small case for the bug. See if you can get at it at some time while we're in there. We don't want the barkeep to wipe it up and we don't want our target to start fiddling with it either. I just hope that hasn't happened yet. I'd hate to think what that little robot is worth. Okay, wise-guy, you ready?"

"Ready as I'll ever be!" he said as pocketed the small case, swung his huge frame out of the Jeep and sauntered off down the sidewalk toward Ali'i Drive. I would give him five minutes and follow him in.

I sauntered over to Sonny's Hideaway Bar a short distance upslope from Ali'i Drive. Its curving outside wall and large portholes gave it a nautical flavour. Indeed, there were two front doors - one on either side of the curving wall between which it said: Sonny's Hideaway - Cocktails. The *Cocktails* part was in blinking red neon. I chose the one on the right, the one the bug flew through on the way in. Inside the door, I paused to let my eyes adjust to the darkness of the juke joint. There was a sour odour that came over me like a fog - the stinks of stale booze, sweaty bodies and cigar smoke. A few grizzled patrons in muscle shirts and tattooed arms gave me the once over, then averted their eyes as I stared them down. A puffy-faced bleached blonde in a tight short skirt and a bouffant hairstyle flashed her rheumy blue eyes at me through glittering inch-long eyelashes. I ignored her.

Through the haze of blue smoke I could see that there was no back door as such. The rear of the dingy bar was backed up against another building. Therefore, no back door.

I noticed Kimo sitting on the far side of the horseshoe bar. It was apparent now that he was in a difficult position in that he couldn't sit at a booth by himself - the bar was the logical place for a solitary drinker. There was no hint of recognition between us as our glances met. The hulking bartender was busy pouring out a shot of hard liquor. He set it in front of a scar-faced man sitting on the end bar stool then slid a glass of beer along to him as well.

Could this be Jake? I hoped so.

The bleary-eyed man swallowed the harsh liquor in one gulp and chased it with a frothy beer. He raised his hairy tattooed forearm and swiped at a dribble of beer foam that ran down the side of his stubbled chin. I went around the horseshoe bar to the right, followed it as it curved around to the left, passing Kimo without so much as a glance at him. I sat in the middle one of the three vacant bar stools that separated them.

"Bud, please," I said to the bartender as he lifted his head in my direction and raised his eyebrows without speaking. He reached down into the cooler below the bar, grabbed a Bud, snapped the top off and emptied half of it into a glass with one practiced motion as he set them down in front of me. I drank thirstily then glanced left, then right.

I gave a hint of recognition to the guy on the right on the end bar stool. "Jake? Jake, is that you?" I asked hoping that I was appearing normally surprised at seeing an old buddy.

"Huh?" said the bleary-eyed man who was in need of not only a shave but also a bath.

"Jake, is that you buddy?" I looked past him, squinting toward the end of the bar, looking for our bug.

"Uh, yeah. Whadya want?" he answered in a tone that was more statement than question.

"Remember me? Your old bud? Long time no see. Can I get you another drink?"

"Uh, yeah, yeah sure," he said, brightening with my offer.

"Bartender!" I called out, "another drink for my old friend Jake here."

The bartender poured out a shot glass of whiskey, brought it over and set it down then swiped his rag at a water ring and some cigarette ash. He missed the spilled beer at the end of the bar. I was glad he was a lousy cleaner.

I suggested we move to a back booth to discuss old times. We picked up our drinks and settled into a scarred old booth with torn red leatherette seats. The tired bench seats audibly sighed through ragged cracks as we sat down.

"So how you been, Jake?" I said as I fed some quarters into the small juke box on the wall at our table, punched selections out of the country menu and waited for the music to play to cover our conversation. A guitar twanged and a gravelly country voice began singing. I noticed Kimo shift over into the bar stool at the end where he could keep a better eye on everything and scoop up the bug off the bar - if it was still there.

"Where do I know you from?" Jake asked as his glazed eyes peered at me through the dimness of the smoky juke joint.

"You dropped a note under my door yesterday, remember?"

"Oh, that!" Jake said peevishly. "I thought you would'a been here a little earlier. I was more sober then."

"Sorry, but the note just said noon."

"Yeah, well . . . " Jake said as the ashes from his stained roll-your-own cigarette fell onto the table, "lately the chances of catchin' me stone cold sober have been slim and none. Didn't used to drink at all what with diving for a living and all. But now . . . "

"How did you know to find me?" I asked.

"Scuttlebutt! You know how word gets around the docks?"

"What info have you got for me?"

Jake glanced around nervously and said in a whisper, "I'm a walking dead man!"

"You're a what?"

"I'm a dead man!" he restated as he moved his head closer to me and emitted a boozer's foul gust of breath.

"Why?"

"They're after me. I just know it. It's only a matter of time!" Jake said as he peered intently at me.

"Who is after you?"

"The guys from the company I used to dive for."

"What company?"

"A company called Island . . . " Jake broke into a wheezing fit of smokers' cough. "Island Pipeline. I know too much about them!"

Intrigued, I pressed for more information. "What is it that you know?"

Jake hesitated and furtively looked around. The bartender was hovering, cleaning an empty booth right behind him. Jake waited until the bartender returned to the bar. The barkeep busied himself by making a phone call.

Jake continued, "What I know is that there were two other divers hired on for this project with me, now both of them are dead and I know I'm next!"

"I heard they were killed in accidents, both of them."

"That's what they think!"

"Why were they killed?"

"Like I told you, because they knew too much," Jake said with large frightened eyes.

"What do you know?"

"It's a long story but when me and the two other guys got hired on for the project - Island Pipeline had the contract to lay pipe for SSEAAL . . . you know who they are?"

"Yes, go ahead."

"Well, everything was goin' along just fine until they asked us to work at the same time on what Island Pipeline called phase two, another project next to the first. We were sworn to secrecy by Island Pipeline about both projects - they got our signatures on paper and all. We stood to lose our pay if we said anything. They said that their technology was highly sensitive and what with industrial espionage and all, well, they didn't want to let any cat out of the bag. Fair enough!"

"SSEAAL said that too?"

"No, Island Pipeline, only Island Pipeline. It was because of their specialized equipment, they said."

"Okay."

"Everything was going along just fine until things started to go haywire. We would lay pipe down off one side of the barge on phase one and at the same time we would be laying new pipe down and connecting it up to the old pipeline off the other side of the barge on phase two. We had just got the new SeaTruck, so it helped speed the work. We ended up working harder and for longer hours to get the job done. Lots of overtime."

"That was bad?"

Jake took a pull on his beer. "Well, no, that was good at first but then it got bad, real bad." He belched loudly.

"How so?"

"Well, even before the projects really started, me and the other guys couldn't figure out why Island Pipeline got a lease on some SSEAAL land out off the highway over a mile from the sea and built a huge warehouse for their base of operations when it made more sense to have built the thing seaside. Anyway, they said that it was closer to the highway and the airport. Fair enough. It kind of made some sense but not enough to be practical, in our minds."

"Go on."

"Yeah, well, like I say. The other two guys and I worked hard, real hard and we worked well together. We had some real good times. Now they're gone. Poor bastards! I really feel for Billy Tucker, he was a good man. Had a real nice wife and then there's Billy Jr., his young son. Heard he was the one got blown out of the water in that explosion out there at Keahole Point. I hope he wasn't a target too! I sure hope not! Lord help us if he was!"

"Then what happened?"

"Well, you see? This second project was supposed to be for SSEAAL but they didn't seem to mention it at all. We were told by the Island Pipeline boss to just keep our mouths shut at all times and to concentrate on our work and to discuss it only with our project foreman."

"And did you?"

"At first we did. Later on we asked a couple guys from SSEAAL some leading questions about the second project but they didn't respond to them at all. We became sure that they had no idea what was really going on."

"So what did you guys do then?"

"Nothing! We just kept on working because the money was so good. But then other things cropped up." Ash fell off the end of his cigarette.

"Like what?"

"Well, for instance, these phase two pipelines didn't go up on shore."

"I thought you said that . . . "

"I did but because Island Pipeline wanted their existence kept quiet the pipes were run up through an ancient underwater lava tube entrance that was located over a hundred feet down."

"The pipes where the steel gate covered the lava tube," I muttered to myself.

"What?" asked Jake.

"Its okay, never mind. Go ahead."

"Anyway, we laid those pipes up that old underground lava tube until we got above sea level."

"Isn't that where there is an ancient heiau just above on the shore?"

"Yeah, there's something up on shore there, don't know exactly what it is. Sign says to keep out. It's kapu, forbidden to enter the grounds or something."

"Where did the pipelines run beyond that?"

"I don't know. The three of us were finished at that point because we were divers, that was our specialty - underwater work - and this was above sea level. There was only maintenance work to look forward to."

"What did you see there?"

"Not much. The lava tube was huge, you could have driven a bus through it and still have room left over for a semi-rig beside it. But above water we could see into the tube. There were faint lights that seemed to show that there was a big cavern that opened up farther upslope from there."

"How far upslope?"

"Don't know, maybe a quarter of a mile or so."

"What was going on there?"

"Don't rightly know. As I say, we were sworn to secrecy and we didn't ask and no one told us. One of the guys thought it might have been some kinda secret U.S. military installation."

"What gave you that idea?"

"Just a guess, pure speculation. But then Billy Tucker died under some real suspicious circumstances. Ray almost got it at the same time.

Bad air! Then Ray took a spear to his heart. I didn't think that the military would get involved in something like that. Especially when another government agency - SSEAAL - knew nothing about it. So I came to the conclusion that it's Island Pipeline's doing. They want to get rid of the people who know about and can finger them for the secret phase two underwater pipeline installation. We were expendable, just slaves, hired slaves though, to be sacrificed for the good of the corporation."

Something like how the ancient Hawaiians sometimes treated their captive warriors during times of war, I thought.

Out of the corner of my eye, I noticed two guys come into the bar. Both wore dark glasses which they lifted slightly to focus their eyes in the smoky dimness of the bar. Both wore dark knit caps on their heads rolled up in longshoreman fashion. Kimo glanced up at them and tracked them as they made their way around the curve of the bar. They selected the empty booth directly behind Jake. They called for four draft and started talking while they waited for their orders. The bartender eventually waddled around the end of the bar with a tray of beer and plopped four down in front of them. It seemed like they were going to be here for a while.

I glanced over at Kimo. There was no indication that he thought these two were anything other than normal bar clientele. I threw a few more quarters into the wall juke box at the booth and blindly hit the buttons. *Honky Tonk Man* began playing. With lowered voices, Jake and I resumed our conversation. "Have you been into the warehouse out off the highway?" I asked.

"No, none of us have. We mainly worked off a tethered barge and occasionally off the Global Sea vessel *Scorpion* if we had to ride the SeaTruck up into its bay or something like . . ." I heard a slight cracking thump over the sound of the music, like wood splintering, and felt a hot flash brush past my arm. ". . . they gaaht me!" Jake blurted out as he was slammed against the table. He looked at me with eyes widened in terror as he tried to stand up.

"What?"

"I'm dead!" Jake gurgled as bright red blood leaked out of his mouth and down his grizzled chin. He clutched at his chest with his bony, cigarette-stained fingers. I watched his life fade out of his eyes as he slumped. Now vacant-eyed, his head hit the table, knocking his glass of beer over onto the floor where it shattered in a spreading pool of frothy amber liquid. Blood from his mouth ran onto the table and dripped over the edge into the pool of beer on the floor. A spreading red stain wet his chest area; his staring eyes, unseeing.

A high-pitched scream came from the blonde floozy at the bar. She froze in her seat. The bartender had already ducked below the bar. The drinkers at the bar dropped low as they fell off their stools trying to scramble for the door.

I looked up to see a handgun with a silencer. It was in the hand of the guy furthest from me in the adjacent booth. He was bringing it up level with my head. Both men had their knit caps pulled down into balaclavas, giving them a sinister appearance. A split second later a bar stool went crashing into the gunman, who gave a painful yelp as the gun was knocked out of his hand, hit the wall beside him and skittered under their table. The second man was reaching for his gun under his shirt as I saw Kimo heave a second bar stool, scoring a direct hit as well.

The thug managed to hang onto his gun.

I scrambled out of the booth, ran around the bar and dove for the open doorway. Kimo was right behind me. His martial arts talents would be useless against a gun. This was one time that we both wished we had been armed. We dashed down the sloping street before ducking into the doorway of a pottery shop.

"Where's your back door?" I asked frantically of the startled Chinese woman clerk who dropped a large vase she had been holding. It crashed into bits on the tile floor.

“No back door, no back door!” she shouted excitedly in singsong English.

“Chief, what the hell is this thing around here about no back doors!” I yelled.

We ran out into the street again, knocking a table display of pottery down to the floor with a resounding crash. The two balaclava-clad thugs from the bar were running down the street after us, guns in hand. Tourists screamed and fell as the two roughly shoved them out of their way. Others walking toward the two hit the ground as soon as they saw the waving guns and the balaclava headgear.

Kimo and I ran across the street into a tee-shirt shop and ducked behind some displays before noticing an adjoining door to the next store.

The two thugs came through the doorway low with their guns pointed dead ahead as they swung their heads from side to side, looking around the shop.

We crouched behind stacks of tee-shirts and made our way over to the adjoining doorway as we tried to stifle our ragged breathing.

The two thugs moved along slowly as they strained to see through the tinted glasses that both of them were still wearing.

We bent down as we shuffled along to stay ahead of them one aisle over. I followed Kimo as he slid through the doorway. We found ourselves in a room full of trinkets and tourist baubles.

No place to hide!

Kimo ran for the street. I followed him. We dashed down the lane toward Ali'i Drive only to find our access blocked by a wall of people watching the passing parade. Glancing behind me, I saw the two thugs in hot pursuit with their guns still drawn. I pushed my way into the throng then onto Ali'i Drive, almost falling under the wheels of a passing float. I glanced back to see our pursuers in a state of confusion. They ran with raised guns as they shouldered their way into the crowd, roughly shoving people aside. People began screaming. Others ran blindly into fellow parade watchers, knocking them down.

The West Hawaii County marching band, dressed in powder blue and white, was just coming along, their melodious marching tune and thumping drums lent a surreal air to the life and death chase we were in.

I glanced around looking for Kimo.

He disappeared.

I looked back. The thugs were still mixed in with the crowd searching for us.

"Hey! Rune!" I heard kimo say. I looked around but couldn't see him.

"Up here!" He shouted again.

I glanced up at the Kona Coffee float. A white banner proclaimed *Island Grown - Hawaii's Own.* A blue flatbed tractor-trailer was decorated with gunny sacks of coffee beans and plenty of thick foliage at either end. Drummers on the float banged a hypnotic tattoo on the skins with stout sticks. The float crawled along but still I couldn't see Kimo.

"Up! Up here!" Kimo called again as he stuck his face out from behind some foliage at the end of the flatbed trailer.

I ran around the far side of the tractor and doubled back, flinging myself onto the flatbed with a western roll. Kimo pulled me behind the thick foliage where we silently watched the two thugs. They were in a frenzy because they had lost us. There were more people screaming as the two hitmen began knocking people out of the way with their gun butts. We saw them run across the road to check the maze of tourist shops that flanked the seashore.

Kimo and I stayed on the float. We kept our eyes peeled for the two hitmen. In a while we passed the farmer's market. I spotted Sarah standing under a spreading shade tree. We startled her as we jumped out of the foliage on the float.

"Whoa!" Sarah shrieked. "Where did you guys come from?"

"We got tired of walking!" I quipped.

"Yeah, we're traveling on the incentive plan." Kimo laughed. "We had an incentive - we didn't want to get shot!"

"What happened?" Sarah asked apprehensively.

"Long story," I said, "but basically we got our info but they got him."

"You're not serious!"

"I'd have been dead too if it wasn't for the Chief here backing me up! He saved my life!"

"Things are really getting too rough. What did you find out?"

"I'll tell you later!" I said. "Kimo, did you find the bug?"

"Got it!" he said as he patted his pocket.

Sarah gave us a lift back toward my Jeep in the upper lot near the cop shop while I fleshed out the story as she drove. A crowd of curious onlookers stood around two police squad cars parked at odd angles outside Sonny's Hideaway. The neon cocktail sign flashed oddly out of sequence with the cop cars' rooftop lights. An ambulance wailed past us and screeched to a halt beside another ambulance already outside the bar, scattering the edging onlookers and drawing more curious parade watchers up the lane from Ali'i Drive.

"Oh, God!" Sarah said in consternation. "The poor man!" She added as she drew her hand up to her mouth. "What a horrible thing!"

CHAPTER TWENTY FIVE

GLOBAL SEA MARINE

KAAHUMANU HIGHWAY, KONA. The huge warehouse stuck out like a wart on a hog's back, sitting out there as it did in the middle of a field of jumbled lava striations and tufts of pili grass. Occasional jet traffic in and out of the nearby Kona International Airport reverberated off the metal sides of the structure. Kimo and I boldly walked through the office door at Island Pipeline - it said so on the sign above and included a "Div. of Global Sea Marine" under the name. The place had a few huge sliding doors for rigs to get in and out but not much else to give it some identity, some purpose for being.

A small office staff was in evidence. They were mainly gadding about but having seen us, got down to the business at hand. They were now peering intently at their computer screens and technical reference sheets.

We approached the receptionist.

"Hi! My name is Rune Erikson," I said as I placed my briefcase on her desk. "We're here from the manufacturers of your SeaTruck. I just flew in from Vancouver last night and I've got to catch a two o'clock flight to Tokyo today where I have another appointment. I'm a marine technical evaluation specialist and this is my assistant Kimo Kekuna. We're here to do an on-sight technical evaluation on your SeaTruck as per the manufacturer's warranty agreement. Any lapses in technical evaluations will, according to your contract, automatically render the manufacturer's warranty null and void. Where exactly is your SeaTruck parked at the moment?"

"I don't know about any . . . " the receptionist started to say.

"What is your name?" I asked as I peered at her name plate sitting on her desk. "Ah, Suzanne Daniels. Miss Daniels! I don't know if you caught the significance of what I just said. Any lapses in technical evaluation will automatically render the manufacturer's warranty agreement null and void. Now our companies had set this appointment up weeks ago and everything was confirmed because of my tight schedule. So you can see that time is of the essence. Now show us where the SeaTruck is parked so we can get on with it!"

"But I don't have any record of your . . . "

"Miss Daniels! It is obvious that you are incapable of fulfilling something as simple as an appointment arranged well in advance. I want to speak to your manager now!"

"But he's at lunch, he's usually gone a couple hours and he has me hold all his calls until he gets back."

"Miss Daniels, I must insist upon seeing the SeaTruck now. My schedule precludes any delay. Any delay renders the warranty null and void."

"But I don't think I can authorize you . . . " she said as she nervously glanced around at her co-workers for support and found none. Everyone had tucked their heads lower and had busied themselves at their terminals, not wanting to get involved in this situation where one could easily find themselves out on the proverbial precarious limb in a windstorm.

"Miss Daniels! Null and void!"

"Do you have a business card?"

"Yes, right here," I said as I pulled the crisp new card from its leather holder.

She read the card quickly. I was glad that I had the foresight to have these made up just in case I needed them. This was just the case.

"Well, okay. I suppose it will be all right, if it was scheduled. They did have some breakdown with it. Come this way," she said, her resistence deflated. She rose from her chair, smoothing the wrinkles on the front of her skirt as she did.

We followed Miss Daniels clicking heels through the doorway into the echoing recesses of the deserted warehouse. Pallets of cable and rope and huge nuts and bolts littered the concrete floor. A large shed within the warehouse stood off to one side. Miss Daniels went up to the doorway of the shed and flipped the light switch, bathing its interior with bright lights. In the middle of it was a SeaTruck which appeared to be somewhat the worse for wear judging by its dings and scrapes.

"That's fine, Miss Daniels," I said as Kimo and I set our briefcases down. "We can take it from here on in. We'll be done in under two hours. No need for you to hang around but if you want to that's okay too. Pretty woman like you is always welcome to watch. Quite boring stuff we do, though absolutely essential!"

"Uh, no. That's okay. I have some files to check and reports to type. You guys just go ahead with whatever it is that you have to do," she said with resignation as she turned and clicked her way back to the front office.

Kimo and I glanced at each other, smiled and started looking over the SeaTruck while waiting for her to leave the warehouse.

"I think we've got about an hour max!" I said to Kimo. "Should be enough time to have a snoop around here."

"Let's do it!" Kimo replied eagerly.

We slipped out of the SeaTruck shed and made our way to the rear of the warehouse where we found more piles of construction materials.

"Where do these trucks unload?" I asked. "I don't see a loading bay!"

"I don't get it either!" Kimo said. "There should be a loading bay somewhere."

"What's that on the far side of the warehouse?"

"Let's check it out," Kimo said.

We furtively made our way over to the other side. There, we came across a locked door. We picked the lock and made our way into a second but smaller part of the warehouse. There we found a small loading bay that was still large enough for two rigs to be loaded or unloaded at the same time. A rig was backed into one bay. We walked onto a ramp and peered into the trailer which actually was a sea container that was lashed down upon a trailer deck. There was almost a full load of locked metal crates and rim-locked metal barrels on pallets. There were no markings to indicate their contents.

"What's that over on the side?" I asked.

"Looks like another cargo door," Kimo replied. "It seems to be well-used too."

"Out the back?" I questioned.

"Yeah, that's odd. It slopes down too."

"Look for the switch to open it. It must be here somewhere." I said as we looked high and low without finding it.

Kimo stood back and surveyed the layout. Finally, he bent down on the floor in front of the door and said, "Pressure plate. Requires a certain amount of pressure to open the door. Usually heavier than one person."

"I'm sure the two of us can trigger the switch!" I said as Kimo and I both stepped on the plate together.

The heavy door slowly rolled up to reveal a tunnel angling downward.

"A tunnel? That's odd!" Kimo said.

"And down to where?" I added.

As we entered the tunnel, we saw that it led into a dimly-lit passageway that swung under the surface in a steady descent. The tunnel had been bored through the ancient lava bed. We walked down the gradual slope until we came across a junction where the man-made tunnel joined a meandering lava tube that was big enough for a full-sized train to run through. Moisture dripped from the ceiling of the lava tube creating small puddles here and there. It was cool but the air was somewhat foul and humid.

There was evidence that this passageway was being used by some vehicle like an ATV as narrow tracks were evident on the fine grit and rubble that was used to fill in the low spots on the floor of the lava tube.

We descended steadily into the bowels of the ancient lava bed. After walking awhile, we heard a distinct hum as though from machinery being operated. Crunching and grinding sounds accompanied the hum as we descended farther. Hugging the niches in the wall of the tube, we neared a glowing, well-lit cavern.

We stopped and peered into the void to see industrial machinery, conveyor belts, pulverizing machines and large water pipes running maze-like throughout the cavern. Workers clad in work-blackened grey jump-suits and coveralls were checking on equipment and monitoring valves and flow meters. What appeared to be a laboratory and an office of sorts occupied a space high overhead against one wall overlooking the whole operation. On a workbench, a bright red beam from a laser device was cutting its way through a rough, dark-brown lump of rock.

"What do you make of it?" asked Kimo as we surveyed the underground complex.

"Don't know. Looks like some sort of rock or ore that is being worked on. Could be that they are grinding ore for a mining operation or something," I answered. "I sure wish that we had the SpyFly back in operation. We could really use it here!"

The laser finished cutting through the rock and the two halves fell apart. A lab-coated man with a shock of salt and pepper hair examined the halves and placed both cut sides down on one of several moving conveyor belts at his disposal. Soon the crunching grinder chewed into the halves with a hammering roar.

A round black textured rock came tumbling down from a sturdy screen that ran through an open water pipeline. It was constructed in such a way as to let gravity tumble the rock out of the gushing water in the pipe down into a holding bin yet still let the force carry the water on its intended route through the pipe. Pipes ran from glass-lined, stainless steel tanks off to one side. Large stickers stuck on other pipes read *Danger!* A logo of a skeletal hand was pasted alongside as well. A decal placed alongside that listed the type of chemical that the particular pipe carried.

Kimo and I moved back into the shadows of the lava tube as two workers suddenly looked over at a machine that was near us.

"That was close!" Kimo said.

"Yeah, I wasn't expecting them to look over here!" I said. "Let's see what else is going on."

"You want to go farther into the cavern?"

"We're running out of time, let's just lie low here and see what happens."

"Got it!"

The next rock was split in half and placed on another conveyor. This time there was no resulting crunch from a crusher. The rocks were being sorted in some fashion.

"Look!" Kimo said excitedly.

I looked to the far side of the lava tunnel to where he was pointing. A gleaming SeaTruck, like the one Sarah and I had seen under the *Scorpion*, emerged from the lava tunnel alongside the pipelines. It was dripping water as it had just emerged from the sea. There were tool attachments on it that were quite different from those on our SeaTruck. Two pilots worked the controls while two divers, wearing swivel-jointed deep-dive hard suits, sat impassively in jump seats in the bed of the SeaTruck. Bright headlights shot out ahead as it rolled to a stop on the cavern floor.

A discussion followed, apparently about the diver's equipment, accompanied by arm gestures. Shortly, another piece of equipment was delivered to the two divers. One of the workmen removed part of a diver's equipment - a robotic hand - and exchanged it for the replacement. They got back on the rear jump seat while the pilots re-entered the cockpit. They wheeled the SeaTruck into a U-turn and drove back down the lava tube alongside the water pipelines.

"So what was all that about?" Kimo asked.

"Fine-tuning their equipment by the looks of it."

"So where did they come from and where did they go to?" he asked.

"Don't know. Maybe they are being hauled down to the deep in the SeaTruck. Sarah and I saw them a while ago. They're designed just for such type of work as that."

"Maybe they are gathering the rocks off the sea floor and having the pipeline suck them up to the surface," Kimo speculated.

"Could be, but why? There's not supposed to be any viable mineral mining down in the deep around these parts. I can't figure it out."

I glanced over to our far right where small metal crates were being stacked alongside black metal barrels whose rims were being sealed and locked by a worker. These were in turn being placed upon small flatbed trailers which were hooked to an electric tram unit. Finishing loading, the worker jumped on the low tram and drove it up the slope toward us. Kimo and I pressed ourselves into the niches of the tube as the piercing headlights of the tram bounced shafts of light past us. We could feel the ground vibrating as the tram trundled past us with its heavy load.

"Lets tag along for the ride," I said to Kimo as I swung aboard the end of the last flatbed and hung on. Kimo swung up beside me.

We listened to the electric whine of the tram as it pulled us up the slope. Droplets of water occasionally leaked upon us from the rough ceiling. At the junction, the driver diverted his tram into the man-made tunnel where the tram strained with the increased incline then emerged into the ground-level warehouse. The whining noise of the tram was lost amongst the void of this empty section of warehouse after having been reverberating off the walls while in the tunnel. Kimo and I jumped off as he cut in front of the trailer. The driver swung his tram train into an arcing turn that took him up to the higher level of the loading dock.

We hid in front of the trailer watching as the driver got on a forklift and started loading his tram cargo into the sea container on the trailer deck.

Checking my wristwatch, I whispered to Kimo, "Our time's just about up! We've got to get back to the SeaTruck shed before anyone comes by and discovers us missing." We waited until the driver took the forklift into the sea container then sprinted for the door to the other part of the warehouse. We double-checked the SeaTruck shed to make sure it was still lit and deserted.

Picking up our briefcases from where we had left them, Kimo and I returned to the front office. We thanked Miss Daniels for helping us and said that if we hurried, I would just be able to make my flight to Tokyo.

"Have a good flight," she wished me with a wave as we left the front office.

"Thanks," I replied with a smile. We walked over to my Jeep and drove off onto the Queen Kaahumanu highway. A short distance away, I pulled over into a driveway that led to a rough trail over the lava fields. We had a good view of the grounds of Island Pipeline.

"I'm glad the manager didn't arrive back from lunch before we got out of there. It would have been tough to explain ourselves out of that one without having to involve everyone else and possibly blowing our cover."

"You got that right but what now?" asked the Chief.

"We wait and see if that rig moves off that property. If it does, we're onto it like a fog!"

"Yeah. Good idea! See where it goes," Kimo replied.

The hot sun beat down upon us as we sat in the open Jeep. Any length of time here and we would slowly be roasted as the sun got hotter as the day wore on. However, we didn't have long to wait. The cargo doors rolled sideways on the warehouse wall. The rig belched black smoke as it geared up and slowly edged through the warehouse door, up the road to the highway where it turned left and lumbered along toward the airport turnoff.

We slipped into the traffic well back of the rig. But it didn't take the airport turnoff as I had presumed that it would.

"Where are you going?" I absent-mindedly asked of no one in particular.

"Good question," added Kimo.

"Any idea where he's headed?"

"Not really," he answered.

We hung back as the heavy truck rumbled along. At the Waimea junction, the driver bore left rather than going through Waimea and possibly on to Hilo.

"I think I know now," Kimo stated firmly. "There is a marine port for oceangoing freighters near here. I think that's where he's headed."

Sure enough, we followed the rig into the seaport's terminal where it pulled up beside a rusting hulk of a freighter called the *Sun Young*. It looked neither bright nor young; rust had leaked off the after deck and coated the name with stains of streaky copper. It looked like it had seen some rough times; its days at sea were numbered.

We parked in the shadow of a shade tree on the far side of the terminal parking lot. The driver, with his clip board of manifests in his hand, scurried aboard the rusting Panamanian-registered freighter.

Shortly, a worker appeared on the main deck. He climbed into the winch control cab and swung the arm of the winch out over the dock.

The driver came back down the gangplank and connected the winch to the four corners of the steel container. The container was placed on deck with a multitude of others of various colours.

"What I wouldn't give to have a look at those papers," I said.

"Yeah," replied Kimo, "but they're probably phony."

* * * * *

Sheriff Jim Paoluana had just thrown the last file into the out-basket. It was the end of another busy day in a string of busy weeks. Rising from his desk, he stretched and contemplated phoning his wife to tell her that he would be home soon.

He peered through his window into his outer office to see if anyone was waiting to see him. It was empty save for his secretary who was logging-off her computer and locking the drawers on her desk. To hide them, as usual, she threw the keys under her keyboard. She'll be glad to see the end of this day too, he mused as he thought of all the paperwork he had unloaded on her yet again.

Lately he had been just too busy to do a lot of the little things himself and had been forced to scribble a Post-It sticky-note on each item asking her to handle them.

Deep in thought, he worriedly turned back to his desk, stretched again and stifled a yawn. He thought, Christ sakes, this makes one murder, one suspicious death, one industrial accident that was being treated as suspicious, an unexplained explosion with mostly dead divers and one injured surf boarder, and one suspicious car accident that appeared to be two counts of attempted murder. All in one season! Most times we didn't get that much in one year!

There was a short rap on his office door behind him. It suddenly burst open as Kimo and his friend Rune entered his inner office. Lost in thought, the sheriff quickly turned around and gave a little groan as his back protested the sudden twisting motion.

"Sheriff!" Kimo said in greeting. "Sorry to startle you, but your secretary said to just go in as you were wrapping up for the day."

"Kimo, Rune! What can I do for you guys?" the sheriff asked.

"Well sheriff, we thought it was about time that we came in to give you our statement on the shooting at Sonny's Hideaway," Kimo stated matter-of-factly.

"That was you guys that hightailed it out of there?" he asked in surprise.

"Not the shooters," I answered. "We were in the bar though. I was talking to Jake in the booth when they took him out in a permanent way. It was too bad. He knew what hit him too! That's what he was afraid of, why he wanted to talk to me. Any line on the shooters yet?"

"The shooters? I got my guys working on that right now. Got lots of eye witnesses but nothing consistently reliable in the way of descriptions. Everybody's sure they looked just a little different from what the next guy saw."

"Well we don't know who they were but both were wearing knit caps like those longshoremen wear, only they pulled them down over their heads, balaclavas, I think, and dark glasses. Blue jeans and loose cotton twill work shirts. Oh, and work boots. But they didn't look like your typical longshoremen. They looked too skinny and their hands weren't rough either. I can still see that guy pointing his gun at my head and me fully expecting to take the hit in a split second. It was like a bad dream in slow motion. If it wasn't for Kimo here, I would have been a goner, that's for sure!"

Kimo added, "You might lean on the bartender at Sonny's. He made a phone call while Rune and Jake were talking. He was talking to someone in a real low voice but from snatches of conversation and him glancing over at Jake and Rune as he was talking, it could have been him putting the finger on Jake."

"Okay, we'll do that," the sheriff agreed.

"They're keeping you guys pretty busy lately," Kimo said to the sheriff.

"Yeah, I was just thinking," Sheriff Paoluana said. "We got a murder on the books now. We've also got a suspicious death, an industrial accident that is suspicious, and the car accident that looks like it could be an attempted murder. Not to mention the explosion"

"We know about the car accident. What was the suspicious death about?"

"Kids found a scuba diver floating face down in a tidal pool. He'd been shot through the back with a spear gun. No leads so far on that one. Forensic haven't completed their exam findings and at the moment that's just about all we have to go on."

"And the suspicious industrial accident?" Kimo asked.

"That's a strange one!" the sheriff answered. "It appeared to just be an industrial accident. A diver drowned after getting some bad air. It seemed straight forward at the time. Coroner even thought so too! But now, I don't know," he said, shaking his head while looking down at the floor in recollection.

"Why?" I asked.

"For starters, the other diver diving with him at the time should have died along with him. They both had bad air. He managed to somehow stay alive when he recognized the signs in his partner and effect a rescue. He survived, his partner didn't."

"One of the divers, was that the guy who had a wife and a young son named Billy?"

"That's the one! Tucker was his name, Bill Tucker, Sr. Fellow from the hills of Tennessee. Ex-navy man. Wife's name is Marsha, I think. It was sad, real sad, young family and all. He had his whole future ahead of him. Then his wife and son were in that offshore explosion at Keahole Point. So it was a strange start to a series of unusual misfortunes."

"And that was suspicious?" Kimo asked.

"Not in itself. But when the surviving diver was found to be the one who was shot in the back with a spear gun, we started to investigate both incidents together. You see, they both worked for the same company."

"Which company?" I asked.

"A marine contracting company - Island Pipeline - they're new to the islands. They got their start here putting down pipe for SSEAAL. You guys know anything about them?"

"Some," I stated unsure if I should tell him of all our suspicions about the underwater pipeline, the cavern in the lava tube and the warehouse complex off the Kaahumana highway. I continued, "Island Pipeline is owned by Global Sea Marine which is owned by a former North Korean commando by the name of Chung. His full name is Chung Min-Ho. Mr. Chung got his start by going AWOL and smuggling a submarine, a Shark-class, if I recall, out of the north. He told me in Victoria that he let most of the sub crew go ashore but I did some checking and found that, according to the South Koreans, the crew that were expendable were all murdered in cold blood - execution style! This was also confirmed by some western intelligence sources including our own CSE. He later sold the sub on the open market to the highest bidder. Then he got into brokering Russian subs as well. He's now into marine contract and salvage and who knows what else. I had a serious run-in with him in Victoria aboard his work-yacht, the motor vessel *Scorpion*. He tried to have me drowned. I've also had dealings with his thugs there and probably here as well. He is the type of person who will stop at nothing to get what he wants. He is really an extremely dangerous type of guy! Absolutely ruthless!"

"Whew! No kidding!" the sheriff whistled in surprise.

"Want to know something else? Jake, the guy who was shot at Sonny's, was the third diver employed by Island Pipeline."

"You sure about that?"

"Jake himself told me that he was afraid for his life because the other two divers were dead. He figured he was next and you know what? He was right!"

"There's definitely something going on with that outfit then," the sheriff stated as he rubbed his chin.

"You're telling me!" I said.

"Looks like mister . . . what's his name?"

"Chung . . . Chung, Min-Ho."

"Right! Mr. Chung's got some explaining to do," the sheriff stated. "But murder? Why would he have anyone murdered? What's at stake here that would lead to murder?"

CHAPTER TWENTY SIX

CAULDRONS OF FIRE

KILAUEA CALDERA, ON THE FLANK OF MAUNA LOA, THE BIG ISLAND OF HAWAII. We decided to let Sheriff Paoluana and his deputies have some time on their own to investigate the new evidence that we had literally dug up. Likewise, the SSEAAL lab still needed a day or two to conduct their extensive analysis of our samples from the deep. Sarah and I had thought that we had done about all we could do for the time being and desperately needed to take a couple days off to recharge our batteries by doing some exploring and rock climbing. Sarah had managed to cajole Stu, her taskmaster boss, into getting a couple days away from the office. She had cornered him in his office and told him that he could consider this a field trip as she and I would be spending the first day at the Kilauea Caldera and the second day studying caverns and lava tube formations in Hilo.

According to Sarah, there was a rather unique river gorge that was located just outside of Hilo. We would be rappelling down into the gorge to where we could access and explore a lava cavern whose entrance was on a vertical cliff directly under a river waterfall.

We decided to take the southern route, the Kuakini Highway, then the Mamalahoa Highway as it would take us past the Kilauea Caldera where Sarah wanted to make an offering to Pele.

I stopped by Sarah's condo in Kailua and added her climbing gear to mine in the rear of the Jeep. We were both in high spirits as we set off in the early morning mists and tangerine shades of sunrise for the four-hour drive to the Kilauea Caldera.

The Jeep climbed the rise of the western flank of Mauna Loa as we drove south along the Kona coastline. To our left the slope rose ever upwards out of sight. To our right, far below, were Kealakekua Bay and the brilliant blue waters of the Pacific Ocean. Small roadside villages with rundown but picturesque buildings sat every few miles on the serpentine and, at times, cliff-hugging highway. The towns became fewer; dense foliage became interspersed with barren lava fields.

We rounded the most southerly point of the United States. Dropping back down to sea level at Punaluu Beach where the Hawksbill turtles nest, we followed the Ka'u coastline. The land rose again as we tracked the highway inland with Mauna Loa's peak on our left and the Ka'u desert on our right. We crossed the Great Crack which starts at Kapaoo Point and forms a rough hourglass shape with the waist near the Kilauea Caldera and the top part ringing the apex of the more than two-mile-high Mauna Loa. The other end of the immense crack culminated near the Wahaula Heiau on the far side of Kaena Point beyond where the lava rushes into the sea in a billowing toxic cloud of steam and gas.

Turning off onto the eleven-mile-long circular highway around the Kilauea Caldera, we stopped at the information center so that I could get a feeling for the lay of this extraordinary landscape.

We continued driving the mile-high circular highway. It had been patched and rerouted as necessary over the years as new eruptions occurred here and there. Sarah gave me specific instructions to drive until she asked me to pull over at the ancient sacred site of Halema'uma'u Crater, Pele's home, which is a crater within a crater. I pulled over into a parking area.

We walked through the stink of sulphurous steam vents to get to the edge of a precipice which afforded a breathtaking view of a section of the caldera floor some 450 vertical feet below.

Sarah carried an offering of fruit, pig, fish and chicken to appease Pele. Venting acidic vapours rose out of cracks along the trail. More steam vents far below spewed rising trails of vapour out of the crater floor.

"What you have to realize is the power of Pele," Sarah said. "In 1924 this crater was only a quarter mile across when an explosion occurred, doubling the diameter of the crater to a half mile."

"So what happened?" I asked.

"There is a reservoir of molten rock over two miles below us. When the pressure becomes too intense the lava is forced up into the caldera. Sometimes it is forced on the flank below through surface flows and underground rivers of molten rock within old lava tubes. At times the force reaches explosive proportions as happened in 1924. At one time the floor of the caldera was twice as deep as it is now."

"So the immense forces that occur far below cause the explosions?"

"Yes, and sometimes methane gas accumulates underground and is trapped in a large pocket as molten lava rushes down an old lava tube. This frequently causes tremendous underground explosions that rip open the ground as the lava advances and hurls rocks in all directions. Other than that, our volcanoes here in the Hawaiian Islands are not explosive as such when compared to most others in the world."

I gave Sarah some space for a private moment, standing off to one side in respect. She waited for some time in reflection before she flung the food offering into the abyss. The rising wind along the vertical wall of the caldera buffeted the offering as it fell.

Could it be that one of Pele's sisters was playfully toying with her siblings offering?

My thoughts returned to the erotic images of Pele in Kiana's form the night of the luau. Even now I struggled to come to terms with what had happened or what I thought had happened.

Sarah stood alone for a few minutes longer before turning and waving me over to her. We stood together, letting the emotions wash over us. I was waiting for some special sign from Pele but none was forthcoming. I thought it best to let this sleeping goddess lie.

"You can't come this far and not see the lava flowing at the Pu'u Loa," Sarah firmly stated with a bright smile.

"How do we see that?" I asked.

"One way is to go down the Chain of Craters road until we reach the sea. Then we hike along the lava beds at the coastline until we reach the area where there is active flow."

"And the other?"

"Back along the highway toward Hilo, right at the town of Keaau then down to the end of the road near the sea. At one time the coastal road ran right through but the lava flow has cut if off and destroyed many homes and settlements along the way. It was an ongoing disaster that could be rekindled at any time."

"Let's try the Chain of Craters road, shall we?"

"Sure!" Sarah agreed.

It was a twenty-mile trip on a winding road that kept descending. Watching the huge billowing cloud of volcanic vapour was like watching the approach to a major industrial city on the prairies where you can see the towering skyline for a long time before you actually get there. We stopped beside an information sign to take in the enormity of the lava bed we were traveling on.

"What does it say?" I asked as I unpacked my field glasses.

Sarah read, "It says 'Ka uahi o ka mahu ha'alelea i uka,
Ka hala, ka lehua, lu 'ia ia kai.
Ha'aha'a Puna, ki'eki'e Kilauea;
Ko Puna kuahiwi mau no ke ahi,

O Puna, aina aloha!"

"Easy for you to say but what does it mean?" I asked as I swept my binoculars across the stark landscape.

Sarah responded, "It means 'As smoke and steam leave the upland,
The hala, the lehua scatter to the sea.
Puna is far below, Kilauea high above;
Puna's forests frequently flame,
Oh Puna, cherished land!'"

"That's amazing!" I said as I lowered my field glasses.

"It sure is!" she agreed.

"No, I meant your translation!" I said as I turned to look at Sarah. "You translated that really quickly."

"No, I can't translate that fast!" Sarah laughed. "I was only reading what was already written here alongside the Hawaiian words."

I drove the Jeep down to the bottom of the road. Sarah and I walked to the edge of the lava cliff overlooking the sea. A sign stated "Extreme danger beyond this point! Collapse of lava bench occurs without warning causing violent steam explosions and ocean surge." We moved over to a designated lookout and peered over the cliff down to the sea to where a spouting lava fall had been solidified into a permanent arc or as permanent as it can get in this ever-changing landscape.

I thought back to the lava collapse that sent an encampment of Boy Scouts into the sea years ago on this very coastline. This potential collapse here would likely be minor compared to the land slippage that had occurred at that time. I shuddered at the thought.

The road ended abruptly as a six-foot-high bed of lava was frozen in its tracks. A yellow sign stuck off to the right side of the road cautioned, "Hiking to lava flow is dangerous. Terrain is rough and unstable."

Sarah and I put on our hiking boots and set out along the utter blackness of the coastal lava field but not before reading the warning signs that said: "Danger! Hazardous fumes, steep cliffs, rough surfaces, hot lava, flashlight required after dark." And, "Caution! Avoid the steam plume - It is hazardous to your health and may be life-threatening. The plume contains hydrochloric acid and volcanic glass particles which can irritate eyes and skin and cause respiratory distress." Hmm I thought.

Sarah and I climbed the rising lava slope to where it leveled out into an undulating terrain full of crevasses and rough openings. The towering white cloud gave us a marker to walk to as we made our way over the several miles of blackness to the river of fire that ran into the sea.

There was a smoking trail that showed the route that the coursing lava took to get down the slope to the point where we intercepted the flow. I looked upslope and could not see the top of Mauna Loa some forty miles distant and over two miles high as the vog obscured my vision. I looked down at the fiery-red stream with the bright-yellow hot spots that meandered as gravity and terrain worked their effects. Here it spread out, there it narrowed and further still it subducted and flowed under where its only presence was indicated by glowing skylights that afforded us a glimpse into the underground fiery river. We walked over to a skylight and cautiously peered over the edge. The heat rose from the large hole in the lava. The cooling sea breeze provided us with a natural air conditioner. We bent down to examine some fine strands of golden glass that had solidified.

"What's that?" I asked.

"Pele's hair," Sarah replied.

"Really?"

"Yes, strands formed from the molten lava. Different, isn't it?"

"It sure is!" I agreed.

"Careful!" Sarah cautioned me as I moved over to get a better view, "We've got to stay upwind of these skylights. The superheated air and gasses could burn our lungs and permanently damage them, or worse yet, kill us in flash of superheated vapour."

"What did you say causes these skylights to occur?" I asked.

Sarah replied, "They're formed when the flowing lava solidifies, covering itself. This covering then partially collapses in places to form a skylight. Sometimes pockets of the methane gas that I was telling you about explode as the lava hits."

Through the skylight below we could hear Pele's gasping, choking shrieks as the molten lava flowed taffy-like on its way down the slope to the sea.

We became aware of the clattering whine of other creatures, the tourist helicopters as they hovered, affording their paying customers a glimpse of this unique spectacle.

"The choppers make a nuisance of themselves with their noise especially when you need all your undistracted senses to walk here, but that's life, I guess," Sarah said as she shrugged her shoulders in resignation.

"Those old empty lava tubes we just crossed over, were they formed this way?"

"Yes, the same way, only the molten lava passed right through them, leaving a void behind."

"Could they start flowing again?"

"Sure, at any time, especially in this area. You never know where molten lava will flow next. Those recent lava flows in the old lava tubes that we saw in the deep, offshore of the heiau at Keahole Point, are a good example of that."

"Where the pillow lava stopped flowing?"

"That's the one."

We followed the winding stream down to the sea's edge where the lava bubbled and wheezed as it flowed into the water throwing off great rising clouds of hissing steam and fizzing gasses.

The buzzing helicopter that had been here had turned to go back to its base. In the relative silence, we stared in fascination at this steady process. It held our mesmerized gazes better than any lava lamp in a bar did. It was like life imitating art imitating life.

We heard the clattering of another chopper coming toward us from offshore. It changed the pitch on its rotor blades to slow and hover. We instinctively looked up at it as it slowly closed the gap between us. My sixth sense was immediately set off by the sight.

"Something's not right!" I yelled to Sarah.

"What's not right?"

"That chopper. It's not a tourist chopper. It's too small. It's black and there's only two people in it," I said as I saw a flash of reflected light off a pair of binoculars in the cockpit. "I don't like the looks of this. Is there anywhere we can take cover if we have to?"

"Well, no! There's not . . . uh, yeah! In that old lava tube that we looked at over there. Why, do you think they're after us?"

"I just think we're sitting ducks here and that they are seeing if we are the right ones for them to go after."

"I think maybe you're being a little paranoid, huh?"

"My sixth sense is jangling my nerve ends. Something isn't right!" I repeated with increasing nervousness.

"Maybe they're just sightseeing like everyone else. A private chopper and they're using binoculars to get a better look."

"A better look would mean that they would likely drop down really close to the lava where they could feel the heat off it through the skin of the chopper."

"You sure?"

"My intuition doesn't often fail me. Let's slowly make our way back up the slope toward that old lava tube."

"Okay, I'm with you," Sarah replied.

We pretended to examine the flow higher up while we still furtively glanced over at the hovering whirlybird. We moved higher up, nearing the old lava tube that ran next to the existing flow. I glanced back again and caught the glint of metal off what appeared to be a rifle.

"When I say run, you run! And make it a zigzag!"

"Okay!" Sarah replied with a look of consternation on her face.

I looked back again. The chopper was slowly moving up the slope toward us. "Sarah, doesn't that chopper look like the one that tried to tamper with my Harley back in Victoria, you know, the small black chopper."

"It looks about right," she agreed.

"Okay, run!" I shouted as the chattering blades grew louder.

Our running caused the passenger to unbuckle his seatbelt, lean out his side of the chopper and shoot a burst of rounds at us. Showers of sparks flew all around us as the slugs zinged past us and ricocheted off the lava near our feet.

The chopper overflew us as we stumbled into a sloping skylight that allowed us to descend underground. I looked over at Sarah and asked, "You all right?"

"Yes, I think so," she replied as she gasped from the exertion of running.

I peered up through the skylight again and saw the chopper making a swing arc to return. I ducked back down. "Get back and hug the far wall. They're coming back for another run!" The chopper made another sweeping pass over us and returned to hover just back of the skylight. The gunman leaned out the cockpit and fired another burst of rounds into the skylight. Sarah screamed as the slugs ricocheted around the tube. Chunks of lava broke off and added to the bits flying around.

"Move back up the tunnel!" I shouted. The noise of the gunfire reverberated in our ears.

The darkening tunnel had patches of light that leaked through other cracks in the lava tube wall high up near the ceiling as we made our way back.

"It's getting hotter the farther back we go!" Sarah complained, "I think there are some openings farther up the tube that open onto the top of the lava tube that is flowing next to us. That's where the heat is coming from."

"Any chance that we will be caught up in a flow of lava ourselves?"

"I hope not! If the lava flow increases, it could rise and flow through the connected openings near the ceiling. It could pour onto us into this tube."

"Let's keep our fingers crossed that it doesn't happen," I said as I started to sweat from the heat in the tunnel.

"You never know. This slope is honeycombed with old tubes."

"So it's a crap-shoot at best!"

"I'm afraid so," Sarah lamented as she mopped her brow with her palm.

I poked my head up through a small skylight and saw the gunman leaning out of the cockpit with one foot on the skid.

"I got a plan Sarah. But I'm going to have to use you as a target. It's our only chance."

"What do you want me to do?" she asked.

"I want you to poke your head up through this small skylight so that the gunman notices you. Then duck back down quickly. I want to draw the chopper forward over the big skylight where I'm going to try to bring it down with a rock. I'll throw it up through the opening."

"Okay, let me know when you get into position."

I scrambled back down the lava tube, picking up a couple fist-sized rocks along the way. Positioning myself under the skylight, I looked back at Sarah through the gloom of the tunnel. Her face was illuminated by the small skylight above her.

"The lava is overflowing!" Sarah suddenly cried out.

"Okay now!" I commanded. The chopper remained hovering off to one side. They hadn't seen her. "Again!" I shouted over the din of the rotors. This time they saw her before she ducked back down again.

The chopper edged forward. I looked up from my hidden position and could plainly see both men ensconced in their Plexiglass bubble. The pilot was excitedly pointing to where Sarah had popped her head through the small skylight. I saw the passenger with the rifle lean farther out on the skid so as to be ready for his next shot. He had his sights set on the small skylight waiting for Sarah to pop her head out again.

"Stay down!" I shouted to Sarah over the racket from the chopper. I flung a lava rock up through the skylight. It rose in front of the cockpit.

Short!

I cursed my bad throwing.

The startled pilot took evasive action. His craft suddenly veered in response. At the same time the gunman was leaning out from the cockpit with his rifle in hand looking for a pick-off shot. He expected her to show again but didn't expect the pilot to suddenly move the chopper without warning him. The veering motion of the chopper caused the gunman to lose his balance and slide out of his seat, his seatbelt laying useless on his seat. He reached back toward the side of the chopper but the gun in his outstretched hand excessively counter weighted his other arm. His free hand uselessly slid off the Plexiglass bubble. As he fell, he made a desperate grab at the chopper's skid. He was outreached by inches; I could hear his scream over the clatter of the rotors. He fell, landing in a sickening heap, shoulders first, his head at an impossible angle on the rough lava edging the hot stream. His rifle tumbled and landed beside him.

The chopper rose abruptly as the weight of his passenger was removed.

The dead body's weight was enough to shatter the fragile thickness of solidified lava that formed the edge of the coursing molten river.

Both body and rifle fell with the shattered edge into the molten river below. The body blistered and sank as it was pulled downstream.

A chain reaction followed as a small pocket of methane gas was released creating a miniature explosion that sent lava rock debris skyward into the whirling main rotor. The chopper began an out-of-control swing that spun it like a dervish, causing the chopper to keep settling lower.

The pilot looked wildly around.

The chopper settled onto the lava crust beside the glowing river of red. The weight of it collapsed the edge of the overhanging solidified rock, dropping one of his skids downward. The pilot tried to lift the chopper out of the dangerous situation he found it in. For a moment the machine started to tilt back slightly but he didn't have the lift. The chopper slowly slid into the cauldron of fire.

In a reflex action, the pilot let go of his controls to try to shield his face from the intense heat as his machine slowly sank into the fiery red liquid. I ran up the sloping side of the skylight, horrified at the sight. I watched the pilot's mouth working out a silent scream. The rotor blade tips caught the lava rock and sheared off rotating pieces of blade toward me. In a useless reflex action, I ducked down as they flew by, narrowly missing me. I poked my head up again to see the melting chopper start to float and slowly get pulled downstream by the raging river of molten lava.

A tremendous roar occurred as the fuel tank exploded. Lava spewed out of its course as if in a mini eruption but Pele still held her melting prize tightly to her bosom as she bore it down to the sea. A thick, rising cloud of black oily smoke, a newly-broken skylight and a few pieces of broken rotor blade were the only evidence that a chopper had been here. Shaken, I turned to Sarah, held her trembling body in my shaking arms and said, “It’s all over . . . they’re gone . . . they’re gone for good!”

CHAPTER TWENTY SEVEN

RAINBOW FALLS CAVERN

HILO, THE BIG ISLAND OF HAWAII. The road from Kilauea Caldera toward Hilo was running steadily downslope; the scenery, uneventful and the vegetation, scrubby. It gave me time to think things through.

Yesterday, Sarah and I had phoned in to report the chopper crash to the authorities. I had memorized the tail numbers of the chopper after scrutinizing them from inside the lava tube skylight; I was not surprised to find that it was registered to Global Sea Marine. These numbers were dark charcoal gray on black which was the same colour combination of the chopper that we chased through Finlayson Arm in Victoria. That time we were not able to get sufficiently close to the chopper to be able to read the obscure tail numbers with any certainty.

Sarah and I had driven to the Volcano information center where we contacted the police and gave them our statement on the crash incident.

The police were keen to get the information but were disappointed that there was little in the way of crash evidence for them to look at. The Federal Aviation Administration and the National Transportation Safety Board were extremely disappointed. They were particularly disturbed that their evidence had melted and flowed out to sea. I mentioned that there may be some residual rotor pieces and a few bits that may have been blown out of the stream of lava when the fuel tank exploded. Other than that, I told them that I didn't hold out much hope for anything substantial. This seemed to mollify them somewhat. We had an appointment with these authorities in Hilo for later this morning.

Having some time before the scheduled meeting, Sarah suggested that we swing down highway 130 to Kalapana where we could see the other side of the miles-wide lava flow. A collection of small towns and settlements lined the road down to the sea.

As I drove, I thought back to last night, reliving the evening. After phoning the authorities from the information center, Sarah and I had decided to stay at the Volcano House Hotel. We registered and walked through the lobby sitting room where a cheery fire in an enormous fireplace was surrounded by antique furniture.

We showered, changed and went down to dinner in the rustic dining room for a sumptuous meal which included a bottle of Chardonnay. Our table overlooked the huge Kilauea Caldera. It changed colours dramatically as the sun set in the western horizon highlighting the plumes of volcanic gases rising from the caldera floor.

We withdrew for a brandy in the sitting room. The glow reflected off the dark wall panels as we sat in the overstuffed love seat in front of the blazing fireplace. A chill had settled in at this mile-high elevation. The fire and the brandy warmed our bodies; our sensuousness warmed our souls.

We retired to our room to enjoy the spectacular view. Closing the door, I went to Sarah who was standing at the window admiring the panoramic vista of the caldera. She turned and draped her arms around me enveloping me with her subtle scents.

We kissed passionately, hungrily seeking out each other's tongues; slowly we shed our clothes on the carpet. I lingered, tracing her ears and neck with my lips and slowly ran my fingertips over her trembling body. Sarah gently laid me back on the bed and straddled me while continuing to kiss my lips and chest. She gently rocked as I rose to meet her.

Leaning back, she afforded me an erotic view of her porcelain body. Luxuriating, Sarah closed her eyes, letting her silky dark hair cascade down to the bed until she breathed deeply and fluttered her eyelashes as a heightened sense of uncontrollable urgency overcame her.

The caldera began to tremble and undulate. Sarah leaned forward again and was repeatedly rocked deeply. Her muscles rippled as the volcano rumbled; from deep within, a continuous eruption followed until finally the forces of nature subsided with a wanton moan.

We lay in each other's arms. Sarah was contentedly nuzzling, whispering, purring in my ear with feline persistence.

"How did it feel . . . " Sarah began to say.

"Fabulous," I replied. "I was going out of my mind over you."

"No," she continued, "how did it feel to have made love on Pele's threshold?"

"I didn't think about this being Pele's home," I prevaricated.

But I *had* thought about it.

I didn't know how to tell her that without hurting her feelings. It was impossible without exposing such an unusual, mystical coupling with Pele in the form of Kiana, especially at such a precious but awkward time as this.

I couldn't help but think of Pele. This was her home and considering the legends and myths that surround her, I had probably experienced her sexual petulance in that misty nighttime tryst after the Kealakekua Bay luau. This would likely remain one of my innermost thoughts.

"I was thinking . . . " Sarah said after a long while as she twirled my hair around her slender forefinger.

Oh, oh! I thought.

She continued " . . . that my offering to Pele today came at a most propitious time."

"Why do you think that?" I asked as I tenderly kissed her neck below her ear.

"Pele helped us when those guys in the chopper tried to kill us."

"Really?"

"Yes!"

"In what way?"

"With a little help from us, she threw rocks into their rotors and collapsed the crusty edge of the lava that the chopper was on. Then she destroyed them and their machine by melting them and carrying them off to sea."

"You're right! I hadn't thought of it in that way."

"And now she has allowed us the pleasure of the use of her home for our lovemaking."

"Do you think she is capable of remorse?"

"Remorse? Why do you say that? Oh, for her actions you mean?" Sarah asked.

"Yes."

"I suppose so. I suppose that she could show remorse. Why do you ask?"

"Ah . . . uh," I stammered as I fought for something to say that would make sense and draw her away from my innermost thoughts. "Because I've heard that she can also be quite testy and vitriolic."

"Only if you don't appease her or please her. Yes, she has been known to be that way. She is a woman, after all!" Sarah said with a mischievous smile.

"Well, you've convinced me! I'm a believer now!"

"I'm glad."

"And have I appeased and pleased you?" I asked with a faint smile.

"I don't know about appeased because I haven't made any demands of you but you certainly have pleased me!" Sarah said as she kissed my eyelids closed.

"Um!" I murmured sleepily.

She whispered, "Off to dreamland now, my sweet dream-weaver."

My thoughts drifted away as we drove through the monotonous landscape, finally reaching lush jungle vegetation as we turned right at the junction with highway 130. The road took us into the town of Kalapana where we swung to the right down a residential street to make our way over to the lava fields. A flimsy orange and white barricade sat in the middle of the road behind which was a rising wall of solidified lava. A sign upon it solemnly declared that the road was closed. No kidding!

From this point on the lava bed rose sharply to a dozen feet. We parked and walked over to a lady tending to the tangled flower garden in her front yard.

"Are we in the right place to best see the lava plume?" I asked.

The lady rose from her bended knee and said, "You are. You just have to climb that rise here and you can see it plain as day. I'm glad that the flow is there and not still here," she declared firmly as she placed her hand on her hip for emphasis.

"Looks like your place just missed getting engulfed," Sarah said with some consternation.

"By the grace of Pele, yes! It was close and it was scary. The lava curled right around our property line after burying all of our neighbours' properties to the west. Those poor people!"

I looked next door to see a rising two-story wall of black pahoehoe lava. It looked like a cake batter that had been roughly poured out of a mixing bowl and burnt to a crisp in a giant oven. Their neighbour's rusting, burnt-out shell of a pickup truck was poking out of the lava like nouveau art.

Her property was a profusion of tropical plants and twisted jungle vines; somewhere back there, hidden amongst all this vegetation, was a clapboard house.

"Yes, it sure was something. It was beautiful here. The beach was right across the road. Now the beach is a quarter mile away across a plateau of lava flow."

"We're sure sorry to see this happen to you people," I said.

The lady bit her lower lip and replied, "I hope it doesn't start flowing here again. We couldn't sleep knowing that the lava was advancing slowly toward us and when it got closer, why we couldn't even stay here in the house. I don't know if I could handle the constant stress if that happened again."

We left her and climbed the lava rise. In the distance was the rising silver plume that looked like it belonged to a factory complex. In a way it was. It manufactured new land, acres and acres of new land in this one new flow alone.

We drove along the hauntingly beautiful shoreline toward Kapoho. The road was rugged; the vegetation and trees were a jungle. It was paradise.

Lava Tree state park was unique. Here, the dozen-foot-high wall of lava had flowed through years ago and had easily slid out to sea without piling up on the land. The molten rock clung to the tree trunks and burnt them out but left the cooled shell of lava in place of the bark. The lava towers dominated the landscape for all time even though new trees had grown to many times the height of these natural obelisks.

Sarah said, "When the lava flow remains and doesn't slide, tree molds are left behind. Basically they are holes in the ground where the tree trunk was. The mirror image of what this is."

We cruised on down into Hilo where we stopped to give our statements to the authorities. The sheriff was there and the FAA and the NTSB had flown in for the meeting as well. There wasn't much that we could elaborate on that we hadn't already told them about. Climbing into two choppers, we all flew out to the lava stream by skimming the sea along the coastline.

We felt the heat from the molten lava flow through the chopper as we hovered above the stream as it poured into the sea. Landing, we walked around pointing out where the chopper had gone down, how it had broken through the lava edge and how it had melted and flowed down the stream to the sea. There were a few small pieces around the site where the fuel tank had exploded. Forensics said that they thought they would have a go at it and see if they could make a positive I.D. to corroborate my statement in which I had given them the tail numbers of the craft. We departed to go back to Hilo.

"Well, that about wraps this part up for me," stated the chief investigator that was sent out by the NTSB to delve into this accident. "We got their statements, we got their maps, we've been out to the site, we got some evidence but I'll be damned if I know why Global Sea Marine hadn't reported one of their choppers missing yesterday! They are still dragging their feet and haven't returned our call yet!"

I conveniently evaded answering that question, a question that begged the answer that I already knew except that I still didn't know the ultimate reason why Global Sea and Chung were on a killing rampage. Certainly they had stepped up their campaign against us. They had started off benignly, trying to kill by making their attempts look like accidents. Now they were bolder in their attempts on our lives, no doubt as they grew more desperate. Something appeared to be coming to a head.

But what?

Perhaps we had touched on one of their raw nerves. Was this raw nerve located in that cavern under the heiau at Keahole Point?

Or were we completely off track?

"C'mon! Lets go climbing!" Sarah said as we left the Sheriff's office. "We've still got all afternoon."

"You're right, let's forget about all this and enjoy ourselves," I replied as we got in the Jeep.

"Why don't we stop off at a deli and fix ourselves a picnic lunch to have at the Boiling Pots river?" Sarah suggested. "There is a perfect spot there that overlooks everything."

"Good idea. I'm getting hungry already."

We spread out a blanket and set out our picnic lunch upon it on a bluff overlooking one of the most picturesque and peaceful scenes on the island. Rainbow-hued falls tumbled over a precipice under which was a gaping lava cavern looking like the inside of some gigantic geode, the bottom leading edge of which was only partially edged in river water far below. We were fifty feet above the upper river.

"That is a pretty sight!" I exclaimed.

"Like it?" Sarah asked.

"Like it? This is a real jewel of a place. I've not seen anything like it before. It's unique! I can't wait to go down there and start exploring that cavern."

"Me too!" Sarah added.

I surveyed the scene. "So the river flows along in its own eroded bed over there then drops over the edge in a waterfall behind which is the cavern. In other words, the river flows on top of a huge lava cavern," I said as Sarah nodded her head in agreement. "Then the water falls into that pool below in the gorge and carries on as a river. But then the water disappears then reappears into another pool slightly lower, runs for a short distance and disappears again only to reappear later. What gives?"

"That's why they are called boiling pots. The actual Boiling Pots are upriver from here but below here are some boiling pots as well. Those pools along the river are the pots. The water swirls around the pools before being sucked underground into ancient lava tubes. Later the waters reappear, boiling up to the surface in another boiling pot slightly farther down the river. The river continues for a short distance before being sucked underground through another pot. Then the river flows underground for some time until finally coming out of a lava tube in a cliff wall. There, it becomes a gigantic round waterfall that shoots down into a final pool way down there," Sarah said as she pointed me along to where she meant.

"So I can see why this is a popular spot."

"This is a popular spot, almost right in Hilo like it is, but dangerous too! No one is allowed into the river where the boiling pots are. It's far too treacherous!"

Indeed, it was. But there were a few other people enjoying the view and having picnic lunches like we were. Tourists mainly. A few office workers in business suits or Hawaiian shirts. A couple of guys sitting on a bench occasionally glanced our way as they talked. Other than that, everyone pretty much left us to enjoy ourselves.

After lunch Sarah and I had a short nap on the blanket under a tree to rest before our descent into the gorge. Sunlight filtered through the branches and dappled our skin. A slight silky breeze cooled and caressed us.

We got our gear out of the Jeep and began to set up. We would be using static ropes as we didn't want our lines to stretch on our rappel down into the gorge. Nor would we want them to become elastic on our way back up when we would be using ascenders to climb up the rope. We would each descend on our own double static ropes as two ropes are infinitely safer than one, especially with the knife-edged lava walls!

We put on our harnesses. I slipped a sheathed knife on as well and selected a sturdy tree trunk to anchor our lines to. It sat directly over the falls. We used our blanket to cover the rough edge of the lava rock so that our ropes wouldn't be cut through. Throwing the lines over the edge, we made sure that they were long enough to reach the bottom of the gorge. There is not much worse than to run out of rappelling rope half way down!

Sarah would be going down on a pyramid belaying device while I selected a figure eight for myself. We added ascenders to our gear slings, snapped our helmet straps in place and clipped our carabiners into our belaying devices to attach us to our ropes. We slipped our leather gloves on.

"Ready?" I asked Sarah.

"Ready," she replied as we backed out over the precipice and let the rope take up our weight as we got into position to rappel down the cliff. We tried to go down in tandem but found that we occasionally bumped into each other so I said I would keep descending a little lower than she did, though both at the same rate. This worked fine as we inched our way downward. What little scree Sarah knocked loose, fell harmlessly off to one side. I looked down to my right at the upper river.

We descended to a point where we were level with the upper river. We could feel the thundering pulse of the flow of the water as the top of the falls ran over the edge and cascaded into the gorge below. A light mist off the falls was borne on a slight updraft; the sunlight was refracted into a rainbow around us.

"You okay?" I called up to Sarah just above me.

"I'm fine! Isn't this just the greatest?" she called back. "This is just like climbing down a rainbow!" she added.

"What a rush! Do you think there'll be a pot of gold waiting for us at the end of the rainbow?" I asked.

"Maybe we'll find the pot of gold in the cavern."

"The rock is getting a little slippery with all this mist so we'll have to be careful of our footing."

"It's not too bad though if we take it slow and easy."

We were now descending to a point just below the top of the waterfall, still quite some distance from the pool at the bottom of the gorge. When we reached the bottom, we would have to swing in to touch down on a ledge. We could use it to gain access to the cavern behind the waterfall because the pool below was too deep and fast to maneuver around in.

I looked up at Sarah to see how she was doing. My eye caught some slight movement at the very top of the bluff. Then a moon-faced head peered over the precipice at us and stared emotionlessly down at us.

My blood ran cold. We were halfway down our 200-foot descent.

What is that idiot doing around our setup? I thought. Doesn't he realize that to do so is dangerous?

"Somebody's up there at our lines," I quickly called up to Sarah.

"You don't suppose that they are part of that . . . "

"I hope not . . . " I felt one of my ropes twang a little then it suddenly slackened and fell down on top of me, stinging my face as it hit with full force. "Lookout!" I shouted a warning to Sarah. "They're cutting our ropes. You better . . . " was all I managed to get out as my last rope suddenly went slack in my hands and I was falling. In a reflex action I shot my hands over to Sarah's taut ropes and grasped them, feeling the ropes slide through my gloved hands with a sickening odour of burning flesh before I managed to stop my slide. My gloves were toast!

Sarah screamed, "Rune! Rune! You okay?"

"For now!" I shouted up to her. "Rappel down to me!"

She did.

A second face appeared above us on the bluff as we both felt one of her ropes twanging as it was being cut through from above. So there were at least two of them. "Look out! They're cutting your rope too!" I yelled as Sarah slid down to me.

"What can I do?" Sarah screamed.

"Can you swing in and get a foothold?"

"I can't! There is nothing here to grasp on to!"

"I'm clipping onto your harness sling and we'll both drop as quickly as we can before they get to the last rope." The first rope slackened and smacked into our helmets with a resounding whack.

We were hanging by the thread of a single rope.

"Let it go!" I called to Sarah. We accelerated downward on her remaining rope but we were too late. The rope slackened and fell with us as we plummeted the remaining distance to the waters of the gorge far below.

"Noooo!" I screamed out in anguish.

It felt as if we had hit a brick wall when we hit the water feet first. Tethered to each other's harness as we were, we plunged far below into the cool, dark waters as we were pushed down into the depths by the force of the waterfall. I could hear the sonar-like sounds underwater and could feel the pressure of the depth on my eardrums. My feet hit the bottom of the pool. I instinctively pushed off the bottom but struggled with the extra drag from Sarah as her feet had not reached the bottom before I pushed upwards. My lungs were bursting from exertion as I kicked the last stroke to reach the surface. Sarah popped up right beside me.

We greedily sucked at the air and sputtered as we swallowed some water. I tried to make some sense of the ropes that still entangled us.

Drawing out my sheath knife, I desperately cut at the jumbled ropes as we kicked to stay on the surface. I was making slow progress cutting the ropes as we slowly floated along.

Sarah looked downstream and gasped, "The pots, look out, the boiling pots. They'll suck us down!"

"Let's swim for the cliff!" I said as I coughed to expel some water. Awkwardly, we stroked our way sideways but it was no use. The pull of the vortex was too powerful for us. Increasingly faster we were drawn into the middle of the swirling pot.

"Hang on!" I shouted as I felt our legs sucked down and our bodies whirled around like in some giant washing machine. It was wet, cold and dark as we were sucked along this subterranean lava tube. Our helmets bumped the cratered walls as we rushed along. Suddenly a strong light blinded us as we bubbled up into a pot in the lower pool where we again surfaced and sucked at the air after what seemed to have been an interminably long time under water.

I choked, "You okay?"

Sarah sputtered, "Yeah, you?"

"Yeah, we've got to swim."

"Okay . . . swim," she agreed as she floundered.

"Swim! Let's try to swim!"

"Okay!" she gasped again. "Swimming," she added, redoubling her efforts as we were again pulled downstream by the current. But our tandem effort was holding us back. Before I could untangle the ropes and unclip us, we were drawn ever so slowly toward the vortex of the next boiling pot.

"Hold your breath!" I shouted. "Here we go again!"

We both drew deep breaths as we were sucked underground into this lava tube that threatened to be our watery grave. This time we were sucked along in total darkness like rag dolls, caroming off the walls as the tunnel twisted and turned. We crashed into each other and hoped that our harnesses would not snag as we slid downward in this black hell. The sound of the rushing water was deafening.

Suddenly brilliance!

Was this how it was when you died, a brilliant light?

We were riding a raging waterfall spout as the river shot out of a cliff wall, arcing downwards, like tea being poured from a pot, into a large, placid green pool far below. The spout dragged us to the bottom of the pool before releasing its watery grip on us.

Sarah and I bobbed back up, amazed that we were still alive. We anxiously scanned the surface of the pool for its vortex. But there was none, for this placid pool emptied not underground but over a lip on the far side. Still tethered together, we dog-paddled our way over to the edge of the pool. We clung to the lava rock there, too tired to even haul our sodden bodies onto that flat surface. We lay there, panting like a couple of run-down prey.

Sarah asked quietly, "You okay?"

"Yeah, I'm okay. You?" I asked as I lay my head down on the smooth wet rock.

"Yeah . . . okay."

CHAPTER TWENTY EIGHT

BRAINSTORMING

KAILUA-KONA, THE BIG ISLAND OF HAWAII. I poured myself a large mug of coffee then took cautious sips of the hot liquid as I shuffled across the thick carpet from the kitchen toward the lanai. My image in the floor-to-ceiling mirrored wall in the living room kept pace with me as I went. I looked as bad as I felt. My body was bruised from the pummeling I took after being swept downstream underground into the boiling pots. I tried to work the soreness out of my muscles. Pulling the sliding glass door open, I breathed deeply of the heavy sweet air that was laden with the exotic scent of plumeria.

I pulled up a deck chair and sank heavily into it. The warm morning sun was peeking over the mountain casting long palm tree shadows across the stillness of the blue pool. Hearing a whirring sound, I looked up into the reaching branches of a single gnarled koa tree. I saw what Kiana had told me days ago was an ‘Apapane, a blush-red and gray bird. It had come to a rest in one of the lower branches where it called to its mate with a slurring whistle. She had said that it sometimes nested within lava tube skylights. It whistled and chirped and buzzed and clicked in a fascinating vocal repertoire. Finished, it quickly moved on. The magical spell of the moment was over.

Kiana! I thought of her - a beautiful woman with a charming personality. In the prime of her life, yet afraid for her life. That was no way to live. She had balked at having a 24-hour bodyguard. I couldn’t blame her. Kimo couldn’t blame her either. We compromised. She was to call Kimo if she was going to be alone when she was going anywhere, even just to school.

I took another sip from my coffee mug, the bite of the hot coffee had lessened as it cooled. I leaned back, clasping my aching hands behind my head as I enjoyed the moment, savouring all that surrounded me. Then reality set in again as my thoughts went back to Chung and his henchmen. They had been trying to take me out of the picture for some time without any success but given enough chances, sooner or later they would succeed. Lately, I had been on the defensive, dodging them as I went about gathering information from here and there. It all

seemed to lead right back to him and his secret underground operation.
Maybe it was time for us to strike.

* * * * *

"We have some interesting results from the analysis of the water samples that you and Sarah brought up from your second dive," Dr. Stuart Kerrigan, Director of SSEAAL said as Kimo, Sarah and I sat in his office that morning. "The surface water samples were normal, a little higher in some substances but essentially normal. However, the analysis of the water taken from the chasm was interesting."

"How so?" I asked.

"Well, the concentration of methane gas for one."

"Methane! Are you sure?"

"Yes, we're sure," Sarah stated. "We've retested our samples."

"Yes, it's common to find traces of methane but not usually in this heavy a concentration," Stuart said.

"Okay, so there is a high amount of methane gas there. What does it mean?" I asked.

"When Stuart said that it is not all that uncommon, he is right," stated Sarah. "What happens is that pockets of methane gas are naturally trapped underground. Now and then advancing lava flows hit these methane pockets and cause explosions of some considerable force, enough to rip open the ground and hurl rocks some distance. What we saw a couple days ago below Kilauea Crater, where a methane explosion threw up some rock at that helicopter, was a minor explosion."

"But what does it mean here? Did this cause the Keahole Point explosion?" I asked.

Stuart said, "We don't know. What we do know is that there is an unusual concentration of methane gas rising up from the chasm and through that layer of the ocean where the warm and cold seawater meet."

"We also took note of the fact that there was an underwater shelf that had tilted, tumbled and slipped downslope recently," Sarah interjected. "It was at least a quarter mile long."

"Yes," Stuart said, "that was very interesting. Exactly when it happened is a matter of conjecture."

"What are you saying?" Kimo asked. "That the shelf may have caused the explosion?"

"We don't know that either. What we do know is that there is a high concentration of methane gas in that area, the area of the explosion and that a tumbling shelf slippage occurred at some point," Stuart said.

"And there is some evidence of recent lava flow at the site as well," added Sarah.

"So what you seem to be saying," I postulated, "is that there could have been an underwater explosion. It could have been brought on by an undersea lava flow hitting a pocket of methane gas and causing an explosion which may have been the straw that broke the camel's back, so to speak, and tumbled the shelf downslope."

"Perhaps," stated Dr. Kerrigan, "but that is pure speculation at this point. More likely it collapsed under its own sheer weight, with or without the aid of an earth tremor or quake. We'll have to check the records for that time frame with the guys at the seismic monitoring center up on Mauna Kea. However," Stuart continued as he leaned back in his chair, "the other water samples you gave us that were taken from the area where that outfall pipe ends - at the level where warm surface water meets the cold water of the deep - were unusual . . . most unusual."

"In what way?" I asked.

"The tests on the other water samples from the level where that pipeline flows out showed a variety of chemicals including acids."

"But, Sarah, I thought you said that acids can form around lava flows, acids such as sulphuric and hydrochloric," I said.

"True," replied Sarah, "but not in these concentrations and then there are other types, chemicals, for instance."

"I don't understand," I said. "What other types?"

"Cyanide for one. In concentrations much greater than normal."

"Cyanide!" Kimo whistled in surprise.

"Not only cyanide, but a veritable witch's brew of contaminant chemicals," stated Dr. Kerrigan as he worriedly rubbed his forehead.

"How did all that get there?" Kimo asked.

"We have no idea," Stuart said. "What we do know is that it did not come from any of our operations here nor did it come from any of our associate businesses. They are all signature-monitored constantly for use in just this type of situation."

"Who would use chemicals of that nature?" I asked.

Dr. Kerrigan thought a moment and said, “The only thing that I can relate that group of nasty chemicals to is a tailings pond at a mining operation. But there is no mining operation here as such. That’s the puzzling thing!”

“Now hold on! I’ll be willing to bet that it’s coming from the cavern,” I interjected. “Kimo and I scouted around at the Island Pipeline warehouse off the Queen Kaahumana highway. The one that’s a division of Global Sea Marine’s worldwide operations.”

“Yeah, it was eye-opening,” stated Kimo.

“And what we found was an underground tunnel leading to a lava tube that led us to a cavern which we estimated was somewhere close to the shore here.”

“Yeah, maybe under the heiau, maybe a little upslope from it,” Kimo said.

“A cavern, you say?” Stuart asked, his curiosity now piqued.

“A cavern. Right up the slope from the heiau. They have some sort of operation going on deep down there.”

“Right, they were cutting rocks down there,” Kimo said.

“Some of them were set aside, just cut into halves, while others were cut and sent to a rock crusher,” I said.

“Why that’s preposterous! I’ve seen nothing around there at all!”

“Not on the surface but far below, in the cavern.” I said. “It’s there, all right!”

“Really? That’s hard to believe!” Stuart said. “Sounds like a type of mining operation to me. But from where did they get the rocks?”

“They came out of a large pipe,” Kimo said.

“Yes, a large pipe that ran up from the lower slope of the lava tube from the shore,” I said.

“But we have no pipes running up the shore at that point,” Stuart exclaimed. “All that is there are some old abandoned pipes and they don’t come anywhere near the surface any more.”

“Of course,” Sarah interjected, “the pipeline that Rune and I saw running into that underground lava tube on our last dive. That’s it!”

“What’s it?” Stuart asked.

“Well, that’s where the rocks are coming up from,” Sarah said. “Remember? I asked you about that abandoned pipeline that was near the heiau. Rune and I found that it was reconnected so that it ran into an underwater lava tube.”

Stu nodded.

“Right,” I said. “Those rocks on the sea floor. Those funny looking ones, brown or black potato-shaped. What did you call them, Sarah?"

"Nodules!"

"Nodules?" exclaimed Dr. Kerrigan. "But there are no commercially-viable nodules around these waters! It's too expensive to bring them up!"

"Well," I said, "maybe Chung has found some that are or maybe he has found a commercially-viable method of mineral extraction. You did say that nodules were high in manganese."

Kimo said, "He used a SeaTruck. Maybe he used its ease of getting divers down to enable his operation to gather these nodules with minimal cost."

"While at the same time working on contract for SSEAAL," Sarah added.

"He just brought in another SeaTruck on his work-yacht," I added. "It appears that he used his marine contract with SSEAAL to instal his own pipeline onto an existing one to mine the seabed."

"But he's not allowed to! He can't get a permit! This is a marine sanctuary here!" Stuart said, his voice rising in anger.

"Right! Therefore, the secrecy. Whatever he is after is so valuable that he is willing to go to these lengths to get it!"

Sarah said, "Or ruthless enough that he just doesn't care, just like those huge trawlers that suck up all species of fish in their nets!"

"Or like those drift nets on the high seas," Kimo added.

"I don't like where this thing is taking us. We're talking a marine sanctuary here for God's sake!" Stuart said as he thumped his desk in disgust. "And how in the hell am I going to explain this to the WOOPS delegates."

"WOOPS?" I questioned.

"World Oceanic Organization on Pollution of the Seas. The delegates, of which I'm one, have an upcoming conference in Kailua and a meeting in our facility right here. I'm the keynote speaker at the dinner at the conference windup," Stu said dejectedly. "This is extremely embarrassing!"

"They were mentioned on TV. Getting back to the explosion," I interjected. "What I don't understand is that from all eyewitness accounts of the kids and the mother on shore and from the pilots in the air, the explosion didn't appear like your typical fireball explosion. There were bubbles and white vapours and mists and fog like sea smoke. And there was thunder and heavy rumbling from below. Then the surface waters turned irridescent green, then electric blue and finally a yellowish-red colour as the explosion occurred. There were bright lights that flickered as the mist streaked upslope from the sea.

"The divers and crew in the dive boat didn't survive except for those two divers from Wisconsin and they can't recall exactly what happened before the explosion. They were both somewhat preoccupied. The fellow did see the bubbling waters and the rising mist just before he blacked out. We know that afterwards the survivors had a hard time breathing while the rest of them died from asphyxiation and not from the immediate physical effects of an explosion. There were some scorch marks along the hull of the boat but it wasn't burnt or damaged otherwise. Weird huh?"

"Maybe not so weird," Dr. Kerrigan said as leaned forward in his chair. "Let's assume that the underwater shelf broke off, tilted a little, and slid downslope some ways."

"But what about the lava flow. When would that have occurred?" I asked.

"I don't know," Sarah replied, "but as I said, there was evidence of fresh lava on the broken shelf."

"You mean a new lava flow?" Stu asked.

"Yes," she replied.

"Right! On our sweep of the chasm, it ran along the bottom," I added.

"Fresh pillow lava," Sarah said as her arms formed a pllow-like shape.

"It doesn't matter at this point if it was a factor or not," Dr. Kerrigan said as he carried on with his supposition, "we can figure that one out as we go along. Okay, lets say that for whatever reason, the shelf tumbled down, be it from the force of a lava flow or from gravity or from an earthquake, or a combination of that. We may never know what actually happened down there. But if you had to guess, what do you think would happen?"

"What would I guess happened?" Sarah repeated. "Well, first of all there would be quite some turbulence in the sea as the shelf tumbled."

"In what direction would this turbulence go?"

"Probably in all directions."

"And one of the directions would be . . . ?"

"Sideways."

"Yes, and that could account for some of the pipeline anchor shifting. And some of the turbulence would also be directed upwards."

I stated, "That could account for the rough bubbling water just prior to the explosion."

"Yes," Dr. Kerrigan replied, "and the white mist?"

"Why, methane gas!" stated Kimo.

"Perhaps! Methane gas, maybe other gases as well, rising from the fracture where the shelf broke off a few hundred feet down."

"And the rumbling?" I asked.

Sarah replied, "An earthquake or from the shelf tumbling or sliding downslope."

"But what about the colours? The greens, the blues, the yellowish-reds?" I asked.

"Okay," answered Dr. Kerrigan, "let's suppose that there are chemical contaminants being dumped into the sea - effluent from a mining operation."

"Right!" Sarah cut in, "probably coming from the pumping out of effluent at the two-hundred-foot level."

"Let's say that the chemical effluent is deliberately disposed of at that level so as to become trapped between the cold and warm layers of the ocean," Kerrigan said.

"That can happen?" I asked.

"Yes," Sarah said.

"The chemicals would not show up on the surface but would eventually be carried away by the deep ocean currents that we know occur here and throughout the Pacific."

"That's right." Sarah agreed.

"Surface currents can be deflected down by the earth's rotation."

"And rotating ocean currents carry these chemicals widely."

"They can rotate their deadly mixture for years," Stu said as he scratched his ear lobe deep in thought.

"And internal waves."

"Yes, they form between the warm and cold layers of the ocean."

"What about segregated waves?" Sarah pointed out.

"They too can hide toxic effluent at depth."

"So," I interjected, "at 300 feet down, the shelf breaks off and goes tumbling and rumbling downslope for a hundred feet or so. Methane and other gases are released. These gases rise and mix with the chemicals that were being released at the 200-foot level. The turbulent upward-welling wave, a small tsunami really, forces everything up to the surface. There was a volcanic underwater vent suspected of wiping out a rare species of fish in Singkarak lake on the Island of Sumatra. The scientists suspected that nearby Marapi Volcano had spewed out poisonous gases that killed hundreds of tonnes of endangered Bilih fish. But I thought I was told that gasses would be absorbed into the sea."

"In much deeper waters but not from just a few hundred feet," Stu said.

"Right," Kimo said, "just like that lake in South America, I think it was. The one where an earthquake triggered the release of gases trapped near the bottom of the lake. It happened the night before market day, so the village people including the market farmers were asphyxiated."

"I recall that now that you mention it but what would ignite it there?" Stu asked.

"Maybe the exhaust from the dive boat set it off," Kimo said.

"That's logical," Stu said.

"But why wouldn't it burn the people in the dive boat?" I asked.

"Perhaps there wasn't enough methane gas, maybe the gas was spread out or scattered along the surface of the sea. The explosion may have gone outwards, linear, in a chain of very small explosions instead of in one huge fireball," Sarah said.

"And the colour?" I asked.

"Perhaps it was from the various chemicals reacting with one another, the methane and the air and the water," Sarah guessed.

"And the streaking mists could have been the smoke after the methane and chemicals exploded and burned," Kimo said.

"We'll probably never know exactly what took place but that is a fair assumption," Dr. Kerrigan stated.

As I sat near Dr. Kerrigan's desk, my eyes flickered over the cigar humidor with the exquisite marquetry that sat upon his desk. I admired the skill of the maker and glanced at the solid-gold global emblem that sat upon its lid. Stu followed my gaze and declared, "I had Anne turn the cigars over to U.S. Customs Service but I kept the humidor. It's too nice to get rid of."

Suddenly, it clicked! The global emblem! It was that of Global Sea Marine! Only the name was missing.

Intrigued, I leaned forward for a closer look at the emblem. Its raised globular surface contained a mesh-like background upon which the solid gold continents were affixed. Taking a magnifying glass from Stu's desktop, I peered into the mesh.

It was a listening device!

And good old Harry back at ORCA unwittingly had one just like this one sitting on his desk too!

I hurriedly scrawled the words - “IT’S A BUG!” - on Stu’s notepad and held it up to be read.

Stu’s eyes widened, his jaw dropped. He cursed silently, “That bastard!” with only his lips forming the words. He grabbed the magnifying glass from my hand and leaned forward for a closer look.

But the damage had already been done!

CHAPTER TWENTY NINE

VANISHED

KAILUA-KONA, THE BIG ISLAND OF HAWAII. The jangling within my brain was persistent. From within the fog of sleep, I struggled to make sense of the intruding sound. My eyes flickered open but still could not figure out where I was. I bolted upright in bed fighting the dizziness of rising too suddenly from a prone position. The jangling sounded again.

The phone!

I leaned over and shook the receiver off the cradle, held it to my ear and grunted.

"Rune?" a female voice asked.

"Yeah. Sarah? What's up?" I sleepily asked.

"It's Kiana!" she said in a scared voice.

"You're Kiana?"

"No! It's about Kiana."

"Sorry, about Kiana? What happened?"

"I just got a call from Kiana's parents wondering if I knew where she was. They've been up all night. Kiana was supposed to call them last evening and didn't."

"Maybe she just forgot."

"No, I don't think so. And there's still no answer at her condo either."

"What time is it?"

"Just after five."

"Okay. Just sit tight. I'm going to phone Kimo and see if he's heard anything. I'll call you right back. Bye."

"Bye."

I immediately dialed. "Kimo! Rune! You heard from Kiana?"

"No man! Why?" he answered groggily.

"I think she's missing. She was supposed to phone her folks last evening. Never did. No answer at her condo either!"

"What time is it?"

"Uh, just after five," I said as I double-checked the time on my watch. Why don't I swing past your place and we can start looking for her? This doesn't sound too good."

"I'll be waiting. See you shortly."

"Yeah."

I dialed again.

"Sarah? No word?"

"No!"

"Damn! Look, Kimo and I are going to start looking for her."

"I'll keep trying her place and maybe you can drop by there and see if her car is there," said Sarah.

"Is she still driving that green rental?" I asked.

"No, she turned it back in when she bought her replacement car," Sarah said.

"What kind of car did she buy?"

"That's just it! I don't know! She just got it yesterday from some dealer."

"This is going to complicate us finding her," I said with resignation. "I hope this fellow Chung isn't involved in this," I added as a foreboding thought came over me. "We'll also swing out along the way to Kealakekua Bay."

"Keep in touch."

"I will."

Kimo and I swung out to her condo. We leaned on the buzzer but got no answer. Neither was there a car in her parking slot. We even woke the caretaker to check the condo. It was empty, no sign of a struggle nor any clue as to her whereabouts. Her bed hadn't been slept in either. We followed the road out to her parent's place but there was no sign of a car going off the road.

A dead end.

Kimo and I were going to get together for a meeting with the sheriff after breakfast but now breakfast was on hold. He did have other plans for later in the day too. A couple of Navy SEAL response boat units out of Pearl Harbour would be stopping at Kailua Pier on exercises. Kimo, our chief, knew their Chief McGillicuddy who had one of the units under his command. Based in San Diego, their boats had been airlifted by C5 heavy transport plane just for this series of exercises. They had a dinner planned and a get-together later in the evening at a Kailua nightclub.

So much for his social life!

If we couldn't find Kiana or if she didn't just show up, we were in for the long haul.

We dropped by Sarah's place but still no word there. She was going to stay by the phone in case anyone phoned. Sarah was fighting back tears and stifling a sob as she said she was worried that Chung had got to Kiana. I was inclined to agree with her. Privately, I had regrets that we had acquiesced to Kiana's request that she didn't need any protection yesterday because she didn't plan on being alone. She had said she would call Kimo if she found herself in need of security. He had said to call at any time through the day or night. Well that was the plan anyway. Obviously, the plan didn't work. Hindsight!

* * * * *

"Rune! Kimo! Good to see you guys again," Sheriff Jim Paoluana said as he ushered us into his office. "How is it going? Coffee?"

"Yes, black, sugar please."

"Kimo?"

"You bet! Black, no sugar."

The sheriff poked his head out the door and asked his secretary if she would mind getting them some coffee. "Two black, one with, and my usual please," he said as he sat back down.

A minute later she pushed the door farther open with her hip and set down a tray with the coffees.

"Great girl!" the sheriff said after she left, "and don't think that I get treated this way all the time. Most of the time I'm the one getting her the coffee. I keep her busy with paperwork and then there's the phones. So what's the latest?" he said as he leaned back in his chair.

"The latest," said Kimo with a worried look on his face, "is that Kiana has been missing since last evening."

"Missing? No one called me! What's happened?"

Kimo related the story to Sheriff Paoluana as we knew it so far.

"You guys sure she just didn't go off the deep end?" the sheriff asked. "There was that talk, you know."

"We don't think so," I said, "she's been pretty lucid and there have been some attempts on our lives the last while that I think will convince you that we've got a major problem on our hands. I went on to fill the sheriff in on the rope-cutting incident while rappelling out at Hilo and the chopper attack and subsequent crash downslope of Kilauea Crater. He knew about the chopper crash but didn't know the background on it. These events of the last few days raised his eyebrows considerably. "Now taking all these things into consideration, I think that our Mr. Chung is definitely behind all of this."

"I agree!" Sheriff Paoluana said. "Why don't we concentrate on finding Kiana? Then we'll go after Chung. If he's involved in this one too we'll be after him in any case. In the meantime, I'll have my deputies scouring both the town and the countryside."

"Thanks, sheriff," I said.

"What kind of car is she driving?" he asked.

"I don't know. She just bought another car yesterday. We haven't seen it yet."

"Deputy!" barked Sheriff Jim as he leaned out his door. "We got a missing person. Kiana . . . yeah, Kiana Kilolani. You got the file from before. Generate a missing person file and get right on it. It's urgent!"

"Sheriff?" the deputy called back from the outer office. "We just got a call from some surfer guy on his cell phone. Says he was going to the beach on one of those trails that run off the side road out past the airport and came across a body in a parked car."

There was a chill in the air. No! We thought. We looked at each other, trying not to break down. Tears were forming in the sheriff's eyes as he sternly asked his deputy, "The body, male or female?"

"He said he wasn't sure, there was so much blood," the deputy shouted from around the corner.

"Ask him to please have another look, but not to touch the body or anything else," the sheriff quietly asked.

There was absolute silence in the sheriff's office save for the deputy's muffled phone conversation with the surfer. The seconds ticked away loudly on the wall clock. Feeling light-headed, I felt that I was on the edge of a nightmare. I looked over at Kimo. His head had sunk and was now supported by his hands, his elbows lodged on his knees. He stared at the floor. The sheriff's face was ashen.

The seconds slowly ticked by on the wall clock.

One minute.

I clenched my fists so tightly that they were white, all the blood having been forced out of them. Tick!. . . Tick! . . . Tick!

Two minutes.

"Yeah," a grunted greeting from the deputy in the outer office. Silence . . . "Okay."

The deputy's chair squeaked as he turned toward the sheriff's office.

"He thinks it's a guy, a younger guy," the deputy finally yelled out. "He says that it was hard to tell as the blood was caked and dried as if the body was out there all night."

Collectively, we sighed and slowly rose with relief.

I backed away from the blackness of the abyss.

"Thanks," I said as we turned to leave, "we'll keep in touch."

* * * * *

I dropped Kimo off at his condo at the Big Island Inn. He had to arrange to have a message for his SEAL buddy, McGillicuddy, left at the Kailua Pier. I was going to stop off at my condo first but I remembered that Sarah would be anxiously waiting for news of any kind and continued to her place. I filled Sarah in on the tense moments we had at the sheriff's office while we waited for confirmation on the gender of the dead body. Sarah shivered and said that she thought that we should at least drive by Kiana's workplace to see if she had shown there or if there was a car there that belonged to her.

She hadn't; there wasn't.

I let Sarah off at her door at her complex, parked the Jeep in the visitor's slot and walked back to her condo.

"Anything?" I called out as I walked in the door. Looking toward Sarah on the phone, I saw her finger against her lips silently asking me to be quiet.

" . . . and that's all she said? Can you hold a moment please?" Sarah put her hand over the receiver and said, "It's a teacher, a friend of Kiana's, she's calling from school. She says that she just remembered Kiana telling her yesterday that she had to drive her cousin out to the airport last night. She thought Kiana said his name was Nicky or Neki. First they were going to pick up her car from the dealer then there was something about picking up a parcel from air cargo."

I nodded and asked, "Did Kiana say anything else?"

Sarah nodded her head sideways and said, "No, I've already asked her that." Turning back to the phone, she thanked the teacher and hung up.

Going over to the Big Island Inn to pick Kimo up, Sarah and I went back to my condo first so that I could check for messages.

The light was flashing insistently on my answering machine. I stabbed at the button.

"You have one message," the machine's electronic voice said. *Hey Rune! Good news. Kiana called and left a message on my machine. She's out at the airport. I just missed her call by five minutes so I've gone out there to pick her up. I tried to call Sarah but there was no answer and I didn't want to leave a message there as I knew I would be calling you at your place if you and she weren't there. Kiana sounded a little strained though. She said something about trouble with her car. I'll be back with Kiana before you know it. Let Sarah know but hold off telling her folks and her brother for now as I want to make sure that she's definitely all right. Back in a flash!*

But he wasn't.

Sarah and I waited. Twenty minutes out there and twenty back. An hour max.

An hour went by. Was he trying to fix her broken-down car?

We walked over to Kimo's condo farther along the complex.

We rang the bell.

Nobody there.

With the help of the manager, we let ourselves in and played back his answering machine. "*Kimo, this is Kiana. I need your help,*" her voice quavered. "*My new car broke down at the Kona International Airport. I'll be waiting in my car at the rear of the long-stay parking lot.*" The message's quality was such that it likely was pre-recorded and replayed over the phone.

"Oh, that doesn't sound like Kiana normally does!" Sarah said as her face wrinkled with consternation. "She sounds as if she is repeating something that she was told to say. This is definitely not how she normally sounds on the answering machine!"

"I hate to say it but I'm inclined to agree with you. Why is her car in the long stay lot and not near air cargo? I smell a rat! And that rat is Chung!"

Think!

"What would Chung do if he had Kiana hostage? Kill her or . . . "

"Use her for bait first!" Sarah said. "The first fish might have been Kimo and if that's what happened, you're next!"

"In that case, if we're second-guessing Chung correctly, there'll be another message waiting for me on my machine."

Just then Kimo's phone rang. We looked at each other for a long second with the instinctive reaction of hesitating to answer someone else's phone. Then we dashed for the phone at the same time, hitting each other's hand in our eagerness. Sarah picked up the phone.

"Hello?" she answered.

"Kimo there?" the voice asked.

"Uh, no, no, who is calling?"

"Sheriff Paoluani. Can I leave a message for him to call me? It's urgent!"

"This is Sarah, Sarah Leikaina, sheriff. Would you like to speak to Rune? He's right here."

"Oh? Sure, put him on."

"Hi, sheriff," I said cautiously.

"Kimo not around, Rune?"

"No," I said. I quickly brought the sheriff up to speed on what we had just found out - that Kiana had told her school teacher friend she had to go out to the airport last night. I told him about the pre-recorded message to Kimo and the message Kimo left me.

"Anybody show back there yet?" he asked.

"No, we're getting worried. They should have been back by now!"

"Well, I've got some new information and it isn't good at all. You know that car that was found out on that trail this morning with the body in it?"

"Yes," I quietly acknowledged as my heart began to pound.

"One of my deputies is out there now. Registration in the glove box says the car belongs to Kiana Kilolani."

I flushed. My head pounded. I saw blackness. . . "Is that the car that she just bought to replace the red one?" I asked quietly.

"It sounds like it is the one."

"Well whose body is in it?" I asked weakly.

"Don't know yet but it's not Kiana, it's definitely a young male though. The deputy didn't want to mess with the body. We got to wait for forensic to get out there first."

"And the trunk, anything in there?"

"Don't know yet, same reason," the sheriff replied. "Besides, he can't find the car keys."

"I can probably guess who the young guy's body in the car is."

"You can?" asked the sheriff with surprise.

"Yes, it's probably Neki, her cousin," I said as I reached for Sarah's hand. She drew close against me, quietly sobbing against my chest. "According to one of the teachers she works with, that's who she was supposed to give a ride out to the airport last night to pick something up at air cargo."

"Aw, that's a shame, that's a damn shame!" Sheriff Paoluana said.

"Let us know as soon as you spring the trunk open."

"Sure thing," the sheriff said quietly. "Do you know Neki's last name?"

"Kilolani, I think . . . I'm not sure . . . yeah, Sarah says Kilolani."

Back at my condo, we carefully opened the front door, while checking for signs of anything amiss.

The red light on my answering machine flashed steadily.

I rushed over and punched the play button. *"Rune! This is Kimo! They got to Kiana. Now they got me hostage. Sorry man. The guy wants to swap for you. I'm at the rock place, the cavern . . . where you and I were. Be here by sundown or else . . . Oh, and be sure to send my regrets to McGillicuddy. I won't be able to make my dinner date with him."*

"They got to Kiana?" Sarah asked. "What does that mean?"

"I don't know!"

"I hope she's with Kimo otherwise she's in . . ." Sarah's voice evaporated with a tremble.

"So, this is it!" I said with finality.

"What are you going to do?" Sarah asked.

"First, I've got to think. We have to mount a strike against them. We've got to get some support and go into that cavern from both sides. What did Kimo say? '. . . be sure to send my regrets to my dinner date.'"

"I think so," Sarah said.

"I know he's already done that. It can mean only one thing."

"What's that?"

"He wants us to alert his Navy SEAL buddy about our predicament." I went on to tell Sarah of Kimo's friend, Chief McGillicuddy, who would be here on exercises with his crew and how they had planned to get together.

"Of course! They can go in from the sea," Sarah replied.

"Yes, no doubt Chung's got his yacht anchored off Keahole Point. They can take him out for sure."

"But what about on land?"

"I haven't figured that one out yet. I'll call the sheriff and see if he can help."

"Good idea but how are you going to go in there?"

"Well, I'm not going to give them the easy target they want. I'm going to go in with the SeaTruck . . . alone!"

"But that's crazy! You can't go in alone! You're going to need me! You're not that experienced in operating the SeaTruck."

"I have to!"

"I'm going with you and that's all there's to it!"

"Easy now! Think about it. Why risk your life too?"

"There is nothing else that I'd rather be doing than this, helping out my friends just as they help me out. Besides you're going to need all the help with the SeaTruck that you can get! There, that's settled!"

I dialed the sheriff's office hoping to catch him in. He wasn't. His secretary said that she could probably reach him on his cell phone or on his radio. I crossed my fingers as time was now running against me and more lives were hanging in the balance.

A minute went by then five.

My phone rang. It was the sheriff.

"Oh, good. You're still there!" he said quickly. "Hold on! I'm on a cell phone. They're not secure. I'll phone you back on a land line in a minute or so."

The phone rang. It was the sheriff on a land line.

"You had called. What's up?" he brusquely asked.

I filled him in on the details and laid out my plan.

"Got any ideas?" I asked.

"So you want to go in from the sea and you got backup from the Navy SEALS."

"No, I hope to get backup from the SEALS," I corrected.

"Look, we're understaffed and underpowered for an operation of this magnitude but we'll be happy to go in from the land side. I'll have to get approval from the governor. But we'll need backup on land. There's an army airborne unit at Bradshaw Army Airport located on the south flank of Mauna Kea. The elevation up there is over a mile high and the terrain is unique to say the least. They fly in and out of there all the time, especially with their choppers. They do tank maneuvers including tank drops up there too. The base commander is a friend of mine. I'm sure that he can help us out on short notice like this. I'll be willing to bet that he is just itching to get into a scrap and have his men see some action. Leave that part of it to me. Now let's phone each other as soon as either one of us firms up their backup because time is running out."

"Got it!" I said then hung up. I turned to Sarah and said, "Call Manny to make sure that the SeaTruck is all ready to go. I'm going to try to make contact with those SEAL units enroute to here from Pearl."

Sarah went over to the phone and quickly dialed the number for Manetti Marine. She impatiently drummed her fingernails on the edge of the coffee table. "C'mon, c'mon," she said.

"Get me Manny! . . . Manny? . . . We need the SeaTruck right away," she barked. "Never mind why! Just see that it's ready to go!"

* * * * *

The U.S. Navy SEALS Special Operations (SOC) Craft MK-V bristling with machine guns - the M60ES, 7.62; the M2HB 50 cal.; the MK19 Mod.3, 40 mm - was an awesome sight to see as it cruised along at 55 plus knots, the plus still being classified. Their gunmetal-gray craft held a crew of one officer, four enlisted personnel and carried sixteen Navy SEALS strapped down into aircraft seats under cover back of the bridge. She is 82.5 feet long and 17 feet at the beam. Even though it displaced 57 tons, it was air deployable for rapid response and could be anywhere in the world within 72 hours from its home base. With its bridge unbolted, it was easily fitted within the huge C5 transport plane. Built in Louisiana, this seahawk-nosed, mean-looking craft traveled 450 nautical miles at top speed or 600 nautical miles at cruising speed propelled by two 2285 horse power German diesel engines and two Swedish water jets. It also carried the latest in radar, GPS units, fathometers, chart plotters and compasses. A Zodiac inflatable boat was always at the ready on a stern ramp for fast personnel deployment.

With this impressive capability, Chief McGillicuddy had originally thought that he was the luckiest man to be put in charge of a craft like this. He saw action in Central America, the Caribbean and in Desert Storm. But like all blooms, this one wilted - rather quickly. For starters, the speed of the craft dropped dramatically in 10 foot seas or 35 knot winds. They had to curtail operations when these conditions were present. In spite of their firepower which included Stingers, grenade launchers and armour-piercing machine gun rounds and personal Smith and Wesson stainless steel revolvers that were capable of being fired underwater, it is the personnel that operate them. They were equipped with crash helmets with slip-down night vision goggles to see their white laser gun-sight lines in the dark. The goggles also protected against laser eye damage. In heavy seas they are jolted around with spine-damaging regularity. The standing joke is that the craft only slowed after the first person got hurt. Sometimes bridge windows broke and consoles became flooded with water; salt water sprayed onto the machine guns regularly. The seasoned crew had bets on when the rookies would see past the macho image and request a transfer to a less-rigorous posting.

But McGillicuddy had stuck it out this long. His transfer would be effective when they returned to their home port of San Diego from this Hawaiian exercise. He wanted some "Mai-Tais, some Chi-Chi's, and some Wa-Wa-hines" and to visit Kimo, his old service buddy in Kailua-Kona. It would be his last hurrah but this kind of action was the last thing that he expected as he took the call from someone named Rune Erikson who said their mutual buddy Kimo was in dire straits.

It took a few calls while they were enroute to the Big Island to get clearance from his superiors to abort their exercise and replace it with this new mission. The request went up the brass listings then back down again as calls were made to the White House, to the state governor, the army, and the sheriff for confirmation then back up the brass totem pole again for approval.

Government protocal and red tape usually made for slow decision-making but in this case it meant everything that the White House was already aware of the mission.

McGillicuddy levered the throttle up a notch to put on more speed. Damn! He thought, anything for my buddy but why does it have to happen on my last mission. Oh, well! It's better to go out with a bang rather than with a whimper. He replotted his course to Keahole Point and recalculated their ETA. There, he would be on the lookout for a work-yacht by the name of *Scorpion* which he was told, a certain dangerous ex-North Korean commando owned.

Setting his jaw forward, McGillicuddy throttled higher. A distinct look of determination came over his face. Frustration hung over him like a cloud - he wished that he was there already. He didn't want to miss out on the action! The adrenalin rush was still there after all these years. Some things never change.

* * * * *

The live shell jolted the tank backward as it exploded in the barrel to loft it on its trajectory. It would be carried from its mile-high altitude on the practice range, over the adjacent Humuula Saddle road to the target on the lower southern flank of two-mile-high, snow-capped Mauna Kea.

Commander Akahani took the urgent call over the headset on his helmet. There was one thing about Ace, as he was affectionately known, he was a hands-on commander. As a result of that and his sense of fairness, his troops would do anything for him. Yes, he would be happy to oblige his superiors, the governor and the White House in this mission. Calling for one of his choppers to pick him up, he passed his binoculars down to the tank crew, climbed out of the turret and slapped at the dust that coated his shoulders.

The chopper settled down amidst a whirl of dust and volcanic grit. Ace returned the pilot's salute and slid into the seat beside him. If only they knew how happy I am to see some action, he thought as they winged over to the army airport ten miles distant. He had scrambled the pilots of a chopper unit for a briefing in twenty minutes. The tank units were put on alert pending his personal briefing.

It was no coincidence that he was eventually given a command right back on the Big Island where he was born and had grown up. He could speak Hawaiian and he knew the lay of the land. These days public relations with the local population were important no matter where in the world an army was based. This was the new age and these matters were of prime consideration.

So he had come back to the land that he loved; he knew every nook and cranny, felt every tremble as Pele made her presence known and had explored many of Pele's lava tubes as a kid. He knew that the land was riddled with ancient lava tubes and caverns, some of which could swallow a tank with little effort and with room to spare. Stressing the point to his green recruits, he told them about the hazards of not looking where they were stepping while in the field on maneuvers. Many had ignored the warning and some had broken ankles and legs.

An unfortunate few had fallen into a lava tube skylight and had lost their lives.

He thought he had seen it all but this underground and undersea mining operation in a marine sanctuary was a horrible crime against nature. And right where he had played as a youngster - in Kona. He mused, the gods would not be happy over this despoiling of their home.

CHAPTER THIRTY

PANA'I

HONOKOHAU HARBOUR, KONA, THE BIG ISLAND OF HAWAII. "And how are my two favourite people doing this beautiful afternoon?" Manny sarcastically asked as he greeted us at the entrance to the SeaTruck bay, "off to the deep?" He emphasized *"the deep?"* by raising his rough voice at the end of the word and chewing it off abruptly.

"Don't even ask, Manny. We haven't got time for any verbal sparring," I replied.

"Whatsamatter? Can't take the heat? Then stay out of the kitchen because ole Manny is just cookin' and in fine form today. I just sold my fifth boat today. How about them pineapples, hey?"

Sarah piped up, "Manny. Look. We've got some serious problems!"

"The doctor's got some serious problems. Well, Doll, no wonder! You keep hanging around with this loser!" he said with a smirk and a jerk of his thumb in my direction.

I picked the rotund little man up by his lapels and held him up against the wall. "Now look, Manny! When we say we've got problems, we mean just that. Don't add to them! Or both of your size nines will be roughly inserted into your size eighteen mouth!" I said as Manny made pleading motions with his bug-eyes to let him down. His arms flailed and his heels knocked against the wall; he made gurgling noises as he slid part way down, causing his throat to jam down onto my fists.

I dropped him. He crashed to the floor in a spluttering heap.

"Manny," Sarah said, "friends of ours are missing. One or two are probably dead. We have no time to waste. We have to find them."

"S.. s.. sorry! I was just trying to . . . I don't know what I was trying to do. I'm sorry. I was only joking. You guys need a hand or anything like that? 'Cause if you do, just say the word. I can have a half-dozen boats out looking in no time flat. Just say the word!"

"No, Manny. I wish it were that simple. We know where they are. We've just got to get to them, okay?"

"But how can I help?"

"How about just staying available in case we need your help later. You never know what may come up."

"Sure thing, guys. I'm at your disposal! And if you need some heavy work done I can get hold of my no-good brother-in-law and some of the boys. You just gotta ask!" Manny said as his face brightened at the prospect.

I called the sheriff from Manny's office. Shutting the door for privacy, I didn't want my agony to show when I got the bad news that I knew I was going to get.

I dialed.

"Sheriff's office," his secretary answered.

"This is Rune Erikson. Sheriff in?"

"Oh yes, he's in. He's expecting your call. Just a moment please."

"Rune!"

"Sheriff."

"Well, you were right. The dead young man was Neki Kilolani. He was murdered . . . shot . . . two bullets through his head. Don't say anything to anyone else, I haven't told the family yet. I'm beginning to hate my job, well, this part of it anyway."

I cringed. Tears flooded my eyes.

"And the trunk?" I closed my eyes tightly, squeezing back the flood, waiting for his answer.

"They say the keys are missing. We got a locksmith on the way out there right now."

"Why don't they just force the damn thing?" I asked, shouting angrily.

"Forensic doesn't want anything damaged, not even the trunk lid," he said quietly.

"That's crazy! What if . . ."

"Rune, there's no movement from the trunk at all. Anything in the trunk is . . ." his voice trailed off.

"Well, okay. We're at Honokohau Harbour with the SeaTruck. I can't wait any longer. We're going in."

"Are the Navy SEALS there yet?"

"No, they're on the way though. Are the army choppers all ready?"

"They say they are. They haven't left yet but they'll be picking me up by chopper in the upper parking lot in a while. With all that's going on we're stretched real thin at the moment as you can imagine. I think it'll just be me in a chopper. I've got no one else to spare. We'll have to get the army to cover the warehouse too."

"Okay. Take care. We'll have to play it by ear because our communication with each other is going to be practically nonexistent."

"Good luck to both of you. We'll hope for the best."

"Thanks. Gotta run."

I opened the office door and shouted, "Manny!" He came at a jiggling trot. I closed the door again. "Look, Manny. I need your help. Get these guys on your radio." I gave him a slip of paper with the information on how to contact McGillicuddy out on the SOC. "Tell them that it's a 'GO'. They'll know what it means."

Manny read the note then beamed as he straightened up, clicked his heels together and snapped a salute at me. "SEALS! Yes Sir!" he replied contritely, happy to make amends and to be of service.

Sarah took the news roughly but shook it off quickly as the dead couldn't be helped now. We had to try to save the living. I knew she was hoping they wouldn't find Kiana in that trunk.

"Ho' opana'i," Sarah said as if cursing.

"What?" I asked.

"I'm going to seek revenge. Pana'i. Revenge."

We quickly suited up in our white jumpsuits and ran the SeaTruck into the placid waters of Honokohau Marina and headed out to sea. We did our preliminary check before diving below the offshore waves.

Off Keahole Point we were chagrined to find the *Scorpion* anchored just off the heiau. It was going to be tougher than we had anticipated. "How are we going to sneak past the *Scorpion* to get into the lava tube?" I asked as we rose to a point just under the surface of the sea.

"I'll think of something." Sarah answered.

I called the Navy SEALS Special Operations Craft. "SOC, this is SeaTruck."

"This is SOC, go ahead," they answered.

"What's your twenty?"

"More than halfway between Kahoolawe Island and the point. About thirty minutes out."

"Okay. We can't wait. We're going in."

"We'll be there! You can count on us! Good luck!"

"Thanks, good luck to you too, out." I turned to Sarah and said through the SeaTruck headset intercom. "We're on our own for now. Any second thoughts about holding off?" The sun was sinking lower in the sky.

"No, if we can just find a way to sneak by them. Look, there's a pod of Humpback whales going up along the coast. Why don't we maneuver closer and follow them as they go past the Scorpion?"

"It'll eat up precious time but we have no other option. It's worth a try. But once we split off from the pod they'll detect us."

"It'll at least buy us some time and get us in closer."

Sarah angled the SeaTruck over and fell in with the Humpback whales as they alternately dove and rose back up to the surface as they headed around Keahole Point toward the Kohala coastline. They pretty much ignored us as we went along with them. The surface water was agitated from their flapping flukes but under the surface the view was superb as we mixed in with these magnificent creatures.

Reaching the *Scorpion*, we split from the humpback pod, angling right and downward, heading directly for the lava tube at the two hundred foot depth where the pipelines ran up it into the cavern.

"Damn! I forgot about the locked steel bar gate covering the entrance," Sarah said as the black entrance hove into view. "Electronic locks. Do you think the robotic arms can snap them?"

"We'll use the laser. It'll be able to melt those bars like butter!"

"I'm not so sure," Sarah said, "but it's worth a try." The underwater lights on the *Scorpion* flashed on, illuminating the seabed around us. "Quickly!" she urged. "They've seen us!"

"Okay, here goes," I said as I pulled the trigger on the laser gun. A brilliant red beam shot out. Playing the beam on a bar, it instantly turned red and parted as the seawater around it bubbled away. I kept burning quickly through one after the other while Sarah held the SeaTruck steady. The gate fell away, tumbled onto the pipe then slid off and lodged on the sloping seabed.

We shot forward into the darkened maw of the lava tube just as the ship's underwater doors slid open.

"They know we're here now. So much for our stealthy entrance."

We rode the top of the pipelines up the sloping tube using our roll bar gravity jets to maintain negative buoyancy. As we rose, the occasional turbulence bounced the SeaTruck into the roof of the lava tube. *Wham!* We hit again. It was like riding a wild roller coaster and a log-flume ride all in one. The roll bar wheels saved us from serious damage.

The tube widened as we got closer to the cavern. We shut off the gravity jets, slipped the SeaTruck off the pipelines and shot up the side of them until we reached the surface of the water. We cautiously ran the SeaTruck along the lava tube floor up to the edge of the cavern where we parked it in the shadow of an enormous pump.

Machinery hummed. Water pumps gushed prodigious quantities of seawater up from the deep through a maze of clear acrylic pipe within the cavern. Other pumps forced effluent and saltwater out to sea at depth. Conveyor belts ran slowly along carrying sliced black textured rocks of various sizes. Technicians worked at the controls for various rock grinders and chemical leaching tanks.

Sarah and I were still in our white jump-suits - not conducive to stealth. We kept low, hugging the perimeter as we scouted the premises. There was no sign of Kimo or Kiana. Neither was Chung to be seen.

"What now?" Sarah asked as she turned to me.

"Let's check out the office area up there," I said as I pointed up four floors to the top of the cavern. "The other day Kimo and I got as far in as the end of the tunnel on the other side of the cavern, so I know the layout over there."

We used the noise of the mining machinery, the grinders and the pumps to cover us as we moved along, low and slow.

Suddenly, I heard Sarah's muffled gasp.

As I turned to her, I felt the ice-cold barrel of a handgun against the back of my neck. A silent pair of Chung's thugs had snuck behind us, their movements also covered by the cacophony of the operation. I smelled the distinct odour of garlic. It was old *Garlic Breath*. I had last seen him as I was being dumped into the Victoria Inner Harbour through the bottom of the *Scorpion*.

Suddenly the rock crushing machinery ground to a halt. The conveyor belts stopped. A familiar voice came over the loudspeakers. "Welcome or as they say in Hawaii, aloha! Mr. Erikson, Dr. Leikaina! No need for subterfuge. You were expected! Did you not get Mr. Kekuna's message? Welcome to Global Sea Marine's subterrane mining operations. It's so nice to see you again, Rune, after all, we thought that we had lost you in Victoria when you unexpectedly went for that late-night swim in the Inner Harbour. Once again you are my guests!" he crowed.

We looked around for the body that belonged to that familiar voice but could find none. The voice started again, "Are you two looking for me? Well look up high. Still can't see me? Here, let me turn some lights on," he said with a maniacal laugh. High up, near the cavern ceiling, was a control room. Chung's grinning moon face was now visible under the glare of the harsh lighting. An expansive bank of controls and video screens flashed behind him. A catwalk ran from there, hugging the perimeter near the ceiling and following the clear seawater pipes. It continued across to pipes and equipment in the center, bisecting the cavern four stories up.

"Where are Kiana and Kimo?" I shouted up to him.

"You'll have to come up here if you want to find out," he said over the loudspeaker as he motioned to a steel staircase.

We were pushed along, the gun butts prodding our backs. As we ascended the steel staircase, our footsteps rang out with a clangor. We reached the fourth story and approached Chung. "Where are they?" I demanded. "I want to see them now!"

"Mr. Erikson. Such demands from someone who is in absolutely no position to demand anything!" Chung admonished. "Such rude behaviour! And from a guest at that!"

"I want to know what you have done with our friends!" I shouted.

"We already know what you did to Neki, you murderer!" Kiana shouted.

"The kid just happened to have got caught in my net. He was of no use to me," Chung sneered.

"You dirty bucket of slime!" I shouted at him.

"But your other friends are safe and sound. In fact, I have given them added protection during their stay here," Chung answered with a sneer.

"I want to see them for myself, to see that they are all right."

"Then Mr. Erikson, you have only to turn around to do that."

Sarah and I whipped our heads around frantically searching for our friends but we could not immediately see them.

"Where?" I shouted menacingly at Chung.

"Right there, can't you see? On the catwalk in the middle of the terrane."

A spotlight flicked on, highlighting two jumbo-widths of clear acrylic two-meter-long pipe. They were attached to an acrylic effluent outflow pipe at a forty-five-degree angle. My blood ran cold as I recognized Kiana squirming, trussed up in one pipe and Kimo struggling, hogtied in the other.

"Kiana's here!" Sarah exclaimed.

"And Kimo!" I added.

"Rune!" sobbed Sarah as the full realization of their predicament hit her like a runaway Mack truck. "No!" she wailed in frustration.

"You're insane!" I shouted at Chung. "What are you trying to do with them?"

"I like to keep my bait fresh, Mr. Erikson, and now that I have caught my fish, I no longer have a need for stale bait."

"What are those pipes you've got them in?" I asked hoping to buy some time.

"They are pipe connections that are used to feed residue back into the depths from which they came. Recycling at its best."

"But what do you intend to do with Kimo and Kiana?"

"What do I intend to do with them, you ask? Why just watch. I like to amuse myself by seeing how long it takes for someone to extricate themselves from a difficult situation."

Chung turned to talk to one of his armed staff. "Mr. Nolan! Why don't you show our guests exactly how this is done? Mr. Nolan is one of our technicians here at Global Sea Marine." Motioning to the two thugs, Chung commanded, "Tie Mr. Nolan and put him in a pipe to see how long it takes him to Houdini his way out. Maybe he can be an inspiration to the other two who seem to have done little in that regard." Chung kept his gun trained on the two of us. The thugs disarmed Nolan and took him to the middle catwalk.

"Mr. Chung, I'm not sure I underst . . . " Nolan cried out as he was roughly pushed along, bound with duct tape and placed within a third clear acrylic pipe.

Much to Nolan's consternation, the thugs slid the pipe with him in it down an inclined slot next to the other two. They attached it onto the main outflow pipeline with a snap connection.

Chung expounded, "Mr. Nolan has been a loyal employee of this company since the day that we started our Hawaiian operations. I demand loyalty from all my employees. I also demand respect. In Mr. Nolan's case he has shown me great disrespect of late. It seems his loyalty to Global Sea is being subverted by his diarrhetic mouth in spite of him having signed a company non-disclosure-of-secrets affidavit."

Nolan squirmed as he heard this pronouncement from his boss. Beads of sweat like condensation on a cold glass of beer in the tropics shone on his brow under the harsh spotlight played upon his trussed form. He fought against the duct tape that held him immobile in the cramped cylinder. "No!" he screamed out in fright as his situation became more desperate.

"You were attempting to place our company in jeopardy. Now try get out of this situation that you find yourself in, Mr. Nolan," Chung laughed as he signaled to his thugs by closing the points of his thumb and forefinger together. They snapped an end cap on the capsule, stifling Nolan's frantic pleas as they did. Chung waved his forefinger sideways.

Nolan's terror-filled, bulging eyes swung wildly around, vainly searching for an escape route.

The thug pulled the lower end cap sideways opening the bottom of the capsule to the rushing waters in the outflow pipe. Nolan twisted as he tried to wedge his body against the inside of the clear pipe. Time stood still as we watched his duel with death unfold. His muscles began to tremble. He weakened. He shook. His purchase became tenuous then slackened. Nolan's taped hands struggled as his fingers clawed at the smooth capsule. His body slowly slid down the incline in spite of his Herculean efforts and was sucked into the clear outflow pipeline. He only succeeded in delaying his death slide by mere seconds.

We could only guess at the intensity of his scream as his body was pulled like a rag doll into the raging stream of seawater in the pipeline. Sarah screamed, giving sound to his silent one. His face was contorted in horror as he flowed along the maze of clear pipes. Kimo and Kiana stared, wide-eyed, in shock and horror knowing that their fate was sealed.

They would be next!

We followed his whipping movements down the pipeline, swirling and curving around as he was sucked along in the stream, ever downward. Reaching the bottom of the maze, his limp body disappeared into the huge pump connected to the main pipeline that ran down the lava tube to end some two hundred feet below the surface of the sea. I felt sick with the realization of what had just occurred.

"Murderer!" Sarah screamed.

"You are a madman, totally evil!" I shouted at Chung. "You don't deserve to live, you lunatic!"

"On the contrary, Mr. Erikson, it is you who I don't intend to let live! You have been making a nuisance of yourself. It has already cost me a helicopter not to mention the crew! You have been meddling in my business for far too long. Now it is I who hold the winning hand!"

"We'll see," I replied.

"You have been distracting me from my work here. It was an unfortunate set of circumstances that led to the explosion offshore. Consequently, we are far behind in our production quotas in this operation. Just watch how I take care of my distractions!" he snarled.

Playing for time to work out some sort of rescue, I asked, "So how did you manage to come upon this cavern?"

"Why, opportunities, of course! I am an opportunist!" Chung proudly boasted. "One of our divers grew up here and had stumbled upon this place as a youngster. He mentioned it to me when I hired him for the original pipeline contract that we had with SSEAAL. As it turned out, it was tailor-made for our mining operation. A mining permit was out of the question. I produce my own electricity here. No one else knows about it. It was deserted except for some old bones I found down here."

"Bones?" Sarah asked.

"Yes, human bones. Picked clean, they were. Someone must have got trapped or lost down here at some point," Chung said.

"It sounds more like this was a burial ground for bones prepared by a kahuna. Do you mean to say that you disturbed the bones?"

"Yes, well, they were the first things to go when our outflow pipes started operating."

"Didn't the fact that there is a heiau aboveground near the shoreline suggest to you that there was a conflicting issue here?" Sarah asked.

"That is above, this is below," he laughed.

"Do you realize that this was very likely a sacred burial ground, that those bones could have been royalty's bones, maybe even King Kamehameha's bones? They've never been found."

"Yes, it's sacred all right . . . to me!" Chung roared with laughter.

"Exactly what is it that your company is doing here?" I asked.

"It is simple! Quite simple! Recently scientists dredged up nodule samples from the ocean floor between here and New Zealand that contain a higher concentration of gold than found in some inland mines. While we were installing the first set of pipelines for SSEAAL, I decided to check out the seabed here for minerals. Sure enough, there were areas of the deep seabed that contained high concentrations of nodules. They were high in manganese as well as gold, cobalt, copper, nickel, zinc and other minerals. Though it is these minerals which are our bread and butter, it is the discovery of a new mineral which could make me wealthy beyond even my wildest dreams. Now that we have the SeaTruck line of technology which can ease the descent and ascent of divers using special deep-dive suits, we have the ability to economically gather these nodules and mine the seabed."

"This is all just for minerals?" I said in disgust.

"This is all for mankind!"

"This is all for profit!" I thundered at the former North Korean.

He shouted, "This is for mankind! I'm a new breed of prospector searching the seabed for minerals. I got lucky and struck it rich! I found a rare new mineral, it will command a high price for its properties."

"You're justifying murder because you've discovered a new mineral?" I asked incredulously.

"Not just any mineral. This one is of particular interest to those countries with space programs. Just think! I'll have the Americans, the Russians, the French, the Japanese and the Canadians bidding against each other for exclusive use of this new mineral. Global satellite communications companies too! Whoever wins will have the edge in space exploration and communications for all of the twenty-first century. It's that important. Up to now, they have only wished that they had a mineral like this. And I think I've found the mother lode. If the seabed field proves itself, there will be enough mineral to realize a practical application. If I am correct, this new mineral, which I have named Chungite, has the ability to deflect smaller bits of space debris - tiny rocks, sand grains and other space junk, the type which occasionally puts Earth communication satellites and exploration satellites out of commission. Think of the security of continuous communication, think of the money saved when satellites are no longer destroyed by small space debris. For instance, every year, around the middle of November, we pass through the Leonids, a spectacular meteor shower which has its radiant point in the constellation Leo. There are almost a thousand satellites orbiting in space at any given time. They involve military surveillance, navigation, the Internet, banking, pagers, cell phones, satellite phones and news services. All these satellites could be and some have been damaged and put out of commission as they pass through these billions of particles as small as the size of a grain of sand which are traveling at over 250,000 kms. per hour. Remember the loss of the Canadian TV satellite a few years ago?

"But murder? You are absolutely nuts! Think of it! Murder!"

Chung shrugged this off and continued, "Throughout history man has had the need for gold. Our world depends on new discoveries. I am supplying this newly-discovered *gold* for the market. I also supply old gold. It is there for the taking. So why not?"

"But murder?"

"We mine copper. Manganese too! There is a burgeoning market for manganese."

"A new market for manganese?" I scoffed as I played for time.

"Yes, in your own country even," he replied with relish.

"My country?"

"Yes, there is a new market for my manganese. Under the NAFTA agreement manganese is going to be added to the gasoline that your country consumes. Think what that will do to the market price of manganese."

"Manganese was banned as a gasoline additive by the Canadian government."

"Under the North American Free Trade Agreement rules the courts have recently decided that your government cannot ban this additive. To do so would be against NAFTA and therefor unfair to outside business. And to reinforce that opinion, the courts, under NAFTA terms, have ruled that your country will pay all legal fees that have been incurred in fighting your government's ban. Ha! Ha! So I am able to supply what is going to become a more-sought-after commodity."

"So, is that what you were having hauled out in barrels to the freighter?"

"Yes. We refine what we can here, gold, copper, whatever and ship that and partially-refined ores containing the new rare mineral as well. Most everything we find has some value! There is very little waste."

"It sounds like you are doing to the seas what clear-cutting is to forests and strip mining is to the land," I said.

"So? It's there for the taking. We take! What we don't use, we return to the ocean. That's recycling."

I shook my head in disgust. "So you use those acrylic capsules for getting rid of the waste?"

"They are connectors. We use them to load the outflow pipe with effluent. In this case capsule number one has been launched for recycling into shark food with numbers two and three ready for launch. Get it? For launch! It's a joke. Ha! Ha!" laughed the lunatic.

His words chilled me. I kept him talking, biding for time. "What happens to the chemicals that you use in your refining operation here?"

"We recycle them as well."

"How?"

"We feed them into the outflow pipe. The sea eventually disperses the chemicals."

"Do you use cyanide in your operation?" I asked knowing that it was one of the chemical signatures that had been analyzed in the water samples that we had collected on our earlier dive.

"Yes, yes," Chung said impatiently. "We use a lot of different chemicals. You must remember, they originally came from the earth as well. We are just returning them there," he snorted.

Sarah spluttered, "What you are doing is committing murder, raping the sea and polluting a marine sanctuary!"

"Ah, women!" he barked, then spat at her in disgust. "You should never have been allowed to stray from the house."

Surprising everyone with her ferocity and sleight-of-hand, Sarah picked up a nearby short length of steel rod and flung it at Chung, catching him with a glancing blow to his head. He screamed with painful surprise at her bold move as he futilely tried to ward it off with his gun hand. The gun that he had trained on us fell to the steel deck and skittered off to one side while the rod fell noisily to the cavern floor far below.

I dove for the pistol and rolled as I snatched at it. Chung, blood spurting from his head wound, raced into the control room and locked the door behind him. It barred Sarah from getting at him in her rage.

Chung screamed orders over the loudspeaker to his two thugs guarding Kimo and Kiana. "Pull the end caps! Pull the end caps!" Horrified, Kimo and Kiana stiffened and braced themselves to keep from sliding down the effluent tube to their death. The two thugs slid the lower end caps open then raced around the catwalk firing shots off at us as they went. Bullets ricocheted and whined around us; sparks flew. I returned their fire with Chung's gun.

I shouted to Sarah to jump on my back as I undid a winch chain that was tied to the catwalk railing. As the two gunmen took cover nearby, I stepped onto the bottom loop of the block and tackle. Sarah leapt onto my back from the top of the guardrail. We swung pendulum-like over the four story void to the catwalk in the middle of the cavern. Bullets ricocheted off the heavy chain we were hanging onto. I felt Sarah slump as a bullet whined and struck her shoulder. She managed to hang on by locking her arms around my neck. I turned and shot at the two men, wounding one, causing him to cry out in pain and sending his gun spinning to the cavern floor far below. It chinked off machinery as it fell. The other thug, pinned down, was silent. We tumbled onto the center catwalk as the block and tackle swung up to the guardrail.

Here, Kimo and Kiana lay trussed in their acrylic coffins. Wounded, Sarah bent low, struggling to hang onto Kiana, trying to keep her from sliding to her death. I pulled Kimo's hands up to the edge of the clear acrylic pipe. He hung onto the rim. A short burst of rounds ricocheted off a pipe near my head and slammed into the acrylic pipe that Kimo was in, creating star burst cracks in it. I watched flecks of blood stain the side of his shirt. Turning, I fired off another round at the shooter, then heard him scream in pain. I helped pull Kiana out of her acrylic coffin. I handed Sarah my Olfa knife. Sarah slashed at the duct tape bonds on Kiana's legs. She tossed the knife back to me then led Kiana to safety behind a metal housing on the catwalk. I reached over and pulled Kimo out of his pipe. I slashed at the bonds on his legs so he could get to safety. Another pick-off shot slammed into the housing just as we squatted behind it.

"Good to see you man!" he exclaimed as he rubbed at his wrists after I freed them as well. "For a while there I thought we were goners!"

"You okay?" I asked.

"Yeah, why?" Kimo asked.

"You got hit just now!" I replied.

"Where?" Kimo asked. I pointed to the spreading red stain on his shirt. "Surface wound . . . I hope."

"Nice aim, Sarah!" Kiana said as she exulted over her release from her acrylic coffin. "I didn't think we were going to get out of there," she shuddered.

"We're not out of the woods yet!" I said.

"Did you get word to my buddy McGillicuddy in the SEALS?" Kimo asked.

"Sure did!" I replied. "By my reckoning, they'll be all over Chung's yacht offshore any minute now."

As we stayed hunkered behind the steel housing, Sarah and I told Kiana about Neki's death. She collapsed, tears flooded her eyes. Sarah comforted her the best she could. Kimo raged at Chung.

"I remember Neki on the day of the luau," I said softly as tears misted my sight, "he was such a fun-loving guy with his impish character. I'll always remember him cavorting in Kealakekua Bay that day. He was totally carefree. Now he's a free spirit."

I told them what Chung had just said about his mining operation and how he had disposed of ancient bones that he had found in the cavern.

Kiana, in a daze, said, "Now it all starts to make sense to me."

"What makes sense?" Sarah asked her.

"My dreams. The white sticks and stones. The white sticks were actually bones. Maybe I had a vision about the bones down here being disturbed. They were violently thrown about!"

"Your dreams! That's right!" Sarah said.

"But I also dreamt about these gray stones rolling down, tumbling around me, rumbling and clunking as they caromed off each other and rushed toward me. And it was hot, very hot. Bright rivers of lava swirling at me while this tall figure in a yellow cape would roar at me, then laugh. Remember me telling you?"

"I remember," I said as I peered at the shooters around the corner.

Another bullet whined past us. I returned the fire.

"What's that?" Sarah suddenly asked as she cocked her head to one side.

"What?" I asked.

"Did you feel that?"

"Feel what?" I asked.

"That distant rumble," she answered.

"The lights are swaying," Kimo exclaimed.

Suddenly the machinery came to life again as the conveyors moved along and the rock crusher was fed with the rock that had been on the belt.

"I think it's just the machinery," Kimo shouted to us.

A gunman was advancing toward us, with pistol in hand. It was Garlic Breath. Wounded, he was in a mad-bull rage.

I fired off a shot at him as he rushed us from the far catwalk. The shot spun him around, twisting him over the guardrail. Wounded, he fell, landing on the slowly moving conveyor belt below. Dazed, he was slowly drawn nearer to the rock crusher. He screamed as he realized his fate. Then his scream was cut off as he was yanked into the rock crusher's maw. There had barely been a crunching sound as bright red blood and soft tissue leaked out the bottom. Frightened, the other wounded thug slunk back into the shadows.

There was a distinct rumble heard over the grating of the machinery. The cavern shook, rocks fell off the conveyor belt and plummeted to the cavern floor. Chung's armed workers and accomplices scrambled around, looking for their own escape route.

Suddenly, I felt a red-hot slam against my right leg. I cried out in pain. I was hit in the fleshy part, just above the knee. I had allowed it to rest just beyond the corner of the steel housing. Peering around the corner, I figured that it was only a covering shot. I was right. Chung had gotten another pistol and had fired off a round, nicking my leg. He tried to make a run for it. Carrying a small air tank and regulator, Chung ran out the side door of the control room and plunged into an open spiraled flume of clear acrylic water pipe. It was his personal emergency escape chute. The flowing seawater in it carried him down to the cavern floor as if he were using a water slide.

Blood running down my leg, I fired off a couple rounds with the gun, piercing the acrylic pipe as he slid down into a deep spiral that ended in a pool on the cavern floor. Showers of arcing water traced the bullet holes in the pipe. The placid pool below was now wrinkled with small waves as the ground vibrated and shook harder; bits of machinery tumbled into the void, pieces from the lava ceiling came loose and fell in a cascade of scree.

Chung waded out of the pool below. More pieces of metal and light fixtures crashed to the floor below, throwing the cavern into spasms of darkness. Arcing electricity shorted out in crackling bursts of blue.

The center catwalk swayed. One end wrenched loose, dropping one story. It caught on a sloping conveyor which ragged at the broken metal, bouncing us around. We grasped at the sloping handrails.

Kiana screamed as she missed the handrail and slid toward the edge of the tilting catwalk. Kimo lunged, grabbed her arm and pulled her back.

More lava rock fell from above. They crashed onto the machinery below with a resounding clangor.

The rumbling intensified. A whole section of the cavern ceiling fell down, allowing a wide shaft of twilight to fall into the now-dim cavern. Part of the falling ceiling hit the other end of the catwalk, breaking our link with the perimeter. We were precariously stranded four floors off the cavern floor. What wasn't hit and torn apart was bent at a crazy angle, held only by a flimsy attachment to the shuddering machinery. The warm, humid air rolled down into the cool cavern from the dark blue evening sky above.

Looking below, I caught sight of Chung frantically trying to get our SeaTruck maneuvered out from under the ledge where we had driven it.

Now a new sound took over. It was a whooshing rush of hot air from the cavern below, like some desert wind whipping out of the upper lava tube. To the growing rumbling sound, a clunking sound of deep proportions was added.

Overhead, clattering rotors drew our eyes up into the darkening blue sky to see an army helicopter hovering. I could just make out the faces of the sheriff and a Hawaiian pilot in the lead chopper cockpit. A crewman began lowering a rope down from the chopper's winch, threading the needle through the gaping hole in the cavern ceiling.

"They're lowering a rope with slings on it to pull us out of here!" Kimo shouted over the din. Conveyor belts were now spinning off their rollers and streaking for the cavern floor far below. "I'm going to try to grab the line," he said as he lunged at the rope over the bent railing. I hung onto his belt as he leaned out. "Got it!" he shouted after his third attempt was successful. "Okay! Drop the loop over your head and under your arms, then hang on," Kimo shouted to Kiana over the din. "Gravity will hold you in as long as you don't put your arms up."

I helped Sarah into her sling. Her shoulder was bleeding from a surface graze. Kiana rose first with Kimo on the sling right under her. Sarah rose next. I followed all three on the sturdy single rope. We swung out. The four of us rose like fish hooked on a longliner's line.

The hot air gushing up at us from the cavern below was being met by the wicked downdraft from the chopper above. The buffeting was throwing us around as we tried to hang on and dodge falling debris.

Meanwhile, Chung had gotten the SeaTruck turned around far below us and was heading for the downslope lava tube where he could escape to the sea.

The rumbling intensified.

Kimo gave the thumbs up to the chopper. We were slowly hoisted upward just as the catwalk we had been on broke loose and fell in a crazy slow motion to the cavern floor. The grating sound of twisting metal momentarily filled the air.

Dangling in mid air, we still had not cleared the thick new skylight. Sarah, who was just above me on the rope-sling, called out to us, "I can see the lava tube glowing up the slope. What's happening?"

"I don't know!" I shouted up to her as I tried to staunch the flow of blood from my wounded knee.

"It's started, I know it!" Kiana exclaimed.

"What's started?" Kimo asked her.

"The gods . . . they're angry!" Kiana cried out.

"What do you mean?" I asked.

"My dream. It's starting to happen. I know it!" she cried out again.

There was an eerie low moan that emanated from the far reaches of the higher end of the lava tube, as though from Mount Hualalai Caldera itself. It was like a sigh that had its decibels increased tenfold then steadily increased again until it became a pulsing and then a roaring whine.

"What is that?" Sarah shouted with trepidation.

"Its starting!" Kiana screamed as she kicked her dangling feet in panic.

"It's what?" I asked straining to hear over the noise.

I got no answer from her.

We cleared the skylight and in the dimness of twilight, saw the Navy SEALS' grey special operations craft bobbing in the darkened sea. Their guns were trained on the *Scorpion* anchored off surf-lashed Keahole Point. Their Zodiac was rafted onto the starboard side of the work-yacht whose crew were being held at gunpoint on the main deck.

But then I got the answer. The shockwaves shook us to our very souls.

The roaring whine grated on our ears as a rushing holua sled swept out from the upper lava tube and through the cavern as though it were a high-speed bullet train roaring through a subway. A regal figure of a man sat upon the sled, a yellow cape trailed off his shoulders like saffron smoke in a jet's slipstream. The smoking holua sled arced upwards, shooting through the new skylight beneath us like a rocket in a hail of brilliant sparks and smoky contrails then continued ever upwards until it became starlike in the indigo evening sky.

The flash of heat and turbulence from the holua sled's trajectory sucked at our bodies as we slowly rose toward the chopper.

The cavern below shook. A distinct rumbling and clunking occurred as dozens of meter-high grey stone balls caromed down the sloping lava tube toward the cavern. The noise reverberated throughout the lava fields. The stone balls shot through the tube like buckshot out of a gun barrel. They smashed men and machinery in the cavern before piling up against the opposite wall, some finding their way farther downslope into the lower lava tube. The stone balls bowled everything over in their path as if they were merely tenpins.

We were still being winched up as a heat blast came at us. The lava fields below us creaked and twisted and shook. Like a screaming banshee from the bowels of the earth, a fiery figurehead of a woman howled and shrieked as she burst forth through pockets of ancient air and exploding choking gases. The fiery female hurled the Global Marine electric tram into a twisting spiral as though it were a crazed roller coaster. It blew off sparks from melting metal wheels running on bright rails of molten rock. Shooting down the lava tube into the dark cavern in a brilliant display of exploding fireworks, a blazing river of yellow and red lava surged behind her, burying machinery and pipes.

Pele lay glowing, gasping and moaning as she settled into the far recesses of the cavern and flowed down to sizzle the sea in the lower lava tube. She gave off a lasting satisfied sigh as she cooled, filling the void to the very top of the cavern skylight.

* * * * *

If you go down to the sacred heiau behind the SSEAAL lab near Keahole Point in Kona and look up the slope toward Mount Hualalai as we did early the next morning, you may notice a wide circular patch of fresh ebony lava just below a skylight. It lies tomblike underneath the ancient rusty lava bed from tens of thousands of years ago, both of which are under the old black a'a lava bed from just two hundred years ago.

"Just being here is giving me the shakes," Kiana declared as we walked across the ancient lava bed toward the buried cavern. "To think he had Neki murdered just because he had no use for him."

"That horrible murderer Chung, I hope that he is buried down there in that lava tube for good," said Sarah.

Kiana broke down, sobbing. "Oh, Neki! Neki! Neki!" she wailed in grief. Sarah consoled her.

"And how many other people has Chung had murdered?" Sarah asked. "We came pretty close to being killed by him as well! I hope that murderer Chung suffered before he died!"

"I spoke to my buddy, McGillicuddy, on the SOC this morning," Kimo said. "They haven't seen any trace of him nor the SeaTruck. His best guess is that the lava got Chung in the lower tube."

"I feel as if I've lived a nightmare!" Kiana said, sniffling with grief. "I still find it hard to believe what we saw."

"We all know what we saw," Sarah said, "but there will be those who will have doubts that it really happened like that. They will think we were under a lot of stress at the time and that perhaps we saw things that looked like something else rather than just nature at work. Still, there's too much of the scientist in me to not want physical evidence to substantiate our vision."

"Well, I know it happened like that all right," Kimo declared as he put his arms protectively around Kiana, "there were four of us that saw it! Okay, so the chopper pilots, the sheriff and the SEALS only saw a blinding fireball shoot out of the skylight into the evening sky but they weren't up close to see it and hear it like we were. They also didn't see the caroming stone balls nor did they see Pele raging."

Reaching the spot where the new patch of vaporous lava lay visible under the ancient rusting lava, we stood on the skylight rim and stared into the shallow void at the cooling mass, each of us lost in our own thoughts. Sarah molded her body against mine as I carefully draped my arm around her tender wounded shoulder.

Feeling a twinge of pain, I dropped my gaze to my bandaged knee. I refocused my eyes on something that caught my attention on the rim of the smouldering skylight. It was a mere smudge of contrasting colour against the earthy bleakness of the wrought lava. I bent down to the rim, picking up a single small yellow feather that had been hand-plucked centuries ago from the underwing of the extinct black Mamo bird. I held it up for all to see in the mango-hued, misty morning light.

COMING SOON

THE SECRET TEMPLE OF KINTAMANI

A new Rune Erikson novel by

Ernie Palamarek

Available in 2000

THUNDERSEA

ABOUT THE AUTHOR

Ernie Palamarek has recently had articles published in magazines and has several works in progress.

Having grown up in the saddle, ranching and farming on the Alberta prairie, he has a keen appreciation for nature's wondrous beauty and its amazing resiliency that counters the eggshell fragility of the environment. Combining his eye for detail with a vivid imagination, he roams the world in search of unique experiences - to listen, to observe and to talk to wonderfully-different people in strange, exotic lands.

He experiences the adventure and journeys through life with his photographer wife, Sharon, who shares his passion for travel. He has worked in public relations for a major newspaper, in a private industry research and development laboratory, in his own businesses, and in the service of a government agency.

The author has lived in Victoria, British Columbia since he was twenty years old. Vancouver Island, a wonderful, temperate rainforest in the Pacific Ocean, is his backyard.

Thundersea is Palamarek's first novel.

ISBN 1-55212-251-4
9 781552 122518